The Unquiet House

The Trevannions

Volume 2

Audrey Morris

M.A. Consultants Limited

This edition published in 2011 by M.A. Consultants Limited
11 Belmore Avenue, Pyrford, Woking, Surrey, GU22 8LN.

Copyright © Audrey Morris

Cover photographs by Mike Morris

ISBN 978-1-903690-02-4

All characters in this publication are fictitious and any resemblance to real persons, living or dead, is purely coincidental.

The Unquiet House is the second book in the Trevannions trilogy.

The Granite House (ISBN 1 903690 01 03), the first book in this series, is also available from M.A. Consultants Limited.

Volume 3 is expected to be published shortly.

With thanks to all my family and friends with special mention for my grand-daughter Katie for her interest and enthusiasm and my daughters Frances and Sara for help with proof reading as well as their encouragement.

Synopsis of "The Granite House"
(Volume 1 of the Trevannions Trilogy)

Barnabas Trevannion marries Eliza Talland and takes her to live in Roscarne, a granite house, she has always admired, situated on a Cornish cliff top overlooking the sea. Her sister Grace is devastated as she is in love with Barnabas and it is difficult for her to live in the same house. Eliza gives birth to twins, Nathaniel and Caroline. Eliza's friend Rose Trewin helps when she can until her mother falls ill and Barnabas invites his troublemaker sister Ewella to come and stay. Grace meets Sir James Treloyan who lives at the Manor and they get married. Grace is furious when Eliza disturbs the wedding by her labour pains and the birth of John. Nessa and Joel follow in quick succession.

Meanwhile Grace is unhappy in her marriage as she remains childless. She seduces Barnabas, hoping to have his child. She becomes pregnant but is uncertain of the father. Eliza finds out and runs away; she is rescued and brought back to Roscarne by Seth Quinn to find that Ewella is setting herself up as mistress of the house, has dismissed Hedra and employed Jael, who eventually becomes a close friend of Eliza. Barnabas wants to hold a reception to celebrate the formation of a tin mine consortium, but Eliza is appalled to find he intends to invite the Treloyhans. At the reception, Eliza spends time with Seth finding him attractive and interesting. Rose is not pleased as she, too, finds him attractive. Eliza discovers Jael in the cellar brewing potions and medicines of various kinds. She cures Eliza's stomach pains and supplies a love potion to Rose who is trying to get closer to Seth.

Eliza's Aunt Gloria and her husband Yelland come down from London to check on their investments in the tin mine. Rose and Seth announce their engagement, but Eliza has mixed feelings. Aunt Gloria advises her to be more conciliatory to guard what is hers, i.e. Barnabas and Roscarne. Jael has premonitions, followed by the death of Grace's husband, Sir James. Seth admits to Eliza that his engagement to Rose is a mistake. Barnabas allows Grace to live at Roscarne. Volume 1 ends with a mine disaster and Seth postpones his wedding to Rose. The flooding of several mines means their closure and Barnabas has to close Roscarne, prior to going to Australia to recoup his fortunes. Eliza and family have to move to a smaller house.

THE UNQUIET HOUSE

PROLOGUE

A mizzling rain began to fall as Eliza and her children rattled along the stony track towards their new house. Her spirits drooped as the day faded and the realisation gripped her that at the end of this journey there would be no return to the light, the colour, the space of Roscarne. Nessa had fallen asleep, her head in Eliza's lap, but the two boys were upright, galvanised by curiosity. John was stiff lipped with disapproval as the carriage swayed and bumped over potholes but little Joel, still only six, could not hide his excitement at this new adventure. Ahead of them, a rickety bridge spanned a stream swollen by recent rain and Eliza muttered a prayer as the carriage bounced over it. What would happen if the rain continued? Already there was little room between the fast flowing water and the arch of the bridge.

Then, suddenly, the house. A stone house, hiding in the darkness of thorn trees. Its windows, empty eyed, gave no promise of welcome. Only the red flowers on a fuchsia bush at the entrance gate defied the gloom, their bright beauty highlighting the harshness of stone, the run down ruins of several barns and outhouses, the domination of weeds and rubbish in the muddy drive. The gate lay on the ground, its hinges broken. The heavy wooden door was ajar and, as the carriage came to a stop, Ewella appeared. Her hair was scraped back and she wore an all enveloping hessian apron. Surprisingly, she had a smile on her face.

'I've managed to light the range!' she announced, triumphantly. 'We can have hot drinks for the children. Jael is sweeping out one of the rooms and we can lay down the mattresses and bedding for them. The twins are helping Mathey.'

'Are we all going to sleep in the same room, Mama?' asked John, screwing up his face as if he had sucked on a lemon.

'Just to begin with,' said Eliza. 'Ewella, I have brought provisions for supper which perhaps we should have early before the light goes completely.'

'We do have oil for the lamps and plenty of candles. I made sure of that,' Ewella assured her. The driver of the carriage unloaded their baggage in haste, and then surprised them all by his speedy departure, shouting at the horse and cracking his whip.

'As if demons were after him!' said Ewella

Eliza entered the front door of her new home. The iron monster was indeed alight and giving off sulky warmth. The floor had been swept, if not scrubbed, and wooden chairs had been arranged around the big wooden table, a table which had taxed Mathey's ingenuity in its transport from the kitchen at Roscarne. A brief picture flashed before Eliza of that comfortable room where Mrs Kershaw, their cook had held sway and produced such wonderful feasts. The roast goose. The squab pies. Saffron cakes. How they would miss her.

'The other furniture and bits and pieces are round the back,' said Ewella. 'Mathey made several journeys and brought all he could before Barnabas closed Roscarne.' She frowned. 'Just like my brother to do everything in such a hurry and with no real thought for others!'

'Let's eat now,' said Eliza, not wanting to think about Barnabas and Roscarne. 'I feel exhausted.'

Ewella bustled around the kitchen, in her element. This was not the discontented, easily slighted Ewella of Roscarne. She was faced with a challenge which had brought out all her latent domestic skills.

'Are we going to have supper all together?' demanded Nathaniel rushing in ahead of Caroline. Eliza nodded. The children all looked at each other in delight.

'So we are not babies any more, Mama,' said Caroline.

2

1

Eliza stood and looked out of the window she had just cleaned. In spite of her best efforts it was still blotched and smeary and what little light there was outside filtered in with difficulty. She sighed in exasperation. Already several months had passed since, unhappily and unwillingly, she had come to take possession of this house and still she felt no lighter in spirit. With her were her five children, the twelve year old twins, Caroline and Nathaniel, John who had at last reached double figures and let everyone know it, and the two younger ones, Nessa and Joel. Also with her were her Uncle Tobias, her sister-in-law Ewella and Jael Tregonning, the young girl from Liskeard, no relation but a valued member of her household. It was Jael who had been there to help Eliza face her loneliness after Barnabas, her husband, had sailed for Australia. At the same time Rose, her best friend and long-time companion, had also left, bound for Arizona where she was to be married to Seth. Seth Quinn. The name still sent shivers down Eliza's back.

Time had passed slowly since the Trevannions had been forced to leave Roscarne, their granite house on the cliff, to Eliza the most beautiful house she had ever seen, a house she had learned to love with fierce devotion. But the disasters facing the Cornish tin mining industry had spread inevitably to the Trevannion mines, resulting in the closure of many. A flood of unemployed miners and dispossessed owners, Barnabas Trevannion among them, hastened to Hayle and Bristol and Liverpool to board ships for the far corners of the new world – Australia, South Africa, America, anywhere with a thriving mining industry. Men from Cornwall were in demand and welcomed for their expertise; some made their fortunes and others gleaned new ideas for their return home. Eliza hoped desperately that Barnabas would come home within the year as he had promised. However the few brief letters which had come for her did not bode well. No mention of a return date, no mention of improved finances, only bland assurances that he was well and hoped they were too.

The latest unsatisfactory missive in the pocket of her apron, she attacked the next window to find her view even more obscured by the rain which had been threatening since early morning. The dense tangle of thorn trees which surrounded the house had vanished behind a grey curtain. Sighing, she remembered the views of the sea through the many windows of Roscarne, the storms, the sunsets, pale dawns and bright sunshiny days, the ever changing colours of the water – gunmetal grey, metallic silver, milky blue, singing turquoise and intense, dramatic blue. And she remembered the sounds of the sea in the background, sighing, whispering, lapping, then crashing on the shore in storm winds, booming in the caves below the cliff and, in the background, the eternal rhythm of the rising and falling tides; such memories never failed to bring tears to her eyes. Then there were the pleasures of huddling in an armchair, the heavy velvet curtains drawn, feeling safe and knowing that the granite house would resist all assaults from the winds howling outside.

Now, she and the remnants of her family were exiled to this derelict place in a gloomy valley, hemmed in by thorn trees and bordered by an irritable stream which rushed through part of their land when it rained, seemingly reluctant to remain within its banks.

'It will come through the house one of these days,' warned Ewella, a remark which excited the children who found the darkness and lack of space limiting and welcomed any diversion.

'There is nowhere I can do my schoolwork in peace,' grumbled Nathaniel.

'I know it is difficult,' soothed his mother. 'But Professor Martineau says you are making good progress just the same. And think of all the difficulties he has to face just coming here. He is not a young man but he has to come from Rosmorren in all weathers in that creaky old cart.'

'He was soaked when he came last week in all that rain,' said Caroline, 'and his hands had turned quite blue.'

'Poor old man,' whispered soft hearted Nessa.

'He doesn't have to come to teach us! I don't mind if he stays home!' said Joel.

'You are just an ignorant child,' John put in loftily.

'What's ignorant?'

'Exactly!'

4

'Listen to me,' Eliza said. 'When your father comes back he will expect you boys to be ready to go to school. You have to work hard or he will be seriously displeased with you.'

'Ewella says he's not coming back for a long time,' said little Nessa. 'Do you think he will come soon, Mama?'

'I don't know,' Eliza was forced to admit. 'But I do know that he will return as quickly as he is able.'

'And then will we go back to live in Roscarne?' asked Nathaniel.

'I hope so.' She smiled brightly. 'Now finish the work you are doing before supper.'

'We used to have a dining room,' Caroline complained.

Reluctantly the children trailed back to their makeshift schoolroom next door. There was just space enough for five desks and benches, roughly nailed together by Jed Laity, their handyman. The desks even had lids so the children's slates and books could be kept there, ready for the next lesson, a boon even though the lids creaked and squeaked and Joel delighted in allowing his to drop with a crash that reverberated in the carpet-less room. Caroline and Nathaniel sat down next to each other, both glaring at John who pushed into his place in his usual graceless way.

'I need more room,' he complained.

'You eat too much,' piped up Joel.

John leaned forward and cuffed his little brother round the ear.

'Just hold your tongue, you. You don't know what you are talking about. Mama says I am a growing boy and I need to eat.'

'You should be growing upwards, not sideways,' Nathaniel could not resist a dig.

'And you shouldn't hit Joel, he's only little,' Caroline added.

'Mistress Eliza!' Ewella strode in, making Eliza jump guiltily as she was day dreaming rather than cleaning. Her sister-in-law was as tall and imposing as her brother, Barnabas, but Eliza noted that her hair had none of the Trevannion fire and their removal from Roscarne had carved new lines in her gaunt face. Ewella made a point of addressing her formally, on occasion, probably trying to maintain the illusion that they were still at Roscarne and not living in straitened circumstances in this near derelict house. How could Barnabas leave them all in such circumstances? Sometimes Eliza felt rage sweep through her even though she knew that his journey to Australia was his way of hoping to recoup his fortune. On bad days the thoughts came unbidden that his travels were also a way of escaping awkward times and situations, leaving it all behind him, without thought for his family. Then she would chide herself for unkindness. Of course her husband had made a brave decision to travel to unknown places right across the world.

'Where is Jael?' demanded Ewella. 'That girl is supposed to be helping me in the kitchen today but she has been poking about at the back of the house among the weeds and now she seems to have disappeared.'

'She has probably found some new ingredient for her potions,' smiled Eliza. 'Let me finish these windows and see that the children are working and I shall come to help you. What are we having for dinner today?'

'Some cold chicken left over from yesterday, though it was a right stringy bird Farmer Tull gave us – and potatoes if there are enough left.' Eliza frowned.

'There should be plenty of potatoes – Mathey brought a load from the farm only a few days ago.'

'Yes, but we made cottage pies – which seemed to disappear as fast as stones down a mineshaft,' grumbled Ewella.

'I suppose the children are growing.'

'Perhaps we should try to clear some of the land at the back of the house and grow our own potatoes?'

'Ewella that is a marvellous idea! It will be one less heavy chore for Mathey, carrying those sacks – and save us money as well! How clever of you to think of it.' Ewella blinked. Clever? It seemed like common sense to her.

'Nessa helped me to make a saffron pudding yesterday,' added Eliza. 'That will help to fill everyone.' Ewella shrugged. Off she went to search for Jael, without success as Eliza found when she descended to the kitchen.

'How strange. She usually tells someone if she is going to look for plants.'

An hour later and everyone – or almost everyone as Jael had not reappeared – was sitting at the wooden table in the kitchen. Uncle Tobias hobbled to his big chair at the head of the table and sat down with a sigh of relief. Eliza could see that his arthritis was still bothering him but he did not complain. How well he had adapted, she thought affectionately, forced to leave his comfortable room at Roscarne to share the bleak kitchen with them all, to endure the noise made by the children, who sounded sometimes like squabbling hens in a farmyard. His only refuge was a damp cubby hole adjoining the sitting room, a far cry from the comparatively opulent study he had left. And not a word of protest from him. But she did worry about him. He coughed more than before and his movements were noticeably slower. Nothing wrong with his appetite however, she noted with a smile. Dinner over, Mathey left to fetch eggs and milk from the farm with instructions from Ewella to ask for another chicken but it had to be a better specimen than the last one.

The rain had eased so Eliza bustled the children outside for a walk in the fresh air. There had not been much time for just walking in the past months because all energies were directed towards making their living space habitable. They had no maids so the children had chores to do as well as their schoolwork while Eliza and Ewella worked till they fell, exhausted into their beds. The house had been scrubbed from roof to ground floor. The rubbish left in the kitchen and the outside courtyard had been cleared and the weeds pulled up. Jed had mended the wooden gate and he and Mathey had tried to repair the stone wall but both were frequently called for other duties and so progress was slow. Mathey had to keep the rickety cart in working order though it was Caroline who cared for the pony, feeding and grooming him. She had named him Trembles because he was so nervous. She spent a long time talking to him and soothing him in the broken down stone barn which was his shelter. Her twin, Nathaniel, was responsible for maintaining piles of wood at the side of the house, wood which was partially protected by an old tarpaulin sheet. He also took a hand in chopping the wood and feeding the range, a monster of iron, which lurked at the back of the kitchen. He was justifiably proud of the muscles he was developing.

Jael did not reappear until late afternoon, creeping in quietly. Rain dripped from her hair and down her nose and she was shivering.

     'Jael?' Eliza was concerned to see her in such a state. 'What happened?'

7

'I-I'm sorry to have been so long...' Jael's teeth were chattering so much she could hardly speak. 'Mistress Eliza, I must tell you. I have been looking for somewhere else to live. I cannot stay in this house.' The chilling statement hung in the air.

'But why? What have we done? You were happy to live here with us at first.' Eliza could not believe what she was hearing.

'Yes. I am happy with you. But I have to move out.'

'I think you should have a cup of tea,' Eliza said, recovering herself. 'Move closer to the range and I shall bring it to you - and some gingerbread unless John has been in the kitchen. Then we shall talk.'

Jael crouched down in her chair as though trying to disappear. Her pale hair hung about her face in tangles and there were shadows beneath her eyes.

'Jael, have we been working you too hard?' suggested Eliza, but with sinking heart. Clearly, Jael's problem was not to be solved by a cup of tea.

'No.' She seemed to gather herself together. 'I was looking for some herbs in that field behind the house when I found - I found -'

'Well, what? What did you find to upset you so much?'

'A stone. It's right at the back end of the field by the wall.'

'A stone? What kind of stone?'

'A standing stone. We couldn't see it before because the thorn trees hide it. But it is there. And it changes everything.'

'Nothing I could say made her change her mind,' Eliza confided to Ewella. '...I asked her what the stone had to do with it but she clammed up and I could not get another word out of her.' Ewella sat with a frown, digesting this information.

'I knew her mother when I lived in Liskeard,' she offered at last. 'She always was a strange woman and by all accounts Jael is a strange girl. It was her mother who taught Jael about herbs and healing. Then they had a quarrel and Jael left to wander round Cornwall working in fairs.'

'That's right. I met Jael at Llanteglos fair just before Joel's birth. I shall always remember how kind she was to me.' Eliza was silent for a moment remembering that outing when she and Rose had been to the fair to watch Seth Quinn fight. She remembered vividly that it had been Seth who had taken care of her, not her husband, Barnabas. But it was Jael who had warned her that the birth of her baby was near.

8

'I think both mother and daughter were reputed to have "the sight",' went on Ewella. 'There was gossip about witchcraft, but that was mainly to do with her mother. Anyway, Jael wanted to escape all that which is why she left.'

'I don't think you can escape 'all that' any more than you can escape having blue eyes,' said Eliza. 'She knew that hard times were coming to Roscarne before we did and she was very unhappy for a time, telling me that the clouds were gathering.'

'I didn't know that,' said Ewella, sharply. Eliza flushed.

'We - we did not speak much then.' She did not add that she had been well aware of Ewella's desire to oust her as mistress of Roscarne. Her persistent mischief making had not allowed closer relations between them.

Evening came but there was no sign of Jael. Eliza and Ewella cleared up after supper and chased the children to their beds, surprised that Jael was not there for the bedtime ritual.

'Has she gone already, then?' demanded Ewella. 'It's still raining and almost dark.'

'No, of course not. She wouldn't do that.'

But Jael did not return that night. Not till Eliza was bustling about the kitchen, rattling the range into wakefulness and setting the porridge on the hob for the children, did the heavy wooden door open for Jael to slip in. Before Eliza could say anything Jael gave her a hesitant smile.

'Mistress Eliza, I have a solution to my difficulties. I slept in the smaller barn last night and it remained dry in spite of the rain. I can stay here, near to you all, without risk!'

'Risk? Jael, what ARE you talking about?'

'If I stay I shall bring danger to all of you,' Jael spoke slowly, patiently. 'I felt this house was not welcoming when we arrived and now I know about the stone I have to leave.'

Eliza opened her mouth to protest but Jael held up her hand.

'Mistress Eliza, no questions. Please trust me. I am doing what is best for everyone here. You are the nearest thing to a family I have ever had and I am fond of you all. I should never forgive myself if any harm came to you.'

'Such nonsense!' said Ewella.

2

'What about Trembles?' asked Caroline, when she heard that Jael intended to sleep in the barn. A bemused Eliza could do nothing but shrug her shoulders.

'I hope that Mathey and Jed can make one of the other outhouses habitable for him,' she said. 'But I really don't know. You had better ask Jael.' Caroline rushed off to find her and, sure enough, she was already sweeping out the barn. There was a clattering on the stairs and Jed appeared, dragging Jael's bed with him. Fortunately it was narrow and light and there was little wheezing and gasping as there would have been with Mathey. Jael took one look at Caroline's anxious face and put down her broom.

'I'm sorry this has happened so suddenly, Caroline, but I have my reasons. Now, don't you worry about Trembles. Mathey is fixing up the outhouse across the courtyard. He's repairing the roof and he has already fetched a load of new straw from the farm so Trembles will be quite comfortable.'

'Why do you want to sleep in the barn?' Caroline wanted to know. Jael hesitated.

'I feel it would be better for all of us,' she said, briskly. 'It will give us more room in the house and Jed is putting up a wide shelf for me to use for my potions. I shall even have hooks to hang up my drying herbs without cluttering the kitchen.'

'But you haven't a sink,' said practical Caroline.

'I have a bucket,' Jael smiled.

Only partly satisfied, Caroline wandered back to the house to tell Nathaniel what was happening. It was her custom to tell her twin everything though Nathaniel had shown signs recently of being less interested in her chatter and her flights of imagination. He preferred teasing John till he lost his temper or joining in one of Joel's wild games and this alternated with long periods of study where he struggled to come to terms with some new concept and woe betide anyone who interrupted him. Caroline was beginning to find him tiresome.

'Jael didn't give me the real reason why she's moving out,' she said to her twin. 'And poor Trembles is in a much smaller barn.'

'I thought you and Jael were witches in the same coven,' mumbled Nathaniel, gulping down some gingerbread before John found it. 'Use some of your magic to find out.'

'You're always making fun of me. I hate you, Nathaniel.'

Eliza had to admit that Jael had made the barn reasonably comfortable.

'But you have no protection against the damp and the cold in the winter,' she warned. 'You will need plenty of straw. We have no more blankets.'

'I can build a wood fire if I need to,' Jael reassured her. 'Don't forget I spent several years with a travelling fair and I had to rough it then.'

'She looks so delicate,' Eliza fretted to Ewella. 'She looks as if a breath of wind would blow her away.'

'Her choice,' said Ewella, tartly. 'But don't worry about her. Her mother said she was much tougher than she looks.' So Jael moved into the barn, but she kept her reasons to herself. When Eliza tried to question her further, she always changed the subject or made a comment about needing her own space.

Summer was ending and it was time for Professor Martineau to return from a holiday break to resume lessons. The children were pleased to see him as their work had been mostly unsupervised and become boring, Eliza and Jael having been too busy. His old pony pulled the creaky cart into the courtyard and the children clustered round him, joyfully.

'I know my tables,' volunteered Nessa. 'I can recite them all.'

'And I've labelled my collection of shells,' boasted Nathaniel. 'But we haven't any room to put them on show because our shelves are full of books.'

'Nathaniel, you are very lucky that you were able to bring so many books from Roscarne,' said the Professor. 'You have many more than I have in my cottage. But I hope you are taking care that they don't become damp in this house.' Sometimes he found it hard to disguise his disapproval of the living space the family now occupied and his thoughts about Barnabas were less than charitable.

11

'But the books are all stories,' said Nathaniel in disgust. 'We don't have books about biology or books about wildlife or the sea and…' he ran out of breath.

'I shall see if I have some I can bring for you,' soothed the Professor. 'They will do more good here with you than in my bookcase. Perhaps it would be a good idea to get Jed help you to put up more shelves and then you can display your shells as well.'

'If Mama lets me. Jed always has a lot to do. But I can find some wood at least.' Nathaniel cheered up at the thought of doing something practical to remedy the deficit.

'What about you, Caroline?' asked the Professor kindly.

'I've read 'Nicholas Nickleby' and have just started 'The Old Curiosity Shop.'

'Well done. You'll be ready to start 'A Christmas Carol' before Christmas really does come.' Nathaniel snorted but Caroline smiled a self-satisfied smile. It was a smile that hid her perusal of what was really important and interesting to her.

'How about you, Joel,' he asked. 'What have you been doing?'

'Not a lot,' admitted Joel.

'That will change when our father returns home,' jeered John.

Eliza's worries about Jael were driven from her mind when an unexpected visitor appeared. A burly man, smartly dressed in dark coat and brocade waistcoat, pushed impatiently at the still rickety gate and strode into the courtyard. Eliza was horrified to see that his fine leather boots were covered in thick mud and he was dripping wet from the steady rain.

'Mistress Trevannion?' the man demanded in tones of irritation. Eliza nodded.

'I am here on behalf of your sister, Lady Treloyhan. I have some matters to discuss with you, if you please.'

'Please come in,' said Eliza, coolly, rather resenting his tone. She was conscious that she had been caught at a disadvantage, still in her faded work dress; however her caller seemed in worse shape, his fine clothes mud splashed and his temper only just under control.

'Negotiating the muddy reaches of this track has been appalling!' he complained. 'The potholes are monstrous and I have had to leave my pony and trap near the bridge. Perhaps your man could help me to pull the wheels free when I leave?' His tone made it seem like an order. Eliza inclined her head.

'We have no man on the premises,' she said. 'Jed Laity is our handyman but he does not live here and Mathey is too old to do such work.' This was not strictly true but she was loath to see hardworking Mathey utilised like a carthorse for the benefit of this abrupt stranger. He did not pursue the matter.

'I will get straight to the point,' he said, sitting with certain distaste on one of the wooden chairs. 'I am Edgar Tallack, brother-in-law to Austol Treloyhan. As you know, your sister, Grace Treloyhan, is living at the Manor by kind invitation of Austol and his family.'

'As she is widow of the late Sir James, that is her due,' said Eliza.

'That may be so, but we have a problem. She has given birth to her baby before time –'

'I had no idea!' cried Eliza. 'Why did no one inform me? Is she well?'

'I was told that there was a rift between you and your sister.'

'Yes – but she is still of my family. Tell me – how is she? And the baby?'

'They have both survived the birth but are now struggling to regain their health. They need nursing. This is the problem we face.'

'How is it a problem?' Eliza was surprised. 'Grace has money – as has Austol, I am sure. They have the means to pay the doctor and hire a nurse!'

Edgar Tallack sat back in his chair and heaved a sigh. This was proving more difficult than he had expected. Grace Treloyhan's sister seemed to be every bit as awkward as Grace herself. Also, Eliza's self confidence was unnerving. After all, she was a woman – and living in straitened circumstances at that but she was addressing him as an equal. A little more deference would have been in order. Annoyed, he was about to embark on further explanations of his 'problem' when there were two interruptions, one after the other. First, Uncle Tobias appeared, rubbing his eyes sleepily after dozing in his small study.

'Let me see now – I know you,' he said, eyeing their visitor. 'You are Edgar Tallack, Austol's brother-in-law.'

'And you? Tobias Trevannion, I believe? Uncle to Barnabas Trevannion, late of Roscarne?' Uncle Tobias nodded. The two men stared at each other, their mutual distrust and dislike thickening the atmosphere of the kitchen. Eliza was shocked – it was so out of character for Uncle Tobias to be discourteous – but before she could say anything the door opened again and Ewella appeared.

'Professor Martineau has finished lessons for the morning,' she announced, observing their visitor with curiosity.

'Ewella, please will you see to the children until I am ready.' Eliza made no effort to introduce Ewella, feeling that first she needed to find out more about this Edgar Tallack and what he wanted. It was seldom Uncle Tobias was so unwelcoming.

'It is a matter of space,' Edgar resumed, stroking his abundant whiskers.

'Space? But the Manor must have at least twenty rooms!'

'Indeed – but Austol and Eulalia have seven children, there are nannies, their tutor and governess, myself – and all the maids of course.'

'Of course.' Eliza waited. What did this man want?

'So perhaps it would be helpful if Lady Treloyhan, your sister Grace, could return to her family to be looked after......?'

'Out of the question!' cried Uncle Tobias, his face turning red with anger.

'You see where we live – and the state of this house,' said Eliza, quietly. 'Though much improved it is still damp and I feel not suitable for a new baby and a sick mother.' The nightmare of being forced to live in the same house as her sister Grace, after all that had passed between them, had reared up to haunt her.

'What is the real reason for this – this ridiculous suggestion?' snapped Uncle Tobias. Edgar looked affronted but the old man wanted an answer.

'My sister, Eulalia, is not at all well and it is too much for her running such an unwieldy household 'Uncle Tobias remained silent. 'Austol is – is too busy to be of help. He also has business acquaintances as guests ... I am sure I do not need to continue.' Some of the swagger had left him and he sounded really concerned about his sister.

Eliza came to a sudden decision. Whatever the reasons, the family at the Manor did not want Grace and her new baby. Therefore she should

14

come home to her sister and family. They would manage somehow. The quicker she saw the back of this less than pleasant man, the better.

'Very well. However I should like to come to the Manor and discuss this with Grace. I am not sure she would be amenable to such an idea. We have had problems in our relationship – '

'Blood is thicker than water!' interrupted Uncle Tobias firmly. Edgar nodded and Eliza realised from the appraising look on his face that the story of the rift between the two sisters had reached him.

'I should like to offer you some refreshment,' she said, terminating the discussion. She would not allow this man to discomfit her or see her shaken.

'If you have brandy?'

'Certainly. I also have a brush if you would like to clean off some of the mud.'

'My valet will do that.'

'If you need help to move your pony and trap perhaps ask Farmer Tull. His farm is about a mile along the track after you cross the bridge.' That should erase his look of hauteur, she thought.

'Have you a boy I could send – I cannot possibly walk all that way in this weather – and the mud!'

'I'm afraid not.' At this juncture, John appeared. Eliza wondered if her beloved son had been listening at the door.

'I'll do it, Mama,' he offered. More surprises. But John was curious. He had caught the glint of a gold watch and observed the ornate rings on this stranger's hand. Obviously a man of means.

John scurried off and Edgar sat back, comfortable at last, and savoured his brandy. Uncle Tobias watched with disbelief. There were few bottles left in his private store and, left to him, Tallack would have been offered tea or some such drink – but to see his precious brandy going to a complete stranger, one who would never have been given house room in Sir James Treloyhan's time, furthermore a man who was trying to eject his unwelcome guest without care for her wellbeing, was more than he could stomach. He stomped off to his 'study' and banged the door. Eliza winced as she came back into the kitchen. That door was likely to come off its hinges before too long. She then became aware that Edgar was studying her rather too closely.

'Your husband, Mistress Trevannion – gone to Australia, I believe?'

15

'Yes.'

'Is he due to return soon?'

'I am not sure exactly when.' Eliza's answers were as short as she could make them without being impolite.

'A rough place, Australia. Full of convicts, rogues and thieves.' The colour rose to Eliza's face but she ignored his blatant rudeness.

'Australia has opportunities for those in mining. They need Cornish expertise...'

'Of course. And your husband left you to live here, on your own?'

'The journey would have been too difficult for young children. We thought it best.' Eliza could feel herself beginning to stammer. This odious man had no right to pass judgement on Barnabas.

'Next time I shall come on my horse – leave the pony and trap at the manor.'

'Why should there be a next time, Mr. Tallack?'

3

Eliza planned her visit to Treloyhan Manor with great care. She intended to make a better impression on Edgar Tallack, he of the superior attitude and scathing comments, and she needed to feel at her best for her forthcoming encounter with Austol Treloyhan and his family. And, of course, with Grace, her sister. How sad that their relationship was so fraught. Eliza sighed. Try as she might, she could feel little affection for the one who had so betrayed her. However she was determined that she would do the best she could for her sister, even if it meant that she would become part of their already crowded house. No gratitude from Grace would be forthcoming. She was sure of that.

'Uncle Tobias, I can't go to the Manor in a cart,' she said. 'What can I do?' Uncle Tobias thought a while.

'I have the answer!' he announced. 'I will send Mathey with a letter for the Lanivets. They will lend us their pony and trap, I am sure. They have been so kind to us already.'

'The mud is still too deep from here to the road – '

'So Mathey will take you in the cart as far as the road and then you can pick up the pony and trap! It will be a bumpy ride but I'm sure Mathey will manage it.'

That problem solved, Eliza turned her attention to her wardrobe. Her deep blue silk dress was in a box under her bed. She remembered Rose admiring it. However, she had little choice and knew that she would have to wear it as the claret velvet was for the evening and the two twill dresses not smart enough. The blue silk would do. Though she spent most of her days in her work dress, which was already faded and threadbare, it was comforting to have some remnants of her life at Roscarne to fall back on.

'You need a hat,' said Ewella. 'And your hair should be put up properly. I'm sure Jael would do it for you.'

'I haven't a hat.'

'I have one you can borrow.'

So Eliza was driven off in the cart, her hair beautifully coiffed and its severity artfully softened by a few escaping ringlets, Ewella's hat perched austerely on top.

The pony and trap was waiting and the Lanivets' man insisted on driving Eliza to the Manor where he promised he would wait as long as was necessary. Summoning all her courage, Eliza knocked on the studded wooden door. A maid opened it and ushered her into one of the beautiful rooms with long windows, still with the pale curtains chosen by Grace so long ago, such a contrast to the prevalence of dark velvets in grand houses. A fire was crackling in the grate, welcome warmth after the chilly ride. Grace would not want to exchange such comfort for life in a near derelict house in a muddy valley, Eliza thought ruefully.

'Ah, Mistress Trevannion.' It was Edgar, smiling a welcome, which was an improvement on their last meeting. Eliza did not miss his sharp eyed scanning of her person but smiled back sweetly and ignored it. Basically she thought this man was a boor and there was no hiding it. But it was Austol she wished to meet and the sickly Eulalia – and of course, her sister Grace and the new baby. The door opened again and this time Eliza had a shock. It seemed at first that Sir James had returned from the dead. The same tall spare figure, the same noble profile, the same grey eyes. But on closer scrutiny, the mouth was looser, the grey eyes colder, and the smile less genial. Introductions over, Austol offered excuses for his wife who was still unwell and confined to her bed.

'I should like to see my sister, Lady Treloyhan,' said Eliza, directly.

'She will be down in a moment,' assured Edgar, 'Meanwhile, we should discuss…'

'No, Mr. Tallack. I should like to talk to my sister first. Alone, if you please.'

Both men looked taken aback at the temerity of this female but agreed, rather unwillingly, that the sisters should take tea in the drawing room together.

'Please remember that she has only recently given birth to her second child and is still rather weak,' said Edgar.

'I care only for my sister's welfare,' Eliza responded. Who was he to instruct her how to treat her own sister?

Austol nodded briefly and left Eliza in the drawing room. Edgar made as if to follow, and then hesitated.

'Mistress Eliza, we too, want only the best for Grace.'

'For Lady Treloyhan,' corrected Eliza, in cold tones. Edgar was discomfited.

'I assure you, we are family and your sister is very happy to be called by her first name.'

'So happy that she wishes to live elsewhere?'

'No, she has no idea ..... perhaps I should put you in the picture,' said Edgar resignedly. He sat down opposite Eliza and leaned forward confidentially. 'I told you she was in need of nursing – as is the baby. She is not just weak after a difficult birth but is – wandering.'

'Wandering?'

'Suffering hallucinations.'

'What kind of hallucinations?' Eliza exclaimed, horrified.

'She has it in her mind that Austol is James, her husband. She calls for him to send Eulalia away – which has caused my sister considerable distress, as I am sure you will understand. She is dismissive of the children and screams if she should meet one by accident. The older girls understand but the younger ones are confused. Richard, her five year old boy, is the only child she allows near her.'

Eliza sank back into her chair.

'How dreadful,' she whispered. 'I am so sorry such a thing should have happened. And I am sorry that I did not understand at first.'

'I - we - thought that it would be too much of a shock to you to convey this directly. We spoke to the local physician who feels that she would benefit from specialised treatment but then we decided that perhaps time with you would help. It must be hard for her to live in this place where she lived with James and to find everything so different. Austol has become very impatient, and is angry that Eulalia has been so affected that she has taken to her bed.'

Edgar looked concerned enough for Eliza to feel that perhaps she had misjudged him. Or perhaps he was worried that he and his sister would not be able to remain at the Manor if the marriage should fail. Such an unkind thought. No, she would give Edgar the benefit of the doubt.

Edgar took his leave, saying he would arrange for tea to be brought in for the two sisters. Now for Grace, Eliza thought, preparing herself for a meeting that was bound to be difficult. The door opened and in came a small boy who came over to Eliza and offered his hand. 'How do you do? I am Richard. And you are my Aunt Eliza.' He looked at her solemnly and Eliza was enchanted. No hint of Barnabas, no red hair, just a little blond boy with big blue eyes and delicate features. This was a meeting she had dreaded but her reaction was one of pleasure.

'Oh Grace,' she said as her sister entered. 'Your son has the face of an angel – and such good manners!' A frail looking Grace summoned a hesitant smile at such praise.

'I am very proud of him,' she murmured. 'I don't know what he thinks of the new baby as yet. She is upstairs with her nanny but you may see her later if you wish.'

'I should like that,' agreed Eliza. She scrutinised her sister. 'Mr. Tallack tells me that you have not been well?'

'I don't know why he keeps saying that. I know my health is improving.' Indeed she appeared to be quite normal, Eliza thought. Her fragile beauty was not dimmed though her skin had a translucent quality, an indication of recent illness.

'James will not be pleased with me if Edgar insists that I am ill.' Grace said abruptly. 'He must stop saying so!' Her eyes sparked with sudden anger and Eliza's heart sank.

'Grace, surely you don't mean James? Austol is now head of the family because James is - er - a - ' Eliza floundered.

'You mean you think that James is dead? Oh no. He is still here,' said Grace, with a certainty that chilled her listener. 'The problem is that his brother is here too and with so many children you would not believe. James has been too kind letting them stay. He should go – and so should his sister, silly Eulalia.'

This was worse and worse. Grace seemed lost. She was uncertain whether she was in the past or the present and she had tangled both like skeins of knitting.

'Grace,' Eliza leaned forward and spoke gently. 'Would you like to come for a while to live with us in the new house – it's a very old house of course,' she added hastily. Grace lit up, her eyes like candles.

'Will Barnabas be there? I should like to come back if he is there.'

20

'No. I'm sorry but he is away in Australia.' Eliza kept her voice steady. 'But Uncle Tobias is there, Ewella and Jael and the children of course.'

'Children! What children!'

'My children. There are the twins, Nathaniel and Caroline, John, Nessa and Joel. Richard could play with them.'

'Out of the question. I don't like children and Richard does not like to play.'

'I should like to meet other children, Mama,' said Richard, seriously. 'You won't let me play with the ones here......'

'Richard! Quiet!' The little boy subsided and Eliza ached for him.

'I shall go up to my room. I have a megrim coming on. Perhaps you could see the baby another time. No, Richard' as her son tried to follow her. 'You stay here and entertain our guest.' And she was gone.

The little boy looked at Eliza pleadingly.

'My Mama is not well,' he said. 'I should so like to come and play with your children but she does not like me to play.'

'Has your Mama been ill for a long time?' asked Eliza, gently.

'Oh yes. A long time. But Mr. Tallack helps to look after me. He is very kind. He plays games with me when Mama is resting.'

An unexpected side to Edgar, thought Eliza. Perhaps he was anxious for Grace to move out so that Richard would have playmates – as he certainly would in the cramped conditions of their new house. Of course it was wrong of Edgar to have hidden the nature of Grace's illness but she could understand how difficult it was for him, probably worried about his sister, Eulalia and the reactions of his brother-in-law, the impatient Austol.

The subject of her musings came in, following a maid carrying a tea tray.

'Where is she?' he demanded.

'Gone to lie down because she has a megrim coming on,' replied Eliza, trying not to take umbrage at his peremptory tone.

'Well – what do you make of her?'

'Not in front of Richard,' she reproved.

'Richard – go and find the housekeeper and tell her that I sent you. She will find you milk and saffron cake if you ask her nicely.'

Richard nodded and left the room – so quietly and obediently for a small boy that Eliza wanted to call him back and hug him. But of course that would not be correct behaviour.

'I should very much like Grace to come and live with us,' Eliza offered. 'She will find it very different from the Manor but maybe the change will benefit her.'

'That is very kind of you.' Edgar sounded relieved. 'I do realise now that perhaps you are not as cold hearted as your sister seems to think.' He paused. 'All this talk about her cruel, uncaring sister is obviously part of her illness – her 'wandering'. Now that I have met you I know that the description of you is all part of her imagination.'

Eliza was brought up short. Cruel? Uncaring? So this was how Grace thought of her and talked of her. No wonder Edgar had been so unpleasant at their first meeting. Whatever else had her sister been saying?

'It is true that there has been a rift between Grace and myself,' said Eliza, carefully. 'But I should like you to know that there has been no unkind action on my part.'

'Of course not.' Edgar became jovial in his relief that this pretty woman was not the uncaring creature her sister had described. He went on, 'I should like to ask you if I might visit you to see how Grace has settled – and Richard. I am very fond of Richard.'

Eliza began to feel as muddled as her sister. From her first impression of Edgar as an arrogant, opinionated man, he had now metamorphosed into being caring and even kindly. Then he surprised her even further.

'I have dismissed the Lanivets' man and told him that I shall be taking you back to your home. I have ordered the carriage. It is the least I can do after all your trouble.' He held up his hand to avert protest. 'Furthermore, I shall see to it that Grace and Richard travel in comfort to you - probably in a week or so to give her time to pack – and get used to the idea.'

It would be the last comfort she would experience for a while, thought Eliza, grimly. To accustom herself to life in their house after the luxury of the Manor would be difficult. And what would happen if her mind deteriorated even further? It seemed that Edgar read her mind.

'If there is no improvement in her condition, Austol is willing to send her to London to a consultant physician.' A bewildered Eliza had to revise her opinion of Austol as well.

4

'Are you out of your mind, Eliza!' demanded Ewella, too angry to be polite. 'How can you think of having Grace in this house after all she did to you! And bringing two children with her!'

'She is my sister,' said Eliza, wearily. 'Now she is no longer welcome at the Manor I feel bound to offer her shelter. What happened was a long time ago – I cannot brood about it for ever.'

'Where do you intend to put them? We might have managed when we lived in Roscarne but even with Jael hiding out in one of the barns we have no room here.'

'Ewella, let us put our heads together and work out the best way to do this,' suggested Eliza.

It was not often that Eliza turned to her sister-in-law for advice and Ewella was suitably mollified.

'Perhaps we could move Trembles again,' she offered, not meaning to be taken seriously. But Eliza was horrified.

'Grace is going to need care and the children will need looking after,' she said. 'We shall have to put her where we can be vigilant without being too obvious.'

'Why? Is she ill?'

'Not exactly. But she gets a little muddled at times....'

'Oh my goodness! You mean she is deranged!'

'It's not as bad as that,' said Eliza irritably. 'Edgar says that living somewhere else, other than the Manor, would probably help to return her to reality. It has not been helpful that Austol looks so like his brother though I believe his temperament is – not the same.'

'Edgar says....Edgar says....' mimicked Ewella. 'I thought he made a bad impression on you when he came to call.'

'He did. But first impressions are not always correct.'

Uncle Tobias was not best pleased when he heard the news but his concern was for Eliza.

'That sister of yours led you a merry dance in the past. And did she bother to come and see how you were managing here in this damp, mildew riddled hole while she was in luxury at the Manor? No she did not.'

'There were reasons,' said Eliza soothingly. 'Don't worry Uncle Tobias, I have Ewella and Jael to help me and the children are older and more responsible.' Uncle Tobias frowned in doubt, then jumped to another subject:

'Better tell that Jael to make up one of her potions. The one she gave me for my rheumatism did me a power of good. Clever girl she is.'

'She is indeed,' nodded Eliza, relieved that his attention had been diverted from Grace's shortcomings.

'I believe that Professor Martineau is coming to supper tomorrow. He knows what is going on at the Manor. He'll tell us the news.'

'Uncle Tobias! You are wanting to gossip! Shame on you!' The old man laughed gleefully.

'The Professor told me last time that he is tutor to all seven of Austol's girls, even the young ones, and there's not a brain between them!'

'I'm sure he said no such thing!' Eliza was scandalised. But she was pleased to note the old man's good humour and his greater ease of movement. She must remember to mention this to Jael.

It was the next day that Caroline contrived to puzzle and frighten her mother at the same time. She was curled up on the windowsill of the schoolroom, the others having left and it was there Eliza found her.

'Caroline! It will be suppertime soon. Why are you still here?'

'I'm looking at the thorn trees and the woodland beyond. I wish we could see the sea.'

'We are not far from the sea. Jed Laity tells me that there is a path down to the shore from the bridge but it is steep and overgrown and often very muddy. Still, we could try to find it one day.' She tried to sound encouraging because Caroline was looking unusually pale and miserable. The little girl took a deep breath.

'Mama, this house does not want anyone else to come and live here. Aunt Grace should stay away.'

'You are talking nonsense Caroline. I know it won't be comfortable to have so many in such a small house but Aunt Grace needs our help.' Eliza spoke soothingly

24

'This house will push her away. That's what will happen.' Caroline jumped down from the windowsill. 'Just like it is pushing us away.' And she was gone.

Eliza looked out of the window. What a strange idea for a little girl to have. Not so little of course. She and her twin, Nathaniel, were twelve years old. Perhaps it was Jael's influence still, lingering on. The two of them had always been especially close and though Jael was seldom there now, living in the barn as she did, Caroline still contrived to see her. However they had less contact than before and Eliza had hoped that the 'fey' stage Caroline had gone through was past. She remembered her fixation on dark clouds and water, followed by the uncomfortable coincidence of the flooding at Carn Trevose – and then at Wheal Eliza. An impressionable Caroline seemed so receptive to Jael's premonitions.

It was quiet in the kitchen. A huge pot of stew bubbled gently on top of the range; Ewella had been busy and Eliza was grateful. She had other matters to attend to. She crossed the courtyard until she came to Jael's barn where Trembles had been. A striped, rough woven hanging covered the entrance, which provided some privacy but would not keep out the chills and damp of winter. Something would have to be done. There was no answer when she called Jael so, carefully, she pulled the hanging aside. Daylight spilled into the barn and she could see several wooden shelves scattered with phials, bowls, cups, herbs and flowers in vases. Jael had made herself at home. Stubs of candles and one oil lamp showed that she had some light; a rough wooden table and chair indicated more of Jed's handiwork. Eliza did not wish to pry into Jael's living space any further but she was disturbed by the paucity of comfort. Poor Jael. At least in the house there were solid wooden doors and some furniture from Roscarne. The range, the 'black monster' so named by Nessa, emitted some warmth; there was a sink and cold water and oil lamps for the approach of darkness. Jael had to fill her bucket from the pump in the courtyard and she had no fire. This would not do, Eliza decided. She and Jael needed to discuss ways of improving her living space.

She looked round the courtyard and shivered. As dusk approached, the thorn trees seemed to be crowding even closer and she had the feeling that the house was battling to maintain its space in the gloomy valley.

She could hear the stream complaining as it rattled over pebbles and was grateful that at least the rain had stopped. Perhaps she should go and look at the standing stone that had so worried Jael. She found that the land at the back of the house stretched much further than she had realised, and was bordered by a granite wall with gaps like missing teeth where stones had become dislodged and displaced. Towards the far border, the weeds, the thistles, the thorn bushes, grew even taller and there was no sign of a standing stone. She pushed her way through the tangled vegetation, marvelling at the strong growth on such poor soil. Then she found it. In a tangle of hawthorn, buckthorn and thistles it stood and, for a moment, Eliza felt that it was a sentient being, entrapped by the trio of witch trees whose thorns scraped and squeaked over the granite and whose bone-like branches whipped round it when the wind blew.

'It is impressive, isn't it?' Jael spoke softly as if she might be overheard.

'You startled me!' gasped Eliza, drawn back from her fancies. 'But yes, it has a presence. It may be just a granite stone but it makes me feel – I don't know – as if it has power.'

'I feel the same way,' Jael said. 'It is contemptuous of the enemies around it and protective of its ground. I see a shimmer of colours around it' – Her voice became softer, stranger in tone. 'The wind and the rain and the trees will not be able to harm it.'

'We are talking about a stone,' said Eliza, with a half-smile.

Jael came to share supper that evening. Caroline could not hide her delight that she was there and insisted on sitting next to her. Everyone complimented Ewella on her tasty stew which elicited a satisfied smile.

'It's a rabbit stew – Mrs. Kershaw used to make them back at Roscarne,' she said.

'Where did you get the rabbit, Ewella?' demanded John.

'Farmer Tull, of course.'

'I'll wager the poachers catch them on his land and then sell them back to him,' put in Uncle Tobias.

'I don't like eating rabbits,' Nathaniel blurted. 'Remember poor Nibbles?'

They all remembered Nibbles, the rabbit Nathaniel had rescued and the ensuing row with his father.

'Well, it's rabbit or nothing this evening,' declared Ewella. 'The larder is empty.'
Eliza hid a smile. She knew that youthful hunger would overcome Nathaniel's scruples.

'Has there been a letter from Papa?' asked Nessa. 'He doesn't write very often. I think he should be coming back to us soon - perhaps that's why.'
'There was a letter this morning,' replied Eliza. 'But it was not from your father – it was from Lord Treloyhan at the Manor. He wants me to visit Aunt Grace there before she comes to stay with us.'
'You have been there once,' said Caroline. 'Why do you have to go again?'
'I can't explain that.' shrugged Eliza. She had no intention of telling the children that their Aunt Grace was 'wandering' in the head and had declared she did not want to leave the Manor. She did not have a sister, she had told Austol and Edgar and so she could not move in with her, could she?

Summoned to the Manor, a visit she viewed with some trepidation, Eliza was reconciled to the idea when Edgar let her know that of course he would pick her up and drive her there – provided the rain had not rendered the track impassable. It was kind of him, she decided and she would use the journey to find out a little more about his sister, Eulalia.
'I understand Grace is now unwilling to come and live with us at – at –' with a shock, Eliza realised that there was no name for the house other than the 'Hidden House', a name given to it by the children. Surely it had had a proper name when it belonged to the Lanivets? She must find out what it was. Edgar had not noticed her pause. He was negotiating the pony and trap over the bridge, a difficult manoeuvre as the trap had narrow wheels which threatened to catch in the gaps between the wooden boards, gaps which were less difficult for the cart which Mathey used to drive them.
'Her attitude changes with the wind,' declared Edgar. 'Sometimes she is excited by the idea, then she will burst out that no one wants her and she would prefer to stay confined in her room and not see anybody at all. Other times she will run, crying to Eulalia, and demand that she leave the Manor because James is not her lawful husband. We have tried to make her realise that Austol is NOT James,

but his brother and that, sadly, James is dead. Then she has hysterics but still accuses poor Eulalia of stealing her husband.'

'Oh dear!' was all Eliza could find to say. 'But Eulalia is ill, I understand. How is she now?'

Though eloquent on the subject of Grace, Edgar seemed unwilling to discuss Eulalia.

'Obviously my sister is upset by Grace,' was all he would say.

Eliza was ushered into the same beautiful room as before and had time to admire the view of the gardens while Edgar went in search of Austol. It was early autumn and the Virginia creeper which draped over the Manor like a shawl was already in full colour, reminding Eliza of Roscarne. How she missed Roscarne! And the sea! Where she lived now was near the sea but separated from it by a barrier of thorn trees and tangled woodland. None of the family had yet found a way through and it was only the distant roar of the waves on stormy days that reminded her of its presence.

'Mistress Trevannion! You are so kind to come and see us again.' It was Austol, impeccable of dress and austere of manner as usual. 'We shall take tea here if that is agreeable to you and then perhaps we can persuade Grace to come and see you.'

'Thank you.' Eliza became monosyllabic in his presence. His eyes were disquieting, she thought. Edgar had disappeared and they were alone.

'Mistress Trevannion, I understand that Barnabas Trevannion, your husband, has been away in Australia for some considerable time, now? Do you expect him back in the near future?'

'Yes, no, I don't really know...' stumbled Eliza.

'Have you heard from him recently?'

'Last month,' she replied. In fact it had been two months previously but she was not going to admit that to Austol. 'I am prepared to look after Grace without help from Barnabas,' she declared. 'And if it proves too difficult then we shall consult a physician in London as you suggested.'

Austol nodded. Surprisingly he then changed the subject.

'I understand you have five children. Tell me about them.' It was a command rather than a polite query but Eliza was always happy to talk about her children.

'The twins, Nathaniel and Caroline are twelve, nearly thirteen years of age. John is ten, Nessa is seven and Joel is six.'

'So you have three sons,' he commented, unable to hide a certain bitterness in his voice.

At this juncture, Edgar entered the room.

'Grace – Lady Treloyhan' he began, sketching a brief bow to Eliza. 'I believe she is in a good mood and very willing to take tea with us.'

'Very good.' Austol sat back in his armchair but Eliza could sense that he had not taken his eyes away from her. Those cold grey eyes with strange musings in their depths. Edgar seemed ill at ease but relieved when the door opened and Grace made her entrance. All smiles, dressed in pale blue silk with her hair caught up with silver combs, it was difficult to believe there was anything wrong. She took Eliza's hands in hers and said simply. 'My sister. My sister, Eliza. You have come to look after me, have you not?'

'I hope you will come and stay with me,' said Eliza gently. 'And then I can certainly look after you.'

'It will be like old times,' declared Grace. 'Will Rose be there? And Barnabas? I look forward to seeing you all. I should like Mrs. Kershaw to make me some of her saffron buns. They were so good.'
Eliza looked despairingly at Edgar but he shook his head.

'Grace,' said Eliza firmly. 'You know that Barnabas is in Australia. And Rose has gone to Arizona with Seth Quinn and they are now married. But you will see Uncle Tobias and Ewella and the children, of course.' Grace was beginning to frown but Eliza went on persuasively. 'We are living in a much smaller house now, but you will have the best room and it will be such fun to be together again. Come and try it for a while and see if you like it.'

'I think I will do that,' said Grace. Abruptly she changed the subject. 'Do you know that Eulalia has stolen James from me? And Edgar is always cross with me? .....' and she was off into childlike rantings while her listeners looked helplessly at each other.

'I shall get a room ready for her,' said Eliza. 'She must bring her own bed and bedding and there will be no room for a nanny. We shall have to care for the baby between us.'

'I hope the complete change will help her,' said Austol but he did not sound convinced. 'The alternative is probably care in a special hospital.....'

'Absolutely not!' said Eliza fiercely.

Austol escorted Eliza to the front door, waving the parlour maid away.

'I am delighted that we have come to this arrangement,' he said. 'I do not like to say this in front of Edgar, who is very sensitive on the subject of his sister, but I am beginning to feel that Eulalia's condition is deteriorating.....'

'I am so sorry to hear that,' Eliza replied. She was feeling acutely uncomfortable. Austol was holding her hand and standing rather too close. Considerably taller than she was, he was bending over her, restricting her space. She could smell cigar smoke and, faintly, cologne. And those eyes – cold, grey and calculating. She felt that he wanted something from her, something more than the removal of Grace from the Manor. How she could ever have imagined that he resembled his brother, James, eluded her. The inner man inhabiting that familiar frame was a different creature entirely. And she could not wait to get away.

5

Grace, Lady Treloyhan, sister to Eliza and Aunt to her five children, arrived in some state in a carriage - a small carriage admittedly but the narrow track did not allow for anything large. Her escort was Edgar on his fine bay horse and behind, her baggage followed, carried more ignominiously by pony and cart. It was clear, by Edgar's expression that he would have preferred to distance himself from this duty and that feelings of disdain warred with those of concern. Everyone in the house except for Jael, who was elsewhere, crowded outside to see this arrival. Edgar opened the carriage door to allow Grace to alight but, Eliza was disconcerted to see, she was not alone. The nanny followed, carrying the new baby and then little Richard tumbled out.

'Grace, welcome to our house,' Eliza managed. 'Caroline will show you up to your room.' Grace smiled sweetly and followed Caroline, the nanny and Richard trailing behind.

'Edgar – I thought we agreed there was to be no nanny! We do not have the room!' Eliza hissed.

'It was the nanny or no Grace!' snapped Edgar, whose patience had obviously worn thin. 'Grace refused point blank to leave without her and was on the point of having hysterics when Austol insisted we take both of them.'

'How could he insist on such a thing?'

'He was threatening to have Grace taken away to some place where they look after people who are – who are – ' Edgar was unable to finish his sentence.

'People who are considered mad, you mean,' said Eliza, bitterly.

'No, those who are suffering from nervous illnesses,' said Edgar firmly.' But Austol is difficult to deflect from his decisions. He is allowing Grace to live with you in the hope that she will recover her senses.'

'And if she does not?' Edgar shrugged. 'He will send her away.'

'He has no right to do that!' cried Eliza. Austol could not do that to her sister.

'He has the doctors in his pocket!' Edgar sounded bitter.

There was only one solution. Grace, who had been given the most habitable room in the house, would have to share with the nanny, Richard and the new baby. It was not an arrangement she was used to and the beds jostled uncomfortably in the small space, but she was in sunny mood and made no objection.

'This is just till we go back to Roscarne, is it not?' she smiled. 'I am so glad to have Nanny Hannah with me. She is wonderful with the baby and Richard adores her. I can help by arranging my room – putting clothes in the wardrobe and my rugs on the floor. I am rather surprised, Eliza, that there are no carpets up here? Is it a new fashion?'

'She is far worse than I ever envisaged,' Eliza groaned to Ewella. 'She will soon realise that there are no curtains either. And Richard will have to sleep on the floor until we can find a bed small enough to fit in next to hers.'

'She has been living in a world of luxury and has not yet broken out of it,' agreed Ewella. 'We shall just have to do our best with her when she realises and hope that we can keep her happy.' Eliza looked gratefully at her sister-in-law. Ewella was not usually so optimistic.

'We shall have a good supper tonight,' Ewella went on. 'That Edgar has left us some fine provisions – including a ham that is almost too big for the range. But not quite!' she finished. 'I shall get it cooked, never fear. We shall have plenty, for a change.'

'Let's make it a celebratory feast!' Eliza cried. 'The children will enjoy that too.'

Mathey and Jed carried in all the contents of the cart while Ewella busied herself at the range. Nanny Hannah stayed upstairs with the baby and Eliza sat with Grace who was looking increasingly bewildered.

'I thought Barnabas would be home,' she said plaintively. 'Will he be back for supper?' and Eliza had to explain all over again that Barnabas was in Australia and that Rose was now married to Seth and was in Arizona. Further explanations were interrupted by the entry of Uncle Tobias, someone Grace recognised and she greeted him delightedly. Then the children, with Richard in their midst, came in, ready for supper. The benches from the schoolroom had been pressed into service to enable everyone to be seated; only Uncle Tobias had the luxury of a cushion. Eliza looked at the long wooden table which

32

looked quite festive with candles but she could not help contrasting it with the polished furniture, the snow white linen tablecloths, the silver, and the crystal glasses that had been usual in Roscarne. She sighed. Finally, everyone was slotted into a place at the table. The children were unusually quiet, sitting upright and sedate as was Richard. It was only when Ewella started passing round dishes of potatoes and vegetables that they began chattering among themselves. Only Richard stayed silent.

'Of course, at the Manor, we ate without speaking,' said Grace. 'And Richard had his supper in the nursery with Nanny Hannah.'

'I like it better, here.' Richard broke his silence. He looked angelic, his blond hair so light and bright in the gloomy room. He was a beautiful child and Eliza found it difficult to remember that his birth had been the cause of so much unhappiness for her.

'Hush, Richard,' said Grace. 'Children are to be seen and not heard. Especially at mealtimes.' She spoke in the irritable voice she seemed to reserve for her son.

'Grace, you will find we are less formal, here,' said Eliza hurriedly. 'But we hope that you will settle happily with us. Nathaniel, Caroline, John and Joel – and Nessa, of course – ' she looked at them sternly. 'You will please look after Richard.'

'Yes, Mama,' they all chorused. Only John looked sulky at the prospect. It seemed that Richard was to get all the attention.

Later in the evening, the children in bed, the dishes cleared away and Uncle Tobias back in his little room, Eliza, Ewella and Grace sat close to the wood-fire and chatted. Grace seemed quite normal most of the time, only lapsing into a muddle occasionally. It was then that Jael came in, having missed supper. She brought a blast of cold, damp air with her.

'Don't worry, I have had something to eat,' she assured Eliza, rubbing her cold hands as the warmth of the fire reached her. Grace smiled at her and Eliza began to believe that this visit would not be a disaster.

'Tell us all about life at the Manor,' Jael suggested when the talk stuttered to a halt. Eliza was immediately on the alert. Would this be wise? Ewella, however, looked eager and greedy for information.

'What sort of a man is Austol?' she demanded. Grace frowned.

'He is an impostor!' she burst out. 'My husband, Sir James Treloyhan, should be the head of the family at the Manor but Austol has usurped his position. Also, he has allowed his stupid sick wife to take over from me - from ME. I am the Lady of the Manor, not silly Eulalia! And now she is sick. And her seven girls have no one to oversee them except for Nanny Hannah and she is here with us. That will teach him!' Jael looked stunned by this tirade but Ewella wanted more.

'Surely your husband is – is not with you now? So Austol has to take charge?' Grace ignored the implied question

'Austol should go. But he won't go. He is not a nice man and very unkind to Eulalia.'

'We should not be gossiping like this,' interposed Eliza, but Ewella would not let the matter rest.

'Unkind? But how?'

'He wants a son but she has given him seven girls and only one son – a weakly one by all accounts. He is always reproaching her for this. And now she has taken to her bed and that makes him even more cross. I think she stays there just to escape him.'

'I heard that she is really sick and has bad headaches,' said Ewella.

'Oh yes. And Austol won't let the doctor come and see her.' Grace sounded more and more childlike in her listing of Austol's misdemeanours and Eliza determined to put a stop to the questions.

'Grace, you have had a very tiring day,' she said. 'Perhaps you would like to retire to your room. We can catch up with all your news tomorrow. I hope that you will be comfortable and that your baby will sleep through.'

'Do you not have a name for her, yet?' queried the indefatigable Ewella.

'No. I shall have to consult James before I decide.' Eliza's heart sank.

At last Grace was upstairs in her room, being fussed over by Nanny Hannah.

'I'm glad Nanny Hannah is here with Grace after all,' said Eliza. 'She is wonderful with her.'

'I'm afraid your sister is like foam upon the sea,' said Jael. 'She is blown every which way according to the conversation.'

'Do you think she will ever return to her right mind?' Eliza agonised. 'She is so convinced that James is still alive and she does not retain explanations.'

'Perhaps rest and this change of scenery from the Manor will help,' Jael said.

'With three more mouths to feed, no one, not even Grace, will have time to do much resting!' was Ewella's tart contribution.

There was not much rest to be had that particular night, either. Eliza was just drifting off to sleep having managed to block out Ewella's stertorous breathing when there was a commotion from Grace's room. The door burst open and Grace stood there, wild eyed, with Nanny Hannah close behind her.

'WHO is crying?' she demanded. 'Someone keeps crying and won't stop.'

'Oh Grace, it must be one of the children having a nightmare,' Eliza rubbed her eyes.

'I've checked on the children and they are all fast asleep,' said Nanny Hannah virtuously. 'And the baby hasn't stirred.'

'They must stop! Whoever is crying must stop! I can't sleep!'

'I can't hear anything,' said Eliza, sitting up in bed.

'Nor me,' said Nanny Hannah.

'Grace, you must have been dreaming yourself. You get back to bed and I'll bring you a hot drink.'

Eliza went downstairs as Nanny Hannah ushered Grace back to her bed and was just mixing one of Jael's herb teas when Uncle Tobias appeared in irritable mood.

'One of those children is crying! Can't you stop them? I'm trying to sleep.' He was a sorry sight in his nightshirt, which hung on him as he had lost weight in the short time he had been in the new house. His grey hair awry, his whiskers unkempt, he tore at Eliza's heartstrings. Poor Uncle Tobias. Barnabas had not been kind in his closing up of Roscarne and disappearing to Australia. The old man deserved better.

'We all do,' she thought.

Peace returned as Grace and Uncle Tobias slept, soothed by the herb tea. But Eliza stayed awake, worrying. She worried about Uncle Tobias' health. She worried about Jael in her cold barn. She worried about

Grace and Richard. And she worried that she had not heard from Barnabas for over two months. Neither had there been news from Seth and Rose in Arizona.

'This can't go on,' she thought. 'What if the money Barnabas left does not last?' It was only when she had made up her mind to travel to Truro on the following day to see Cubert Petherwin, the solicitor, to question him on the exact state of their finances that she was able to fall asleep. But sometime later she awoke with such a jump that she could feel her heart racing. She sat up straight in bed. Something had disturbed her but she had no idea what it was. It was cold and the black square of window showed that dawn was nowhere near. Ewella was fast asleep, her red hair hardly showing beneath the coverlet. She was about to slide under the covers again when she heard it. Someone was crying. With a sigh of exasperation she tiptoed next door to the children's room. All was quiet there. She pushed open the door of Grace's room. It creaked loudly and Eliza froze. But there was no sound from within and nobody stirred.

'I'm imagining things,' she scolded herself; nevertheless she crept down the cold stone stairs to the kitchen. The fire in the range was still giving out a little warmth but there was no one there. Jael must be still in her barn and Uncle Tobias still asleep in his little room. She sat down at the table, letting the warmth lull her back to feeling sleepy. There was no sound anywhere.

The grey light of dawn was suffusing the kitchen when she woke up. She lifted her head from her arms feeling her neck and shoulders ache in protest. What a place to fall asleep. She would creep back to bed and make the most of the short time remaining before she had to rise and put breakfast on the table for her houseful. Outside the wind was strengthening and branches from the thorn trees were scraping against the window.

'I'll get Jed to cut those back,' she thought. Quietly she opened the door, wondering if Jael had yet woken but her blanket awning was still in place. She shivered as the cold air rushed in and closed the door again quickly. In the following brief quiet she heard it again. Someone was crying, a heartbroken, hopeless sobbing, that made her feel incredibly sad.

6

'Mistress Eliza! You look so pale! Are you not well?' Jael was crossing the courtyard, with an armful of grasses and herbs and came upon Eliza leaning against the stone wall, gazing out at the woodland. It was unusual for her to be unoccupied at that time of the morning. Eliza essayed a laugh but it was not very convincing.

'I had a poor night's sleep,' she confessed.

'Why?'

'Grace heard somebody crying and so did Uncle Tobias. Fortunately they only woke me and did not disturb anyone else.'

'One of the children having a nightmare?'

'Well, no. They were all sound asleep when we looked.'

'Oh.'

'Jael, don't you feel hemmed in by these thorn trees?' demanded Eliza, changing the subject. 'It's a lovely sunny morning but the branches obscure the light and bar the way across the track. We seem to be in a valley of darkness and I long for the light as we had at Roscarne.'

'What you need is a taste of the sea,' said Jael. 'Why don't you follow the path by the bridge? It does reach the sea eventually.'

'I can't. I have a thousand things to do,' said Eliza, dolefully.

'Nonsense!' said Jael, forgetting she was speaking to her mistress. 'The children are with Professor Martineau, Ewella is preparing lunch and Uncle Tobias is looking through some old maps he brought with him. They are all busy and you are not needed.'

'And Grace?'

'Oh, Grace. She is still in her room. Nanny Hannah will take care of her. Go on. You deserve some time on your own, something you have not had since we moved here.' Though Jael was so much younger than her mistress her tone had the determination and drive that Eliza had lost in her sudden reversal of fortunes.

Persuaded, Eliza set off. Jael, meanwhile, stared long and thoughtfully at the house. The dark windows gave away no secrets; they seemed to stand guard and repel all who wished to enter. Those already inside could not be heard through the granite walls, no cries from the children, no Ewella shouting. The only sign of occupation was the cart that had brought the Professor that morning. Presumably the pony had been turned out into the fields at the back to graze. Looking abstracted, Jael hurried towards the barn that had become her home. Something was wrong. The house was not welcoming to its new occupants and this was manifested in several ways – the unfriendly façade, the strange crying and the encroaching darkness which she was sure was more than just the approach of winter. She could not be responsible. She had removed herself from the house. What more could she do?

Some days without rain had reduced the volume of water rushing down from the moor and the stream burbled along quite happily. Opposite the bridge, Eliza plunged into the darkness of the wood, pushing aside low branches and avoiding the knee high thistles where she could. Even so her dress was being snagged and pulled and her legs scratched. The thought of seeing the sea again kept her going, stumbling through mud-filled potholes, over barriers of fallen branches, strewn boulders and sudden changes in the downhill gradient. In one small clearing, she stopped and listened. She could hear the busy chatter of the stream so knew she was still on the path. Here the low branches were covered with lichens and moss and everywhere hung a strong smell of damp and rotting vegetation intermingled with the acrid tang of wild garlic. No smell of salt, no sound of the sea as yet. It seemed the path was leading her through the darkness of fairytales and she was beset by demons ands trolls in the shape of thorn trees and dark leaved bushes. But having come so far she was determined to keep going. A trailing branch cut her face but she brushed the blood away impatiently. Find the sea she would. No imagined horrors would bar her way. A little further and the trees opened on to scrubby grass and bracken. She was out in the open. And before her was the sea.

She was still high up and she realised that she had followed a fork in the path that led away from the stream with its stepped waterfalls that splashed down into a narrow valley on her right. Before her spread the wide sky and a limitless expanse of blue, shimmering with sunshine. Such light after the darkness of the path. Such space. There were no ships on the horizon or small boats fishing, no children on the shoreline. No one. The sea was in gentle mood, lightly rippled like silk. Delighted,

Eliza perched on a boulder and stared around her, absorbing the atmosphere, and basking in the autumn sunlight. A cluster of pointed rocks and islets just off shore caught her eye and she realised that she could climb down to their level and approach even closer to the water. The scramble down over tussocky grass tore another hole in her dress but she did not care. The unladylike nature of her little expedition brought back her girlhood and reminded her of the many hours she had spent on the shore close to the breaking waves. Sometimes too close. Several times she had underestimated the advance of the tides and she laughed at the memory of her rescue by Seth. Seth. No, she would not think of him. Barnabas then. She had seen him for the first time when he had shouted a warning to her from the cliff and saved her from a further wetting. She needed to be more careful in this empty place; there would be no one to rescue her here.

Childishly she dabbled her hands in a rockpool, watching as the anemones waved their fronds hopefully. Little fish whisked away and hid under weed but the snails stayed still, clinging to the sides of the pool. She would bring the children down here, she thought. They would love it even though the walk along the path was long and difficult. Feeling strengthened and invigorated she climbed back up to her boulder. She would sit in that peaceful place a little longer. Eventually, resting her head and stretching out with a sigh, she fell asleep. The sun was lower in the sky when she woke. A veil of cloud was drifting over the water, muting the colours and wreathing round the rocks which looked even more like teeth. Sharp teeth. Fangs. She shivered. A last look around and she climbed towards the path back to the house.

She was hardly into the trees when the thin, contorted trunks closed in, thorny branches laced together against the sunlight. All too quickly, darkness wrapped around her. To make any progress she needed to push her way along the path as the gradient, now upward, seemed steeper, the mud and stones conspiring to hinder her. She slipped and slid along, grasping tall weeds occasionally to maintain her balance, reassured at least by the sound of water that she was following the stream. Out of breath, she stopped in the small clearing she remembered from earlier and it was there she felt a change in the atmosphere. The smell of rotting vegetation was as strong, the burble of the stream as loud but all of a sudden she was cold even though the perspiration from her walking was still damp on her forehead. She shivered. Insidiously, the feeling crept over her that she was not alone. Perhaps there were other walkers on the path ahead; soon she would hear them, she thought, trying to rationalise her nervousness. But no one appeared. The darkness thickened as she continued walking; a branch whiplashed across her face. Panic set in. Would she ever reach the end of this trail? Surely she should be back to the bridge by now. Used to the rustling of the leaves, the plashing of water she became aware of another sound. Voices whispering. She listened, desperately trying to make out what was being said. Then a louder voice whispered. 'Leave. Leave the house.'

'What do you mean? Who are you?' Eliza quavered. There was no answer. Emboldened, she spoke loudly. 'If you want to say something – show yourself.' Then a bolt of sheer terror transfixed her. With absolute certainty she knew she did not want to see the owner of the voice. She needed to get away, to return to the house.

'Mama, you don't look very well,' said Caroline who met her at the gate. 'We had lunch a long time ago and Ewella is cross.'
Eliza smiled at her twelve year old daughter who had been looking out for her and was pretending that she had not. 'The path to the sea was longer than I thought, Caro. Don't worry I feel perfectly well.'

'Your dress is all torn and you are covered in mud - and grass!'
'It was quite a difficult walk,' Eliza allowed.
Ewella was cross as Caroline had said but it was not because she had missed her lunch.

'I declare, Eliza, you have no thought for anyone but yourself! Professor Martineau wanted to talk to you about the children but where were you? No one knew! Then Grace wanted you – but we could not find you! And here am I buried in pots and dishes! And no one here to help!'

'Jael knew I had gone for a walk,' said Eliza mildly.

'A walk! You have time for walking with all the chores we have to do? You were spoilt at Roscarne with nannies and maids. Here there is only me – and Jael and she does not put in an appearance very often. Too busy concocting medicines and peculiar potions!' Ewella had worked herself into a fury. How like her brother Barnabas she was, Eliza thought. Eyes flashing, nostrils flaring, red hair on end.

'I'm so sorry to have put you to extra trouble, Ewella. I shall make sure you know where I am going next time.'

'Yes, well…..' Her sister-in-law simmered down. She was a conundrum, Eliza thought. There were times when she felt that Ewella really hated her and then other times she seemed as concerned as Rose had been. Oh how she missed Rose, now so far away in Arizona. And she missed Barnabas. She missed his daily presence, the bulk of him in her bed, his infectious laugh, his arm around her shoulders. And she knew that he adored the children even if he tried too hard to discipline them.

For the evening meal, Ewella had concocted one of her stews and the delicious smell brought everyone together in anticipation. Uncle Tobias hobbled out of his 'study', rubbing his hands together, Jael came in from the barn, the children were called and rushed in with their usual alacrity and even Grace and Nanny Hannah put in an appearance. Fortunately the baby was asleep. Eliza noticed that little Richard was overcoming his shyness and had actually pushed in front of John. A brave thing to do as John was still quite pugnacious when he considered his space to be violated. However he let Richard sit next to him and this dispossessed Nessa from her usual seat. Her wide smile disarmed everyone as she wriggled on to another chair and looked around the table, quite unperturbed.

'We are as crowded as pilchards in a net!' grumbled Joel. 'What shall we do when the baby is old enough to join us?' What indeed. Eliza hoped that by then Barnabas would have returned and they would be moving back to Roscarne.

'Lady Treloyhan,' said Jael softly. 'Are you going to name your baby soon?' Grace looked up with a dazzling smile.

'No. I shall wait for James to come back and then we shall choose a name together.'

'But Sir James is dead!' John exclaimed before anyone could stop him.

'Shut up, John!' hissed Nathaniel.

'Oh no.' Grace smiled sweetly. 'James is not dead. He has merely gone away on his travels. He does this occasionally. Baby and I will just wait patiently till he returns.'

There was an awkward silence. Uncle Tobias broke it by complimenting Ewella on her stew which put her in a good mood and diverted attention from Grace. As if to make up for John's unfortunate remark, the children were extremely well behaved during the rest of the meal and the words 'please' and 'thank you' hovered over the table like hungry gulls.

As Eliza busied herself at the sink, cleaning dishes and platters, she mulled over Grace's denial that her husband was dead, a fact she did not seem able to face. In many other ways she seemed accepting and peaceful. The former Grace, of course, would not have suffered the privations of their present daily life, the plain food, the lack of adequate heating, the cramped sleeping arrangements, the absence of maids, but for the present she was content to put on a pretty dress and sit by the window, watching Nanny Hannah deal with the baby. Help in the house she did not. Cook she would not. Eliza was just thankful that there were no tantrums and that she seemed not to miss the Manor at all. There was one puzzle still to be solved. Where was Grace's money, the money settled on her by James Treloyhan in his will? Grace had never mentioned it and Eliza was reluctant to do so, feeling that it was nothing to do with her. She knew that Nanny Hannah was being paid by Austol but surely Grace had private means?

Outside, dusk was falling. Ewella lit the oil lamps and began to shoo the children to bed. It was Caroline who was unusually obstructive. Finally Eliza lost patience.

'Caroline, what is the matter with you this evening? One excuse after another and here you are still down here and everyone else has gone to bed. You are twelve years old – nearly thirteen – and too old for these childish ways.'

'Mama - I - I don't want to go upstairs. I shall feel sad.'

'Please explain what you mean,' said her mother.

'There is someone who cries all the time and I don't know who it is. I asked Jael but she doesn't know either.'

'Why did you ask Jael? She doesn't sleep here.'

'I thought she might know. She has the sight.'

'Oh Caro, I'm sure it is someone having a nightmare,' said Eliza, helplessly.

'Mama, you know that is not true.' In a clear voice, Caroline pinned down her mother's evasions. 'It is not one of us in the house now - so it must be someone who used to live here.'

7

That night, though Eliza remained awake, there were no more sounds of crying and no whispers. She had managed to reassure Caroline by blaming the wind in the chimney though she did not believe her own words. No doubt Caroline did not believe them either but she was still comforted enough to fall asleep. The morning brought sunshine bright enough to spear through the thorn trees and the kitchen window; breakfast was cheerful as a result and the children chattered more and squabbled less. Ewella doled out the porridge with a smile and Uncle Tobias congratulated her on reaching the correct coagulation of the milk and oat-flakes which, he insisted, Mrs. Kershaw had never managed.

The sunshine brought them unexpected visitors. George and Thomas Lanivet, the twin brothers who had so kindly given them the house to live in, arrived in their smart pony and trap. There were anxious smiles on their rubicund faces as they clattered into the courtyard. The journey had disarrayed their white hair and ruffled their whiskers, the pony was spattered with mud and obviously the journey had not been without incident.

'Mistress Trevannion, we hope you will forgive us that we arrive without warning!' cried Thomas, helping George down from the trap.

'But of course. We are delighted to see you,' replied Eliza. She had quickly untied her apron to step forward and greet them. They were, after all, her family's benefactors in spite of the reservations she still held about the state of the house.

'We wished to ascertain that you are all safe and well,' added George. 'We promised Barnabas that we would do that.'

'Please come inside,' said Eliza, hoping that all was cleared up in the kitchen. She need not have worried. Ewella, with great efficiency, had scurried round and put the last few dishes away as soon as she heard the arrival of the pony and trap.

The Lanivets entered cautiously – 'almost as if they expected someone to jump out at them,' Ewella said later. George, in particular, seemed uneasy, looking over his shoulder once inside and casting furtive glances at the closed door.

'I think we should stay in the kitchen.' Eliza was apologetic. 'There is no fire as yet in the other room and it is much warmer in here with the range alight.'

'Splendid. That will do nicely,' said Thomas heartily. 'I wonder if I could ask your man to attend to our pony? It is a longer journey than we remember and a struggle along that track which has become even more rutted and potholed.'

'I'm afraid Mathey and Jed are fetching supplies from Truro,' replied Eliza. 'But Caroline will look after it. She is in charge of Trembles, our pony, and is very capable.'

'You have no one else to help?' queried George, looking puzzled. 'Barnabas assured me that he had arranged for sufficient servants to attend you. Surely there was much to do to make the place habitable and to clean up before you arrived. Is that not so?' he appealed to his brother.

'Certainly we had no help apart from Mathey,' Ewella put in, frowning. 'It seems my brother was very lax in his duties to his family! We arrived here to find the house in an advanced state of neglect. Quite clearly no one had been near it for some time. And there were rats and mice scampering about!'

'I seem to remember that – we left the house in rather a hurry,' said Thomas. 'I am aware it was some years ago but – '

'But we did not wish to return,' George interrupted. His brother gave him a warning look before he could say any more.

'Ewella, perhaps we may offer these gentlemen some refreshment,' suggested Eliza. 'I am sure that in the rush to close Roscarne and packing for Australia, the matter of preparing the house was overlooked.' Her voice was soothing. She intended to allay the anxieties felt by the brothers. Clearly they were not at fault.

'I shall fetch Caroline,' muttered Ewella, conscious that perhaps she had been less than tactful. 'And Grace, of course.'

'Grace? Is Lady Treloyhan here with you?' The twins spoke together in tones of astonishment.

'Surely you do not have sufficient room!' gasped Thomas.

'We have overcome the difficulties,' Eliza said cheerily. 'I know it is rather crowded but she is my sister and she needed us. She has little Richard and her new baby with her and of course they are very welcome.' She decided not to mention Nanny Hannah.

'We understood that Austol Treloyhan had invited her to stay at the Manor. Surely that would have given you more space? Oh dear, it seems that we are the ones who have been lax in our duties!' Thomas spoke gravely. George nodded, looking in need of reassurance; he had the air of an old collie dog unable to round up his sheep.

'Please believe me, we are very grateful for your kindness,' said Eliza. 'It would have been so difficult to find a suitable house in such a short time.' She sat down, smoothing her dress and trying to act the welcoming hostess.

'Now please tell us what is happening in the outside world? We are quite isolated here. I am sure Uncle Tobias would be interested in mining news in particular.'

'Tobias! He is here as well?' Thomas threw up his hands, looking really disturbed. 'My dear Mistress Trevannion this is too much for you, surely!'

'No,' said Eliza obstinately. 'He is a member of our family also and we could not be without him. In fact it is time for him to wake from his nap so I shall go and alert him that you are here.'

Uncle Tobias was delighted to see these old friends and time sped by as they exchanged news about the increasing popularity of the railway which had reached Penzance, the opening of new hotels to cater for increasing numbers of tourists and, of course, the latest developments in the mining industry.

'We should have come to visit you all much earlier,' Thomas said, abruptly, rather interrupting the flow of talk. 'But we have moved to Pendeen. Quite a long drive away.'

'Pendeen?'

'Near to Geevor Mine. You know the area, Tobias. We have an interest there and we are hopeful that our investment will prove profitable.'

'Also this house proved rather costly in these times and we prefer a smaller house' put in George. 'Fewer servants needed.'
Eliza glanced at Ewella. This was worrying news indeed. It indicated that the Lanivets were possibly having financial difficulties. Would they want their house back? Nervously she broached the subject but as one the twins exclaimed with force:

'Certainly not!'

'We shall NEVER come back here,' said George impressively.

'We are happy at Pendeen – which is also not far from Wheal Charlotte, where mining has recommenced,' Thomas hastened to explain. 'Carnglaze is yours for as long as you need it.'

'Carnglaze? Is that the name of the house?' Thomas nodded.

It was then that Grace made her entrance, an entrance reminiscent of old times. She was wearing a lacy white shawl over an aquamarine dress in taffeta which rippled round her like water. Her hair was piled high in twists and coils and Eliza realised that Nanny Hannah had other talents apart from baby care. Lovely as ever, in spite of her pallor, she made Eliza feel diminished. It was an unworthy feeling and Eliza knew that, but still she wished she were not in her work dress of grey twill. Thomas and George rose from their chairs, obviously delighted to greet the beautiful Lady Treloyhan. Her magic seemed to work on young and old alike, thought her sister, repressing a sigh with an effort.

'My sister and Ewella are taking such good care of me,' said Grace. 'I am glad to be living here with them and not at the Manor.' Eliza could see that the eyebrows of both Thomas and George were raised so far they disappeared into their hairline. They were wanting to ask more but manners forbade such questioning. The conversation rattled on and Uncle Tobias was pleased to share one of his precious bottles of brandy with his guests.

'Very fine, Tobias,' said Thomas, sitting back as far as he could in his hard chair. 'I see you are not without your necessary comforts.'

'I am very comfortable here,' said Uncle Tobias, stoutly. 'And I am looked after very well by these ladies. I have no complaints.' Eliza wanted to hug him. Then Grace made a comment that acted like a stone thrown into a pool.

'I'm afraid I have a complaint to make. At night there is often the sound of someone sobbing which is very upsetting. My sister assures me it is only the wind in the chimney. I wonder did you experience such an unusual problem? I really would like it to stop.'

There was a shocked silence. Then both Thomas and George spoke at once.

'My dear Lady Treloyhan – how very annoying – '

'Perhaps a handyman could look into it – examine the chimney?'

'I shall ask Jed to see what he can do,' agreed Eliza, hurriedly.
There was a pause then Grace bade them all goodbye and swept out,
declaring she had to see to her baby. Uncle Tobias retired to his 'study'
having pressed their guests to call again very soon. After the Lanivets
had taken their leave, Ewella and Eliza looked at one another.

'They looked quite disturbed,' said Ewella. 'What was all that
nonsense about someone crying at night?'

'It's not nonsense.' confessed Eliza. 'I have heard it.'

'Eliza! Don't you start hearing strange things. Nothing has ever
woken me.'

'No.' thought Eliza. Ewella was not the kind to be intimidated
by voices in the night. She decided not to mention Caroline.

'The Lanivets seemed very determined not to move back here,'
Ewella went on. 'I do wonder why?' Eliza shrugged.

'They could not break the arrangement they made with
Barnabas?' she suggested. 'They are respected gentlemen. They would
not cast us out.'

Grace did not appear again for the rest of the day but little Richard
joined John and Joel who were playing with a ball in the courtyard.
Nessa sat on the wall watching them and cheering when Richard
managed to extract the ball from the other two. He looked very frail,
particularly next to John, who was heavily built, but he was faster on his
feet. John, however, used his bulk to barge into both Joel and Richard,
eliciting screams of: 'That's not fair!' The screams and shouts were too
much for Ewella.

'WHY are you making so much noise!' she scolded, appearing
at the door. 'Well brought up children should be quiet and well
behaved! What will your father say when he returns! You seem to have
forgotten all his training.' The children looked abashed. It was true that
at Roscarne they had seldom had so much unsupervised time but since
they had moved to their new house this had changed. Eliza and Ewella
were busy attending to household chores and the general management
of their life there, which took up many hours in the day. Many of the
tasks were unfamiliar after their time of comparative ease at Roscarne
and doubly difficult without servants. The younger ones in the family
had proceeded to take advantage of their unaccustomed freedom. Even
Nathaniel and Caroline were on an unauthorised wander down to the
stream with Trembles the pony.

47

'I shall have to speak to Mistress Eliza,' said Ewella, reverting to formality. 'This just will not do.'

'We are not disturbing anybody,' said John sulkily. 'There's no one around here to worry about a little noise.'

'But there is someone who keeps crying. And there is another grumpy voice telling us to go away,' put in little Richard, seriously. There was a shocked silence.

'I haven't heard anyone!' snapped John.

'You are talking nonsense!' said Ewella, almost at the same time.

'I've heard voices,' piped up Nessa, determined to defend Richard. 'Someone crying and there is a lot of whispering. Mama says that I've been dreaming but I don't think I have.' The children looked at each other uneasily. Ewella retired from the fray. In her opinion it was all the fault of Jael and her strange ideas.

'Potions and charms and suchlike,' she muttered to herself. 'No wonder the children are addled like bad eggs. Witches and ghosts and frightening stories! It is time my brother came home to take charge!'

8

Ewella was in a bad mood. The range had turned sulky and disinclined to give out much heat and as a result the kitchen was chillier than usual. The whole house seemed cold and damp even though it was not yet November.

'We need some better wood,' she muttered fiercely as she raked out the ash. 'Jed or Mathey will have to go gathering.'

'Jed and Mathey?' said Eliza, who had just come in. 'I've sent them both to Farmer Tull. We need a chicken and eggs – and he has promised us chicks in the spring to raise ourselves. That will be good for the children especially. And they have to bring the milk.'

'Then Nathaniel will have to go hunting for wood. I do not have any spare time,' said Ewella grumpily.

'May I go too, Mama?' begged Caroline. Eliza looked uncertain.

'We can carry much more if there are two of us,' she added, with perfect logic. Eliza laughed.

'Go on then but don't stray too far from the house or get lost.'

'Get lost!' said Nathaniel with scorn as they scurried across the courtyard. 'Where could we possibly go wrong?'

'Why can't we get down to the sea and find some driftwood,' suggested Caroline. 'That would be better wood than these thorny branches - and it would be more fun!'

'I think it's quite a long way down that path that Mama found – but we could try.'

They came to the stream chuntering busily downhill and found the path with ease.

'Rivers and streams all flow to the sea,' said Nathaniel, leading the way.

'If you are going to try and give me a geography lesson you can go on your own,' snapped Caroline, trying to disentangle her skirt from a thorn bush.

Fortunately for the two children the few days of sunshine had helped to dry some of the muddier patches and they found the path much easier to navigate than their mother had. They stopped by the little clearing where branches, draped with moss and lichens, trailed low and tangled over the stream. Here the sun could not penetrate and a pervasive smell of damp and decay hung in the air.

'I don't like this spot,' shuddered Caroline. 'Look, I've come up in goose bumps. Please let's go on.'

'Don't fuss Caroline. You're only cold because the sun can't reach us here.' Nathaniel resumed his trek along the path. He decided that he would not tell his sensitive sister that he, too, had felt the abnormal chill and he set a fast pace so that warmth would flow back into their limbs. Soon, like Eliza before them, they broke out suddenly into the open.

'The sea! The sea!' chanted Caroline in delight.

'We're too high up still – we have to get down to the beach,' her brother said, scanning the cliffs to find the easiest way. Their enterprise was rewarded. A twisty path he had spied spilled them on to the sand where they found piles of driftwood scattered above the high water mark.

'The wood seems to be quite dry,' said Nathaniel, delighted. 'It must have been left here after a storm and the tide hasn't reached it since.'

'Mama will be pleased with us,' observed Caroline as they picked through the debris, making a pile of the best wood. 'But we won't be able to carry much of it all that way back.'

'I've been thinking about that.' said Nathaniel. 'I intend to use hessian sacks for next time. There are lots in one of the barns that have been used for straw and feed. Mathey won't mind if we take two.'

'If we're allowed a next time.' It had dawned on Caroline that they would have been away for some hours and might well have worried their mother. They turned with one accord and made for the path up the cliff.

'At last.' Perspiration beaded their foreheads as the two finally reached the house. Sure enough, Eliza was standing by the gate, Jael with her. They were both looking towards the house and, strangely, hardly registered the fact that the children had returned home. It was Ewella who rushed out with cries of joy when she saw what they had brought back.

'Jed will chop it all up,' she said. 'You have done well.' Nathaniel decided he would build on his success and find Mathey to ask about the hessian sacks, with a view to further wood gathering   down by the sea. It was unusual to receive praise from Ewella and the prospect of further freedom attracted him.

'Mama and Jael say that we have been very helpful,' confided Caroline to Nathaniel.

'That's what they said. But did you notice that they were not really attending to us?' Caroline nodded.

'Sometimes they each seem to be two people - one listening and the other far away, thinking about something else.'

'You have hit the nail on the head,' said Nathaniel, with respect. In fact Eliza and Jael had been discussing the voices. Both Uncle Tobias and Grace had complained again, convinced that the children were the cause, but Eliza and Jael knew they were not.

'Ghosts?' Jael said, quite seriously. Eliza was eager to deny the possibility.

'I know that Cornwall is full of such stories but they ARE just stories.'

'Perhaps not ghosts then – maybe spirits? Or even just impressions left in the house by previous occupants? Shades, shadows, spectres….?'

'I don't like to think of anything like that.' Eliza was definite. 'If the children become frightened or Grace is affected we should have to leave.'

'I do wonder why the Lanivets left here in such a hurry.' Jael mused. 'It is possible that the voices had something to do with it.'

'Next time we see them I shall ask,' said Eliza. 'But we cannot afford to move so I hope you are wrong…..oh, I do wish Barnabas would come home! All this talk of ghosts and spirits has made me nervous.'

'Any news?' asked Jael, delicately.

'No. I have not heard for three months. I'm sure it means he is travelling to another part of Australia and settling into another job – or maybe he has been ill!' Panic struck as the possibility occurred to her. Then she shook her head decisively. 'No, we would have heard. I shall go and talk to Uncle Tobias. He will take my mind off all this – this strangeness.' She turned to go but had another thought. 'Jael, do you think this has anything to do with the standing stone?' Jael looked uncomfortable.

'I don't know,' she said. 'There are so many standing stones in Cornwall and many of them have stories and legends attached to them. Like the Merry Maidens near Lamorna.'

'Oh?'

'The story is that they were young girls turned to stone for dancing on the Sabbath – and the single stone nearby is the Piper who played for them.'

'That is just a story,' said Eliza, uncertainly.

'Yes, but there are so many such stories all over Cornwall. Strange, don't you think? This land of granite has the past, good and bad, imprinted on every stone. So many myths and legends – ' There was a pause and her next words were wrenched out of her. 'I worry that people like me are disturbing – they attract the past and wake forgotten memories, invoke evil in some form...'

'Stop!' cried Eliza. 'I am sure, Jael, that you could not bring evil with you.'

'I am taking no chances. We don't know what the standing stone signifies – whether someone is buried there from the recent past or from long ago – or maybe it is nothing. Just a pillar of granite. But I do know that I could become the focus of forces we don't understand. That is why I will not live in the house.' Eliza shook her head as if to clear it of cobwebs.

'Jael, we must stop all this surmising. Maybe the sounds are just the wind in the chimney after all .... now I must go and cluck over Ewella's chicken. She tells me it is the best one yet from Farmer Tull.'

The next morning, the sun shone in with cheerful zest. The fire in the range was burning particularly well and all the family, apart from Jael, had gathered round the wooden table, downing Ewella's porridge with relish. Eliza looked around with satisfaction. Spirits, forces of evil - what nonsense. Thank goodness for sunshine that banished the creatures of darkness and allowed the mind to build barriers against unknown forces.

'It is important that I visit the solicitor soon,' she said to Ewella. 'I have been meaning to go for several weeks but Truro is such a trek and there is so much to do here.'

'Why don't you send a message to Edgar Tallack and see if he can help? I'm sure he would be willing to drive you. You can't go all that way in a cart with Mathey,' Ewella responded briskly.

'You should not go in the cart, Eliza!' put in Grace, shocked. 'What would the villagers think!'

'There are no villagers near here,' Eliza assured her. 'The only house within call is Farmer Tull's and that is nearly a mile away. Rosmorren, I'm afraid, is nearly as far as Truro.' She smiled at Grace. Her sister did not often join them for breakfast, though she always sent Richard down and it was encouraging to see her looking more like her former self. There had been no petulant outbursts or tantrums of late and she seemed sunny and sweet tempered. Unnaturally so. An unkind thought, Eliza scolded herself.

Before Eliza plucked up sufficient courage to send a message to the Manor, she was surprised to receive a large envelope with a gold seal from that very place. In it was an invitation for Mr. Tobias Trevannion and Mistress Eliza Trevannion of Carnglaze House to attend a reception there. No one else was mentioned. She took it in to Uncle Tobias' room.

'I don't want to go,' she declared. 'Grace has not been asked and she will feel slighted, I'm sure. Also Ewella is Barnabas' sister – surely she should have been invited?' Uncle Tobias shook his head. He could see the prospect of a sumptuous meal and fine wine being snatched away and such treats were infrequent.

'Eliza, I do feel that we should endeavour to maintain good relations with the Manor,' he said. 'Austol and even that reprobate, Edgar, can be of help to us. And we may meet some old friends again. I should like to find out the latest news in the mining community…?' He looked pleadingly at his niece. Of course she gave in. She could not resist her Uncle, he who had suffered a summary removal to Carnglaze with such stoicism and who had settled in so bravely with the minimum of fuss. Grace it was who surprised her.

'Thank goodness I don't have to go!' she exclaimed. 'That creepy Edgar and his mad sister - they have put a spell on James, I know. He is not kind as he used to be.'

'Even the thought of going back to the Manor seems to have muddled her up again,' Eliza sighed to Ewella.

The prospect of attending a reception at the Manor brought back memories of the party the family had attended when they were still at Roscarne. She remembered the welcoming lights pouring out from that gracious house, Sir James, so tall and dignified, greeting his guests,

Grace, at her most beautiful, beside him. And she herself had arrived with Barnabas, her husband and her friend Rose. Eliza sighed. Such a wonderful time. How was it possible that adversity could strike and change everything? That fate would lead their lives along different paths in different directions, breaking relationships, fragmenting families? Then there was Roscarne, the house they had been forced to leave, the house that reached out to her even now, whose granite beauty and breathtaking aspect had filled her with happiness. How she missed Roscarne. And its proximity to the sea. She thought longingly of Marietta Cove, of Marah Cliffs – of the sea in wild mood, rearing waves shattering white on the rocks then peaceful, still as silk in shades of blue. She had met Seth by the sea. He was a secret she hugged to herself. Then came the painful day when she found out that Barnabas had betrayed her. Nothing was the same after that. Sir James died in a distressing accident. Wheal Eliza and other mines closed and Barnabas left for Australia, hoping to recoup his fortunes. At the same time Rose and Seth left for Arizona to be married. She had felt bereft, left alone with five children to manage as best she could. Such a tangle of events, interwoven like matted seaweed on the foreshore and she was left, trapped and helpless in those strands.

9

'Someone who used to live here...' Words which rose like fish to the bait as darkness fell. Eliza lay awake, waiting to hear if there would be a recurrence of the voices. Earlier, in the daylight, she had dismissed the sounds, telling herself it was imagination – or the wind in the chimney – or someone having nightmares, but then Caroline had heard them also. And Grace. Not only that, but the way the Lanivets had looked at one another, clearly disturbed by the story, and then their rather hasty exit was strange in the extreme. Surely they should have been more interested in the happenings at the house, particularly a house that belonged to them? But no. Another thought struck her. They had been adamant that they would not return to the house. 'Never!' George had said. 'We shall never live in Carnglaze House again!' It was not a far step to surmise that something had frightened them off.

Eliza woke next morning feeling unrefreshed but relieved that she had heard nothing more during the dark hours. She did not mention the matter to Caroline and was relieved to see her squabbling as usual with John over the breakfast table.

'Ewella, today I must go to Truro and talk to the solicitors,' she declared. Such a trip would certainly take her mind off ghostly voices. 'I need to find out exactly where we stand financially now that Barnabas has been away for such a long time.'

'We need some more money now that we have an extra three in the house,' said Ewella. 'I know that Nanny Hannah is being paid by Austol but what about Grace and Richard? Surely Grace has money left to her by James?'

'I expect she has. But who has control of it? Austol?'
Ewella glanced at her sister-in-law and observed that she was looking pale and drawn. Worries were piling up and the constant round of daily chores was becoming an increasing burden. Some extra money would be helpful! Then an uncomfortable thought struck her. Perhaps Eliza's pallor was a lingering reminder of her ill health when they had been at Roscarne. Ewella's conscience received an unwelcome jolt. Hastily she

dismissed the thought from her mind. It would do no good to revive such memories of her earlier misdeeds.

Eliza's plans were disrupted however. She came downstairs in her blue silk dress and her warm velvet cape ready to take the cart with Mathey for the long journey to Truro. Trembles had been harnessed and was eager to go on such a fine autumn morning but it was not to be. Edgar appeared, leading his horse along the last part of the potholed track.

'Mistress Eliza!' he called cheerily. 'It seems I have just caught you! And where are you going?'

'Truro,' said Eliza, shortly. She was not sure how she felt about Edgar.

'You are never going all the way to Truro in that cart!' Edgar was scandalised. 'Please allow me to offer you our carriage. I am sure Austol would be delighted to help. Your journey would take half the time and be much more comfortable.'

'I - I' Eliza was at a loss for words.

'Allow me to drive you to Truro tomorrow. I have come a long way to enjoy a conversation with you today...' he smiled winningly.

'Very well. Please come in that I may offer you some refreshment,' said Eliza, rather glad that she would not have to suffer the bone cracking ride in the cart. Mathey, too, was relieved and took himself off to do some less demanding hammering.

Eliza looked warily at Edgar as they sat in the room adjoining the kitchen. It was bleak even though a fire sputtered feebly in the grate. Ewella bustled in with a tray of coffee and Eliza felt a spurt of grateful affection for her sister-in-law. There was no doubt that she was a much changed person from the one she had known in Roscarne. Occasionally the storm clouds would gather and her eyes would flash fire but more often she would be trying to please and, with a determination Eliza wished she herself possessed, meet the problems of day to day living in their new house.

'I made the ginger biscuits,' Ewella announced before sweeping out. Edgar laughed.

'She is a character, your sister-in-law!'

'And so like Barnabas,' Eliza added. Edgar looked interested.

'Have you heard from him recently?'

'No,' Eliza admitted, 'But I expect a letter any day now.'

'You must be lonely without him?' Edgar insinuated softly. Eliza deliberately misunderstood him.

'Oh no. It is not possible to be lonely in this house! We all jostle together like pilchards in a net, as my son Joel put it. This is why, as I am sure you will understand, that I hesitated to subject Grace to the lack of space here after her time at the Manor.'

'I do understand, I assure you,' said Edgar earnestly. 'And Austol is most appreciative, especially after all your troubles with your sister.'
So, both Austol and Edgar knew the story of her rift with Grace. Eliza felt touched by the frost of betrayal yet again. Everyone saw her as a lonely wife, deserted by her husband. Would what happened ever die a natural death or would the gossip go on for ever? She sighed. She could look at Richard and see a lovely child without a hint of Barnabas in his colouring or his physique. But then, neither could she see any hint of James. The boy seemed entirely his mother's son with his pale skin, his delicate features and his blond hair. A beautiful boy in his own right and, she felt, the identity of his father irrelevant. Possibly.

'I see I have upset you,' said Edgar, anxiously. 'I have no wish to do that.'

Eliza sat up straight in her chair. Pride came to her rescue.

'What do you wish to talk about?' she queried, her tone cold.

'I thought you would like to know that the reception at the Manor is being held to honour Austol's only son who has been fighting in the Transvaal War. He was wounded and has been invalided out so we are all looking forward to welcoming him home to Cornwall.'

'Uncle Tobias is delighted by the invitation and is looking forward to the evening. But why has Austol invited me? And does this invitation include Grace?'

'Certainly not!' said Edgar. 'Austol does not want to disturb Grace. He is incredibly relieved that there has been an improvement, however slight, in her state of mind. But he was most impressed by you and wishes to see you again. Furthermore he is hoping to introduce you to some of your old friends!'

'Old friends?'

'Come along and see,' Edgar encouraged, then added slyly, 'Also he would like to find time to discuss finances with you. He realises that you have taken on an extra burden and he hopes to recompense you. He has charge of Grace's money as I expect you know. Of course Grace is in no condition to manage on her own. Please do not be offended – this is only until Mr. Trevannion returns.'

'I am not offended – but rather relieved,' said Eliza, frankly. 'We have been wondering how we were going to manage.'
She watched Edgar lead his horse out of the courtyard and mount, turning to wave her a cheery goodbye. He was a man she could not fathom. He had reason to be angry with Austol for his treatment of Eulalia but was still willing to run his errands and sing his praises. Then he had not asked to see Richard even though he had declared his affection for the boy. And certainly he had not wanted to see Grace.

'A reception?' said Ewella, surprised. 'I don't trust that Austol. He is playing some devious game. I only met him once but I thought he was a cold fish – with untrustworthy eyes. He has some scheme in mind and it won't be to benefit you.'

'The cold fish has a son and seven daughters,' replied Eliza with a smile. 'I shall have to go if only to see about the money. He has control of Grace's money and we need some of it.'

'I have been thinking,' said Uncle Tobias. 'Perhaps you were right after all. We should not go to this reception.' Eliza looked surprised.

'What changed your mind, Uncle Tobias?' she asked.

'Most of the local gentry will be there and they will be curious as to the whereabouts of Barnabas,' he said bluntly. Eliza coloured.

'I don't know where Barnabas is or what has happened to him but I cannot avoid every one until he deigns to put in an appearance.'

'I don't want you to be upset.'

'That is very thoughtful of you,' smiled his niece, 'But I have hopes of discussing our financial situation with him, now that we are looking after Grace.' Uncle Tobias looked alarmed.

'Don't sign anything,' he warned. 'Not until Cubert Petherwin has looked it over.'

'I won't. We'll just talk.'

When Jael heard about the forthcoming visit she reacted in her own typical way.

'Wear this,' she said, giving Eliza a necklace of rowan berries. 'You remember the one Hedra's mother gave you? It is to protect you from harm.'

'I remember,' laughed Eliza. 'Jael, that necklace did me no good. Everything bad still happened!' Jael was unmoved. 'Wear it to please me,' she said. You can hide it under your collar.' So, to please Jael, Eliza took the necklace.

'Will you look after Uncle Tobias when I am away?' Eliza asked. 'And even more importantly, I think Caroline needs a friendly eye. I am worried that she still hears voices.'

'She does,' said Jael. Eliza was surprised at her certainty.

'What do you think is going on?' she asked, shakily. Jael paused before she answered.

'I do not know, Mistress Eliza. It is possible this house is haunted. Voices alone won't hurt us. But what will follow? I don't know.' Her matter of fact tone was at odds with the enormity of what she was saying. Eliza almost choked. This was her fear confirmed and no facile explanations would make it not so.

'I don't know what I should do,' she whispered. 'Are the children in danger? Should we move away from here?' Jael shrugged.

'Where could we go?' she asked. 'I think we should stay and hope that Barnabas comes back soon and we can move to Roscarne again.'

Eliza sat in the chair near to the feeble fire. She could not face the kitchen where Ewella was clashing pots and pans. She needed to think. Her family was living in a house which was possibly haunted by restless spirits. There was one who cried and sobbed and engendered terrible feelings of desolation. There were whispers. And there was at least one angry one who claimed the house and certainly did not want to share it. Anger was a destructive force, to be feared, Eliza was sure of that. She looked round the bleak room in the dull light coming through the window, feeling helpless and, she had to admit, full of dread.

10

The heavy wooden door of the Manor swung open and a wave of voices and music broke over Eliza and Tobias. The light poured out revealing a crowd of guests in the great hall and the room beyond. So many people. The ladies swirled and twirled in multicoloured silks, taffetas and velvet and glittered in diamante collars, a recent fashion, and bracelets, tiaras and swinging earrings. Eliza could feel her stomach tighten with nervousness. Rather wistfully she recalled the receptions held at Treloyhan Manor while Sir James was still alive and Grace had not yet proved so deceitful. How friendly they had always been, how welcoming their hosts. And of course, Barnabas had been there. She remembered his tall figure in his formal jacket and the defiant, flame like red of his hair and how his snapping blue eyes could warm with affection when he looked at her.

'Don't you worry, Eliza,' whispered Uncle Tobias, bringing her back to the present. 'I'll wager there is not a real diamond amongst them.' Eliza choked back a giggle. How astute of her Uncle to know how she was feeling.

'Mistress Trevannion – and Mr. Tobias Trevannion – welcome.' It was Austol – Eliza could not think of him as Sir Austol – looking immaculately groomed and almost as handsome as his brother before him. In a high collared shirt and dark jacket he was straight-backed and austere, as James had been; his eyes, she noted, at odds with the warmth of his welcome, were cold as stones.

Edgar had disappeared after escorting them to the front door but Austol preceded Eliza and Uncle Tobias into the main reception room.

'I should like you to meet my wife, Eulalia,' he said, formally. A small woman in an unbecoming yellow silk dress held out her hands to Eliza with a smile, a smile that lacked all warmth that appeared on demand and then vanished at once. She was pale and her skin had a yellowish tinge as if she had been in the tropics. Her dark hair, pulled back into sparse ringlets, showed white streaks and lacked life as if she were a much older woman. The ostentatious pearl and diamond collar she wore seemed too heavy for her thin neck. No wonder Edgar was worried about her, Eliza thought. She looked as if she should be confined to her bed. Before she could enter into conversation with Eulalia, Austol took her arm and led her firmly away. Tobias followed and then stopped with an exclamation of pleasure. It was one of his mining cronies. Eliza was pleased to see him light up with eagerness and launch into mutual reminiscences.

'Someone here to see you!' Austol announced. Eliza could hardly believe her eyes. Aunt Gloria, her mother's sister! As she lived in London, visits had never been frequent and her niece, overwhelmed by her new circumstances, had not written to inform her of Barnabas' expedition to Australia.

Aunt Gloria bore down on them, resplendent in blue velvet and pearls, her hair still that unlikely shade of red but her smile warm enough to cheer Eliza.

'My dear, you should have let me know!' cried Aunt Gloria. 'I have been so busy nursing Yelland through his dreadful jaundice that I have not given anyone else a thought. Most remiss of me and I am so sorry.' Eliza smiled at her with delight.

'I am so glad to see you, Aunt Gloria. I hope Yelland is getting better?'

'We-ell.' Gloria looked doubtful. 'We shall see. But my main purpose in coming down here is to visit you and Grace. I wanted it to be a surprise. Austol has told me how difficult it has been with the closure of the mines but I had no idea that Barnabas had taken off for Australia. Just like him – always acting on impulse.'
There was no point in trying to defend Barnabas. Aunt Gloria knew him too well. But was she aware that Grace had been ill and that she was now living with all the family in Carnglaze, their new house? Some shrewd questioning and Gloria had dragged it all out of her.

'Hallucinations!' she exclaimed. 'How are you managing, my dear? This will not do at all. She must come to stay with me in London and I shall find a doctor for her.'

'Aunt Gloria, you have Yelland to look after,' said Eliza firmly. 'I am managing quite well because Grace is not spoilt and demanding as she once was – ' Aunt Gloria looked sceptical. 'No, really, she has settled in with us quite happily. I feel that the change of scenery – her removal from the Manor and all its unhappy memories – has been beneficial. We have hopes that she will return to normal with us. I think that to uproot her again so soon would be a mistake. But I do thank you for your offer, Aunt Gloria, it is so kind of you.'

'Nonsense!' said Aunt Gloria. 'You two girls are part of my family and I intend to do anything in my power to help you. Now, I must speak to Austol again and find out what is happening with Eulalia. I always doubted their chance of happiness when I first met her. She does not have the backbone of granite required to deal with someone like Austol. And I believe that she has been suffering from some protracted illness and now has little to do with her children. So nice to see you again, my dear.' And she was off, searching for her host.

Edgar, who had tactfully left Aunt Gloria, Eliza and Tobias to their various conversations, now returned with three glasses of mulled wine. Eliza accepted gratefully and Tobias took the opportunity to settle himself into a comfortable chair, waving the others away. It was clear he wanted a little rest. Edgar and Eliza chatted rather awkwardly. She had the feeling he was trying to bring up a subject he found awkward but then Austol loomed up beside them and shouldered him to one side. Edgar sighed and stepped back.

'So good to be reunited with your Aunt Gloria,' stated Austol. 'She will help you to escape that dreadful place you are living in.' His self-assured tone brought out Eliza's innate obstinacy.

'All is going reasonably well,' she said sweetly, pushing away the memory of ghostly voices. 'If I could discuss the state of Grace's finances with you that would help me more.'

'No doubt, no doubt,' said Austol dismissively, 'But not at a party, my dear lady. We shall make an appointment before you leave.' His tone changed. 'Mistress Eliza, permit me to congratulate you on your appearance. I wish you could advise Eulalia on her dress. She is aware of current fashions but is entirely without colour sense.' Eliza could hardly believe her ears. Such a disloyal statement. Poor Eulalia.

'I have little choice in what I wear,' she said acidly. 'This is the only evening dress I possess. Where I live there is no room for a vast wardrobe of clothes.'

'In that case, I must attribute your success to your personality rather than your dress,' Austol continued smoothly, apparently unaware of the deliberate snub. 'Now,' taking her arm and leading her away from a hovering Edgar. 'Tell me about your children. I am most interested in the way you are raising them.'

'As you know I have seven daughters. Seven!' he exclaimed, not trying to hide the bitterness in his voice.

'But you have a son?' interjected Eliza.

'Yes. You will meet him later. He is on leave after the fighting in the Transvaal and is staying here for a few days. He tells me he is not going back there – but we shall see about that.' Austol almost seemed to be talking to himself and Eliza sensed that he was a troubled man in spite of the façade he displayed to the world.

'Professor Martineau has told me about your children – let me see, three boys and two girls? He says that they are remarkably advanced for their age and work hard even when he is not present.'

'Yes. That is true. He gives them work that really interests them and so they enjoy continuing with their studies. Unfortunately we are without servants and so I am kept busy, as is Ewella, and neither of us has the time to help them. We are fortunate that the Professor is such a good, enthusiastic teacher.' Austol looked at Eliza with new respect.

'The Professor is coming to teach my daughters once a week - I would have engaged him for longer but he tells me that he finds them very tiring. That I understand – so do I. In fact the word I would use is tiresome.' He sighed. 'The alternative is to find a school for them but Eulalia will not hear of it. So they spend their time doing needlework, chatting about fashions and studying music with Edgar. Their devotion to their studies is such that not one of them can play a musical instrument with any precision, or hold a sensible conversation and the eldest, Ebrel, informs me that as Latin and Greek are dead languages there is no point in learning them!' Austol's voice was incredulous. 'They do not realise that they are in the fortunate position of having a father who believes in educating his daughters as well as his sons.' He gave Eliza a quick look. 'Of course I am aware that I am in a minority.' Eliza was surprised into giving Austol her first real smile.

'My father always said that. He and Aunt Gloria took care that Grace and I had tutors and regular lessons.' Her sudden animation and the way her face lit up with delight had a powerful effect on Austol. Already attracted by this lively young woman and intrigued by her history, he had a glimpse of the former Eliza, of how she was when she was happy and not burdened with so many worries. The contrast with the sickly Eulalia did not escape him.

Before Eliza could enlarge on the topic which really interested her, there was a commotion at the door and a renewed outburst of chattering. A young man in red tunic and navy trousers with a red stripe and carrying an impressive helmet with badge and spike under his arm, strutted into the room and was immediately surrounded by many of the young ladies in the gathering. So this must be Austol's only son, reflected Eliza. He was clearly enjoying the attention when his father beckoned to him.

'Kenwyn. I should like to introduce you to Mistress Trevannion.'

With a flourish, Kenwyn bowed to Eliza and then, having given her a brief greeting, excused himself. No doubt she was neither young enough nor attractive enough to retain his attention, she thought drily. The frown on Austol's face, however, was daunting. The relations between father and son were evidently fraught. Eliza was beginning to feel uncomfortable. What did Austol want from her? He had a large and difficult family to contend with and an estate to run – why did he wish to spend time with her?

Later, having been escorted into supper by Edgar, she tried to ascertain what was going on.

'He wants to see you again,' said Edgar, frankly. 'That is why he will not discuss Grace tonight.'

'Why should he want to see me again?'

'He admires you.'

'Nonsense!'

'Oh but he does. He admires the way you are managing life away from Roscarne. He admires your kindness and loyalty to Grace. And he is jealous of the way you are raising your children so they have all the virtues!'

'That is absolutely not true. They are normal children with their fair share of faults! I take it from this that you and Austol have been gossiping about me!'

Edgar had the grace to look sheepish.

'True. It's all my fault because I sang your praises and aroused Austol's interest. Unintentionally I may say!' Eliza was speechless. Awkwardly, Edgar hurried on, realising that he had been indiscreet. 'He would like you to be a friend to Eulalia and that is something that would please me greatly. My sister is lonely in this vast place.'

Then a not entirely welcome voice from the past interrupted them.

'Oh Mistress Trevannion – Eliza! How exciting to meet you here!'

It was Morwenna Tregadillett, hurrying towards them with Nicholas puffing behind her. Edgar stared at the newcomers with distaste. It was clear he had no idea who they were.

'Edgar, perhaps I could introduce you to Morwenna and Nicholas Tregadillett – Nicholas is the Minister from Rosmorren and a friend of the family.'

Edgar looked as if he wanted a high tide to wash them away. He had been trying to talk to Eliza but there had been constant interruptions. The name Morwenna, however, had caught his attention. He remembered Austol referring to her as a useful source of information about the local area. He watched her gushing excitedly to Eliza and noted the reserved way that lady responded.

'Have you heard the news about Rose? Of course, you must have. Is it not wonderful! After all this time being single and childless...'

'I have not heard from her for some time,' said Eliza, carefully.

'She is carrying a child! Even though she is quite – quite old to be a mother she must be so pleased. We heard the news from a member of the Church at Rosmorren. One of Nicholas' parishioners, you know,' she added for Edgar's benefit. 'He has just returned from Arizona. Apparently Seth Quinn is doing very well out there – his gold mine is prospering!'

Morwenna's voice drifted into the distance as Eliza tried to comprehend what she had just said. It could not be true. Surely it could not be true. Rose and Seth – Edgar, watching her, saw her turn ashen. He moved quickly to her side but she recovered herself and was able to chat inconsequentially to the two of them until another acquaintance called them away. Then she sank into the nearest chair. Rose and Seth. Of course they were man and wife. Why should she feel so shocked and betrayed?

'I shall fetch you a brandy,' said Edgar.

'Morwenna brings back unhappy memories,' offered Eliza, by way of explanation.

'Must you go so soon?' complained Austol, as Eliza asked for her cloak. 'There are so many things I wish to discuss with you – never mind, we must make another appointment to take tea together and then we shall not be interrupted.'

Eliza nodded. All she wanted to do was to leave Treloyhan Manor as quickly as she could without being rude. Austol's approval was crucial to Grace's welfare, both socially and financially and he could not be slighted. A sleepy Tobias announced that he was ready to leave.

'I have ordered the carriage to be brought round,' said Edgar, 'and I shall escort you back to your house.'

'Oh no, Edgar - thank you but no. There is no need. The driver knows the way. In any case I have a headache - probably the brandy,' she tried to laugh. 'I should prefer to remain silent on the journey.'

'But – ' began Edgar.

'Edgar, there is no need,' said Austol in a warning tone.

The carriage rolled along as smoothly as the road allowed. A bright moon shone into the window and Eliza tried to order her chaotic thoughts. How was it that Morwenna was always the bearer of bad tidings? And then, with a shock, she realised she had not bade farewell to Aunt Gloria. This was really upsetting and she felt tears spring to her eyes. Neither had she seen Eulalia who had disappeared early on, apparently unnoticed by her husband and her brother. What a strange household it was. The carriage turned on to the track that led to the house. Eliza rapped for the driver's attention.

'Please put me down here,' she said. 'I wish to walk the rest of the way.'

'Is that wise?' asked the driver, concerned for his passenger.

'Of course. The area is deserted and I am in need of fresh air.'

'Do you wish me to accompany you?' Uncle Tobias had woken up.

'Oh no, Uncle, thank you. There is no need.'

'But – '

'No buts. I have made up my mind.'

The driver helped her down, much against his will, and drove on with Tobias, shrugging his shoulders at such wilfulness from a woman.

The moon lit up the track so that Eliza could avoid the worst potholes and she set off at a brisk pace, energised by the fresh night air which whisked away her unhappy thoughts. She crossed the bridge over the unusually docile stream and approached Carnglaze House. The carriage passed her on its way back from leaving Tobias, at a fast pace. The driver was risking injury to his horse on that potholed surface, thought Eliza. It was only then that she began to feel uneasy. The thorn trees were crowding closer and the moon was gradually obscured by spiky branches. A night bird called harshly, startling her. She slowed her pace as the darkness deepened and the track narrowed, again giving her the feeling of being hemmed in, of having to fight her way through unseen barriers. Ahead, the black shape of the house detached itself from the lighter darkness and came into view. There were no lights. Of course they would all be asleep. But what about the voices? The uncomfortable thought crept into her mind in spite of her effort to enjoy the fresh air. She tiptoed across the courtyard, pushing away the feeling that all those empty windows were, in fact, watching her. Not welcoming but repelling. Beginning to shiver, she felt for the big doorkey underneath a stone by the front door. Clumsily, she fitted it into the lock. The resounding clunk it made in the emptiness of the night made her jump. Then she became aware of another sound, a background sound, a familiar sound. She stopped and listened. Then smiled with pleasure. It was the sea.

11

The next day Eliza awoke late and found that Tobias had not surfaced for breakfast.

'You must have had a good time you two, to be so tired,' Ewella said, rather sourly.

'I'm sorry, Ewella, Everything should not have been left to you.'

'No matter. We managed. The children were especially well behaved. I saved some porridge and there are eggs if you wish.'

Eliza shuddered. The wine from the previous evening had left her feeling decidedly queasy and Ewella could not prevent a grim smile from twitching at the corner of her mouth.

'Perhaps just a cup of tea?'

'Ewella, you are more than kind. I feel I don't deserve it. What with Austol and Edgar and Morwenna - '

'Morwenna!'

'Yes, Morwenna. She was the last person I expected to meet there!'

'I shall join you for a cup of tea,' said Ewella, intrigued. 'The children are awaiting Professor Martineau in the schoolroom, Tobias is still asleep and goodness knows where Jael has disappeared to - but I look forward to hearing what happened last night.'

Eliza laughed. Ewella was in gossip mode.

'Someone else was there, someone you know. Aunt Gloria has come down especially to see us.' Ewella frowned. Aunt Gloria she regarded as an interfering old lady who had disapproved of her place at Roscarne and had made it plain that she considered her no better than a servant.

'I expect you were glad to see her. She is a relation after all,' Ewella said stiffly.

Eliza sighed. Ewella was still so prickly sometimes. So she went on to chat about the dresses and Uncle Tobias' delight in meeting old friends.

'What did you think of Austol?' interrupted Ewella.

'He's a strange man. I'm not sure I can make him out at all. But Edgar – I like him much better than I did when I first met him – '

'Just as well,' said Ewella, glancing through the window. 'Here he is. I thought I heard a horse coming along the track.'

'Oh NO! Not again!'

'I'm sorry to intrude on you, yet again, Mistress Eliza,' said Edgar, balancing on the edge of his chair. 'I bring an assortment of messages from the Manor.'

'An assortment? How strange!'

'Your Aunt Gloria would like to visit you before she returns to London next week – '

'Visit us! Oh no! She will be appalled at the lack of space and she will never understand that we are managing.' Edgar shrugged his shoulders in acknowledgement.

'She is insistent,' he said. 'I feel she is a lady who is used to having her own way. Also she wants to see Lady Treloyhan and Richard and the baby of course.'

'Of course,' said Eliza, hollowly.

'Then Austol wishes you to take tea with him in order to discuss finances – and, finally, Eulalia would like you to visit at your convenience and take tea with her and meet the girls. I might say that would really please me.'

'Could I not meet them all at one time? Eliza asked, desperately. Edgar did not deign to answer that one.

'Eliza, I may call you Eliza, may I not? When your sister was staying with us she wished me to call her Grace and I hope that you also will care to dispense with too much formality.' Eliza could only nod. The prospect of receiving Aunt Gloria at Carnglaze filled her horizon so that she had no room to ponder over anything else.

Edgar delivered Aunt Gloria to Carnglaze the very next day. Gallantly he handed her down from the pony and trap and, through the window, Eliza watched her look slowly around the courtyard. While it was tidier than before it still had an air of neglect, not helped by the stones which had broken free from the wall and the gate which had been mended several times but still sagged awry. The granite walls of the house, dark with rain and the vacant windows, Eliza knew, did not promise a welcome. There were puddles and mud before Aunt Gloria could access the front door and her face plainly registered her disapproval.

'My dear Eliza! I hope this visit is not too inconvenient. I am hoping to hurry back to London as Yelland is not yet well and I do not trust him to take his medicine when he should.' She clasped Eliza in her arms and gave her a powdery kiss.

With a cup of tea in her hand, Aunt Gloria glanced disparagingly round the room.

'To think Barnabas has left you to live like this! It is too bad!' she declared.

'There are many who live in far worse conditions, especially after the closure of so many mines,' murmured Eliza. Her Aunt ignored that.

'Now I should like to see Grace and judge for myself,' she said. 'I presume she is here?' Eliza's heart sank. What effect would this have on her sister? Her return to health, both mental and physical, was precarious. However there was no escape. Edgar had disappeared into the kitchen where he was regaling Ewella with stories from the reception so there was nothing else for it. Grace came down at Eliza's bidding, dressed in one of her pretty blue gowns. Her hair was up and a necklace of pearls gleamed at her throat.

'Why, Aunt Gloria!' she cried. 'What a lovely surprise!' Behind her came Nanny Hannah with the baby in her arms and Richard clutching her skirts.

'Grace, my dear, how lovely to see you. Pretty as ever! And Richard! What a beautiful child!' Her exclamation echoed the way Eliza had reacted. Grace smiled complacently.

'And the baby? What have you called her?' Aunt Gloria asked. She knew perfectly well that Grace was refusing to name her until James returned. Which, obviously, was not going to happen. Grace shook her head.

'But Grace, she is a bonny baby! And she must be nearly five months old! You must name her! She should have a beautiful name - a flower name!' Grace flinched as Aunt Gloria prattled on, remorseless as ever. Her niece was certainly not going to continue with this – this delusion if she, Gloria, had anything to do with it. But they were interrupted. Jael had returned. After the usual greetings Grace burst out excitedly – 'Jael, we are trying to think of a flower name for the baby!' Eliza and Aunt Gloria exchanged looks of surprise. There was no keeping up with her mercurial moods.

'May I make a suggestion?' said Jael, carefully. 'This name, a lovely name, has just popped into my mind. It IS a flower name, a Cornish flower name.....Elestren – which means 'Iris'.' Grace clapped her hands like a young girl.

'That is perfect! How clever of you, Jael! And she does have eyes as blue as any iris!' The dead James was forgotten. Only Eliza felt touched with foreboding. How capricious that Grace had changed her mind so completely. How strange that the name should come to Jael – just at the appropriate time.

Again there was an interruption. This time it was Ewella, red-faced with rage.

'It has begun raining again and all the washing is still outside!' Eliza and Jael responded to the cry with alacrity and rushed outside to rescue the lines of washing, mainly children's clothes, which Ewella had hung out with such care earlier.

'She ought to have seen the clouds gathering,' giggled Jael, grabbing towels and bedding from the bushes. Meanwhile Aunt Gloria beckoned Grace to her side, waved away Nanny Hannah and the baby and began to talk to her in an undertone.

The awkward visit behind her, Eliza was again at the Manor, balancing a cup of tea. She refused a biscuit and, firmly, an offer of brandy.

'Business first,' said Austol, 'I have made out a cheque drawn on Lady Treloyhan's account and I hope you will find this a satisfactory recompense for her time with you. She does know, of course, and is in agreement.' He handed over a crested envelope.

'Go on, Eliza, my dear, open it.'

She did, reeling from the sudden intimacy in his voice. The contents were a shock.

'I cannot accept all this,' she protested. 'Grace has only been with us for a short while.'

'I am hoping she will stay with you for longer,' said Austol. 'In any case, I know that you have a struggle looking after everyone at Carnglaze – though I am sure that Barnabas will take matters in hand when he returns. Will that be soon?' The question was tacked on as if it were an afterthought.

'I have not heard recently,' Eliza was forced to admit. She forestalled his quick sympathy. 'But I am sure his return cannot be long delayed.'

'I am pleased to hear it,' he said, his silky tone indicating his disbelief. Eliza had a sudden urge to flee as fast as she could. This man was a threat in some way. She put the envelope down on the table.

'Please write me a cheque for a smaller amount,' she said coldly. 'It is kind of you to offer so much but it is not necessary.'

'It is your sister's money,' Austol pointed out. 'You are taking nothing from me if that is your worry.' Eliza felt he was laughing at her. Again she felt awkward and wrong footed. Austol stood, looking down at her, so tall and elegant, his eyes cold while his mouth smiled. So might a fox approach a rabbit, gently, but determined.

'Come – I should like to show you the progress we have made in the garden.' He took her arm in a firm grip and led an unwilling Eliza through the conservatory which was lush with the coloured blooms of exotic plants that she had never seen before. Then to the garden where the escallonia hedges and the clustered canes of red dogwood reminded her of her former home. She was conscious that he was naming the more unusual plants and describing their origins but she had blanked him and could think of nothing but Roscarne. It was only when she realised that again he was too close, his body touching hers as they progressed down a narrow path, that she stopped abruptly.

'Thank you for showing me the garden,' she said. 'I should like to go home now as it is getting late and I wish to help in putting the children to bed. I am sure Edgar will be waiting to drive me back.' She did not miss the momentary flash of annoyance that crossed his handsome face. Reluctantly he dropped her arm.

'As you wish. I look forward to seeing you again when you visit Eulalia and the children. I am afraid she is very fragile at the moment and seems to spend more time in bed than out of it. But the girls will be delighted to meet someone new.'

As Eliza rattled back to Carnglaze with Edgar, she wondered how she could extract herself from her next visit to the Manor. She was uncomfortable with Austol.

Edgar was glum and uncommunicative on the drive back but Eliza was grateful for the silence. Austol's behaviour would have been understandable if she had been a young girl – or even a servant girl. But she, Eliza, the mother of five children and past the first flush of youth, surely could not be attractive to Austol! But she had felt stalked, there was no doubt of that. Edgar helped her down at the gate of Carnglaze and she thanked him for his help.

'I shall pick you up at the same time next week for your visit to Eulalia,' he said. 'Try to talk to her alone and discourage Austol from being present.' He hesitated. 'In fact, I advise you to be careful of Austol.' More he refused to say.

Eliza was met at the door by Ewella, flushed and hair loose and shedding hairpins.

'I don't know what you will say to this,' she said.

'What IS the matter?'

'Aunt Gloria has taken Grace to London with her and left Nanny Hannah, Richard and the baby here with us!'

12

'I'm sure I don't mind,' said Nanny Hannah. 'She never did much for that baby. Anyway I shall have more space and so will Richard.'

'Has she taken all her clothes with her?' demanded Eliza.

'Oh yes. She were more worried about her clothes than baby Elestren here. I think she 'ave taken a big case full.' There was a look of disapproval on Nanny Hannah's plain face.

'What was Aunt Gloria thinking of?' fretted Eliza to Ewella.

'She said she would write,' said Ewella. 'She also said that she thought a little pampering would help Grace.'

'Pampering! That's all she's ever had!' scowled her sister. 'She always wanted to go to London and now her wish has been granted. But to leave Richard and little Elestren!'

'She always was selfish,' Ewella pointed out. 'She is just behaving as she used to. Maybe this return to her old self is a good sign.'

Eliza watched little Richard carefully but he did not seem to be troubled by his mother's absence. Seven year old Nessa, always a helpful little girl, took him under her wing, and helped him with his reading and writing as well as making sure he was not bullied by John. Nanny Hannah seemed quite content looking after baby Elestren and clearly enjoyed being in absolute charge. Any mention of Grace elicited a click of her tongue. Eliza insisted that she should eat downstairs in the kitchen with the rest of the family, which also earned her disapproval but pleased her none the less.

In due course the letter arrived from Aunt Gloria, apologising for leaving so speedily.

'I needed to get back to Yelland,' she wrote 'and Grace was so wistful, remembering the times she had wanted to come to London after her wedding. Please forgive me, Eliza, but I thought it might help her and you, also, in your crowded house.'

'She means well,' offered Jael, laying out a series of little vials and bowls and bags on the kitchen table. 'I expect she was able to catch the coach for Truro which links up with the one to London and which would have saved them both a lot of time and uncomfortable travelling.' She stood back to admire the array on the table. 'Look at all these medicines and potions I have made up. There's a fair at Penzance next week so I hope I can sell them. It means I shall be away for a few days.'

'You have been busy,' said Eliza, forcing herself to smile. 'I hope the weather stays fine for you but I feel winter is on the way.'

'Don't worry about me,' said Jael. 'I'm just sorry to leave you and Ewella to manage all the chores. But now Nathaniel and Caroline are bringing in the firewood that should help. Perhaps John could do something. He is quite old enough now.'

'He won't like that,' interjected Ewella. 'He puts all his energy into avoiding any kind of work. Except for schoolwork. He tries hard at that.'

Eliza sighed. A difficult life was about to become more difficult. And she had to visit Eulalia for tea. She was in no doubt that Austol would contrive to be there.

'Eulalia is not very well again,' said Edgar, anxiously, on the drive to the Manor. 'She wanted to cancel the tea but Austol wouldn't hear of it.' Eliza felt quite sorry for him. Even though he was impeccably dressed as usual, his whiskers drooped and there was no sign of the arrogance he had displayed on their first meeting. He seemed to be able to put on different personalities like a cloak, she thought, and discard them as easily. However his care for his sister reflected well on him. She decided that perhaps she had misread him earlier and that, in fact, he was quite a nice man. Which was not how she felt about Austol. Handsome, charismatic, indubitably male in his appeal - but not nice. She was relieved that he was not at the Manor when she and Edgar arrived but was uneasily aware that he might eventually appear. Then he was wiped from her mind when she saw Eulalia. It was a shock. She lay on her chaise longue like a wilted flower, her face unnaturally white, daubed inexpertly with powder. An unbecoming silk cap covered her hair completely.

'I'm losing my hair,' she explained, with a catch in her voice. 'I don't know what to do. I'm sure Austol will be even more displeased.' Her voice cracked and Eliza felt a wave of sympathy sweep over her.

'Not only that – but what will Kenwyn think of me? His mother, always ailing!'

'Have you a doctor in attendance?' asked Eliza.

'No. Austol won't have one. He says that my illnesses are all in the mind and that I must try to be more positive. Meanwhile I am suffering stomach pains and nausea – THAT cannot just be imagination.'

'Indeed not,' said Eliza indignantly. How cruel Austol could be. An idea crept into her mind.

'Mistress Eulalia – may I bring a friend of mine to see you? She makes medicines of all kinds and has helped me in the past. Perhaps she could find something that would alleviate your symptoms.'

'Oh yes,' cried Eulalia. 'I am so miserable I would be willing to try anything! But you must not tell Austol! If he thought that your friend was trying to cure me after what he has said he would be exceedingly enraged!'

'What would enrage me so exceedingly?' said a voice at the door. Austol had entered silently in a way that Eliza considered extremely bad mannered.

'Mistress Eulalia feels that you do not approve of casual visitors,' she said, hastily. 'I was proposing to bring a friend of mine to see her. She also suffers with her health and would find it comforting to - er - talk about it.' Eliza offered up a little prayer for forgiveness for such a falsehood. Austol was unfazed.

'It is true. I do not care for casual visitors to the Manor. But, my dear Eliza, I am sure that anyone you would bring would be most acceptable. And if the visit should cheer up my sick wife, all the better. Eulalia, my dear, how are you feeling just now?'

Eulalia looked stunned. Eliza was even more sure that Austol was not in the habit of asking tenderly after her health.

'I am getting better, Austol. Mistress Eliza has cheered me immeasurably.'

'Good. Good. You must come again, dear Eliza - and soon.'

Jael was still away in Penzance when Eliza returned to Carnglaze. She offered Edgar a hot drink before his return journey as the weather had turned colder.

'You are very kind to keep driving me to the Manor,' said Eliza, when they were both sat by the fire. 'I was pleased to see Eulalia and would like to go again soon, when Jael returns.'

'Splendid!' said Edgar. 'More adult company would cheer her, I am sure. Austol is not very welcoming to the ladies around here except at grand receptions. He seems to keep my sister rather isolated.' Edgar gazed gloomily into the fire. 'I have been worried about her wellbeing for some time but Austol refuses to discuss it.'

'I hope to bring Jael to see your sister,' said Eliza, bracingly. 'And, to my surprise, Austol was all in favour.'

'You seem to have put him under some sort of enchantment,' said Edgar, perking up. 'He appears to agree to anything you suggest. That is not the usual Austol! Perhaps you will find a way to make Eulalia better!'

'Edgar, I shall be able to do no such thing!' said Eliza, sharply. 'I am hoping, however, that Jael will have some suggestions.' Edgar had to settle for that.

Jael returned the next day in good spirits.

'It was crowded at the fair and I managed to sell almost all my medicines,' she confided. 'I shall have to set to and make some more. Tomorrow I shall go collecting herbs.'
Eliza smiled at her eagerness.

'I have a new patient for you,' she said and recounted her visit to Eulalia.

'I'll come with you, of course,' said Jael, 'It sounds as if she does need help.'

The dusk outside was deepening and Ewella was chasing the children to bed. Eliza smiled to see that even little Richard was trying to evade her, a sprite in blue pyjamas dancing round the kitchen. Ewella herself was enjoying the game and Eliza could only marvel at the change in her from the old days at Roscarne.

'Mama?'

'Yes, Caroline.'

'I want to tell you something – something strange.' Caroline was looking very serious. 'You know those voices and the crying we hear sometimes?'

'Well, yes.' Eliza could not deny the truth of this.

'Do you know the crying has stopped! Ever since Aunt Grace left to go to London, the crying has stopped.'

'That IS strange.'

'But that's not all,' Caroline said, eagerly. 'Someone was singing a nursery rhyme yesterday night. It was very late but I heard it quite clearly. It made me feel cheerful instead of sad.' Eliza looked carefully at her daughter. So tall and slender, growing up so fast. Her hazel eyes were steady and implored to be believed.

'Perhaps it was Nanny Hannah singing to Elestren,' she suggested.

'No. It was one of the voices. I'm not making it up, Mama.'
That night, Eliza strove to stay awake to hear the voices, voices that seemed a part of the household, sometimes sad, sometimes frightening. But all was quiet. She had been up to see Nanny Hannah who had assured her that all was well with Elestren and no, she had heard nothing to disturb her at night.

The next morning Eliza awoke to a chill in the air that made her unwilling to rise from her bed. The first frost of autumn had arrived and left a tracery of white over the windows. Her immediate thought was for Jael in her barn, which was partly open to the air. The need to see her impelled her to dress hastily and envelop herself in a shawl. Ewella was already in the kitchen seeing to the fire and the big copper kettle was singing on the range.

'I don't know how to thank you enough, Ewella,' said Eliza. 'You are a tower of strength to this family.'

'Porridge will be ready shortly,' said Ewella, looking pleased.

'I'm going to see Jael – I think she might have been cold last night.'

'Don't you worry about her! She has a fire going already, large enough to roast us all. Perhaps you could take her some porridge since she prefers not to come into the house.'

'I'm fine,' said Jael when Eliza appeared. 'I have fresh straw on the ground, which is warm, and a thick blanket for my bed. And look at my fire! As soon as the sun rises I shall go collecting - I predict that the frost will be gone by midday. I'm just thankful that it is not raining again.'

'Amen to that,' said Eliza.

78

Days passed as Jael went foraging and then pounding and mixing in the barn. She seemed contented and she and Eliza shared coffee and hevva cake to fend off the cold. During one of these times Eliza mooted the idea of going to visit Eulalia in the next few says.

'She sounds very poorly to me,' said Jael doubtfully. 'I don't know if I could help her. It would be better if she wanted a love potion - or a charm for protection – '

'That's it!' interrupted Eliza. 'Protection against Austol! That's what she needs!'

Edgar was delighted to hear that Eulalia was to receive two visitors and reported back that Austol was amazingly amenable. Edgar was in an affable mood as he drove the two of them to the Manor, commenting on the cold sunshine and brilliant blue sky.

'I feel you will both do my dear sister a power of good,' he said, cheerfully.

Eulalia was clearly excited to see Jael and patches of red appeared on her pale face.

'Are you a doctor of some kind, Mistress Jael?'

'That I'm not,' said Jael. 'But I am able to see that you are not at all well. I do not understand why your husband has not called in a doctor from Truro or Penzance!'

'Neither do I,' said Eulalia. 'He cares for me quite well otherwise. He has given me a personal maid. He comes in to see me every evening with my sleeping draught and he is kind enough to sit with me until I fall asleep. Oh, and he brings me news of my girls – he will not allow them to disturb me.'

Eliza and Jael exchanged looks. Austol's way of caring for his wife was strange. Surely Eulalia would want to see her girls?

'Do you think you can help me in any way?' Eulalia demanded at last.

'If you will allow me, I shall come back with something for you,' said Jael, soothingly. 'Meanwhile I should like you to wear this necklace of rowan berries next to your skin. Don't let anyone see it – not Austol, not Edgar, nor your maid.'

'Oh thank you! But what is it supposed to do?'

'It is meant to protect you from harm.'

'Oh Jael, you must be a witch!' and Eulalia's laugh rang out. Jael frowned.

'Please wear it in the way I ask or it will do you no good,' she said firmly. Then the expected interruption came.

'How pleasant to hear you laugh, Eulalia, my dear. Your visitors must be doing you some good! Ladies, please come again.'

'We shall do that,' said Eliza, briskly.

Not till they reached Carnglaze and Edgar had departed did Jael say anything Then she burst out: 'I hope I'm wrong. I may be wrong but....'

'But?' prompted Eliza.

'I think she is being poisoned. And the poison could be arsenic! She has all of the symptoms – losing her hair, nausea, abdominal pain – and I noticed but I don't know if you did – her breath smelt of garlic.'

'Surely not,' said Eliza, quietly. 'If she is being poisoned it must be Austol as I don't believe Edgar would try to poison his sister. He really seems to care for her. But Austol! I do not like him and I do not feel easy in his company but to think of him poisoning his wife is a nonsense! Remember he is Sir James' brother and from a good family. Besides, whatever reason could he have?'

Jael shrugged. 'Many good families have black sheep,' she pointed out. 'And I believe a permanently ailing wife can be a great irritant to some men.' She forbore to add – men like Austol.

'How can we find out for sure?' Eliza looked desperately at her young friend who seemed so sure of herself and so knowledgeable about many strange things. She was sitting by the fire, her silvery eyes fixed on the flames, her pale hair hanging over her shoulders, looking not much older than Caroline. But for once, her certainty had left her.

'I don't know,' she admitted.

13

'I am so pleased to see you!' cried Eulalia as Edgar ushered Eliza and Jael into her sitting room. 'I have been feeling so much better since your last visit – I think you must have done me some good!' She was sitting in a chair rather than lying on her chaise longue, wearing a lavender coloured silk dress with a silk gauze stole round her shoulders. Her thin hair had been swept up and ornamented with jewelled combs.

'Austol is so pleased at my improvement,' she said eagerly. 'I am trying to follow his instructions and think positively. And Kenwyn will be back again next week so I must be better by then.'

'We are happy for you,' said Eliza cautiously.

'Such a pretty dress,' chimed in Jael.

'Ladies, I shall leave you to chat,' was Edgar's hasty contribution as he left the room.

This was Jael's opportunity.

'You are looking very pale,' she said, in anxious tone.

Eulalia smiled. 'I have a clever new aid,' she said confidentially. 'My maid found it at the market and it seems to work well.' She lowered her voice. 'It is a special wafer that will soon make me as pale as any aristocratic lady in Cornwall!'

Neither Eliza nor Jael knew how to respond to this but the same thought occurred to both of them. It was not Austol who was poisoning his wife. The silly woman was doing it to herself.

'It seems your rowan berries have been a force for good,' Eulalia trilled. 'I shall continue to keep them safely. Better safe than sorry.'

'Perhaps it is not a good idea to swallow something so unusual and untried,' said Eliza. 'Goodness knows what those wafers may contain. All kinds of potions and ointments are sold in the market and many are worthless – or worse, poisonous. The rowan berries should keep you safe without using unknown remedies.'

'Rowan berries won't help my complexion,' replied Eulalia, obstinately. 'I admit to using powder occasionally but the effect is not so good.' She ignored Jael's careful scrutiny and changed the subject.

Edgar drove two silent ladies back to Carnglaze. He was puzzled as there was a change for the better in Eulalia and he thought they would be pleased. But they said nothing. He had worried about his sister for so long that every slight change in her well being affected him, engendering anxiety and fear. Contrary to Eliza's early cynical assessment of his motives, his concern was real.

'What can we do?' demanded Eliza, as they waved him off at the gate. 'If we tell Austol he will be so enraged I cannot bear to think about it. And do we have the right to interfere in her private life – to stop her taking unproven medicines?'

'We must do something,' said Jael. 'We cannot allow her to continue ingesting arsenic like this.'

'Arsenic! Is that what is in the wafers!'

'Yes. Arsenic. A known poison!' A shocked Eliza was reduced to silence. Jael went on: 'She is showing some of the symptoms already – just like I noticed the last time we came! Also she is losing her hair although that began before she started on the wafers. But then I know that sometimes face powder, too, contains traces of arsenic and goodness knows how long she has been using that. But the wafers are more deadly – and the combination of the two could be lethal.'

'Pehaps Edgar could persuade her not to take them – he wants her to be well.'

'Good idea. You flutter your eyelashes at him next time he calls and enlist his help. All you need to say is that the wafers are possibly dangerous. He could remove them from her room and forbid her to take any more.'

'I'll try. He is fond of his sister and wants her marriage to Austol to be successful so I'm sure he will help.'

'He will have to be careful that Austol does not find out.' Jael warned.

The evenings were drawing in and it was already full dark after supper. Eliza and Ewella supervised the children's bedtime finding them all unusually willing to climb the stairs, each with their candle. Nanny Hannah had already put Richard into his bed and Elestren into her cot and all was quiet in their room. Caroline and Nessa slept in the same bed, in the adjoining larger room, as did Nathaniel and John. Only Joel had a small bed of his own, mainly because he was so restless nobody could sleep with him.

'Right, candles out,' said Ewella.

'Why don't we have stories any more, Mama?' asked Nessa, sleepily.

'Because Jael is not with us,' said Eliza. 'And now you are all in the same room it is difficult to think of a story that would please all of you at once.'

'Ewella has never told us a story. Perhaps she would?' Nessa persisted.

'If you tell them a story I shall go and put all the supper dishes away,' smiled Eliza. A pleased Ewella nodded.

'I'll try to think of a suitable one,' she said.

Eliza found that dealing with the evening chores allowed her a peaceful time to order her thoughts, to think about Eulalia and Edgar. She looked up when Ewella came down the stairs, clattering in a bad tempered way.

'Where is she?' demanded Ewella.

'Who?'

'I don't know if it was Nanny Hannah or Jael. Someone looked in and then closed the door rather sharply as if we were creating a disturbance. It spoiled my story.'

'No one has come down here,' said Eliza. 'Jael is still in her barn and I would have seen Nanny Hannah. You know it is rare for her to leave her room after Richard and Elestren are settled.'

'Oh well,' said Ewella, 'I must have been mistaken. But the children heard the door close and asked who it was.' She shrugged.

Later, Eliza and Ewella sat on either side of the dying fire, trying to sew before they went to bed. Eliza was darning socks and Ewella was hemming a sheet. The oil lamp began to flicker and Eliza put down her needle gratefully.

'More oil needed,' said Eliza. 'Time for bed, I think.'

The door opened, creakily, as usual. It was Caroline, a pale ghost in her nightgown, her hair flowing over her shoulders. Her eyes were wide and apprehensive.

'Mama,' she said, hesitantly.

'Caroline? Why are you not sleeping?'

'It - it wasn't Nanny Hannah who looked in. Nor Jael.'

'Oh? '

'It was a lady in a white gown with dark hair in a braid over her shoulder. She's not a lady I have ever seen before.'

'Caroline, you must be imagining things!' said Eliza, gently. 'Or perhaps you were dreaming.'

'Oh Mama, I was not dreaming!' and Caroline threw herself into Eliza's arms. She was shaking.

'Did any of the others see this lady?' asked Ewella sternly.

'No.'

'Then you must have been dreaming!'

Caroline looked in disbelief at Ewella and then burst out:

'Not everyone sees everything! The lady looked at me and I saw her quite clearly. I would know her if I saw her again. Oh, I want Jael! She would understand.'

Eliza looked helplessly at her daughter. It was clear she was telling the truth.

'Whether you were dreaming or imagining, Caroline, there is no lady here. Just us. And we are coming up to bed so you can, too, quite safely.'

'I don't feel unsafe, Mama.' Caroline was indignant. I think the lady was looking for something. She looked worried and sad.'

'What nonsense,' said Ewella, rising from her chair. 'I think it is bedtime without a doubt. I know that I am very tired.'

Eliza followed Ewella up the stairs, holding Caroline by the hand. She tucked her in next to Nessa who was snoring gently.

'We'll talk to Jael in the morning,' said Eliza.

As Ewella began breathing deeply, Eliza looked round the bleak room, lit only by her own candle. Shadows gathered on the walls, shifting restlessly as the candle flickered, coalescing in the corners into areas of greater darkness. The room was not one to be welcoming to the sleepers. Granite walls, hard floors and a pervading cold, whatever the temperature outside. What was it Caroline saw? A spirit from the past? A figment of her imagination? She wondered, not for the first time, if the house could be haunted. A stray draught from the window blew the candle out. The ensuing blackness did not encourage further musing and Eliza fell asleep, dreaming of strange women wandering through the room. One of them, with a waterfall of dark hair over her shoulders, fell to her knees beside Joel's bed, putting her hand on his forehead. In her dream, Eliza tried to stop her but she found she could not move, as is the way of dreams. She woke with a start, relieved to find herself in her own bed next to the reassuringly solid form of Ewella. Then she heard it. A voice chanting a well known nursery rhyme. 'Silver bells and cockle shells – and pretty girls all in a row. And she is mine…mine…mine…' the voice faded away.

A bright morning sun, though touched with frost, was enough to chase the night glooms away. Caroline seemed her usual self, taking it upon herself to get the schoolroom ready for Professor Martineau, who was coming that morning. Joel was dancing around declaring that somebody had taken his slate while Nathaniel and John were helping Nessa with little Richard. For once all was calm. Eliza and Ewella were clearing away the breakfast dishes when Nanny Hannah made an appearance.

'We've finished breakfast,' said Ewella, surprised. Nanny Hannah shook her head.

'I couldn't eat a thing!' she declared. 'I had such a bad night. Which one of you came in to see Elestren? I woke up just as she started crying and it took a long time before she went to sleep again!' She sounded reproachful rather than angry. Eliza shook her head.

'Neither one of us came into your room,' she said. 'You know that we would knock for your attention first.'

'But someone DID,' persisted Nanny Hannah. 'And more than that, whoever it was tried to sing to Elestren – a nursery rhyme I think.'

'You were obviously dreaming as well,' said Ewella caustically.

'What do you mean?' Ewella explained about Caroline's 'vision'.

'A GHOST!' squeaked Nanny Hannah. 'Oh this is too much. I don't want to stay in a house with a ghost!'

'Don't be alarmed,' soothed Eliza. 'I've never heard of a ghost who sings nursery rhymes. You know, it might have been Caroline sleep walking. She is nearly as tall as an adult.' Nanny Hannah looked unconvinced but the potent mix of sunshine and the children chattering in the schoolroom worked to calm her.

'I shall keep an eye on Caroline,' said Eliza. 'She is of the age when she is likely to sleep walk.'

Nanny Hannah helped herself to a bowl of porridge and retreated back upstairs to Elestren. Eliza and Ewella looked at each other.

'Sleepwalking? Do you really believe that?' asked Ewella.

14

It seemed that Caroline had not waited for Jael's arrival but had gone in search of her. She had disappeared after breakfast much to Ewella's annoyance.

'That child should be helping me this morning,' she grumbled. 'It's her turn. I want to change the beds and get the washing ready for tomorrow. I can't do it all.'

'I was going to prepare the lunch,' said Eliza, 'but I shall help you first. We really do need another pair of hands around here.'

'I can help,' said Nessa. 'I'm nearly eight.' Eliza looked fondly at her daughter. Nessa was such a willing child. She rarely cried or had tantrums even when John had been teasing her. Which reminded her. Where was John? And Nathaniel?

'They've gone to the sea!' cried Joel. 'They are going to collect more firewood because Ella said she needed lots of hot water.'

'They should have asked me first!' exclaimed Eliza. 'Just because it is not a school day they think they can do what they like!'

'A kind thought, though,' said Ewella.

At last Eliza was able to tackle the lunch preparations. She had decided to make a chicken pie, using the left-overs from the roast chickens they had had the previous day. Though she had often watched Mrs. Kershaw back at Roscarne, she had not realised how much was entailed in the preparation. Her own mother had seen to all the cooking when she and Grace had been younger – and we were playing the piano and embroidering, she thought bitterly. How she regretted that they had not helped their mother more – and learned more of the art of cooking.

'What are you making, Eliza?' asked a small voice. It was little Richard. Eliza was concerned to see that he was pale and that his beautiful blue eyes looked sunken and bruised.

'Richard – what is the matter? Are you not feeling well?' she said. He shook his head, but remained silent.

'Come and sit down with me,' said Eliza, trying not to sound too alarmed. 'See, there are some ginger buns left. Would you like one?' He nodded and ate it in small bites, staring at the floor. Eliza could not resist it. She took him on her lap, knowing well that both Nanny Hannah and Grace would disapprove.

'Has John been bothering you?' He shook his head. She rocked him gently.

'If you tell me what is wrong, perhaps I can help you,' she said.

'I don't like the lady!' he blurted.

'Tell me, Richard, what lady are you talking about?' She spoke very softly, not to frighten him.

'She keeps coming into our room – an' she won't go away....'

Nessa was enlisted to look after Richard and play games with him.

'He has been dreaming and hasn't slept well,' Eliza explained. Nessa's motherly instincts took over and she devoted herself to Richard and soon had him absorbed in a game and laughing delightedly when he won. Meanwhile Eliza wrapped a warm shawl around her shoulders and went in search of Jael. She found her, sitting with Caroline on bales of straw in the barn. They were talking very seriously.

'Mama, we want to tell you something,' said Caroline. 'Jael thinks the spirit lady is looking for her baby. And I think so, too.'

'I'm sorry to involve Caroline in this,' said Jael 'But she is aware of what is happening. I think we have to decide what to do next.'

'Yes, we do,' sighed Eliza and explained that Richard, too, had seen the lady. It was strange to be talking of such things in the light of day as if they were ordinary occurrences. But ordinary they were not.

'We cannot allow the children to become uneasy – and Nanny Hannah is already alarmed. Caroline, you won't talk to the others about this, will you? You are the eldest and you seem to be ...er...'

'Sensitive,' supplied Jael.

'Sensible is the word I wanted.'

'I won't say a word,' Caroline promised

'Perhaps we should talk to the Lanivets, first of all. They may have some idea of who used to live in this house and what may have happened,' Jael suggested.

'Yes,' agreed Eliza. 'Our problem is that the Lanivet twins have moved to Pendeen, along the coast. That is a long journey by cart. There is no help for it. We must enlist Austol and Edgar to help us.'

'Are you off to the Manor again?' grumbled Uncle Tobias. 'All this to and froing will wear out the cart wheels as well as poor Trembles. He'll soon feel as old as I do.'

Eliza felt a pang of conscience. She had had little time to spare for him and he had been rather quiet, disappearing to his small room after meals and, she realised, missing out his usual daily walk.

'Are you not feeling well, Uncle?' she asked.

'Oh, I am quite fit,' he assured her 'But – ' he hesitated.

'But – ' Eliza encouraged.

'I don't want to make a fuss. But I do not like this house. The walls in my room seem to close in on me and at night the darkness is thick and unfriendly. That is the only way I can describe it. If I come into the kitchen I am in Ewella's way – or the children are there all higgledy-piggledy and making a noise.' He stopped abruptly. 'I am sorry Eliza, I know that you are doing your best in the circumstances but I have to admit that I miss Roscarne more than I ever thought.'

Eliza was horrified to see a suspicion of tears in his rheumy eyes.

'Oh Uncle Tobias!' she cried. 'I am so sorry you feel like that. You are in the middle of a small house, full of people and bustle and noise. Of course you miss Roscarne! We all do. But soon, I am sure, Barnabas will return and we shall be able to go back there.'

'I hope you are right,' muttered the old man. Eliza watched him shuffle back to his room, his shoulders bowed and an air of despondence wrapped round him like a cloak.

Trembles was not required to negotiate the potholed track that time as Edgar himself appeared, leading his bay horse, its coat gleaming in the winter sunshine. Debonair in a tan driving coat and plaid vest, whiskers smoothed and his brown derby sedately perched on his head, Edgar looked every inch a gentleman.

'Ladies!' he cried, doffing his hat. 'You look so serious on this sunny day.'

'I have no doubt I should look less serious if I had woken up in a comfortable bed at the Manor,' said Ewella tartly. 'However, I shall go and fetch you some refreshment.' Edgar looked abashed.

'Is something wrong?' he enquired, handing the reins of his horse to Mathey.

'No, nothing – oh, yes, everything!' Eliza burst out. 'It is such a lovely day and we are stuck in this gloomy place and we all miss

Roscarne.' And she told him about Uncle Tobias. Edgar looked suitably serious. Perhaps she could tell him of their fears. 'Not only that – but I believe we are being haunted. There is a lady in a white dress who used to cry at night, at least I think it was her, and now she sings nursery rhymes.' She was disconcerted when Edgar burst out laughing.

'Surely you don't believe in such nonsense,' he said, wiping his eyes. Then a glance at Eliza's white face made him realise that his reaction had been inappropriate. 'I am so sorry, my dear Eliza. But you must agree that the idea of a singing ghost is rather difficult to take in. What else has happened?'
Eliza told him everything and saw the smile disappear from his face.

'So you want to visit the Lanivets and ask them a few questions? In that case I shall write to them and arrange a time. Of course I shall take you in the carriage. Austol will be only too pleased to help you after your good work with Eulalia.' A welcome change of subject. Eliza was already regretting that she had confided in Edgar.

'How is Eulalia?'

'Quite well – but rather dreading the return of your sister. She is frightened of Grace and her moods.'

'When is Grace coming back? I thought she would be staying longer with Aunt Gloria.'

'Next week. This is the reason for my visit – to tell you that Lady Conyers will be accompanying her and will stay a few days. At the Manor, naturally.'

'No room for even a mouse, here,' said Ewella, appearing with a tray of tea.

'Mistress Trevannion, I see you have made some more of those wonderful ginger biscuits!' Edgar said and was rewarded with a smile, albeit a rather vinegary one.

Ten days later Eliza and Jael were on their way to Pendeen with Edgar. Ewella was nursing a heavy cold but luckily the children were with Professor Martineau for the morning. Nanny Hannah kept to her room saying she wanted 'none of they germs' from Ewella. It was a cold, sharp morning, the sky icicle blue and the moor against it dark and undulating like a sleeping fairytale dragon. The Lanivets' cottage was down a steep, winding track flanked by sparse hedges of thorn trees bent almost double by the prevailing wind. Gaps in the hedge provided glimpses of the cliffs falling precipitously into a rock strewn sea, a restless sea of perpetual movement whatever the tides and the wind. The cottage was partially sheltered by growths of gorse and more thorn bushes but still Eliza felt that it was dangerously exposed, perched like a gull on the cliff.

'I don't think I would feel safe in a storm,' she said to Jael. 'It looks as if a gust of wind could send the whole building over the edge to the sea below.'

'I am surprised that they choose to live here rather than retain Carnglaze,' replied Jael, thoughtfully.

'Carnglaze has no view. This view is wonderful!'

'But imagine how it could be on a stormy night with the wind howling in the darkness! I should not like that.' As if to illustrate her point, a sudden rough gust of wind blew Edgar's hat from his head and sent it bowling down the grassy slope and over the edge of the cliff.

'Anything would be better than Carnglaze,' said Eliza flatly.

The Lanivet twins, Thomas and George, were waiting at the door to greet them with welcoming smiles.

'Of course you already know Mr. Edgar Tallack from Treloyhan Manor? He kindly offered to bring us as it is a considerable journey,' said Eliza. She went on to introduce Jael, to make Ewella's apologies and to pass on regards from Uncle Tobias. 'He felt the journey would be too much,' Eliza explained. 'In fact he is not very well at the moment and we are concerned.'

'The lack of light in the winter,' said Thomas. 'That is what it is. Something we always noticed at Carnglaze – which makes living here so different.'

'Very different,' echoed George. 'Perhaps Tobias should move somewhere where there is more light.'

'He would not like to be away from the family, I think.'

Later, sitting round a comfortable fire, Eliza broached the subject of Carnglaze again.

'I should like to ask you something,' she began, hesitantly. 'When you lived at Carnglaze, did you notice anything strange? Did you hear any unusual noises?'

'Well – began George.

'You mean the sobbing noise that you mentioned to us on our visit,' said Thomas, quickly. 'I thought you were going to consult a builder to check the chimney?'

'That is not sufficient explanation,' said Eliza. She recounted the sobbing, the singing of nursery rhymes, the closing door with no one there and the fact that both Caroline and Richard had seen – well – '

'A lady!' said George, sitting forward in his excitement. 'I knew it! I saw her but Thomas would not believe me. He thought I had been drinking brandy!'

'I think you were suffering from nerve strain,' said Thomas stiffly.

'We were wondering whether you knew the people who lived at Carnglaze before you?' put in Jael, who was getting impatient.

'Let me see.' It was Thomas at his most ponderous. 'Our family has been at Carnglaze for generations...'

'Just before us there was Uncle Caswol – he lived there on his own,' said George, eagerly. 'And before that there was Petroc – and he had a family, didn't he, Thomas?'

Thomas looked uncomfortable and Eliza felt they should pry no more. But then, fears for her children made her continue.

'Was someone in that family very unhappy?'

'Most families are unhappy at some time in their lives,' said Thomas, with finality, and it was obvious they would learn no more.

'I have an idea,' said Eliza, on their journey back. 'Perhaps we should look at the headstones in the graveyard. I feel that Thomas was very defensive when his family was mentioned and we might find out what happened to them.'

'And the local minister might know something,' added Jael. 'Perhaps Nicholas Tregadillett could introduce us.'

'Yes – but we must make sure Morwenna does not find out and spread it all over the county!' Edgar smiled indulgently at his two fellow passengers. He was not a believer in the supernatural but he deemed it undiplomatic to ridicule their ideas so he kept quiet. Eliza's approval was important to him. At the gate of Carnglaze they found Caroline waiting eagerly, hoping to hear what had happened at the Lanivets. Before they could even greet her, something happened that turned Eliza's world upside down. A large black horse appeared, picking its way efficiently along the track and past the potholes. The rider, in impeccable black coat, white pique shirt and black leather boots of undoubted quality, dismounted and came to greet them.

'Eliza, my dear,' he said. That flopping black hair - it could not be.

'Seth!' she gasped.

15

Eliza found she was trembling so much that she could hardly stand. The colour fled from her face and then rushed back, making her feel like a schoolgirl.

'Seth, what are you doing here?' she stammered. Oh, where was her poise, her ability to deal with the unexpected, to cover surprise with a cool look. She was conscious of Jael and Caroline staring at the newcomer and then smiling in the pleasure of recognition. Recovering sufficiently to string a few words together Eliza croaked a welcome and invited him in.

'Where is Rose?' was her first question. 'Why did she not write to me?'

Realising that this was going to be a difficult encounter, Jael took Caroline's arm and led her into the kitchen, leaving Eliza and Seth in front of a sulky fire. As soon as they left, Seth leaned forward and clasped Eliza's hands in his.

'I have so much to tell you, Eliza my dear, and I have been impatient to see you again and explain a lot of things.' Gently, Eliza withdrew her hands. This would not do at all. Her heart was beating so loudly that she felt he must hear it – and after all, she had to remind herself, he was married to Rose and a prospective father. And she herself was wife to Barnabas Trevannion, though he was so far away and seemed to have forgotten her.

'Rose is at the Galleon hotel in Penzance,' Seth rushed on, 'She has not been well lately and needs to rest. But she is hoping that you will come to see her.'

'I have heard that she is with child,' Eliza responded flatly, evading the plea. 'You must be happy and I am sure that Rose is delighted.'

'No.' said Seth, his voice grave. There was a long pause. With a palpable effort he continued, 'Rose lost the child before we set out for home shores. She has been sad and unwell ever since the loss so I thought a trip back to Cornwall might lift her spirits. I know she wishes to see you above all else.'

'I thought she must be totally immersed in her new life when I did not hear from her.' Eliza tried to keep the hurt out of her voice. 'To tell the truth we have had such difficulties to deal with here that I did not make enquiries as I should have done.' She did not elaborate. Her real reasons were clear to her and, she hoped, to no one else. She had wanted to put both Seth and Rose out of her mind. There was no time for jealous brooding and useless longing for what could not be. In this respect, the daily hardships of living in Carnglaze had helped to divert her thoughts quite successfully.

'I am surprised, Eliza, to find you living like this,' said Seth, looking round in a rather disparaging way, taking in the uncovered floor, the rough walls, the cracked glass in one window, the lack of any softening fabrics. 'Barnabas said he would see that Carnglaze was made habitable for you. And I see that he has not.'

'He went off in too much of a rush to catch his ship,' said Eliza hurriedly. 'I do not think he had any idea how difficult it would be to pack five growing children, Uncle Tobias, Ewella, Grace, two children and a nanny in such a confined space.'

'Grace? Surely she is not living with you!'

'She lived at the Manor for a while,' said Eliza steadily. 'But she, too, has been unwell and I thought it best that she stay with us. Now she is visiting Aunt Gloria in London.'

'And her child? A little girl, I believe.'

'She is thriving. Her name is Elestren.' Eliza was about to enlarge on this when she realised that perhaps Seth would find the subject painful. 'And you, Seth? You look very well. Prosperous in fact.'

Seth grinned cheerfully and settled back into his chair.

'Straight to the point, Eliza. As always! Yes, my gold mine has been very productive and rewarding but now lacks challenge. I find that both Cornwall and tin mining are more attractive to me. I have sold the mine 'Very profitably, I may add, and here we are. I would like to join forces with Barnabas again as soon as he returns. That will be soon, I hope? Rose does not yet know that I intend to stay in Cornwall but she has been suffering from such home sickness that I have the feeling she will be overjoyed.'

Eliza felt her throat constrict. Seth and Rose back in Cornwall! How could she live with the thought of them nearby when every fibre of her being longed for Seth, just as before. There had been no diminution in the intensity of her feelings for him. Seeing him at the door, it was as if the many months had rolled back and they were together again on Marah Sands when she had felt his care and concern for her. However, obviously Seth had come to terms with his marriage to Rose, a marriage about which he had voiced serious doubts. In his married life and with a successful goldmine had he found the time to miss her presence at all? Had he ever really cared for her? The word love she avoided. Eliza realised that he was looking at her in a speculative way, his dark eyes revealing nothing. She summoned all the reserves of strength left to her. He should not find her pining and sad – that would be too much! Before she could respond the door creaked open and Uncle Tobias appeared.

'Seth, my boy! What a surprise to see you! How long are you staying?' And the two of them were off, exchanging news of Arizona with news of Cornwall. Mining orientated of course. Eliza crept out, knowing that she would have to provide food for everybody as Ewella, unusually, had stayed upstairs, with red nose and streaming eyes, her temper uncertain. She needed a hot drink and vapours to inhale. Then Jael took over.

'Mistress Eliza, I have a herbal medicine that will help Ewella – I shall fetch it from the barn.'

Professor Martineau appeared, marshalling the children before him.

'A good morning's learning,' he beamed. 'Young Joel still has trouble staying in his seat but he is improving.'

'He's as annoying as a sandfly!' muttered John. Fortunately, his mother did not hear him.'

'Mistress Eliza, I should like a word if you have the time,' said the Professor, as the children trooped in to interrupt Seth and Uncle Tobias.

'Of course,' murmured Eliza. 'Please do have some refreshment before you go and then we can talk.'
Seated at the kitchen table, away from everyone, the Professor seemed uneasy.

'I don't know where to begin,' he said. 'It is rather a strange subject and you may think that I am exaggerating.'

'Please go on.'

'You have a problem – a serious problem in this house.'

'Our ghost!' exclaimed Eliza, involuntarily. The Professor looked relieved.

'I was worried that the subject would give you a shock,' he said.

'Not anymore,' she replied. 'There is a lady who has been sobbing – that was our first introduction but now she is singing nursery rhymes and sounds much more cheerful.'

'It is not a laughing matter,' said the Professor, refusing to return Eliza's smile.

'There is more here than a simple haunting. I have been doing some research and apparently this house and the land around it has been a focus for supernatural activity for centuries and you should be aware of that. Your lady looking for her baby is a comparatively recent, and, dare I say it, minor manifestation. Probably harmless.'

Eliza stared at him, hardly able to comprehend what he was saying.

'How do you know that? Are you just guessing?'

'No. Not so long ago this house belonged to Caswol Lanivet. He had a housekeeper, a pretty little thing. I think her name was Mathilde if I remember rightly. The rest is rumour and gossip, but it seems she had a child and the child died. Caswol denied any involvement in her life and threw her out. She went into the workhouse in Penzance and died there soon after.'

'Oh, the poor girl!' exclaimed Eliza.

'A sad story,' agreed the Professor. 'But the gossip did not end there. When the Lanivets took over the house, they hired a servant who only stayed a few weeks and then left, declaring the house haunted. She, too, heard sobbing and actually saw what she said was the ghost of Mathilde. Thomas and George decided that this poor sad spirit should be exorcised and apparently a priest from Truro came and held a special service at Carnglaze. They tried to keep it quiet but you know how rumours travel.'

'Obviously the service did not manage to lay the spirit to rest,' protested Eliza.

'The exorcism did not work, certainly. But the priest refused to return, declaring that he was powerless against the ancient forces gathered here. The Lanivets always denied that there was any such problem but they, too, as you know, moved out rather hastily. Which is why you and your family are here rent free.'

'Did Barnabas know of the stories?'

'I doubt it. Thomas and George never divulged anything to anyone. I only know because of my friendship with Father Anselm, a travelling minister, who put me on the right track with my research.'

Eliza was bursting to ask more questions but just then Jael returned with her medicine for Ewella.

'Ewella will be good as new very soon!' she promised.

'I must go,' said Professor Martineau. 'We shall talk further another time.'

The children waved the Professor on his way and then trooped inside. Nessa laid the table, Nathaniel built up the fire and Caroline helped her mother to dish up the herby pies that Ewella had made the previous day.

'Stay for lunch,' said Uncle Tobias to Seth. 'There is seldom enough but it is always tasty.' Seth laughed.

'I must get back to Penzance,' he said ruefully. 'Rose is not well and will need me. Besides she is very anxious for news of you all.'

'Nonsense! You cannot travel all that way without some sustenance!' Uncle Tobias would not countenance a refusal so Seth sat down with them all, not realising that he only had a chair by reason of Ewella's absence and that Uncle Tobias had not been joking when he said that there was not always enough.

'What is in this pie?' demanded John, a lapse in manners which would not have been tolerated by his father at Roscarne

'Herby pie – herbs,' said Eliza, promising herself that she would take John to task. They all laughed.

'I know there are nettles in it,' said Caroline, 'because I gathered them. And they stung my hands.' They all laughed again and then began squabbling over the size of each helping.

Eliza bustled about, conscious all the while that Seth was watching her. The babble of the children became fainter, like the receding tide, and it was as if the two of them were quite alone. She was unaware that Uncle Tobias was sending shrewd glances in her direction and Jael wore a worried frown. The children laughed and chattered as they usually did in the crowded confines of Carnglaze and Eliza wondered if Seth noticed the difference after the stricter routines in Roscarne. But then he would have no idea how difficult the move had been for her and how she had had to adapt to living in a near derelict house without her husband but with the children and Ewella and Uncle Tobias. Jael, of course, was sleeping in the barn which was a help, but there was still the problem of Grace, her children and the nanny. Not for the first time she wondered how Barnabas could have left her in such straits. Would Seth have done such a thing? Comparisons would not help, she chided herself, as she gave Uncle Tobias the last piece of pie.

At last Seth had gone after promising to come back and take her to see Rose. It was with relief that Eliza heard the sound of his horse's hooves diminishing in the distance. She could not have borne the tension for much longer. She and Jael began to clear the kitchen and she was able to confide her conversation with the Professor. Jael nodded her head.

'I don't know what we can do about it,' she said. 'There must be some way that such an unquiet spirit as Mathilde could be put to rest. But...' she hesitated.

'But what?'

'That would not be the end of it, I feel.'

'That is what Professor Martineau just said.' Jael nodded her head.

'I feel this is an unusual house in an unusual, special place. It has such an atmosphere. There is more going on here than we can imagine. Don't forget about the standing stone. That itself is an indication.'

'Indication of what?'

'Possibly a more ancient haunting. This house is so unwelcoming. We have all felt that it seems to push us away. I have a great belief in those feelings that the atmosphere here sometimes brings to the fore. There is possibly evil here – not just a poor, lost servant girl looking for her baby.'

'In that case,' exclaimed Eliza, 'If you and the Professor both think there is danger – we should move!'

'Where to?' asked Jael. 'We are rather a large family. I don't think you should make any decisions until Barnabas returns. Luckily the children and Uncle Tobias seem unaware of anything besides the occasional outburst of nursery rhymes and they seem to have accepted that as part of the house.'

'Caroline was nervous at first,' agreed Eliza. 'But that is not all. Little Richard has actually seen the girl!' Jael did not seem surprised.

At last, all was quiet in Carnglaze. Jael had scurried off to her barn, declaring that she had work to do. Uncle Tobias was in his little room and the children were in bed. Eliza sat before the dying fire, unwilling to brave Ewella's snuffles and snorts. Perhaps she would sleep in the chair rather than that. The fire sank lower and her candle began guttering. Soon it would be out. Her eyelids closed; she was tired and ready to sleep in spite of the unforgiving hard wood of the chair. But sleep eluded her. She had pins and needles and sensed it was getting colder. Outside all was quiet, no rustling of leaves or raging of wind. Just silence. But inside the stone walls of Carnglaze, she began to realise, all was not quiet. There were voices whispering and they were not the voices of the children. The emptiness of the room, the blackness, seemed peopled by evanescent shapes; the smell of weeds, wild garlic and rotting vegetation assailed her and she remembered the fear she had felt on the way back from her walk to the sea. This was the same. She wanted to run but could not move, pinioned to her chair by the thickness of the dark and the disharmony of whispering voices.

16

Eliza was overcoming her night fears by digging a vegetable patch at the back of the house, ready for the spring. Fresh air and the bright day would restore normality. Usually this activity gave her time to order her thoughts and plan what needed to be done but not this morning. Her mind remained chaotic, so beset was she with other worries. She could see that Uncle Tobias was in low spirits, partly because his joints ached and also because the discomfort and damp of Carnglaze was affecting him more as the winter advanced. Ewella, usually such a stalwart help, was still coughing after her cold and it seemed that as the days passed so the cough became more sepulchral and her mood more irascible. Jael did not complain – she never did – but Eliza knew her home in the barn was becoming untenable as the temperature dropped and the rain teemed down, occasionally turning to needles of sleet. As for Professor Martineau, he had been forced to miss several mornings' lessons because the track had become a morass of puddles and mud. Fortunately the children were in good health, even Richard, who looked as if the wind could carry him away. Thank goodness his sister, Elestren, was a bonny, rosy cheeked baby. Nanny Hannah was looking after them with great devotion, for which Eliza was thankful, and everyone was used to the sight of her dumpy figure, wrapped in a calico apron, hurrying up and down the stairs, never stopping to chat.

A watery sun peeked through the clouds as Jael appeared round the side of the house and suddenly the world seemed brighter.
'You are looking very serious, Mistress Eliza,' teased Jael. Eliza raised a smile, glad to see her.
'Just worries about the house and everyone in it,' she said lightly. 'A haunted house, no less. How did Barnabas find a HAUNTED house for us?'
'I don't think Barnabas was at fault,' Jael replied. 'His family needed a smaller house. This one was offered by the Lanivets free of any payment. A neat solution.' There was a pause. She twined a lock of her fair hair round her finger. 'I feel sometimes fate plays with us humans,

plays unkindly with us.' With a shock, Eliza remembered similar words from Seth when they had walked on the sands below Roscarne.

'You have another worry, have you not, Mistress Eliza?' She fixed her mistress with a slanting look. 'What about the return of Mr. Quinn?' Eliza could feel herself blushing.

'I look forward to seeing Rose,' she said, digging her spade into the soil with angry vigour. Silence again. Jael looked searchingly at her mistress but Eliza kept her head down.

'If it rains much more the stream will overflow and then we shall be in a pickle!' Jael offered, after a pause. Eliza threw down her spade and pushed her hair back from her hot forehead.

'I have been worrying about that, too. I must see that we have sufficient food stored in the house. But where will the money come from!'

'Surely you can use the money Austol gave you from Grace?'

'I refused the first draft. It was too much. Grace is not even living here at the moment and Austol is already paying Nanny Hannah. I do NOT want to be indebted to that man. I did take the lesser amount for the children but I should keep it for emergencies.'

'A flooded track and no food would be an emergency, would it not?'

'I suppose so.' Eliza sounded so gloomy that Jael put an arm round her.

'I think it is time we had tea and saffron biscuits,' she said, hopefully.

'No biscuits. Ewella is not well and she hasn't been baking. That cough is getting worse and worse.'

'I shall try to do something about that,' said Jael. 'An infusion of blackberry leaves will help. And she must eat my blackberry jam as well.'

'Must? You need to approach Ewella more tactfully!'

'Mama, the postman has left a letter for you!' cried Caroline. 'Do you think it is from Papa?'

'I don't think so, Caroline,' said Eliza, hiding a smile. The envelope was large and lavender coloured and it exuded a fragrance redolent of Aunt Gloria. It could be from no one else.

'I have sad news,' Aunt Gloria wrote, in her flamboyant script. 'I am afraid that my dear Yelland has passed to a better place. The jaundice became too much for him, weakening him over the last few months.'

'Poor Yelland, how sad. And poor Aunt Gloria,' Eliza murmured, genuinely moved. She could remember how bravely Yelland had consigned himself to the creaky cage that took tin miners down to the lower levels in Wheal Eliza – and his beaming face as he surfaced, thrilled by the experience. She returned to the letter.

'Grace is still with me and I am finding her a great comfort so I hope her continued absence is not too inconvenient for you. You will be pleased to hear that she seems to have improved in health and that her periods of confusion are rare, so much so that she has little desire to return to Carnglaze, deeming it dark and uncomfortable. That is sensible thinking! She tells me she is quite happy to leave the care of Richard and Elestren to you and Nanny Hannah for the time being.' After a line of exclamation marks there followed the caustic remark: 'We certainly have the old Grace back, do we not!'

Eliza could not help but smile at Aunt Gloria's understanding of her niece's character. She herself was not put out that Richard and Elestren were to be without their mother for longer. Neither child had exhibited any upset at her absence and Eliza was more than happy to add the two of them to her own family. She was particularly fond of Richard who often appeared at her side while Nanny Hannah was attending to Elestren. But poor Aunt Gloria. She must write back to her immediately.

'I find it difficult to believe that sister of yours!' croaked Ewella. 'A rabbit has more concern for its offspring!' However, Eliza was focused elsewhere.

'I have been thinking. It would be dreadful if we were cut off by winter weather so we need to lay in stores of food. I intend to use the money Austol had given us.' Jael sighed with relief and Ewella was diverted from her grumbles.

'That small room at the side of the house will do for food storage. It is too cold for anything else and cold is what we need,' went on Eliza. 'I shall speak to Mathey and see what we can do. Meanwhile a visit to Farmer Tull might prove useful.'

'Perhaps I can store my jams and pickles there as well – and then I shall have the space to make some more,' suggested Jael. Jams and pickles! Eliza was delighted.

'The boys should collect more firewood,' put in Ewella. 'Some of that could be stored round the back of the house.' So it was that when Professor Martineau arrived unexpectedly he found his pupils scattered and busy. Nathaniel, John and Caroline were off down to the sea to find driftwood. Joel was 'helping' Nessa and Ewella with the household chores in between dashing to visit Jael in her barn to watch her brewing her various mixtures. Mathey had taken the cart to the market at St. Just to collect apples and vegetables while Eliza was still digging potatoes. Luckily Tobias came out to welcome the Professor and provide him with some refreshment after his long journey and the two of them settled down for a chat by the kitchen fire, during which conversation he did not mention his concerns about Carnglaze.

Meanwhile the three children were busy on the shoreline gathering driftwood and collecting it in the hessian sacks Nathaniel had brought. It took quite a long time as the tide seemed to have dredged up more seaweed than wood. Not only that but the joy of being by the sea encouraged them to play instead. Screaming and shouting into the emptiness of the shore, they played wild catch games, skimmed stones, balanced on the stepping stones across the stream and, finally, built a dam, trying to divert the water along another course to the sea. It was an afternoon of space and freedom. At last, tired and covered in wet sand, Caroline sat back on her heels and looked out to sea. And received a shock.

Look!' she squeaked.
The horizon had disappeared as had the nearest headlands and the sun's rays were being slowly defeated by an advancing grey cloud. The sea was still; suddenly it seemed as if a giant hand had dowsed the lamps, darkening sea and sky.

'A sea mist!' said John.

'More like a sea fog!' corrected Nathaniel. 'Let's go. We need to find our way.'

Hastily the children hefted the sacks of wood over their shoulders and hurried along the sand, making for the rocky climb up to the path which led back to Carnglaze. As they reached it, scrambling up wildly, so the first tendrils of mist curled round them, overtaking them, winding round them and leading them on, wraithlike shapes blending into dense fog.

'Watch your step, you two,' said Nathaniel, his voice anxious. 'If we slip on these rocks we'll never get back and no one will be able to find us either.'

'It's like a wall,' said Caroline in wonder. 'A wall you can push through!'

'Keep your eyes on the path!' snapped Nathaniel. He felt guilty that he had allowed his sister and younger brother to be overtaken by such danger. He led the way, followed by Caroline and John brought up the rear, limping slightly on his twisted foot. With relief, Nathaniel realised that they had reached the path and, with care, there was less danger of losing their way. In spite of the mud and slippery rocks, the slidey stones, in spite of the thickening fog, and encroaching darkness, they were making progress.

'While we can hear the stream we know we are on the right track,' Nathaniel said.

'The sound is getting fainter,' Caroline complained.

The quiet was broken by a screech from John and a wild scramble among stones. A moment's inattention and he had slipped down the bank into the stream.

'John! John …. are you all right?'

'I'm still alive!' was the grumpy answer.

'Hang on – we'll get you out. Keep shouting because we can't see you.' Nathaniel put down his sack and lowered himself over the edge, immediately disappearing from Caroline's view. She could just hear the boys' voices, Nathaniel exhorting, John complaining. She, herself, seemed to be in an area of silence. The mist drifted round her, closing in; she was aware of the damp, cold feel of it as it caressed her neck and face, soft as spider webs. The boys' voices receded, muted by the mist. She began to shiver, inexplicably frightened. Not for John and his fall as she knew Nathaniel would help him. Not because of the mist, scary and strange though it was. But the place. She remembered the place. She could not see it, hemmed in by mist, but she knew where they were. They had stopped in that clearing surrounded by contorted, lichen covered trees, branches spreading snakelike in a vain search for sunlight, the clearing where she had first felt the strange cold. And she could feel it again. Not the normal chill of a dank and misty day but a cold that seemed to stop the blood flowing in her veins that sapped her strength. The silence thickened about her and then she heard them. The voices. Sibilant whispers, scolding, threatening, increasing in volume. She clapped her hands over her ears.

'Go away! Go away!' she shrieked. 'I don't want to hear you!'

'Caroline – what's the matter? What are you fussing about?' Nathaniel appeared, reassuringly solid, dragging a groaning John who looked as if he had been rolled in mud.

'Come on, we must get back before it gets any darker – and we have to keep hold of our sacks or this trip won't have been worthwhile.' Caroline was still trapped in her nightmare, unable to move and could only mutter about voices and cold. Nathaniel decided it was time for more drastic measures when she refused to look at him and only stared beyond him at the strange swirls of fog. He slapped her face hard.

'Nathaniel!' protested John, but not very forcefully. He was almost pleased that the twins were in conflict. Usually they were in agreement and he was the one on the outside.

The trio continued their walk in silence, scrambling and sliding as before. But now Caroline refused all offers of help. Head down, she led the way, letting Nathaniel support John as best he could. Finally they came to the junction of the path and the track which led past Carnglaze and soon the black bulk of the house appeared out of the gloom.

'Now for it!' said Nathaniel.

But their welcome was not what they expected. They could not even get near to the fire to dry their wet clothes because sitting on either side were Edgar and Seth. There was no sign of Ewella, Jael or the other children, nor of Uncle Tobias. Only Eliza was running distractedly between the two men, offering refreshment, tidying the table, her embarrassment clear.

'I was hoping to take you to the Manor, Eliza,' said Edgar, sulkily. 'Eulalia has had a bad turn and wishes to see you.'

'Surely a doctor would be more suitable,' was Seth's frosty comment.

'No one is going anywhere in this weather,' said Eliza. 'There is no sign of it lifting and I feel you will both have to stay the night. These chairs by the fire are all I have to offer you.' Seth nodded his head.

'Thank you, Eliza, but Rose will be worried. I am sure my horse will be able to find its way along the track to the road.' This seemed to cheer Edgar.

'I should be happy to accept the offer of a chair,' he said, brightly. 'Austol will realise what has happened and we can get to the Manor in the morning, I am sure.'

Eliza pursed her lips. She was about to point out that she might have made other plans and was not at the beck and call of those at the Manor – but it was poor Eulalia who wanted her. She would have to go.

'You three,' she said, turning to the children. 'I can see you have had a muddy scramble to get back. Why were you so long?'

'We did get a lot of driftwood, Mama,' said Nathaniel virtuously.

'And he had to slap Caroline to keep her going,' said John, with equal virtue. Eliza looked at her daughter. But Caroline's face was closed. There would be nothing forthcoming from her. Oh, why was she left to manage alone? Why was Barnabas not back to help her?

17

'I am so sorry to leave you now,' said Seth at the door. Eliza nodded.

'I understand. You have to get back to Rose.'

'No need to worry,' called Edgar. 'I shall be on hand to help if the fog persists.' This information did not seem to please Seth. He lowered his voice.

'Eliza, please do not go to the Manor until the weather improves. Mr. Tallack seems to think that his pony and trap can manage the track while it is still muddy but it is dangerous. Even my horse will have difficulty and it is a strong animal.'

'Do not worry. I shall be in good hands,' said Eliza, sweetly and was gratified to see Seth scowl. Just the same she felt a pang as his horse vanished into the mist. For Rose, he was willing to make the long and arduous journey back.

Just then Jael appeared from her barn, the fog biting at her heels like some pet dog.

'I have made a special tonic for Eulalia,' she said, with satisfaction. 'And I have the infusion of blackberry leaves for Ewella. She will soon be baking again.'

'Marvellous,' said Eliza, absently. Jael gave her a sharp look.

'Mr. Quinn has gone?' she queried. 'I thought I heard his horse.' Eliza did not rise to that.

'I must get the children hot drinks before bedtime,' she said. 'And Uncle Tobias – perhaps you could take in his hot toddy?'

'Of course.' She went in to the kitchen and was startled to find Edgar ensconced by the fire. He, too, was pleased to accept the offer of a hot toddy.

'I'm not used to a house as cold as this,' he said apologetically.

The next day dawned bright and clear as if the fog had acted like a dishcloth and wiped everything clean. The sky was cloudless; the wet leaves of the trees and bushes shone as if polished and even the large puddles in the courtyard and on the track reflected blue. Coming downstairs, Nanny Hannah squeaked in surprise when she found a strange man asleep in the chair. Hurriedly she collected the milk for Elestren and disappeared again. Eliza came down, donning her large calico apron and Edgar woke. He staggered to his feet, looking crumpled of clothing and creased of face, not at all the usual debonair Edgar. Eliza smiled at him.

'I can heat you some water in the kettle if you like?'

'Bathroom?'

'No. Not in this house. There is a cold water pump in the courtyard.'

Edgar pulled a face but obediently ventured outside. Then Professor Martineau appeared, surprisingly early, considering the state of the track but soon he and the children were settled in the schoolroom. Ewella began to bustle about the kitchen still looking pale.

'I think I had better stay with her,' said Jael. 'If she does the cooking I can do the rest. Please take the tonic for Eulalia and give her my good wishes.'

'I don't know what I should do without you,' said a grateful Eliza.

Edgar and Eliza arrived at the Manor muddy but in good spirits. The blue sky and benign sun had cheered them both. However Austol received them so gloomily it felt as if the clouds had rolled in again.

'Eulalia is being quite unreasonable,' he said, fretfully. 'She forgets who is the master here and that a wife owes support and loyalty to her husband.'

'What has happened?' demanded Edgar.

'Grace and Lady Conyers are arriving soon. That is what is GOING to happen!' Austol reverted to his usual disapproving mien and the atmosphere thickened with unsaid complaints and accusations. Edgar looked angry.

'We shall talk later,' said Austol stiffly, glancing at Eliza. 'Meanwhile Mistress Eliza and I will take sherry in the morning room.' Firmly he took Eliza's arm and led her away, leaving Edgar disapproving and uncertain.

Eliza could not fault the way Austol looked after her. He placed her in a comfortable armchair next to the window which looked out on a dazzling view of the sea and rang for sherry and some delicate saffron biscuits. Politely he thanked her for making the uncomfortable journey and apologised for his frequent demands on her time.

'I have to confess that I do not know what to do about Eulalia.' Eliza was about to point out that neither did she but Austol held up his hand to stop her.

'You see, she does not trust Grace and her latest outburst has been because she is returning to the Manor. I feel it only fair to tell you that the story of your sister and your husband has reached her' – Eliza felt the colour creep into her face – 'I am telling you this because my wife is capable of blurting it out and offending you. I feel you have probably suffered enough already. I only wish to warn you. Of course I know – hence my reluctance to offer Grace shelter at the time Roscarne was closed.'

Austol's voice contained some plea for understanding but his eyes were cold and metallic as ever. He edged his chair nearer and put his arm around Eliza's shoulder. What did he want? Eliza began to feel that she was the plump hen and he was the fox enticing her to come closer. But for what? She resisted the impulse to run squawking to the door.

'It is good news for me that Aunt Gloria is coming to visit,' Eliza said carefully. 'She writes that Grace is much improved and has fewer muddled episodes. Do I understand that you do not wish Grace to stay at the Manor anymore?'

'No, no! I have not made myself clear! It is not I who wishes it. It is Eulalia! She is fearful that Grace has designs on Edgar – or even me! Anything to cling to the Manor and live her life as it was before. Grace, however, has come to her senses sufficiently to regard Carnglaze as beneath her. Apparently she shudders at the thought of the discomfort there.'

Eliza felt the beginnings of a cold anger. Was she never to be free of Grace's misdeeds?

'I feel sure you and Edgar between you will be able to reassure Eulalia,' she said, firmly. 'As for Grace, you and she will have to decide where she lives. Aunt Gloria may be of some help. Of course Grace is always welcome at Carnglaze but she has to realise that it will be crowded and uncomfortable as before and that will not change until Barnabas returns.'

Austol looked speculatively at Eliza. She made an attractive figure, straightbacked in her blue silk dress, colour in her face from the drive in the cold. The light from the window encircled her head like aureole and her blue eyes sparked with anger she could barely contain. A lady of spirit, Austol observed.

'Perhaps I should see Eulalia?

'Yes, of course.'

The window was shut in Eulalia's room and the air smelt stale. All was in a state of disarray – clothes were strewn over the floor, empty glasses left on the side-table and the bedcovers were rumpled untidily. It was clear that the occupant of the bed had been throwing things across the room as several smashed ornaments littered the beautiful dark blue carpet.

'I don't want to see anyone!' came a voice from beneath the covers. 'I do not want ANYONE in my room!'

'Mistress Eliza has come to see you,' boomed Austol, infuriated by the behaviour of his wife. 'Perhaps she can talk some sense into you.' And he strode out, leaving Eliza to deal with her. However, Eulalia remained under the covers so Eliza sat down on the chair next to the bed and prepared to wait it out. Her gaze roamed round the room, noting the heavy blue velvet curtains, the solid furniture, the decorated mirrors. Eulalia had not been stinted, that was clear. Her eye lighted on something half under the dressing table. It was the necklace of rowan berries, the red ribbon frayed as if it had been torn off and some of the berries scattered. Just then, Eulalia groaned and sat up.

'Oh, Mistress Eliza, I am so sorry that you find me like this! But I am in such pain!' She did indeed look beaten down and ill. Her hair was disarranged, her bald patches revealed and her face had the yellow tinge that Eliza had observed before she powdered it white.

'Perhaps I can help you,' said Eliza gently. 'Tell me how you have been feeling?' And Eulalia did, grateful that someone was prepared to listen.

'I think she is really ill,' Eliza reported to Austol. 'She does need a doctor.'

'I shall see to it straight away,' said Austol. 'It has been difficult to separate the truth of her various illnesses and tantrums from the reality. The last doctor I called recommended sedatives. He felt her symptoms were nervous in origin.'

'Perhaps another doctor might have a different opinion,' said Eliza. What was the matter with this man? Surely he should have been trying harder to find the cause of his wife's obvious distress? If he felt concern he was disguising it well. Edgar, however, looked really alarmed when he joined them.

'I suggested another doctor before – you know I did!'

'Eulalia is my wife, Edgar, and I shall do what I think fit,' Austol replied.

Eliza insisted that she should return to Carnglaze, saying there was nothing more she could do. She wanted to distance herself from the Manor and the unhappy family within.

'You must stay with your sister,' she said to Edgar. 'Perhaps one of the servants could drive me to Carnglaze.'

'Yes, of course,' said Edgar hurriedly. 'How kind of you to understand.'

Eliza did not feel kind; she felt she was running away. There were strange undercurrents here swirling beneath the surface that she could not comprehend. She would have avoided further visits to the Manor had Grace not been involved and now Aunt Gloria was to appear once more with Grace in tow.

'They will come for me again very soon, you mark my words,' she said to Jael.

Her prophesy was correct. Edgar appeared the very next day. Though it was chilly, autumn was still making a brave stand against the onslaught of winter and the sun shone, but with less strength.

'That Edgar is coming along the track,' reported Ewella in disapproving tone.

'Not again!' snapped Eliza. 'I want to check all the children's clothes. They are beginning to look like ragamuffins and I must do some mending. And the boys' shoes need to go to the cobbler very soon. That means a trip to Zennor. I do not have time for Edgar.'

'I'll meet him and try to head him off,' suggested Jael. 'I could say that you were very busy with the children as Professor Martineau is not coming today.'

'That won't stop him,' sighed Eliza. 'He is a very determined man.'

So Eliza found herself driving to the Manor with Edgar who was in a strange mood – alternately irritable and scolding the pony and gloomy. He had assured Eliza that his sister had been crying out for her and wanted to see her again at once. Austol, meanwhile had sent for Doctor Trevell, all the way from Rosmorren. To complicate matters, Aunt Gloria and Grace were travelling down from London on that very day.

'Austol is not often unable to deal with difficult matters,' confided Edgar. 'But I am afraid Eulalia has tried his patience once too often. We had a letter from Kenwyn saying that he would not return to the front – which is desertion of course – and Eulalia cried and screamed and became totally hysterical. Austol intends to travel to the Lake District where Kenwyn is staying with a friend and insist that the boy return to his regiment.'

'What does Eulalia think?'

'She is distraught that her beloved Kenwyn has done something so disgraceful but at the same time she is pleased that he will not be returning to battle. Of course Austol is beside himself with rage.'

'How do you feel about Kenwyn?'

'As the only boy he has been badly spoilt and what he has done is not surprising. Just in character. From being proud of him, Austol has taken to muttering that he should have been another girl for all the manly tendencies he has exhibited. Naturally he blames Eulalia which is hardly fair. He has had no real fatherly training from Austol......' Edgar relapsed into silence, probably feeling that he had said too much.

'Poor Kenwyn,' said Eliza, rather to her own surprise.

Arriving at the Manor, the door was opened by a maid who looked taken aback to see Eliza.

'Lord Treloyhan has just left,' she said, bobbing a curtsey.

'We are here to see Mistress Eulalia,' said Edgar, shortly. 'Please arrange for some refreshment to be brought to the morning room.'

'Yes, sir.'

Edgar led the way to Eulalia's room where they found another maid sitting on a chair outside the door. She jumped up when she saw Edgar.

'Please zur, the master said as I should stay here to listen to Mistress Eulalia – and to stop the girls from disturbing her. She 'ave stopped screaming now and 'ave bin quiet for some time.'

'Thank you,' said Edgar. 'You may go now.'

He knocked gently at the door but there was no answer. With Eliza at his heels, he tiptoed in.

The room had been tidied and Eulalia lay peacefully under the covers, her head turned away from the door.

'Perhaps we should leave her to sleep?' said Eliza softly. Edgar shook his head.

'No, we need to wake her and talk some sense into her while Austol is not here. If she continues to behave so badly I am afraid he will send her away.'

'And send you away as well,' the uncharitable thought jumped into Eliza's head.

'Eulalia?' Edgar spoke less softly. 'Wake up, Eulalia. Mistress Eliza is here to see you.' Eulalia did not stir and Edgar grimaced.

'Eulalia!' he said loudly. Eulalia did not stir.

A cold shiver of apprehension shook Eliza. She leaned over the bed and took Eulalia's hand. The hand remained inert in hers. And cold. At Eliza's horrified expression, Edgar pulled down the coverlet and touched Eulalia's cheek. Then, beginning to tremble, he felt her neck. Nothing. Stricken, he swung round to face Eliza, his eyes imploring. She met his gaze and shook her head slightly. With a groan, he stumbled to a chair and covered his face with his hands.

18

For a moment, Eliza was at a loss. What could she do to help Edgar? She had left him alone with Eulalia and was waiting in the corridor when the parlour maid hurried towards her.

'Dr. Trevell to see Mistress Eulalia,' she announced and the familiar figure of the doctor from Rosmorren appeared. Eliza could have hugged him. It was a comfort to see his familiar figure. She waited while Dr. Trevell and Edgar conferred, then decided to retire to the morning room. There she curled up in one of the comfortable armchairs and tried to order her thoughts, thoughts that followed their own path without her volition. How sad that Austol should be away when his wife was dying. Sad, or fortuitous? And Edgar? His grief had been real and yet there had been no signs of shock – just a heart broken acceptance. She herself had been called in. Why? As a witness? Her musing was interrupted by the entrance of Dr. Trevell.

'Mistress Eliza. I am delighted to meet you again, though at an unfortunate time. I have given Mr. Tallack a light sedative as the poor man is grief stricken. I am really surprised they did not call me sooner!' He shook his head. He was about to say more but thought better of it. Instead he looked searchingly at Eliza and changed the subject. 'Has there been any word from Mr. Trevannion, my dear?' Eliza shook her head. 'It is time that young man returned to Cornwall,' Dr. Trevell continued. 'I hear that you have been living at Carnglaze and that is not wise for any of you. The sooner you leave that house the better!'

'We are rather crowded,' Eliza allowed, 'But we are managing.' She was puzzled that the doctor had expressed himself so strongly. After all, there were many poorer households in the district. Dr. Trevell patted her on the shoulder. 'I must be off. So many babies being born just now. I do not mean to alarm you, but if you need help or advice, my dear, please get in touch with me.' These words, added to Dr. Trevell's grave countenance, did alarm Eliza but she could not question him as he hurried away.

Eliza was relieved to be on the way back to Carnglaze at last. She knew that Aunt Gloria and Grace would be arriving later in the evening but

114

felt devoid of the necessary energy to wait for them. They would have to decide how to proceed without her. Nothing was easy or straightforward and she was beginning to feel even more overburdened. Then there was Dr. Trevell and his reference to Barnabas. That had stung. Also, his disapproval of the family living at Carnglaze had been strongly worded. Strange.

'I knew something bad had happened,' said Jael, fussing round Eliza with tea. 'But poor silly Eulalia, dead! It seems my protective charm did not work.'

'Mama! Mama!' It was Caroline. 'I've been waiting for you. I had a funny feeling you were sad! Are you sad?'

'Yes, just a little,' she said, gently, smoothing back her daughter's brown hair. She explained that Eulalia had not survived her illness. Caroline had never met her so the news made little impact but she was obviously pleased that her mother was back and skipped off to complete her schoolwork. Jael disappeared to her barn and it was only then that Eliza realised she had not confided the comments made by Dr. Trevell.

Soon Eliza and Ewella were busy with the evening meal. Uncle Tobias tottered out of his small room and declared himself delighted that food was on the way.

'I am relieved that his appetite is so good,' confided Eliza to Ewella. 'All thanks to your good cooking!' Ewella smiled with pleasure. It was a hard life at Carnglaze compared with Roscarne but it was good to be appreciated.

'I hope I did the right thing,' she said. 'I sent Mathey with all the children's shoes to the cobbler in Zennor. He has promised to have them ready in three days.'

'Oh thank you, Ewella! I suppose the children are all bare footed now?'

'Not quite. I made them rough socks from some hessian sacking. John is complaining but the others think it is funny! Joel said that he always wanted to be barefoot like some of the farm boys and refused the socks.' They laughed together.

'I shall use some extra candles tonight and patch their clothes,' declared Eliza. 'You have inspired me to a task I find uncongenial in the extreme and which always takes me a long time because I am so unskilled with a needle.'

'Mistress Eliza,' said Ewella purposefully. 'Surely there is money for the children to have new shoes? Penzance has many shoe stalls in the Market where we could find good shoes at a reasonable cost. Caroline and Nathaniel have nearly grown out of theirs; it won't be long before the others follow suit.'

'You are quite right, Ewella,' sighed Eliza 'They all need shoes – and we do have the money – but I have been spending as little as possible. I just don't know how long we need it to last. I must consult Cubert Petherwin, the solicitor, but that means going all the way to Truro. However, shoes are very necessary – I realise that. But Penzance! That, too, is quite a long way.' She did not add that Rose and Seth were in Penzance and she did not want to risk meeting them. 'Perhaps we could buy shoes in Zennor?'

'No shops there – only the one cobbler.' said Ewella. 'I think he only makes those hefty boots that farmers wear. But there is no need to be concerned. We can measure the children's feet here and I will go with Mathey to buy them.'

Eliza heaved a sigh of relief. She would not have to look over her shoulder in the narrow streets of Penzance.

The next morning – a drizzly day, grey and cold, Ewella set off with Mathey in the cart. She was cheerful at the thought of escaping the chores for one day at least and Eliza had promised to take over the cooking. Some sunshine or at least dry weather would have been preferable but nothing could dampen her good mood. Left alone, Eliza began to scurry round the kitchen, raking the range so that it gave out a good heat and arranging clothes still damp from washing around it. Then she made a stew from a rabbit Jed had brought her, eking it out with potatoes and turnips and flavouring it with some of the herbs from Jael's supply. Uncle Tobias had had his breakfast but always welcomed a hot drink in the middle of the morning, so that was next. Then, as the stew was for the evening meal, she planned to serve the children and the Professor baked potatoes at lunchtime. She had no time to cook anything more. Start patching the clothes she must. It was a task that would last well into the evening.

Thus engaged, the table strewn with clothes and cottons, Seth found her. She looked up and there he was at the door. Immediately she felt the colour mounting to her face, conscious of her hair awry and her fingers bloody from the clumsy needle she was using.

'Mistress Eliza – I trust I find you well?' Seth grinned.

'Very well,' she replied, trying to gather her dignity around her as protection. It was no use. The look on his face told her that he sensed her discomfort and it amused him.

'I have come to take you to Penzance to see Rose,' he announced. 'The rain has stopped and the sun is struggling to shine. The break will do you good.'

'No doubt,' said Eliza, drily. 'But I am unable to leave the house at the moment. Ewella is on her way to Penzance right now, Jael is looking for herbs somewhere and I must tend to Uncle Tobias, the Professor and the children. Lessons will soon be over and they have to have their lunch.'

'This afternoon then?'

'I'm afraid not.'

Seth was unfazed by the rebuff. He leaned back in his chair and smiled persuasively.

'Then may I hope that you will accompany me tomorrow?'

'You are not going to drive all the way back to Penzance and then return for me again?' demanded Eliza. 'You will be spending more time on the road than with Rose!'

'Maybe. But perhaps the journey will be worthwhile?'

Before Eliza could say yes or no there was a thunderous knock at the door.

'Surely not Mr. Tallack again!' frowned Seth, losing his teasing manner. But it was. Not the debonair Edgar with ready smile but a sombre man, his shoulders rounded against the vicissitudes of the world.

'Mistress Eliza. Mr. Quinn.' He nodded greeting to them both.

'You had better sit down here,' Eliza said. 'You are aware we have no parlour.' She felt sorry for Edgar who was obviously grieving for his sister and was ashamed of her impatience. She was cross with Seth for assuming that she would be free to follow him whenever he snapped his fingers and even crosser when she realised that his manner was positively antagonistic to poor Edgar.

'Seth, you need to know that Mr. Tallack's sister, Eulalia, has just passed away,' she said, and observed that Seth looked suitably shocked and managed to mumble condolences.

'I am really sorry to intrude, Mistress Eliza,' said Edgar, desperately. 'I am again in a position where I need your help. Lady Conyers and Mistress Grace will be arriving early tomorrow morning and I have made no preparations for them. I have been unable to reach Austol to tell him the sad news and I need to go to Truro tomorrow to fetch the undertakers. I wonder if you would consent to take charge of the Manor during my absence?'

Eliza was taken aback. Problems were arising like bubbles on a stagnant pond and she realised that she was not going to escape them so easily. Poor Edgar sat there, grey faced and his eyes full of pain. Of course she would help.

'Seth, could you see if Jael is in her barn and ask her to come here?' she said briskly.

'I shall go and talk to Nanny Hannah and Uncle Tobias. Oh, and inform the Professor.'

Nanny Hannah, immured in her tiny nursery, was feeding Elestren. There was no sign of Richard. She looked up, surprised to see Eliza.

'I – I will try to help,' she said anxiously, looking as if Eliza had asked her to jump off a cliff. 'As soon as Elestren is asleep I shall come down.'

'Oh thank you,' said Eliza, fervently. 'Ewella will be back before dark and I am sure Jael will help you. There is a stew prepared for the evening meal and then the children will have to be supervised going to bed. Joel often needs a little persuading,' she added. Nanny Hannah looked panic stricken but nodded her head. After talking to Uncle Tobias and explaining what was happening, Eliza returned to the kitchen. Seth and Edgar were there with Jael.

'I do not understand why your housekeeper cannot supervise arrangements at the Manor,' Seth was saying.

'We have no housekeeper. Austol dismissed her in a temper before he left,' Edgar answered, with a heavy sigh. 'Mistress Eliza, if my request is too awkward – '

'No, Edgar. I shall come at once,' Eliza assured him. 'Seth, please convey my regrets to Rose. I hope to come and see her on another day.' Thus firmly dismissed, Seth took himself off in an ill-humoured mood. He sensed that the former closeness between Eliza and

118

himself had evaporated and he was not sure why that should be. It never entered his head that his marriage to Rose might have had something to do with it.

Edgar was silent on the long journey back to the Manor. Dusk was falling and it was still cold but the skies had cleared. Cosily wrapped in a fur rug, Eliza had time to think. Should she have acceded to Edgar's request? He was becoming altogether too dependent on her and it seemed as if he came trotting to Carnglaze at every opportunity. However she recognised that the poor man was reliant on Austol for his place at the Manor, a place become uncertain now that Eulalia was no more. He must be feeling adrift and unsure of the future. Her perception of him had changed, she realised. She remembered his first visit and his arrogant manner towards them all, a manner, she now realised, probably an unconscious imitation of Austol's autocratic behaviour towards those he considered his inferiors.

The next morning, it did not take as long as she had feared to organise the Manor. There was no doubt that it appeared neglected and unwelcoming. No wonder Austol had dismissed his housekeeper. Two maids were put in charge of lighting fires and putting fresh linen on the beds in two large bedrooms overlooking the sea. Another maid was charged with cleaning Austol's room and polishing the furniture. The cook she found lounging at the kitchen table, drinking tea, but soon set her to work making pies for supper, ensuring her cooperation by asking her advice about menus and treating her as a person of some importance. The parlour maid, much to her indignation, found herself lighting fires in the dining room, main reception room and entrance hall; Eliza in full swing was hard to resist. She found two kitchen maids huddled in the scullery and set one to work in the entrance hall, cleaning and polishing and the other to buffing the fine mahogany banisters on the stairs. She told them that she knew these tasks were unusual for them but were to be completed before Austol returned. Their master would certainly be pleased. Not that she had any real idea how Austol would react, indeed he might not even notice. Next, she went out to the conservatory where, sure enough, there were beautiful blooms in spite of the cold autumn weather outside. There was no sign of any gardener so she collected enough flowers herself to decorate the dining room table and fill the large vases in the entrance hall. She was satisfied that the flame coloured dahlias and white lilies as well as the crackling fire would make the spacious hall welcoming. Edgar, meanwhile, returned from the undertakers and, sunk in gloom, had retired to a large armchair with a glass of brandy.

'Edgar,' said Eliza gently. 'I have to return to Carnglaze now. Perhaps one of the manservants can drive me back?'

'Mistress Eliza, please stay! How can I face Austol with this terrible news! I should welcome your support.'

'Edgar – I have responsibilities of my own. The children need me – especially just now. I am so sorry for your loss but I cannot help you with Austol. It may possibly be several days before he returns. Furthermore you seem to have forgotten that Aunt Gloria and Grace should arrive soon. They may turn up this evening but, knowing Aunt Gloria, it is more likely that they will spend the night in a hotel. Whatever they do, the Manor is in readiness and the cook has prepared a fine meal for tonight.' Edgar sat up straight.

'Which you condemn me to eat alone!' he protested.

Eliza tried to contain her irritability. Really, Edgar was demanding too much of her. He was living in luxury and had no conception of the difficulties at Carnglaze. This clinging to her skirts was tiresome. More dignity was needed. But then, she chided herself, he was mourning his sister. Of course he would not understand her need to get back to Carnglaze as soon as possible. What would he make of a wandering spirit singing nursery rhymes? This was part of life at Carnglaze, fortunately accepted by the children. But the threatening voices? That was something entirely different. Her children needed her presence and nothing would divert her. She looked at Edgar, his hair ruffled, his whiskers drooping, his eyes like a whipped puppy and she was horrified at her lack of feeling for him. What was happening to her that she had become so impatient, so unsympathetic, so quick to look beneath the surface and suspect deceitful motives? It seemed that life at Carnglaze was not improving her disposition! Of course Barnabas' long absence and lack of communication played its part. She must guard against becoming bitter.

'Edgar,' she said, with an effort. 'I shall come again soon, I promise, to help you with Aunt Gloria and Grace – and perhaps Austol, if he turns up. Now you have to comfort the girls who have just lost their mother.....'

'They have been sent to stay with the Edgebastons for a holiday. Austol did not want them present when he returned with Kenwyn. They do not know what has happened,' said Edgar, mournfully.

'Oh, Edgar!'

'I shall try to face the new day with more courage,' said Edgar.

19

Eliza was pleased to get back to Carnglaze before full dark. As it was, the manservant from the Manor had to negotiate the track with great care between puddles and potholes filled with mud. Arriving at Carnglaze, a heavy grey shape in the gloom, she thanked him and picked her way across the courtyard, heartened by the light of an oil lamp in the window. An unusual sight met her eyes. All the children were gathered round the table with Ewella and Jael. Richard was there, too, only Nanny Hannah and Elestren were not present. Uncle Tobias had the best seat by the fire but he was not dozing, he looked alert.

'Mama!' cried Caroline, running to her. 'We are so glad you are here!'

'What has happened?' asked Eliza, trying not to show her alarm. 'Ewella? Jael?'

'It's this house! We are not welcome! The house is trying to push us away!' blurted Caroline, before anyone else could say anything. Nathaniel and John looked serious and even Joel was subdued. Little Richard was holding Nessa's hand and looking very nervous.

'You have been playing some silly game,' said Ewella, sharply.

'Will someone please tell me!'

'I'll tell you, Mama,' said Nathaniel. 'When the rain stopped, we all went out to play at the back of the house. We were playing 'catch' and shouting and screaming quite a lot…'

'And we didn't hear the voices at first…' put in John.

'But then I thought I heard something,' said Caroline, 'And I made everyone be quiet – and then we heard them. They were whispering – but whispering loudly if you know what I mean.'

'They kept saying 'Go away. Leave.' said John.

'Danger here….' added Caroline

'The loudest voice was saying 'mine, mine, mine' piped up little Richard. 'And I felt very cold.'

'We all began to shiver,' said Nathaniel. 'It was…quite frightening.'

'I don't want to stay in this house,' cried out John. 'It wants us to go, I know it does!'

Eliza looked from Ewella to Jael for confirmation. It was Jael who nodded. Eliza was appalled. She had come back to find Carnglaze full of frightened children, menaced by a spirit – or spirits – that were strong enough to be heard. Not just someone singing nursery rhymes. Angry spirits wanting them to leave. Something would have to be done. The first thing was to allay their fears.

'We have been in this house quite a long time,' she began. 'And the Lanivets lived here before us and no harm came to them. So I do not think you should worry.'

'They left in a hurry!' put in Ewella, unwisely.

'I expect the house wanted them to go,' said Caroline, her voice obstinate.

'You know that the wind makes strange noises among the trees….' Eliza tried again.

'It wasn't a strange noise. It was words!' interrupted Nathaniel, annoyed. 'And before you say it could have been the wind in the chimney, we were outside, right down at the bottom of the garden.'

'Next to that funny big stone,' put in Nessa.

'I think perhaps we should be honest and say we do not know what is going on,' said Jael, quietly. Her silvery hair shone in the firelight as she leaned forward to warm her hands. 'What we have to do is to decide how we can stop the voices.'

'Yes,' said a bewildered Eliza. The obvious remedy was to leave the house. But they had nowhere to go. And it was winter. It was like being in a bad dream. Uncle Tobias broke the tense atmosphere by standing up creakily and declaring that all this nonsense was making him tired and he shuffled off to his little room.

'I shall make him a hot posset so that he sleeps well,' said Jael. The presence of their mother and the return to a semblance of normality allowed the children to forget their nervousness for the moment and become restless. Nathaniel and John started squabbling while little Richard was hanging on to Nessa's hand and Joel was trying to wrestle him away. Only Caroline sat still and white faced. Ewella echoed Uncle Tobias by muttering 'stuff and nonsense' loud enough for everyone to hear and began to usher them all up to bed.

'Perhaps we could ask the Professor for advice?' suggested Eliza.

'Mmmm… I do not suppose he has much experience with hauntings,' said Jael. 'But he is open minded and knows the district well. We could start with him. Then my mother knows a wise woman in Liskeard.' She hesitated. 'Unfortunately she is reputed to be witch. That is not true, of course,' she added hastily. 'Anyone who is different or who has unusual skills is labelled a witch.' Eliza noticed that her voice had acquired a bitter tone.

'We could ask Dr. Trevell for help. He was very insistent that we should not be living in Carnglaze – so he knows something.' Eliza mused. Jael nodded, her pretty face already tight with thought. She left for her barn and Eliza looked round the empty kitchen. It was becoming familiar, bleak though it was, and devoid of any pretence at elegance. The glow of the oil lamps and the warmth from the range gave it a semblance of comfort, the bare walls and stone floor outside the circles of light receding into the gloom. But what was she doing here with her family? What had Barnabas been thinking of? Why had he not stayed and protected his own rather than escaping to another continent? Sudden rage took Eliza by the throat and shook her so she shivered and trembled with it and blood suffused her face. It was all too much. Her children were crowded together in this menacing house threatened by the unknown; Uncle Tobias was left in her care, his health uncertain and his happiness doubtful, brave old man though he was, and she loved and worried about him in equal measures; Grace was an ever present shadow, lurking in the corners of her life; The Manor and its inhabitants offered problems not solutions – and then there was Seth. And Rose. Eliza rose from her chair, grabbed the one dish left on the table and threw it with all her strength at the wall. With a resounding crash, it broke into a thousand fragments, scattering over the floor. The noise brought Ewella rushing in. The pieces lay in mute evidence on the floor

'Well Eliza, that should have made you feel better!' she said. 'What a blessing we did not bring the good china from Roscarne!' Ewella's dry tones calmed Eliza more quickly than sympathy.

The morning, frosted and bright, brought in Seth as inevitably as the tide.

'Rose seems much improved this morning,' he said. 'She is looking forward so much to seeing you!' There was nothing for it. Eliza could not put off the meeting any longer. In her best blue silk she sat stiffly next to Seth in the pony and trap. Colluding with him, the sun shone with brilliance and the trip promised to be pleasant. However Eliza was still in turmoil. Aunt Gloria and Grace would surely be at the

Manor by this time, the Professor would have arrived at Carnglaze and she so wanted to talk to him and …..'

'Eliza.' Seth broke into her thoughts. 'I can see you are worrying about something. Please tell me and maybe I can help.' Eliza smiled drearily. He and Rose were part of her worries though he seemed unaware of this.

'I am sorry, Seth, to be such poor company. It is true that I have many things on my mind but I, too, am looking forward to seeing Rose and I mean to enjoy this trip.' She smiled brightly at him and they both relapsed into silence. The moors, in autumn colours still, were brown with bracken, patched with the dark green of gorse bushes, their golden blossom long gone, and the purple haze of new heather. Along the roads foxgloves still bloomed among late pink campions and above, the sky arched blue without a cloud. Despite herself, Eliza felt her spirits rise. Carnglaze was crouched in such a dark valley, shadowed by thorn trees, that this light and space was uplifting. Her smile became real, one of enjoyment.

The pony began to labour up an incline, stumbling on stones. Seth encouraged the gallant little creature with a clicking of his tongue and, finally, they reached the top. Spread out before them was an expanse of sea, still as silk, and rising up out of it a fairy tale castle.

'St. Michael's Mount,' said Seth. 'Seat of Cormoran the Giant!'

'Why is it called after St. Michael, then?' demanded Eliza, laughing.

'Apparently the saint appeared at the summit of the Mount – I don't know when. I think he appeared in France as well because they have a similar castle in the sea called Mont St. Michel.'

'You are very well informed!' said Eliza, impressed.

'I have been getting to know Penzance and its local history while Rose has been resting.'

'What about Cormoran the Giant then?'

'Now that is an interesting story – but it will have to wait.'

'I have never seen St. Michael's Mount before,' said Eliza, wistfully. 'What a romantic building and what a setting.'

'We shall go there one day,' said Seth firmly. 'I found out that it is owned by the St. Aubyn family but I believe visitors are allowed. We can cross over the sea by the causeway when the tide is out.'

'What happens if there is a storm, or you find the tide is too high to return?' asked Eliza. Seth laughed. 'I promise you it is a long way to swim!'

'Be serious!'

'I am sure we could hire a boat – or we sit on the shore and pretend we are on a desert island until the tide ebbs.'

'I like the sound of that,' said Eliza.

The pony and trap began to clatter over the cobbles of Penzance. From the main street they turned down a steep alley way that lead to the sea. On the left hand side was the sign 'The Galleon Inn'.

Eliza felt her stomach contract in anticipation. To see Rose again! To see Rose and Seth together! The happy, relaxed mood which had developed over the course of the journey vanished. Seth glanced at her anxiously. He was more aware of her state of mind than she realised and he knew that seeing Rose again would not be easy. But he need not have been concerned. Rose gave such a cry of joy that the happiness of their reunion was never in doubt. They both spoke at the same time and laughed together as they exchanged news and all the old constraints vanished into the air. It was only when Seth brought in a tray of tea for both of them that Eliza had time to scrutinise her friend more closely. She was pale and strands of grey had appeared in her thick brown hair but her manner was animated and her delight at seeing Eliza was unfeigned. She was seated in an armchair by the window and the light showed the lines in her face; the deep green velvet dress and lace shawl spoke of Seth's new wealth but could not hide the fact that she had become very thin. For her part, Rose could see that her friend had suffered since Barnabas had left. Her face was finely drawn and her ready smile appeared less often while her hands were those of a bal maiden, not a lady. Some adroit questioning and Rose had dragged out every bit of news about Carnglaze and the children.

'I cannot believe that Barnabas left you all to stay in a house as derelict as Carnglaze,' said Rose. 'He must have been thrown off balance by the closure of his mines. He always seemed to me to be so caring of his family. A good man and a good husband.'

Eliza felt the unspoken rebuke in Rose's voice.

'I know that so many others live in conditions even more unsuitable' Eliza admitted. 'The tinners and farm labourers crowded in their cottages. Some are so poor they live in nothing better than hovels.

126

Why should we think we are any better? When Wheal Eliza closed, Barnabas lost his money so we have no claim on a house like Roscarne. If he comes back and is still destitute, he will have to sell it.'

'Barnabas will come back having made his fortune,' said Seth firmly. 'He is a determined man of considerable talent. He left in such a hurry because he was keen not to be last in the quest for new opportunities. He wanted to recoup his money and come back to Cornwall and make a good life for his wife and children. And I am here because I want to join him in any venture he has in mind.'

'Good thought. But then where is he? Not a word from him for months!' said Eliza, unable to hide the bitterness in her voice.

On the way back, Seth was brooding and silent. Eliza sat next to him, for once unaware of his physical presence and the way he always made her heart beat faster. She was wondering whether to confide in him about the strange happenings at Carnglaze. But Seth interrupted her thoughts.

'How are things at the Manor?' he asked, with an edge to his voice.

'If you mean how is Edgar – I have not seen him since helping him to prepare the Manor for Austol's return – and for the arrival of Grace and Aunt Gloria.'

'I find it unforgivable that you should be asked to do housekeeping tasks for such as Edgar! Why could HE not organise the servants? Or even set to and do some of the work himself?'

'You forget – he had just lost his sister and was suffering from shock,' said Eliza in reproof.

'Playing the gentleman when he has no right. Correct me if I am wrong – but I believe he is only at the Manor courtesy of his sister?'

'I suppose so. But now she is dead he must be worried about his position,' pointed out Eliza.

'Eliza, why are we wasting time worrying about Edgar when we should be enjoying this journey,' Seth burst out suddenly. 'I am sorry I raised the subject.'

'Yes,' answered Eliza demurely. 'I would prefer the story of Cormoran the Giant!'

'You are laughing at me!'

127

'Perhaps we should talk about Rose. It was lovely to see her and I am grateful to you for taking me.' She hesitated. 'I did notice that she has become very thin.'

'I think that is partly because she was so homesick for Cornwall and partly grief over losing her child. I hope that the fresh air of Cornwall will work wonders for her and return her to full health.'
The trap lurched over a pothole and Eliza was flung across Seth. Blushing furiously, she held on to his arm and righted herself.

'I'm sorry,' she gasped.

'I'm not. I shall look for more potholes,' grinned Seth, losing his serious manner. He glanced sideways at Eliza and noted her flushed face, her bright eyes and her magnificent hair fallen down over her shoulders. What a lovely creature she was. No wonder Edgar was attracted to her. He would like to meet Edgar in the boxing ring and fight him like he used to fight young men at the fair. That would show him. Not that he had any right to feel such infantile jealousy.

'You are frowning again,' reproached Eliza.

'I want – no, I need to see you again. Will you come to visit Rose soon?'

'I should like that.' Eliza tried hard to keep the excitement out of her voice. But only if you promise to tell me the story of the Giant on the way.'

The rest of the journey was silent. Each felt that a step had been taken in their relationship, a step towards each other. As the pony stumbled and slid down the track and the gloom of Carnglaze reached out to meet and enfold them, Eliza knew that troubles of all kinds were waiting for her and the way she was feeling about Seth was not going to help.

20

When Eliza woke next morning she found that Ewella was already busy. It was a dark morning and this had contributed to her oversleeping. Cold and damp seemed to have sneaked in through every opening and moisture was running down the walls making her reluctant to leave the comfort of her blankets where she had snuggled down, dreaming of Seth. Conscience made her drag on her clothes in a hurry and rush down the stone stairs. There she found that the range had gone out and Ewella, in a thoroughly bad mood, was trying to light it.

'The wood is still wet and it won't catch,' she said tersely. 'I told Nathaniel to bring in some new kindling but evidently he did not.'

'Where are the children? Are they still in bed?' asked Eliza, her heart sinking at the prospect of a cold breakfast.

'I thought it would be best to leave them as there is no hot meal for them as yet and it is not a school day. Perhaps you can think of something to occupy them when they do come down as it is not even fit weather for ducks outside.'

'I am sure there will be plenty to occupy them,' said Eliza, surprised. Ewella turned on her, radiating anger. Her sallow face was flushed.

'They were difficult enough yesterday when you were gallivanting off to Penzance! Joel was impossible. He disappeared and took Richard with him. I had to send the twins to look for them and they were such a long time that I was beside myself with worry. Then Nessa was upset by something John said and spent half the day crying!'

'Oh Ewella, I'm so sorry they behaved badly while I was away. I shall give them schoolwork to do when they come down. That will keep them busy. Was Jael not here to help?'

'No. She was off back to her barn. Said she had some herbs to 'infuse' or something, because Uncle Tobias has been coughing and coughing. I went up to see Nanny Hannah because I thought she might like to come down for a change – someone to talk to at least. But she said Elestren was poorly and she would stay upstairs. Then she shut her door quite rudely I thought.'

Eliza was cross. It seemed she could not leave Carnglaze with any peace of mind what with her unruly children and Ewella who was so unpredictable in her moods. Just like her brother Barnabas, she thought, only with less of his charm. Nanny Hannah was another worry. How could the woman spend so much time alone, apart from Elestren? Then there was Jael, helpful most of the time but given to disappearing for long intervals without explanation. And she herself 'gallivanting'? She shook her head in disbelief. The first thing to do was to check on Uncle Tobias but she had hardly formulated the thought when the door banged open and in came Jael.

'I have just the thing for Uncle Tobias' cough,' she said, beaming. 'I've been busy with it since early this morning.' And she held up a phial filled with dark, pink tinged liquid.

'An infusion of blackberry leaves and a few of the last blackberries – that should help him.'
Obediently Uncle Tobias emerged from his 'study' and drank the liquid, pulling a face at the taste. He was as delighted with the unexpected attention he was receiving as much as with the prospect of his cough improving, and he thanked Jael for her kindness.

'Some Cornish winters pass by on light footprints,' he said portentously. 'But not this one. I shiver with cold all the time and the weather will get worse. I feel it in my bones.'

'I hope you are wrong,' said Eliza, patting him on the shoulder. Perhaps she should insist that he spend more time in the warmer kitchen even if he disliked the hubbub of the children?
At last the fire was burning and a cauldron of porridge bubbling. Eliza took some up to Nanny Hannah who was singing happily to Elestren, and then she made sure that Uncle Tobias had his share. There was not enough left for her so she made do with a hunk of bread and scrapings of jam.

The sound of hooves outside heralded the approach of a visitor. This time it was Edgar and Eliza felt relieved. She was not strong enough to endure more of Seth's keen scrutiny for the moment.

'Mistress Eliza, Mistress Ewella,' smiled Edgar, almost back to his old debonair self. The shadows under his eyes hinted at his grief over the death of his sister but he was making a determined effort to put on a good face.

'Lady Conyers and Lady Treloyhan are both safely installed at the Manor and look forward to seeing you soon.' he declared. 'Austol was delighted at the transformation wrought by you, Mistress Eliza, and wishes to thank you in person. So I offer myself as escort whenever you find it most convenient to visit us again.'

'Not just yet,' said Eliza hurriedly.

'I quite understand. But I warn you that if you leave it too long the two ladies will insist on coming to see you here instead. Naturally, Lady Treloyhan looks forward to being reunited with her baby and her Aunt wishes to see you all.'

'Oh no!' Why would they want to visit Carnglaze again? Why would anyone come to Carnglaze unless they had to! If Grace could leave her baby for so long why would she be impatient to be 'reunited' at short notice?

'I expect Austol will join the party,' said Edgar cheerfully. That settled it. Eliza consented to visit the Manor the very next day and bring the twins, Nathaniel and Caroline with her. John was cross that he was not included but his mother pointed out that he was needed to help look after Nessa, Joel and Richard. John preened at this sign of confidence.

'You shall come next time,' smiled his mother.

That night the cold intensified and Eliza found that she was shivering in her bed, even though she was wrapped in blankets. Ewella seemed to be sleeping soundly enough. The door creaked open. It was Nessa.

'I'm so cold, Mama.' She slipped into bed with Eliza to be followed by Caroline. While there was not enough room for comfort at least they were able to keep each other warm. Her daughters next to her, Eliza indulged in bitter thoughts before she fell asleep. The next morning there were frost patterns on the windows and it seemed as if Uncle Tobias was right. Winter was skulking outside like a hungry wolf. The muddy ruts on the track had solidified to iron and the trees looked black and weighed down by the cold.

'It was never frosty at Roscarne, was it, Mama?' said Nathaniel.

'It was, sometimes, but it was lovely and white,' said Caroline.

'The sea warms the land so it does not get so cold,' pronounced Nathaniel. John curled his lip. Just like Nathaniel to show off. He breathed on the window and cleared a little space.

'Mama, there is a carriage coming along our track,' he said. 'It seems to be in trouble!'

Eliza rushed to the door and flung it open, heedless of the blast of cold air.

'Surely Edgar is not coming in such bad weather!' she said. 'I was sure he would change his mind.' The children crowded round her at the door and watched as the carriage lurched and bumped along, finally slewing round and coming to rest with two wheels in the ditch. The driver, in thick all enveloping coat, jumped down, uttering imprecations which carried clearly through the frosty air.

'Such language!' said Ewella stiffly.

Eliza watched, horrified, as several people were helped out of the carriage.

'Aunt Gloria – and Grace – and Edgar – AND Austol,' she said, faintly. 'How could this happen!'

The little party made its way from the stricken carriage, Edgar helping Aunt Gloria and Austol guiding Grace. The driver was left staring disconsolately after them.

'Austol decided it would be best to come and visit you as Lady Treloyhan is eager to see her child,' offered Edgar, by way of explanation as he ushered everyone inside. The look on his face indicated that he was well aware of Eliza's feelings. Aunt Gloria swooped forward and embraced Eliza warmly then went on to exclaim how the children had grown. She was just the same, plump and well corseted, wearing a smart, dark green travelling costume with a matching hat and thick veiling. The lines on her face, thus partially hidden, were overlaid by powder but the twinkle in her eye had not been dowsed by the loss of her husband. Grace stood at the door with a supercilious expression. Austol brought up the rear. As he entered he, too, looked round in disbelief. The interior of Carnglaze was obviously a shock after the opulence of the Manor. Fortunately, Ewella had coaxed the fire to blaze up and there was some semblance of warmth in that bleak kitchen and the arriving company clustered round the flames.

'My dear Eliza, I find it difficult to come to terms with your living conditions,' said Aunt Gloria, whose eagle eye had taken in the lack of floor covering, the lack of curtains and the sparse furniture. 'Do you have another living room perhaps?'

'Yes, but the fire is not lit,' replied Eliza bluntly. 'We usually live in the kitchen to save on firewood.' A faint look of distaste passed across Austol's face.

'Such a wonderful range to give out such heat,' Edgar offered desperately.

'I should like to see Elestren!' demanded Grace. 'I hope she is somewhere warm!'

It was some time later that some sort of calm was restored to Carnglaze. The children were sent to the schoolroom in their coats with work to do and Ewella to supervise. Grace was upstairs with Nanny Hannah and Elestren while Uncle Tobias had joined Aunt Gloria and Austol round the fire. Edgar had been dispatched outside to help the driver and Mathey to right the carriage and Eliza was scurrying round with refreshment for their unexpected guests. Into the already crowded kitchen came Jael wrapped in a striped blanket against the cold. Uncle Tobias greeted her eagerly and thanked her again for the medicine which had helped him so much.

'I shall take the driver and Mathey into my barn,' she said, taking in the situation at a glance, 'The fire is doing well and I can give them hot drinks as soon as they have righted the carriage.'

'I would invite them in here but there is no room,' said Eliza, helplessly.

'And we need to talk!' said Aunt Gloria.

The door opened and Grace reappeared. All eyes turned to her. In pale grey dress and coat, matching hat on her blonde hair, she appeared totally out of place in the confines of Carnglaze. Her whole demeanour rejected her surroundings – and the people within it.

'Austol was right,' she said. Her voice dripped ice. 'I cannot live in this house with my child. It would not be safe. So I have asked Nanny Hannah to pack Elestren's clothes and we shall return to the Manor.' Eliza was ashamed of the twinge of relief she felt.

'What about Richard?' she asked. Surely Grace would want to take Richard?

'Oh, Richard – I do not know. What do you think, Austol?'

'He is happy here,' said Austol smoothly. 'And of course Edgar and I will bring you to Carnglaze as often as you wish to see him. And perhaps Mistress Eliza would see her way clear to visit us at the Manor more frequently to check on you and Elestren.'

Eliza had the distinct feeling that a trap had just snapped shut. What was Austol hoping to achieve? Aunt Gloria looked pleased at the decision and only Uncle Tobias seemed uncertain.

133

'Perhaps you should talk to Richard before you make up your mind?' said Eliza.

'Oh, very well.'

Ewella called the children from the schoolroom. Richard was surprised to see his mother but Eliza noted that he did not rush towards her in pleasure. In fact he hung back behind the others. Only Edgar received a hesitant smile.

'Richard!' boomed Austol, suddenly. 'You would like to come back to the Manor would you not?' Richard jumped at the sudden sound and then shook his head,

'No thank you, sir,' he said politely. 'I should like to stay here with my cousins.' Which settled the matter. Again Eliza felt that Austol was playing a devious game. He had known perfectly well what Richard's answer would be.

Swiftly the kitchen at Carnglaze was emptied of people. Eliza was sad to see Elestren, in the arms of Nanny Hannah, taken away. The children waved at the departing carriage and then trooped off to visit Jael in her barn, Richard following without a backward glance. Mathey appeared in the courtyard leading Edgar's horse and that gentleman perforce had to leave also. Ewella took herself upstairs, grumbling about the need to clear up Elestren's room and Uncle Tobias retired to his 'study'. Exhausted, Eliza sat at the kitchen table. Outside the cold stalked, silencing the twigs, the leaves and even the sound of the stream, usually a background babble. Ewella's footsteps sounded extra loud on the stone stairs as she hurried down.

'What on earth is the matter? You look as if you have seen a ghost!' said Eliza, startled.

'Not seen – heard!' said Ewella grimly. 'You listen!'

And Eliza heard – the sound of sobbing that had been absent for so long. No happy nursery rhymes, just heart broken, despairing sobs.

'The poor girl!' cried Eliza. 'Elestren has gone and she feels she has lost her baby all over again!'

'That is a bit fanciful,' said Ewella, striving for a return to normality.

'That settles it. I shall talk to Professor Martineau in the morning. This must not go on or the children will become really frightened.'

'Not just the children,' replied Ewella, with feeling. In spite of her resolutely pragmatic thinking, the sound of the sobbing had reached her and shaken her.

'I hope this cold does not continue or the Professor will not be able to come here,' worried Eliza.

It was seemed as if it would be another cold night so Eliza arranged for Uncle Tobias to sleep before the fire. She knew that he preferred his privacy but the children were safely upstairs and Jael had left for her barn.

'I worry about you, out there in the cold,' Eliza had said, as she left. Jael smiled cheerfully. 'I have a good fire,' she said. 'I am more likely to set fire to myself!' Eliza peeped in at the children and was encouraged to hear the rhythmic breathing. Wrapped as they were in every woollen garment they could find they were warm enough to sleep deeply. Ewella, too, was already asleep when Eliza slipped into bed. Outside was stillness. No wind in the trees, no scratching of twigs on the windows, even the stream could not be heard. The night was a cold blanket wrapped round Carnglaze and not even the spirits stirred.

21

Gradually the cold unclamped its jaws and a milder west wind brought relief to birds, small animals and the inhabitants of Carnglaze. It also blew in Professor Martineau. Unusually, there was someone else with him, a gaunt old man with such thick bushy whiskers that it was almost impossible to make out his features.

'Mistress Eliza, I should like to introduce Reverend Sithney who has come from the church of St. Mary in the Helston district.' The Reverend executed a stiff little bow, just like someone had pulled strings on a puppet, Eliza said later to Jael.

'Please come in to warm yourselves by the fire,' cried Eliza. It was obvious the long bumpy ride in the cart had taken its toll on both elderly gentlemen. Ewella made haste to provide hot drinks for both as they rubbed their hands, trying to restore their circulation.

'Mistress Eliza,' said the Professor, 'I have taken the liberty of bringing my good friend here to see you about – er – about what is worrying you.' He cast an awkward glance at the twins who were ostensibly writing at the table but their unnaturally rigid backs showed them to be consumed with curiosity about their visitor. Eliza took the hint and banished them both to the schoolroom.

'What is worrying me? And that is?' queried Eliza. The Reverend leaned forward, sharp eyes gleaming beneath bushy eyebrows.

'The haunting – your ghost! I have some experience in exorcism and the Professor here suggested that perhaps I could help you.'

'That is very kind,' said Eliza, gratefully. 'It has been quite worrying for all of us but I am especially concerned for the children.'

'Of course, of course. First of all, may I see round your house and land? I need to get a feel for your situation.'

Eliza, the Reverend and the Professor took a short tour around the house, greeting the children waiting so patiently in the schoolroom and praising their willingness to work. Then they both stood quietly and listened in the room that had been occupied by Nanny Hannah and

Elestren. Eliza hovered behind them, hardly daring to move. Next they proceeded outside and walked round the perimeter of Carnglaze land with slow, careful gait. The Reverend gave a sudden exclamation. They had reached the standing stone. He stood by it for a considerable time, his head bent. He turned to Eliza looking very grave.

'I may be able to help but I am not confident. This is an ancient site as I am sure you have been told.' He looked quizzically at Eliza as if wondering how much she understood. 'I think your haunting may be more extensive than you imagine and, I fear, possibly beyond my powers.'

'Professor Martineau warned us,' said Eliza, miserably.

'Nevertheless I shall try.' The sharp eyes softened. 'I suppose there is no chance of you and your family moving to another house?'

'No. I could arrange for the children to be away for a day but that is all. We have nowhere else to go until my husband returns. Fortunately Uncle Tobias has been collected by the Lanivets for a short break as they were worried about the effects of the extreme cold on him. They are old friends so he was quite excited to be visiting them.' Reverend Sithney nodded approvingly. 'How fortuitous,' he said.

It was decided, much against Eliza's better judgment, that she should ask Austol to allow the children to spend a day and a night at the Manor with Ewella in charge. Edgar could be the intermediary to pass on explanations and this would save the composing of rather difficult letters. However, Eliza realised, with a shiver of unease, that she would be indebted to Austol. More than before. Why this should be such a problem for her she was unwilling to face. She disliked Austol and distrusted him – yet felt, guiltily, that she was being judgmental. To her surprise, Austol was quite amenable, sending a message that his girls were missing their mother and the Trevannion family would be a very welcome diversion.

'Diversion!' snorted Eliza. 'Is that how he sees us!'

'Perhaps you should explain to him how seriously you regard your situation,' said Jael, mildly. 'He has children - he would understand.'

'I do not want him to think that we are taking advantage of his offered hospitality and making excuses to visit the Manor. It all sounds so weird and unlikely.'

'He is the one who has wanted your presence, not the other way round.'

'I suppose so, sighed Eliza. 'And now Grace is back there with little Elestren he will expect us to keep visiting them.'

The following week, Ewella and the children were dispatched to the Manor. Nathaniel and John were delighted at the prospect of good food to eat, a sentiment shared by Ewella, Nessa was hoping for a little girl of her age as playmate while Joel welcomed any change in the usual routine. Caroline, however, wanted to stay with Eliza and Jael. She had realised that something strange was going on and that their visit to the Manor was not just a holiday. Also little Richard proved unexpectedly obstinate.

'I don't want to go,' he pleaded.

'But you would like to see your mother?'

'No. She doesn't want to see me.'

'What about Edgar? You were very friendly with Edgar and he is fond of you.'

So it was with considerable difficulty that all the children finally piled into the carriage sent by Austol. Eliza was left with the memory of Richard's reproachful blue eyes and the way his lip quivered as the carriage door shut on him.

'I feel I have been unkind to him,' Eliza worried to Jael.

'He will soon perk up,' said Jael. 'Nessa will see to that.'

Late evening and the short winter day was already drawing in. No wind and a mist drifting in from the sea. Eliza and Jael sat by the fire waiting for Professor Martineau and Reverend Sithney to arrive. It was very quiet. Without all the children the house seemed to stretch and expand, dark corners remaining out of reach of the firelight. The trees and bushes outside, usually visible from the window, were gradually succumbing to the creeping mist and becoming swallowed into a greater darkness.

'I hope they will arrive soon,' said Eliza, shivering.

'Listen,' said Jael, holding up her hand.

'That is just one horse! Who could be visiting ....?'

It was Seth. Of course. He burst into the kitchen, his lively presence banishing the shadows.

'The mist is thickening,' he offered, cheerfully. 'I do apologise, ladies, for calling at such an hour without warning. Rose has been unwell and this has been the first time in a week that I have been able to leave her.' He looked around. 'Where are the children? Surely they are not all in bed yet?'

Eliza managed to control the beating of her heart sufficiently to explain where they were.

'A strange decision to send them to the Manor,' said Seth, frowning. 'And Ewella?'

'Yes - AND Grace and her children, before you ask.'

'What IS going on, Eliza? I am not just being interfering. In Barnabas' absence I feel that I should keep an eye on you. Help where I can.'

'We have managed so far,' said Eliza coldly. 'But your main concern should be Rose.' At this, Jael crept out quietly, muttering about checking on her fire.

'Rose is in the lap of luxury just now,' said Seth, refusing to be drawn. 'She is wrapped in a fur quilt in a fine bedroom - well, as fine as one can find at the Galleon. But you, Eliza, I am concerned about you.' He caught her hands in his and brought her closer. 'I look after Rose, yes, but my nights are disturbed by you. I think about you, dream about you. Dammit, Eliza, you know how I feel!' Eliza could sense the old attraction weaving its magic around her but she tried to maintain her calm.

'Rose is my friend as well as your wife,' she said, averting her eyes.

'I realise that!' snapped Seth. 'But something drew me here. I felt a compulsion to be near you – almost as if you were in some kind of danger. Now tell me.'

'Carnglaze is a problem for us. We have a resident ghost.'

'I gathered that. I was here when you were talking to Professor Martineau.'

'How matter of fact you are,' said Eliza, annoyed. 'If you heard her sobbing and wailing you would find it distressing as well as frightening. We had a brief time when Nanny Hannah and Elestren stayed here when the ghost sang nursery rhymes and seemed happy - Seth, this is no laughing matter!'

'Of course not,' said Seth, composing his features and endeavouring to look serious.

139

'Now she is back to sobbing. And I, for one, am at the end of my tether. But she is not the only ghost we have.'

'Oh?'

'Both the Professor and Reverend Sithney feel that there are other forces here – forces trying to make us leave Carnglaze altogether. And they ARE frightening.' Eliza went on to describe some of the strange happenings and eerie atmospheres. 'And the result is that the Reverend feels there is little he can do.'

'He will try, though?'

'We are waiting for him now.'

'Then I will wait with you. No arguments. And if his efforts are as useless as I expect them to be – then you will have to move out of Carnglaze!'

'And live in a field I suppose!'

'Eliza, stop being so prickly! You are as beautiful as a rose but your thorns are drawing blood! I have enough money to rent another house for you – '

'No, Seth. You mean well but that is out of the question! We need a house for five children, Ewella, Jael, Uncle Tobias, sometimes Grace and Richard, Nanny Hannah and Elestren and myself. It would have to be a mansion! Carnglaze is not ideal but we have managed to crowd in – like pilchards in a tin, Joel says.' Eliza realised she was beginning to babble. He thought she was as beautiful as a rose! Such irony! And he was unaware. With difficulty she banished the words from her mind. She knew that Seth's solution to her problems was unacceptable because of the continuing close contact with him that would ensue – which she could not voice. But at least his presence in Carnglaze was a comfort. Gently she withdrew her hands from his and moved away. There was no time for further discussion. In came Jael.

'They are coming now.'

Like two black crows Professor Martineau and the Reverend Sithney entered, both in black cloaks, the Professor in his usual threadbare attire and the Reverend adorned with a large silver cross on a chain. Eliza had the strangest feeling that their arrival subtly changed the atmosphere of Carnglaze, that the house suffered a shock of anticipation. She imagined that it was silently girding itself to meet this new intrusion, the same feeling she had experienced on occasion but dismissed as fanciful. Even Seth had lost his mocking look and seemed serious for once.

'Mistress Eliza, we have discussed the matter and feel that we should like to conduct our – er – service where the Reverend experienced the strongest resonance – that is, the small bedroom upstairs,' said the Professor.

'I hope to release this young woman from her endless search for her lost baby,' added the Reverend. 'It would be safer, incidentally, if you all remain down here. I feel the matter of the servant girl should be quite easy to deal with but what else may be invoked I am unable to speculate.'

'Is there anything you need?' asked Eliza, trying to banish the quaver from her voice.

'No, I have everything in this bag.'

The two men climbed the stone stairs, the glow from the oil lamp carried by the Professor dimming as they reached the upper landing.

Eliza sat upright and un-relaxed at the table, noting that Jael, too, was listening anxiously. Seth sprawled in the kitchen chair, his eyes fixed on Eliza, which made her even more restive. She was conscious that her dark hair had become unpinned and was tumbling over her shoulders and her old twill dress was a source of mortification to her And her hands! Hastily she covered them with her long sleeves. It was all Seth's fault that she was concerned about her appearance at such a time. There was a crash upstairs. Then silence. The oil lamp on the windowsill began to flicker. The two candles on the table guttered and went out. Only the fire still crackled and gave out light. Eliza hardly dared breathe. The three of them sat in the gloomy kitchen, not moving, just waiting. Agitated shadows cast by the fire danced over the walls. Then a whisk of wind down the stairs, a touch of gossamer on their faces and suddenly Eliza felt a sharp push. She was jostled as if someone was trying to take her place.

'Don't move, Eliza,' whispered Jael. 'She will go.'

Eliza looked down and found she was enveloped in a white calico apron. Her hands looked different – short stubby fingers and bitten nails. Seth and Jael watched, unbelieving, as the shape of her face changed, her nose becoming snub and her cheeks more rounded. Her beautiful dark hair was no more, hidden by a kitchen maid's cap. A stranger looked at them from Eliza's chair. Jael wasted no time. She leaned forward and shook Eliza vigorously.

'Go away! Your baby is not here. You will not find peace here. Go!'

With a heart rending wail, the invader left Eliza. A flurry of wind whirled round the room and then vanished. All became silent again.

'What happened?' demanded Eliza. She could see that Jael was disturbed and the colour had left Seth's face.

'I think the spirit of the servant girl has gone,' said Jael, slowly. 'But she did stop with you on her way out.' When Eliza finally understood what had happened to her she looked in mute appeal at Seth. He held out his arms and, overcome, she ran into them, hiding her face on his chest. Jael just sat there, deep in thought

22

Eliza, still pale and shocked, sat with Jael at the kitchen table. Seth had gone back reluctantly to Penzance and the Professor and the Reverend had lurched off in the cart. Now was the time to take stock.

'Did I really look different?' whispered Eliza. She was clutching the arm of her chair with such force that her knuckles had turned white.

'Oh yes. Very different! But I have seen my mother chase off a wandering spirit so I knew what to do.' Eliza shook her head and tried to reaffirm her place in the real world. Her dark hair still fell disarranged about her shoulders but her eyes sparkled in a way that worried Jael.

'About Seth –' she began.

'No. Do not talk about Seth,' said Eliza firmly. 'What I want to know is the house now clear of the haunting? Are the children safe?'

'It may be so,' said Jael, cautiously. 'We shall have to wait and see.' But in contradiction, as she spoke, the newly lit oil lamp began to flicker wildly, its flame grew huge and then went out. One by one the candles were extinguished by gusts of wind that blew erratically about the kitchen, making the fire flare up and the cups rattle on the dresser. Eliza trembled in her chair, wishing frantically that she had not persuaded Seth to leave but Jael jumped to her feet. She extracted what seemed to be a handful of twigs from her pocket and held them up in the form of a cross.

'Do what you will but harm none!' she intoned. There was hesitation in the unsettling blasts which snarled about them - then sudden silence. Complete silence.

'What did you say – was it a spell?' whispered Eliza.

'No. Those are words of Wicca. The dark spirits have not all been banished. But at least I think we shall have peace from Mathilde.'

'I am so tired,' said Eliza. 'There is so much to take in and understand. I feel drained of energy.' Jael looked at her with sympathy.

'To bed with you,' she smiled. 'We shall have all the children back tomorrow.'

It was the noise from the children that woke Eliza from a sleep that was, for once, dreamless. The mist, which had lifted unveiled a cold but sunny day.

'Mama, mama, we've had a marvellous time!' cried Nathaniel. 'We were allowed to ride the horses!'

'And we had proper lessons from a groom,' added Caroline.

'Guess who were the best riders!' shouted John. 'Me and Richard!'

'I was allowed to play with the dolls,' volunteered Nessa, more quietly. 'There are lots of girls and they all wanted to join my games.'

'And you, Joel, what did you do?'

'All different things and Edgar showed me the room with the piano in it and I was allowed to play it. Edgar said I was good!'

Ewella was quite pink with pleasure.

'I had a lovely room with a view of the sea and Austol and Edgar were so kind to us.'

Eliza felt a burst of gratitude to Austol for his kindness to her family but at the same time she felt a vague disquiet. How would they settle to the privations of Carnglaze after the pleasures of the Manor?

The children dispatched to their various chores, Eliza and Ewella sat at the kitchen table, Eliza wanting to hear everything about the Manor and Ewella determined to extract all details from the previous evening. But their peace was short-lived. First of all, Uncle Tobias arrived back in the Lanivets' carriage. He was beaming and had obviously enjoyed his stay.

'Thomas and George Lanivet send their good wishes,' he cried. 'They apologise for not coming back to thank you in person but George developed a bad headache – he is prone to them - and Thomas decided that he had better remain to look after him. But they were thoughtful enough to send me back with one of the drivers they use occasionally.'

'Very kind of them,' smiled Eliza. 'I hope you enjoyed the comfort of their cottage – a change from Carnglaze I am sure!'

'Very different,' admitted Uncle Tobias. 'But I am getting used to Carnglaze and at least it is not perched on a cliff ready to be blown into the sea. The way the winds howled round that unprotected headland made me feel quite uneasy.'

'That is one hazard we shall avoid,' said Eliza.

144

'A strange thing, though,' mused Uncle Tobias, helping himself to more tea. 'I had the feeling that George and Thomas would do anything to avoid entering Carnglaze again – even to the extent of making up a headache!'
Eliza and Ewella exchanged glances. A shrewd deduction from Uncle.

There was no time to resume their conversation. Hardly had Uncle Tobias settled happily into his 'study' announcing that all that talking had made him sleepy, when another carriage arrived.
'We are popular this morning,' said Ewella. 'I have not managed any baking so we have nothing to offer anyone.' Eliza was looking through the window
'Oh no! Surely not! Why would they come to visit us!'
'Who is it?'
'The Tregadilletts! Nicholas and Morwenna – do you remember – he is the Minister at Treneglos and she – she – ' Eliza was unable to finish the sentence. Only too well she recalled that dreadful day when Morwenna had passed on the gossip about Barnabas and Grace, and wreaked such havoc in her life. The reason for their visit soon became clear. Aunt Gloria emerged from the carriage, resplendent in crimson with waterfalls of lace.
'My dear Eliza, forgive this visit without warning. I should have let you know but it was all decided so quickly.'
'What has happened, dear Aunt Gloria? You look agitated.'
And indeed her complexion aspired to match her travelling costume.
'Come in, please do. Nicholas and Morwenna, I am pleased to see you. However, has there been some emergency?'
'Indeed yes,' gasped Morwenna.
'They called at the Manor just before I was due to leave,' said Aunt Gloria. 'And they have been kind enough to bring me over here.' She wrung her hands, an action, Eliza felt, most unusual for her Aunt.
'Perhaps you would like some mint tea first and then you can tell me all about it,' suggested Eliza. The three of them were obviously in a state of perturbation, Nicholas nearly as pink as Aunt Gloria and Morwenna's sharp little face pale with shock. Ewella scurried out to make the tea.

Nicholas spoke up in his deep 'ministerial' voice.
'I shall explain.' he said, thus pre-empting his wife.

'We attended the Manor at Lord Treloyhan's request. It appears he wanted us to be there when he spoke to Kenwyn about a serious matter.'

'He often calls upon Nicholas for ministerial help,' put in Morwenna, in a smug voice. Nicholas glanced at her in reproof and continued.

'Lady Conyers was making preparations to leave and Mr. Edgar was going to drive her to catch the stage coach to London and....'

'And?' prompted Eliza

'The most dreadful quarrel broke out between Lord Treloyhan and Mr Edgar – we did not know what to do for the best.'

'To cut a long story short,' interrupted Aunt Gloria, 'Austol punched him. Hard enough to put him on the floor!' Her voice contained unwilling admiration for such a feat.

'Dreadful behaviour from someone in such a position.' said Morwenna, righteously.

'Is he all right?' gasped Eliza.

'He is in bed but has refused to see a doctor,' said Nicholas. 'However, that is not end of it. Kenwyn arrived on the scene, dressed in his uniform ready to depart and spoke most insolently to his father!'

'Then he threatened him with his sword!' Morwenna put in excitedly. 'And shouted that he deserved to be run through – but Lord Treloyhan disarmed him – and unfortunately wounded him. By accident of course. There was blood everywhere!'

'So he, too, is in bed and is also refusing to see a doctor. Austol is not insisting because the scandal would be so dreadful,' said Aunt Gloria, drily. 'And then Grace came rushing down to see what all the noise was about, saw the blood and promptly fainted.'

'She had to be carried up to her room and Richard was upset and the maids are all over the place,' said Morwenna, adding virtuously, 'And Lord Treloyhan has retired to his study with the brandy decanter.'

'So you see, Eliza, you are the one who will have to help them.' Aunt Gloria, calmed by her cup of tea, was presiding over the kitchen like a judge over his court. She had pronounced sentence.

'But what about my children? And Uncle Tobias? I can't just leave them,' declared Eliza, in dismay. 'Surely there must be other friends – relations who could help?'

'I am sure Ewella and Jael can manage here for a short time,' replied Aunt Gloria. 'It has to be you. Austol said no one else was to come to the Manor but you! Rather a clinching argument, don't you think?'

So Eliza found herself in the carriage with Aunt Gloria and the Tregadilletts on the way back to the Manor. Aunt Gloria was to be taken by the Tregadilletts to catch the stage coach to London.

'If I could, I would have stayed to help,' she said. 'But I have an important appointment with my doctor. In any case, I would not be much use as a nurse. Bending over a bed would require an elasticity I do not possess!'

'Dear Aunt Gloria, it has done us all good to see you,' said Eliza, with affection. 'Please write to us soon. Meanwhile I shall try to be useful at the Manor and see if I can restore order out of mayhem!'

'You could do worse than take up residence there,' suggested Aunt Gloria. 'I have a feeling Austol would be delighted. He is lonely and surely anywhere would be better than Carnglaze. There is something about the atmosphere in this house I do not like. And you have insufficient room.'

There was a hastily muffled gasp from Morwenna. Opportunities for spreading gossip were multiplying by the minute. Aunt Gloria turned a gimlet eye on her.

'Of course, Mistress Tregadillett, we shall rely on you to keep all this extremely quiet. I should be most displeased if the Manor or Carnglaze became subjects for gossip.'

'Of course, of course!' said Morwenna hastily. Displeasing Aunt Gloria would be an unthinkable act of bravery. There was a slight snore from Nicholas, who appeared worn out by events.

'Aunt Gloria, I am sure you mean well but it is impossible for me to move to the Manor even if Austol wishes it. Barnabas will expect me to be at Carnglaze when he returns, and as you know, Grace and I are better apart.' She did not go on to say that all the giants of Cornwall could not force her to live there.

Her Aunt sighed. 'It was worth a try,' she said. 'I admire your strength of character for not taking the easy option. But do keep an eye on Uncle Tobias, my dear, he is getting very frail.'

'I will, I will.'

The Tregadillett carriage had rumbled away. Eliza stood in the grand hall way of the Manor and looked about her. A ruffled, ungracious maid had taken her cloak and indicated where she would find the master. To her horror, Eliza saw there was blood still on the floor. She felt angry that the staff of the Manor cared so little. She remembered the gracious place it had been when Sir James had been the owner, how immaculate the rooms, how swift the service, how warm the hospitality. Cautiously she tapped at the door of the drawing room and heard Austol's gruff 'Come in.' He was sprawled in an armchair, decanter beside him, hair unkempt, and the eyes he cast upon her were bleary and red veined.

'My dear Eli - Eliza,' he slurred. 'So glad you could come. Not in a good state …. Kenwyn – not a good son – a deserter – a coward!' His head dropped forward on to his chest and he began breathing heavily. Eliza summoned one of the servants by bawling for help in a very unladylike way. When a maid appeared she was dispatched to find the strongest male servant and with his help Austol was transferred to his bedroom.

'Now, all the servants are requested to come to the hall,' she said crisply. 'They need to hear what I have to say.'

A shuffling, rather mutinous group of servants, maids, grooms, the cook and a valet assembled in the hall. Some looked resentful, some nervous, some defiant.

'I am sure it has reached you that there has been an unfortunate incident here,' began Eliza. 'I am your temporary housekeeper and I wish to give you your tasks. The Manor is looking neglected and this will upset Lord Treloyhan when he returns to good health so it must be remedied. If anyone is unhappy about this they may give in their notice. I need hardly remind you that positions in a grand house like the Manor are hard to come by.' A stir of alarm and an eagerness to please replaced some sullen looks. This temporary housekeeper meant business. And Eliza found that she enjoyed the feeling of being able to run a house as she wished. Soon the cook was busy with kitchen maids preparing the menus she had discussed with Eliza, the maids were scurrying to freshen the bedrooms and clean up the blood and Eliza was making a tour of those in their sickbeds. Grace first, of course.

'What are you doing here?' demanded Grace. She was sitting in an armchair by the window, in a cream and gold robe. There was no sign of Nanny Hannah or Elestren, nor did she ask after Richard. She sat, haughty and uncaring, her beautiful profile like a cameo.

'Are you feeling better?' asked Eliza.

'I am fine, now,' said Grace irritably. 'I really do not know why you are here at all.'

'Neither do I,' was Eliza's thought.

'I need to check on Edgar and Kenwyn. You will have to ring if you need anything.'

'Most times no one comes,' snapped Grace.

Eliza sighed to herself as she left her sister. Grace seemed to have become her old spoilt self.

Next was Kenwyn. He was sitting up in bed, very pale and angry.

'I intend to leave this place!' he informed Eliza.

'And so you shall,' she replied soothingly, 'But I need to check on your wound first.'

He had a slash across his chest, not deep but very inflamed so Eliza bathed it and dabbed it with ointment. Then she wound the widest bandage she could find round his upper body.

'I say, should you be doing this?' asked Kenwyn. 'Should you not have a chaperone?' Eliza patted his shoulder.

'Just you lie down and rest and I shall see that your uniform is cleaned. I suppose you do want to wear it when you leave?' Kenwyn scowled.

'Father insists. But I am NOT going back to the regiment whatever happens!'

'Leave that discussion until you are both better,' advised Eliza as she left him. His handsome young face looked anxious and vulnerable and she wondered how she would feel if it had been Nathaniel or Joel. And how would Barnabas react to one of his sons leaving the regiment?

Now for Edgar. She met him limping down the stairs. When she saw his face she gave a cry of horror. One eye was completely closed with a purple bruise around it and the other was bloodshot. His nose looked as if it could be broken and his whole face was swollen.

'Edgar! Oh Edgar, you should be in bed!'

'Can't abide being in bed,' he responded as well as his battered mouth would allow.

'You look as if Austol has taken an iron bar to you!'

'Where is he?

'Sleeping it off in his room. You need to make peace with each other. You have the girls to think of. Perhaps you should go and sit in the drawing room very quietly and I shall see that you are brought some tea.'

'And brandy.'

'Well, perhaps just a little.'

23

Eliza decided to leave Austol to his drunken sleep and went in search of the children. She found them in one of the ground floor rooms at the back. Nanny Hannah, rather swamped by seven girls of varying heights and sizes, all in white dresses, sat in an armchair with Elestren on her knee. The startled glance she gave Eliza was followed by a smile of relief. The cavalry had arrived. She cleared her throat and tried to speak but only a squeak escaped her. The girls did not even notice, so busy were they with their various pursuits. Two of the older ones were seated at the table, immersed in writing, several smaller ones were playing a game on the floor and one was in a corner with a book almost as large as she was.

Eliza stepped forward and clapped her hands sharply.

'Girls, please will you come and sit near my chair so I may speak to you.' They did so and looked up at her expectantly.

'You do not know me at all and the reason I am here I know is a very sad one. I am so sorry about your mother. I visited her several times here at the Manor and your father thought it would be suitable for me to come and help out for a short while.'

'Are you going to marry our father?' demanded one of the younger girls. Eliza was taken aback.

'No, of course not,' she said. 'I have a family of my own. Perhaps I should introduce myself. I am Eliza Trevannion from Carnglaze and your Aunt-in-law, Grace, is my sister.'

'Carnglaze? That is where Uncle Edgar goes so often,' said a taller girl, with a meaning look at her neighbour.

'One of the maids says it is a haunted house,' said another.

'Nessa comes from Carnglaze,' volunteered a pretty little girl with dark braids.

'And Joel, who played on the piano,' put in the youngest one.

Eliza was shocked. There seemed to be little overt grief at the loss of their mother. Then the questions, so uninhibited, displayed a lack of discipline and she felt that she was already losing control of the little group. Respect for their elders was clearly not one of their virtues.

Rather surprising as she could not imagine Austol allowing such freedom of speech. No wonder Nanny Hannah looked like a rabbit in a pen full of foxes. She decided to find out their names first of all.

The eldest girl, Lamorna, with the sharp nose of the Treloyhans and a mane of brown hair, offered to introduce her sisters.

'How very kind of you,' said Eliza.

'This is Melwyn. She is twelve, two years younger than I am. She likes to ride and is the best!' Melwyn blushed.

'Then this is Kerra. Ten years old and always in trouble. Father gets very cross with her but Uncle Edgar usually takes her part. I don't think she likes reading and writing much.' Kerra looked positively complacent at this less than glowing tribute.

'Elowen' – she pushed forward a small girl with almost white hair and fair lashes. 'Father says Elowen is slow but we think she just takes her time … She is eight years old.' Elowen shrugged. She did not seem put out by the word 'slow'.

'And now, the triplets!'

'Triplets!' exclaimed Eliza. Poor Eulalia!

Three six year olds, Cryda, Tegen and Caja, giggled and pushed each other self consciously.

'Caja is really the youngest – she was born last,' explained Lamorna.

Lunch time came and Eliza insisted that they all sat round the table in an orderly way. She noticed that they ate very slowly compared to her own brood at Carnglaze who fell on their food with the delight of seabirds on fish. Certainly the lunch menu was uninspiring and she made a mental note to speak to the cook. After lunch she suggested that they all find a quiet corner and read their books after which they would go out for some fresh air. They all groaned.

'Mistress Trevannion, have you seen the weather outside?'

Eliza rushed to the window. Feathery flakes of snow were falling from a granite sky and already the expanse of grass at the back of the house was covered in white.

'Never mind, we shall still go out,' she said briskly. Her heart sank at the thought there was a possibility she could be snowed in. Uncle Tobias had warned her that the coming winter was likely to be severe.

'And I shall be marooned here with Austol and Edgar and Grace,' she thought.

The day passed on leaden feet. Unexpectedly the girls enjoyed playing in the snow with the exception of Elowen who just stood and shivered until Eliza sent her in. Then they trooped inside for tea, soaking wet and hair like seaweed, unfortunately meeting Austol who was negotiating the stairs with exaggerated care. He looked aghast at his daughters.

'They are just going to get changed for tea,' said Eliza sweetly. She left them to an unwilling Nanny Hannah and went to check on Edgar and Kenwyn. Both were mending well but declined to join the family for tea and Eliza did not insist. Their quarrels were nothing to do with her. Grace was resting, she was told by Nanny Hannah and Elestren was asleep. Oh well, she had tried. Tea time was a success. The cook had evidently made an effort and baked a variety of enticing biscuits which were demolished with alacrity by the girls, now rosy cheeked, who chatted happily to each other and did not bombard Eliza with more impertinent questions. Austol sat, hawk faced and silent at the head of the table and watched them all. Eliza was sure that she caught a fleeting look of pleasurable surprise on his usually dour face.

'Mistress Eliza, please join me for coffee in the drawing room,' said Austol at the end of the meal. It was a tone that brooked no excuses.

'I should like to apologise for the unfortunate scenes you witnessed on your arrival and particularly for my part in them,' he began stiffly, pouring himself a brandy. 'I am afraid my brother-in-law said something unforgivable and I lost my temper.' He did not mention Kenwyn but went on to talk about his daughters. After the shock of losing their mother he was delighted to see them so happy at play and more settled altogether.

'I have to add,' he said frankly, 'My wife was unwell for a long time and unable to give them the care and guidance they so obviously need. But you, Mistress Eliza, you have worked wonders in just one day.'

'I think you need to employ another nanny rather than rely on Nanny Hannah,' said Eliza, ignoring the compliment. 'She is good with little ones but the older girls need a firm hand.'

'Perhaps they need a governess,' said Austol. 'I remember our talk about the importance of education for women. Professor Martineau did come here for a while but I think seven of them, seven girls at that, were daunting for him.' They both laughed. Eliza began to feel more comfortable with Austol and sorry that he had been left to bring up his family alone.

The next morning Austol sent one of his drivers to take Eliza home in the pony and trap; apparently he felt it would be more suited to the slippery tracks than the bulky carriage. The snow, so unusual in Cornwall, was already melting and it promised to be a slushy drive. Eliza was excited at the prospect of seeing her children again; even a day away was too much. Still adorned with a smattering of white, the trees seemed to watch their progress benignly – until they turned into the final stretch of narrow track which led to Carnglaze. Then Eliza was conscious of a change in the atmosphere. Behind the thorn bushes, jostling with black branched trees to crowd closer, the dark shape of Carnglaze appeared, ominous even in the bright light of day.

'I s'll be some glad to get back before dusk,' said the driver. He pulled up at the gate but declined to bring the pony and trap into the courtyard.

'Not a welcoming house,' he muttered. Eliza watched, without surprise, as he made haste to return the way they had come

All was quiet when she entered Carnglaze. The children were in the schoolroom with Professor Martineau and Richard was helping Ewella to bake. There was no sign of Jael. Sounds of low voices were coming from Uncle Tobias' room. Visitors? Not even the Professor's cart had been visible at the front of the house. She knocked and went in. Then her heart began to pound in her chest. The visitor was Seth. When he turned to look at her there was no smile, no warmth, no relaxing of his taut features. He rose to greet her, made mumbled excuses to Uncle Tobias and propelled her into the next room.

'Eliza! What are you thinking of! Have you lost your senses?' His voice was harsh, his black brows drawn in a frown.

'What on earth do you mean? How dare you speak to me in such a way!' She could not believe her ears. He had the temerity to scold her for some transgression as if he were her father. Or husband!

154

'You have been acting as nursemaid and housekeeper and goodness knows what else to Austol – why should you be there for him? He has a plentiful supply of servants.'

'I fail to see why it is any of your business!' Eliza's voice was icy. 'And what do you mean – goodness knows what else!'

'I should like to have an explanation from you!' Seth ignored her question. 'As a friend of Barnabas I have his interests at heart and he would not approve of what you are doing!'

'And what am I doing? Other than helping out a family in difficult times?'

'You should concentrate on your own family. I am sure you have plenty to do here.' Eliza nearly choked with temper.

'You do not know the circumstances! And I do not intend to explain them to you just now. I am tired. I suggest you go back and look after Rose. She is your responsibility after all, something you seem to have forgotten!'

'Eliza, you are naïve in the extreme!' Seth's dark eyes flashed with anger. Eliza took a step back and subsided into one of the straight backed chairs. She marshalled her arguments.

'And you, Seth, are talking nonsense. You forget, Austol is a relation of mine. My sister was married to his brother. She is now installed at the Manor though Austol has no obligation to shelter her. He is also overwhelmed by family crises – the death of his wife, the rebellion of his son – and all his daughters who need care and education! He felt that I could bring some order there. I am flattered that he thinks me such a capable person – but that is not why I am willing to help!'

The two of them glared at each other. Then Seth grabbed her by the arms and shook her.

'Eliza, Eliza! We should not be quarrelling like this! But you should be intelligent enough to understand that Austol must have an ulterior motive. You should stay clear of him!'

Eliza disengaged herself and stepped back with dignity.

'Seth. I am not an attractive eighteen year old! I am over thirty and the mother of five children. He has no designs on me.'

Seth breathed a sigh of exasperation but his eyes had softened.

'You do not realise how confoundedly beautiful you are! But part of your attraction is your competence, your experience with

155

children, and your ability to handle a difficult household. Austol does not want a feather head like all the pretty young girls of good family round here who are looking for a rich husband. He wants a wife who has all the attributes already – and you fit the bill.'

'WIFE? Are you mad? I have a husband as well you know. And Austol knows!'

'And where is he? Where is your husband? Have you heard from him recently? No. And that is enough to allow Austol to make plans! Edgar said....'

'Ah, Edgar! You have been gossiping with Edgar about me! How could you!'

'I have NOT been gossiping with Edgar. I did have a word with Ewella.....'

'Ewella! That explains it!' Eliza could say no more. Suddenly she felt very tired. Quarrelling with Seth was the last straw. She sat down and put her head in her hands.

24

Eliza sat, still unmoving, at the kitchen table. A contrite Seth had retrieved his horse from the sheltered back of the house and ridden off. Far from thawing, the snow was falling more thickly now so the Professor followed him, leaving the children to crowd round their mother, relieved to see her back with them. Eliza cheered up as she listened to their news and their achievements.

'Professor Martineau says it is time we went to school,' announced Nathaniel. 'He says that Caroline and me and John are ready and he will talk to you about it next time.'

'I don't want to go to school,' interrupted Joel. 'I like it here.' Nessa had a protective arm round Richard and declared that she did not want to go either.

'Richard needs me. I'm helping him catch up with his sums.'

'You can't do your own sums,' sneered John.

Just then Uncle Tobias hobbled into the room.

'Glad to see you back,' he said gruffly. 'Not the same without you. Perhaps we shall get some peace now the snow is falling – no more visitors for a while. Any chance of a hot toddy?'

Eliza laughed. Trust Uncle Tobias to take advantage of any change in routine.

'Nathaniel – please go and get Jael from the barn – and where IS Ewella?'

'Here I am.' Ewella entered carrying a large pile of bedding. 'How am I going to get all these dry today?'

'We shall have to light the fire in the room next door.'

'Mama, we are getting very short of firewood,' said Nathaniel, seriously. 'As soon as the snow clears I shall go to collect some.'

'Very thoughtful,' beamed Ewella.

The snow did not clear and it proved to be a cold night. Sharp edged stars appeared between the clouds and outside the silence was still as freezing water. Inside, Uncle Tobias coughed incessantly and the children tossed and turned, trying to keep warm. With icy feet, Eliza could not sleep. She lay, fretting about their situation. School was too far away even if she could find the money. The immediate problem of firewood, however, could be solved if they all made a concerted effort to find some the next day. A picture of Grace, asleep at the Manor in satin sheets, jumped into her mind and made her grit her teeth. Oh, when would Barnabas come back? Then she berated herself as she thought of all the farm labourers in their cottages, short of warmth, as they were, short of space and short of money. And what about the unemployed tinners who tramped the icy roads looking for work or, worse, spent all they had left in drinking dens. She and her family were not alone in their troubles

Morning came at last, the kind of morning when the cold waited to pounce.

'Dress as warmly as you can,' she said to the children. 'Ewella will have hot porridge ready for us when we get back and Richard will help her.'

'Is Jael coming?'

'No. She is brewing more medicine for Uncle Tobias. His cough is not good.'

The little band set off, carrying hessian sacks and were delighted to find that the snow had broken off large branches and twigs littered the ground. Quite soon they had all they could carry and returned to deposit the wood at the back of Carnglaze. Eliza wanted more.

'Who will come down to the sea with me?' she asked. They all looked at each other nervously.

'We'll all come!' decided Nathaniel, at last, taking the lead. In single file they plunged into twilight amongst the trees and thorn bushes. Twigs cracked sharply and the noise of running water from the stream echoed in the emptiness. The path stretched ahead, swallowed by the gloom.

'We could be the last people in the whole world!' whispered Joel.

'Imagine those ponies with sacks on their backs struggling up this dark, winding path,' offered Caroline, 'and slip sliding in the muddy patches.'

'What ponies?'

'You know! The smugglers and wreckers often used this path to carry the goods they stole from ships stuck on the rocks. Professor Martineau said so.'

'How could he possibly know for sure?' demanded Nathaniel. 'I don't remember anything about smugglers. 'The professor was talking about France and the French Revolution the last time we had a history lesson.'
Caroline stopped in her tracks. Her face was very pale.
'I - I remember that,' she said. 'I don't know why I said what I did about the smugglers. It just jumped into my mind.'
'What are wreckers?' asked Nessa.
'Never mind smugglers and wreckers!' Eliza said sharply. 'Watch your step and let us all try to move a little faster. Then we shall get back to a hot breakfast all the more quickly.'

At last they broke out of the trees and bushes on to the cliff headland and slithered down the path to the beach. The sea was breaking sullenly on the shore and spiteful rocks appeared as the tide withdrew. Eliza was struck by the difference in atmosphere. Last time she had been there it had been all blue sea and bright light but now it was shadowed; the snow had been devoured by the salt water and ill-humoured waves smacked on the sand. The children sensed the change and made haste to fill their hessian sacks with more wood without wasting time and soon they were on the way back to the path through the woodland, the path that did not welcome them.
'It's not fun like last time,' murmured Nathaniel to Caroline.
'I don't like it here either,' said his sister. He noticed that she looked strained and nervous.
They toiled up the path, bent over with the weight of the sacks, unable to look around. It was important to look carefully at each step they took to avoid stumbling over stones or slipping on the ice covered puddles and Eliza was wishing that they had not embarked on this enterprise. For a small fee she was certain that Jed would help them out when the weather improved. It was always gloomy on the path even in the middle of the day and this slowed their progress even more. Trees crowded closer and trailing branches reached out to catch their clothes. John seemed to have the most trouble and spent minutes disentangling himself.
'What was that?' Nessa's voice squeaked in fear. She had not wanted to come at all and this path was scary. They all stopped to listen. Nothing. Suddenly they could not hear the stream. The leaves did not rustle. There were no birds piping, no small creatures scrabbling in the

thickets. They were in enclosed in a silent world. And then it began. The whispering. Voices talking to each other far away, and then closer – and closer. Men's voices, gruff and angry.

'Mine!' hissed one voice, louder than the others. 'Leave…leave…' Other voices joined in, still in low whispers but getting louder. 'Keep away….go away…..leave.'
Caroline clapped her hands over her ears. Eliza wanted to shout at the voices but felt it was more important to get the children back to Carnglaze. She chivvied them on, breaking into their trancelike fear, and kept up a stream of loud chatter all the way back. She was gratified when the whispers grew less and died away as the trees thinned out and the bright light of day beckoned them.

The little party were relieved to stumble into the courtyard of Carnglaze and push their way past the heavy wooden door. Ewella greeted them with smiles.

'Just in time for breakfast,' she said. 'You seem to have a good supply of wood. Well done!'
The lack of response from them all surprised her but Eliza put her finger to her lip. Jael followed them in. Uncle Tobias, wound round with a vast muffler, looked up.

'At last!' he croaked, then peered at them more closely.

'What is the matter? You are all as white as if you had seen a ghost!'

'We are just very cold,' said Eliza hastily. Nathaniel and John both tried to speak but she glared at them. A worried Uncle Tobias was the last thing she wanted.

Ewella built up the fire in both rooms and everybody felt more cheerful as the warmth increased, a feeling bolstered by the hot porridge they received. Jael waited to catch Eliza's attention.

'What happened?' she asked quietly. When the children were occupied clearing away the dishes, Eliza explained.

'It seems our troubles are not ended,' Jael said, seriously. 'Perhaps another word with Professor Martineau might help.'

'I have made up my mind that the children must not use that path again. Do you know, I felt that we were actually pushing our way through a crowd of angry people – but there was no one there. It was really strange – and frightening.' She went on: 'I met Jed and asked him about fetching driftwood for us but he said he would prefer to gather wood from the trees nearby.'

I'm not surprised,' said Jael. 'He is a local man and has probably heard stories before.' Eliza made a mental note to question Jed more closely. Come to think of it, he had been rather evasive and unwilling to look her in the eye.

The rest of the day was spent in clouds of steam from Ewella's drying bedding. Only Uncle Tobias liked it because it eased his throat and chest. Eliza and Ewella baked bread and then turned their attention to pies. Finally, Ewella placed a cauldron on the range with all the vegetables they had left to make a stew. They had no meat. The children were subdued and disinclined to do schoolwork or do any chores so Jael gathered them round and told them stories.

'Do you know any stories about smugglers?' asked John

'Or wreckers?' this was Nathaniel.

'No,' replied Jael. 'But I know a good one about the giants that used to live near here.'

'Baby stuff!' said John, with scorn.

'Then don't listen,' said Jael, mildly. 'The hero of this story is only ten years old so I don't think it would interest you. He was a brave boy who managed to outwit the giant Cormoran who lived on St. Michael's Mount. That is not far from here. Then there is the giant Wrath of Portreath who lived in a cave and feasted on the sailors he managed to catch.' Jael had a mesmeric voice and it was not long before the children were enthralled – even Nathaniel and Caroline.

By the time bedtime came, the children had almost forgotten how scared they had been on their wood gathering expedition; only Caroline lingered downstairs on some pretext until her mother shooed her upstairs. Uncle Tobias declared that he felt much better after Jael's medicine and also retired to bed in good order.

'We have to do something,' said Eliza. 'This house does not feel safe. Neither does the path.'

'Perhaps you are letting your imagination run away with you,' suggested Ewella. 'The dark and the cold can play tricks on one.'

'I think Eliza is right,' said Jael, slowly. 'We need protection and mine is not strong enough. I know what to do. As soon as the snow clears I shall go to Liskeard where my mother is. She may be able to help.' Ewella rose from the table, her lip curled in contempt.

'I used to live in Liskeard,' she said. 'The gossip there is that your mother is a witch – a lot of nonsense of course. Witch or not, what on earth could she do to help us here?'

'I am not suggesting that she could drive the spirits away from here or rescue this house from centuries of hauntings. But she may help to protect us.' Jael's voice was cold.

'I think the only way forward is to leave here. Which means we have to wait for my brother to return.'

'I have been waiting for Barnabas for such a long time,' whispered Eliza. 'Why has he not written? I begin to believe that he is not coming back at all.'

25

The days passed and gradually the cold retreated. A warmer wind brought softness to the air and the desperate need for firewood lessened. Jed brought in armfuls when he could and refused to take any payment. Professor Martineau arrived more regularly for lessons, determined to negotiate the mud. Storms blew in but now they were rainstorms and the countryside changed from white to black. From the moor, melting snow added to the volume of water in the stream and it rushed noisily down towards the sea, threatening to overwhelm the wooden bridge on its way.

'I like the noise it makes,' said Nessa. 'It helps me to go to sleep.'

'You wait till the bridge is washed away and you hear all the wood cracking and splintering!' Nathaniel sounded almost gleeful.

'Then we'll be cut off here!' cried Caroline. 'How will the Professor reach us?'

'Who cares,' muttered Joel.

'What about Edgar and Seth?' had been Eliza's unspoken thought. Problems at the Manor were proving a burden. Austol had despatched Edgar to ask for her presence several times on some pretext or other and when Eliza had demanded irritably why he should do that, Edgar had just shrugged his shoulders. Seth was a different matter. Her heart still skipped a beat when he appeared but she felt pangs of conscience about Rose, Rose who still lingered within the confines of the Galleon and seemed unwilling to make the trip to Carnglaze. Studiously she avoided Seth's intense gaze and his efforts to arrange outings with her alone; if they did go it was always with one or all of the children.

The west wind had brought intimations of spring to Ewella and awakened the dormant urge to clean ready for the new season. Lessons over, she decided that their main room and kitchen would benefit from a concerted effort to scrub and polish and disinfect. The members of her unwilling work force were assigned to their tasks and Eliza decided that she needed to get out of the way. Meanwhile, Jael had gone to Liskeard, refusing to be diverted from her intention to obtain advice from her mother. Eliza sat at the kitchen table and pondered. Then it came to her. She would walk the path to sea again and see what transpired. It was broad daylight, a complete contrast to the gloom of the dark hours and she felt she would be brave enough to face up to any ghostly activity.

Weak sunshine dappled the track and struck sparks from the stream as she made her way to the path. Usually it shocked her how quickly the gloom amid the closely knit thorn trees enveloped her, but today was different. Pale rays of the sun percolated through the vegetation turning the usual grey gloom to green and brightening the clearings. Vivid yellow buds of early gorse and the lively noise of the stream as it rushed on its way to the sea cheered her. She squelched through the muddy patches happily, taking time to wonder if the bridge was still intact. Surely the splashing of the stream over stones and pebbles was playful and pleasant, not threatening as it had been earlier? Even the clearing which had seemed so menacing before allowed her to pass without even a shiver.

'No ghosts here,' she chuckled to herself.

And then the sea. That glorious moment when the path opened out to reveal acres of blue sky and blue water and she could absorb the beauty of it as she had done at Roscarne. She sighed with sudden happiness. Optimism took over. Of course they would return to Roscarne. Of course Barnabas was on his way back with a satisfactory explanation for his long absence. And then she could remove the children from the dangers of Carnglaze. She sat on a rock, her arms round her knees like a young girl, and gazed out to sea. A fishing boat, tiny in the distance, was the only sign of human life. Gulls circled the cliffs, and gannets, their wings folded close to their bodies, performed their spectacular dives. Feeling peaceful at last, she allowed her eyelids to droop and was asleep in an instant.

She woke with aching neck and stiff shoulders but more relaxed in her mind. The scene before her, however, had changed. The sun, hiding behind clouds, had turned the sea to molten silver. The air was still and the birds had gone to huddle in their nests. Along the far horizon lay a bar of black cloud, a frame to the silver, but threatening in its utter darkness. Eliza decided that caution was the better part of valour; storms threatened and more heavy rain would make the path impassable. She made her way back, the gloom of the track welcoming her like the attentions of an unwanted friend. Like Austol, she thought, with a giggle. She pushed her way through intrusive vegetation, her skirt catching on thorns, wondering why the return journey should be so much more difficult. It became darker, colder, noticeably so as she neared the clearing that had frightened her so much on earlier expeditions. The sound of the stream became muted, the birds fell silent and her heart began to beat fast. Not again. Surely not again. But then she heard them. The voices. The gruff voices of angry men, louder than before and seeming to come from behind as well as ahead of her. She stood stock still, unable to move as the air became unquiet around her; solid shapes were pushing against her and she seemed to be marooned in an ugly, angry crowd, and yet still she could not see them.

'Leave.....leave...!' the chant began. 'Traitor....traitor!' and to her horror, a face materialised before her, a face twisted with hate, deepset eyes burning with fury. 'You betrayed us!' it hissed. Eliza thought she would faint. Then her courage returned, fired by anger.

'I have betrayed no one!' she shouted, her voice rising shrilly. 'Leave me alone!' The face vanished but the voices redoubled in strength.

'Leave...leave.... And then, horrifyingly, another chant. 'Die....die....! Let the traitor die!' Clawlike hands were grabbing her, pulling her along, battering her, pulling her hair, the brutal attack more horrible because it was unseen. In the thick dark Eliza could feel her strength ebbing away. She would fall and be trampled by this ghostly band who yet seemed to be as substantial as she was. With a last effort she screamed, but her voice was absorbed by the trees and bushes and did not carry far. Then, to her unutterable relief, another voice broke in, calling her.

'Eliza! Where are you?' It was Seth.

There was no holding back this time. She threw herself into Seth's arms, sobbing and incoherent.

'The voices! The men......they think I am a traitor and I don't understand...!'

'Voices! Men! What men? There is no one here!' Fearfully, Eliza looked up. The clearing was empty of mist, of hostile shapes, of unnatural darkness. A ray of sunlight wavered through the branches And the voices were silent.

'The voices! The ghosts! They seemed so real – and so angry!'
Seth put his arm around Eliza and led her gently along the path, away
from the clearing.

'Eliza, you have been dreaming …… there are no men here!'
Seth spoke firmly. He was alarmed at Eliza's hysterical state and
determined to get her back to Carnglaze as soon as possible.

'Eliza, I feel that this nonsense about ghosts has gone too far.
Perhaps you should talk to Nicholas Tregadillett?'
This was too much. Eliza turned on him, her eyes flashing.

'You call it nonsense! And yet you know that we have had
trouble with a ghost at Carnglaze! Even though you laughed, then,
surely you realise now that this is not just me having hallucinations!
Other people – the children – Jael – have heard voices! How can you
pat me on the back and send me to Nicholas Tregadillett!' Her tirade
caused Seth to slip on the mud and he had to grasp a tree to regain his
balance. He was appalled that his efforts to help had been so
misconstrued.

'My dear, I only meant that a man of God might put such
hauntings in perspective, might give you some idea how to free yourself
from your fears.'

'MY fears? These are not just my fears! This is what is
happening to all of us at Carnglaze!'
Seth fell silent, aware that he had made things worse and that,
somehow, he had been unable to comfort Eliza. He was relieved when
the house came into view.

White faced and thin lipped with anger, Eliza allowed Seth to shepherd
her into the courtyard. A pony and cart stood next to Seth's horse, the
pony peacefully cropping the meagre grass by the gate.

'Oh no, it must be Edgar,' Eliza cried out.

'I doubt it. Edgar would never arrive in a cart. But if it is, I shall
get rid of him,' said Seth, with undue enthusiasm. He did not like
Edgar.
It was not Edgar. Jael and Ewella were sitting at the kitchen table and a
stranger, a woman in a lamentably torn and faded grey twill dress and a
white bonnet, was walking slowly round the room.

'I met my mother on the outskirts of Redruth,' said Jael, by way
of introduction. 'I was hoping to catch the coach to Liskeard but there
she was, walking along the road with the pony and cart.'

'I knew Jael was coming to see me,' smiled her mother. 'So I saved her a long journey. And the pony was tired, poor thing.'

'Travelling in that dress!' said Jael, crossly. 'But then you always were eccentric, mother.'

'You never did give me credit for initiative, my dear,' her mother observed. 'I came at once. I knew it was important. And before you ask – ' she looked pointedly at her daughter – ' I used no spells to find you. I dreamed about you and knew that you wanted to see me.'

'Best keep that to yourself,' said Jael, hurriedly.

'Still worried about me?' teased her mother. 'They have not yet named me as a witch!' Ewella drew in her breath sharply. Eliza was fascinated but Seth did not know whether to laugh or be scandalised. Witches? Ghosts? What was happening to the family at Carnglaze?

The old lady turned to Eliza and gave her a sweet smile.

'I am Mistress Annie, Jael's mother, as you may have gathered. I am sorry to come here so unexpectedly and without invitation but I felt I was needed. Mothers always know when their children need them.' Ewella snorted. Mistress Annie turned to her. Eliza saw that her eyes were sharp and probing.

'Mistress Trevannion, I believe? You, too, come from Liskeard.' It was a statement and not a question. 'I would ask you to disregard the silly gossip that seems to follow those who, like myself, try to help the afflicted by using their knowledge of herbal potions and medicines.'

'Of course,' stuttered Ewella, pink in the face.

'In the same way, I ignore gossip about my fellow creatures – so time wasting and usually unkind.' Ewella seemed to be having trouble catching her breath.

'Now,' continued Mistress Annie, 'I should like to wander round the outside of the house and try to sense what is going on here.'

'I shall come with you,' said her daughter.

'And I must find the children,' said Eliza, suddenly struck by their absence.

'They are collecting plants for me,' said Jael. 'They promised not to stray too far. Nathaniel is in charge ….'

'I should go,' said Seth. 'I feel there is rain to come. Mistress Eliza – I hope to take you to St. Michael's Mount very soon.'

'That would be delightful,' said Eliza, formally. 'Do try and persuade Rose to come as well.'

'Of course,' said Seth. 'Meanwhile I think you should keep away from that path. It seems to play upon your imagination and upset you.'

'Not my imagination,' said Eliza, coldly. 'But thank you for coming to escort me back to the house.' Feeling that he had drawn no closer to Eliza, Seth took his leave. Ewella watched the play between the two of them with great interest. Barnabas should return soon, she thought.

'I need to talk to Mistress Annie,' said Eliza. 'Then you will be free to do as you please. Within reason, John and Joel!' She was pleased to see that Nessa was still hovering around Richard, taking her duty to look after him very seriously. Caroline, however, was a worry. She was very pale and her eyes were bruised and dark as if she had not been sleeping well. As the others left, she remained sitting motionless on her chair. Then she began to speak, not to her mother but to herself. And her voice was not her own.

'You accuse me! But it was not me. I tell you it was not me!' Her voice rose to a scream. 'You are making a mistake! Do not punish me for something that I have not done! No, NO, NO!' And she fell from her chair and lay insensible on the floor.

26

When at last Mistress Annie and Jael returned they found Eliza and Ewella hovering anxiously round a dazed Caroline. Eliza explained what had happened. Ewella decided to make tea for everyone, hoping thus to ingratiate herself with Mistress Annie. Fortunately Uncle Tobias was having one of his increasingly frequent naps and the children were still busy in the schoolroom though Joel did burst in with a complaint and was shooed away.

'I am not sure that I can be of much help,' began Mistress Annie in grave tones. 'I am not surprised that such a thing should happen – especially to Caroline. She is quiet now – ' looking at Caroline sitting silently and gazing out of the window. 'But it may recur.' Eliza could not restrain a gasp of horror. 'There is no doubt that this house and land is the focus of spirit activity and has been for some time – possibly centuries. The standing stone – well, it is an indication and it was wise of Jael to abstract herself from the house.'

'What do you think we should do?' asked Eliza, holding her voice steady with an effort.

'You should move as soon as you can. It will never be a peaceful home for you and your children because unquiet spirits are just that. Unquiet.'

'My mother suggested that perhaps Professor Martineau could research even further back,' put in Jael. 'It might give us an idea of the source of some of the trouble.'

'I have the feeling that there is the weight of a long history here; perhaps there were disturbances before the house was built. Even if the house were to be knocked down, the land would still not be free.'

Eliza listened to this with growing dismay. Mistress Annie seemed to be concurring with the conclusions reached by Rev. Sithney and the Professor that they should move out of Carnglaze. That was the only sensible thing to do. But where could they go? Eliza had an uneasy feeling that Austol would welcome them to the Manor – but that welcome would be shackled to the deep sense of obligation she would feel. Neither did the discomfort of being so close to Austol and Edgar all the time appeal to her. No doubt the children would be welcome playmates for Austol's seven girls and at least Richard would be in the same house as his mother and Elestren .... but .... ? Then there was Seth's offer to rent them a house, an offer fraught with danger. If Barnabas did not return there would be no way of repaying him. In any case, she was forced to admit to herself, Seth himself was the real danger. To be in the same house as Seth – and Rose – was unthinkable. Possibly he would live with Rose in yet another house but again, there would be this burden of obligation. And what would Barnabas think?

Ewella was getting restive. She considered the idea of ghosts not to be entertained with any seriousness. Possibly Eliza was going through some kind of a depressed state because of her husband's absence. Stolid, unimaginative Ewella would have no truck with that. If you were left on your own as she herself had been, you made the best of what was left to you. Eliza, in her view, was excitable, fanciful and particularly sensitive to the changes in her surroundings, more so since she had been left solely in charge of her children and of Uncle Tobias. At Carnglaze, however, Ewella felt vindicated. She had always considered that her erstwhile mistress was not up to the task of running a household on her own and relied too heavily on others. SHE should be in charge of the household. But then, most men were as stupid and unreliable as her former husband, even Barnabas, and she blamed him for leaving them all to fend for themselves.

'If he does not come back soon, he will find that either Austol Treloyhan or Seth Quinn will have penned his hen in a coop. And then what will happen?' Perhaps that would not be such a bad thing. It would clear the way for her advancement in her brother's household.

Mistress Annie was preparing to leave.

'I have instructed Jael to prepare some protection for you all,' she said, ignoring Ewella's look of disbelief. 'I wish you well and will come again if I am needed.'

'How will you get back?' asked Eliza. 'I would ask you to stay but you have seen how crowded we are.'

'Mother can stay in my barn if necessary,' said Jael. 'But there is no need. Mathey will take us to catch the London coach, which stops at Liskeard, and we have plenty of time before the last one of the day.' Eliza called in the children to say goodbye to their visitor who seemed to take great pleasure in meeting them and chatting to them. It was no surprise that Caroline engaged her particular attention.

The very next day, Edgar turned up, smartly dressed and no mud on his shiny boots. His altercation with Austol had left no lasting traces and he was in high good humour.

'Mistress Eliza, I am happy to see you,' he began. Eliza, who was in her raggedy work dress, was less happy to see him. She was still mulling over Mistress Annie's advice and taking advantage of Professor Martineau's presence in the schoolroom to tidy the kitchen. Edgar was a pleasant enough man but he seemed to have little depth, she thought, his moods swinging too easily one way or another. And he tended too much to act as Austol's lackey. Indeed he was on another of Austol's errands that very day.

'You and the children are invited to tea at the Manor tomorrow,' he announced.

'I had been intending to go to Truro to see the solicitor,' demurred Eliza. Edgar brushed that aside.

'Austol has a proposal to make to you – an advantageous one, I assure you. Please do come. The girls will be so disappointed if you do not. Of course he will send the carriage for you.' Eliza could sense the anxiety beneath his bonhomie. Of course he was reliant on Austol's good will to stay at the Manor, particularly since the death of his sister. She sighed. The children would certainly enjoy their trip and she, herself, would welcome an escape from the gloom of Carnglaze. Perhaps tea with Austol would be worth it. What kind of proposal had he in mind, she wondered. 'Curiosity killed the cat,' she remembered her mother saying when they rummaged through the parcels waiting for them on their birthdays.

'Austol does not expect me to come?' Uncle Tobias asked in a worried tone. 'All the children together – too busy – too noisy!'

'I'm sure he understands that,' soothed Eliza. 'You will have a peaceful afternoon.'

'Gallivanting again?' said Ewella, sourly.

'Please come, Ewella – I'm sure you are expected.'

'No room in the carriage,' she said grumpily.

'Mistress Trevannion, I should be delighted to fetch you in the pony and trap,' said Edgar. 'That would be much more comfortable for you.' Ewella was pleased, though she tried not to show it and Eliza was impressed with his unforced kindness. That was Edgar, always surprising. She flashed him a smile before he hurried off, citing urgent business in Penzance.

So the next day they found themselves sitting at the table with all the children, which elicited Eliza's approval. The custom of children banished to a separate room for their meal, as still practised in many households, was not congenial to her. Very small children, yes. But not once they were a little older. She had a vague memory of discussing this with Austol on a previous visit and was pleased that he agreed with her. Ewella, however, felt quite affronted that she was seated between two of Austol's girls and attacked her saffron cake with a grim expression. Austol presided over the gathering, hawk nosed and silent, looking intently at each child in turn, a regard which prevented Joel from pulling Kerra's braids. Then, at the end of the meal, he asked Eliza to step into his study as he wanted a private word with her. The children followed Edgar and Ewella to the girls' playroom, a large, sunny room at the back of the house.

'Eliza – I hope I may still call you that?' Austol gestured to a comfortable looking chair covered in velvet with a gold coloured antimacassar over the back. Eliza found the chair less than comfortable. It had high arms which made her feel hemmed in and to compensate she sat up, stiffly. Austol seemed to find this briefly amusing. He leaned back in his own armchair and studied his guest.

'You will be pleased to hear that Grace is visiting Aunt Gloria with Nanny Hannah and Elestren. She seems almost completely recovered from her nervous problems – and now accepts that I am not James.' As an opening gambit, it threw Eliza completely off balance.

'That is a considerable advance,' she murmured, conscience stricken that she had not enquired about her sister before. He continued, smoothly.

'I am quite happy to offer her a place at the Manor again, when she returns. She is adamant that Carnglaze is not for her.'

'That is good of you,' murmured Eliza. 'I should like to point out that Grace has always made her own decisions in the past and now that she is well again that will continue. I only stepped in to help when she was ill.'

'You mean you are not your sister's keeper,' suggested Austol, with a hint of a smile. 'But now it is your turn to require help. Edgar tells me that you have had hauntings at Carnglaze? And you have been advised to leave the house?'

'Yes.' Who had been talking to Edgar? Ewella? 'But it is out of the question. We are a large household and we have nowhere to go. As soon as Barnabas returns, he will decide what to do.'

'Ah yes, the elusive Barnabas,' said Austol, dismissively. He leaned forward. 'Eliza, you are an intelligent woman. Are you sure he is coming back? Have you never questioned it?'

'Of course he will return as soon as he is able,' cried Eliza, hotly. 'He is a man of honour and would never desert us willingly!'

'When did you last hear from him?' Eliza remained silent.

'For the sake of the children you should move. I have made enquiries and that house seems to have been the focus of supernatural activities for years. The Lanivet brothers were unable to remain there, nor Caswol before them. A haunted house is no place for children. Now, I have a proposition for you. I need a housekeeper. And a mother figure for my girls. You would be ideally suited.'
Eliza tried to protest but he held up his hand.

'And in return, you would all move to the Manor – we have plenty of room – and your money troubles would be over.'

Eliza was bereft of words. Austol watched her, seemingly relaxed, but those cold eyes never left her face. She was the prey of a falcon hovering over her, ready to swoop. He watched the interplay of emotions on her face. The move would be an advantage for the children, of that there was no doubt. Also it would mean that Uncle Tobias would be in better surroundings – of course they all would be – but something held her back. She needed to discuss this with Jael and Ewella and, possibly, Seth.

'Austol, I do thank you for your kind offer but I need to give it some thought.'

'Naturally,' he agreed, without giving any indication of offence at the less than enthusiastic reaction to the idea.

Back at Carnglaze, the contrast between the austerity of their living there and the honeyed comfort of Treloyhan Manor was even more marked.

'What do you think of the idea, Ewella?' she asked wearily, having spent a sleepless night mulling over her conversation with Austol. Ewella looked severe.

'I have no doubt it is a very generous offer – but for you to accept a position as a housekeeper would not please Barnabas at all. If you forget all this nonsense about ghosts and buckle down to our life here I am sure he will be back soon.'

'I thought you would welcome the chance of living more comfortably at the Manor!'

'Then you do not know me very well! I have the interests of my brother at heart and I know he would be furious at you being taken in by Treloyhan like a pauper!'

'It was an honourable offer of employment,' said Eliza, stung.

'Trevannion wives are not housekeepers!' said Uncle Tobias, when he was consulted. 'In any case, the Manor is a strange household and I am not sure that Barnabas would approve. And that Edgar! He had a bad reputation at one time. Some connection with smuggling, I believe. Best to be careful.'

The next few nights were peaceful. The rain fell steadily outside which reinforced the comfort of solid granite walls and a blazing fire. The house seemed to be holding its breath, waiting for Eliza's decision. No ghostly voices disturbed the silence and no shadows lurked in the corners. Eliza, sleepless one night, sat staring into the fire, wondering if perhaps Jael's latest form of protection – a fretwork of rowan branches over the door – was working. Jael, herself, did not give a straight answer when asked for her opinion about a move to the Manor. She hesitated.

'It seems to me that you are surrounded by traps,' she said. 'They all have advantages but there are dangers in all of them.' She refused to elaborate, saying that the choice was Eliza's alone.

27

The rain was still falling, a steady drenching rain that veiled the buildings and the outside world and looked as if it would never go away. It hissed against the windows making it as difficult to see out as if it had been late evening, Eliza thought, as she peered towards the gate. Out of the murk loomed a figure. It was Seth. He came in, dripping with water, his dark hair plastered across his head, rivulets running into his eyes. Eliza did not know if she was pleased to see him or not. She feared a repeat scolding when she talked to him about Austol's offer.

'Come, sit by the fire,' she said, helping him off with his cape. 'I shall ask Ewella to make you a hot drink.'

'Where is everybody? You are usually knee deep in children and visitors.'

'The children are in Jael's barn where she is giving them a botany lesson. We do not expect the Professor on such a day. Ewella is baking while she has some peace and Uncle Tobias is asleep.

'Again?'

'He does worry me,' admitted Eliza. 'Quite often this winter he has preferred to stay in bed rather than get up.'

'This is not the most comfortable of houses for someone at his time of life,' said Seth in sympathetic tones. Eliza realised that this was the perfect opening to a discussion about Austol's offer but before she could say anything he leaned forward and took her hand.

'I have something to say to you, Eliza,' he said, seriously. His dark eyes were fixed on her face and she felt the familiar shiver of recognition. Her heart began to race and her disobedient body wished to draw closer to him.

'I want to tell you how sorry I am that I spoke to you the way I did,' he began. 'I had no right to criticise you or judge you so roughly. Please believe that it was only concern for your well-being that made me act like that. And it shames me to admit it but I think jealousy played no small part.'

'Thank you,' said Eliza, quietly. 'Now I have something to ask you that will make you angry again but I should be grateful if you could just give me an opinion and not make me feel as if I were an opponent in one of your boxing bouts.' She tried to withdraw her hand but he tightened his grasp.

'I am so sorry,' he said softly. 'I promise to listen and respond carefully!' Eliza wondered if he would remain so calm when she mentioned Austol's name.

'I, too, am worried about Uncle Tobias as well as the children,' she began. 'Not just because of our discomfort at Carnglaze. The children are adaptable and have settled in fairly easily and Uncle Tobias does not complain as a rule. But there is something more sinister here. This house is haunted – not just the house but the surrounding land – and I feel unsafe here and, I have to admit it, frightened.'

Seth sat back in his chair. His voice when he replied was gentle.

'I am so sorry you feel like this. I find it difficult to believe that you are in real danger. I know that there have been – ah – incidents but I feel sure there are reasonable explanations.'

Eliza's eyes flashed as she realised the depths of his disbelief. With difficulty she held on to her own temper.

'Seth! You were here when Professor Martineau and Reverend Sithney carried out an exorcism! And you saw what happened!'

'I saw what a hysterical response it evoked in you ......'

'Seth!'

'Let me finish. Expecting something strange to happen, especially in such a charged atmosphere, can actually bring about what is expected. I think that is what occurred.'

The blood drained from Eliza's face and the expression in her eyes alarmed him. So might she regard a large rat.

'I shall fetch you a drink of water from the kitchen,' he said hastily.

'I do not want a drink,' said Eliza coldly. 'Nor brandy if you should suggest that next. I am sorry that you do not believe what is taking place here. Not everyone is sensitive to supernatural activity, the Professor tells me, but I am not alone. Jael, Mistress Annie, Caroline, even little Richard, know that something is amiss in this house. It explains why the Lanivets left in such a hurry and are determined never to return and apparently, Caswol – '

'Yes, yes,' interrupted Seth. 'I know all that. But I do not believe in spirits from beyond the grave. What is important is that you do and something must be done about it.'

'Exactly. And I have been offered a way out.'

There was a silence. Seth sat, deep in thought. Eliza had time to observe the breadth of his shoulders, the comforting bulk of him, the way his hair flopped over his forehead, his sharp nose and those deep-set dark eyes – she stopped herself. This was madness.

'Tell me, then,' he said tiredly. Eliza had the feeling that he knew what she was about to say.

'Austol – he has offered me employment as his housekeeper. Then he will invite us all to stay at the Manor and we can leave this dreadful house.'

'And have you accepted his offer?'

'Not yet.'

Seth seemed to gather himself together to answer her reasonably though he wanted to shout and rail at her for even considering such an idea.

'Please think carefully. Austol is now a widower, not a married man, and even if you have Edgar as a chaperone it is not proper for you. You are not a house-keeper, you are the wife of Barnabas Trevannion and the mother of his children. Imagine the gossip and the damage this could do to Barnabas' reputation when he returns to rebuild his businesses.'

'If he returns!' said Eliza, bitterly.

'I rather think that Austol is hoping he will not.'

'That is nonsense. Anyway, what do you suggest we should do?'

'I could rent you a house elsewhere as I offered before. But I gather that is not to your taste?'

'Barnabas would be mortified if he returned to find me a recipient of such charity! You are a married man and it would be equally unsuitable for me to be a – a – kept woman!'

Seth sighed. 'That would not be the case as you know perfectly well, but I respect your reasons.'

'The Morwennas of this world would be delighted to have such a juicy morsel to whisper about – and it would damage you and Rose as well. It is a kind offer but out of the question. Of course you could offer me a position as kitchen maid when you have an establishment.' Eliza could not resist the barb. 'So, meanwhile, you expect me to stay here with the spirits?'

'Perhaps you are exaggerating the voices you hear and the things you apparently see – '

This was too much for Eliza. Her voice rose an octave.

'Then come with me and experience the walk down to the sea! Perhaps nothing will happen and that would comfort me. Or perhaps the voices will reach you, too.'

'Very well.'

Eliza was surprised that Seth had agreed so easily. She asked Ewella to tell Jael where she was going and ignored her scowl of disapproval.

'Surely you can't go out in this weather! It is still raining pitchforks!'

'It will be more sheltered under the trees,' was all Eliza would say. So she and Seth set off and soon discovered that the waterfall of rain was not the only hazard. Slicks of mud hid the potholes and covered the path, becoming more slippery by the minute. The stream was in full spate, the rushing of its waters louder than the rain.

'Perhaps this outing is ill advised?' suggested Seth. 'Perhaps we should wait for better weather?'

'No,' said Eliza obstinately. 'I am sure the spirits will not be deterred by bad weather.'

'I might be,' muttered Seth but fortunately Eliza did not hear him.

They left the main path and plunged into the tangle of thorny trees and bushes. Immediately they were protected in some measure from the onslaught of the rain but the thickening gloom made their way more hazardous. Now even the rocks on the path were difficult to see and the two of them stumbled and slipped on their way ever more slowly. Then they came to the clearing where the stream dropped away between higher banks and lichened branches hung, contorted and claw-like, over the water. Eliza knew the place well. She stopped.

'I need to get my breath,' she said, feeling her heart beginning to race. She knew that if anything was going to happen it would be here.

'The rain is lessening but it IS getting colder,' said Seth thoughtfully. A silence separated them from the outside world, a silence like a circled barrier, enclosing and imprisoning them. The rushing water of the stream seemed to come from far away. Then the voices began. First whispers then louder. Angry voices loud enough for Eliza to make out the words she had heard before.

'Traitor!' 'Leave – leave the house!' 'Traitor – you betrayed us!' 'You will die!'

'Can you hear them?' Eliza hissed, clutching Seth's arm.

Then another sound. The sound of hooves on stone, incongruous in that welter of mud and water. Eliza shrank back against a thorn tree, dragging Seth with her. She felt rather than saw the animals brush past them. She knew they were heavily laden and then, to her dismay, she heard the rumble of cartwheels. How could a cart possibly navigate this narrow path? She stepped backwards, fearful that she would collide with the ghostly vehicle – then lost her footing and fell over the bank into the stream some six feet below. The water received her in an icy embrace, the fast flowing current sluicing over her face. The last thing she remembered was Seth's agonised shout 'Eliza!'

Faces appeared through a mist; her family were gathered around her and she heard Caroline crying. With a great effort she tried to speak, to reassure them she was not hurt but the slightest movement caused sharp pain and she lost consciousness again. When she next awoke it was to find Dr. Trevell bending over her.

'Dr. Trevell, you must have travelled such a long way,' she murmured.

'Mr. Quinn fetched me all the way from Rosmorren, that is true,' smiled the doctor. 'But when I heard what had happened to you I came as fast as I could. I have examined you and there are no bones broken but you have been unconscious for a considerable time so I believe you must have hit your head – perhaps on a rock. Your thick hair makes any bruising difficult to locate so we shall have to watch over you with care. You have numerous cuts and scrapes which will be painful.'

'Seth?' she croaked.

'Ah yes, Mr. Quinn. He managed to carry you over his shoulder – quite a long way I believe – and Mistress Trevannion is reviving him with brandy. Your children are all here and Mistress Jael is waiting to talk to you.'

Eliza looked around and realised that she was on a makeshift bed by the fire and deliciously warm. Ewella and Jael must have scurried round to make her so comfortable. Dr. Trevell still lingered.

'What exactly happened, my dear? Mr. Quinn tells me that you two were ghost hunting? He saw nothing but I believe you did?'

'Oh yes – I saw, or I think I saw ponies on the path and then - and then I heard a cart and I stepped back out of the way .....' Dr. Trevell nodded his head slowly.

Just then Seth appeared at her bedside.

'I am so glad to see you have recovered consciousness,' he said. 'When you are feeling better we shall talk about what happened. But now I have to return to Rose. She will be wondering where I am.' He made his farewells and Eliza heard his horse leaving the courtyard. A wave of loneliness swept over her when she realised he really had gone. She felt abandoned – a stupid feeling in a house so crowded, she told herself. She must not lose sight of the fact that he was married to Rose. And Rose was not well or she would have come to Carnglaze long since. But even so, his leave-taking had been abrupt and seemed uncaring and the ready tears sprang to her eyes.

The children crowded round Eliza's bed and she had to comfort each one of them and insist that she would be quite better soon. Only Caroline was resistant and it took a while and one of Ewella's saffron buns to stop her crying. Then Jael shooed them away and said their mother must rest and in any case they had important work to do after their botany lessons. Uncle Tobias hobbled in to see her and it was only Ewella who maintained her look of disapproval.

'What do you think Dr. Trevell would make of you and Mr. Quinn out walking together! Have you no sense, Eliza?'

'Ewella – I do not need a scolding! We were trying to ascertain if that path is really haunted – and it is! Please take my word for it. We are surrounded with unquiet spirits!'

28

Several days passed peacefully, allowing Eliza to recover from her fall. She was still covered with bruises and scrapes but her headache had gradually abated. Edgar had come to call but Ewella refused to let him in, giving him a terse explanation of Eliza's illness. Then the next day a driver from the Manor arrived with a huge bouquet of hot house flowers and a card from Austol and 'family'. Of Seth there was no sign. Eliza tried not to let her hurt at this dominate her thoughts. With or without Seth's advice, she would have to decide what to do. 'Unquiet spirits are just that – unquiet.' The words repeated themselves in her brain, reinforcing her desire to get away. Real life was difficult enough without facing the extra pressure of the supernatural and she had her children to think of. Caroline, she knew, was the most sensitive one and then little Richard had actually seen one of the ghosts. No, they must leave.

Jael had been running backwards and forwards from her barn to the house with a worried expression on her face. Finally she crept in to Eliza and sat by her bed.

'Mistress Eliza,' she began, always a sign that she wanted a serious discussion. 'Do you think your Aunt Gloria would be able to help?'

'No,' said Eliza decidedly. 'She is without Yelland and while I know she is comfortably off I would not ask her for anything more. She has already paid for my education and that of my sister and I do not want her to know of our present predicament.'

Jael nodded. 'I understand that. But you will have to decide what you are going to do and the sooner the better.'

'Why do we need to hurry?' queried Eliza, rather shaken by this urgency.

'My mother did say ....' Jael hesitated and then went on with a rush. 'These ghosts – or spirits, whatever you like to call them – are not just unhappy wanderers in the spirit world – they are angry. It seems they want the house to be left empty and my mother said......'

'What did Mistress Annie say?' prompted Eliza.

'They will not stop until you do what they want. Which is to leave. I need to warn you, though, we are in a strange situation here. One haunting – a fairly recent one – appears to have responded to exorcism and is here no more.'

'Poor, sad girl, looking for her baby,' agreed Eliza.

'But now we have angry men!' Jael went on. 'And they are not confined to the house but apparently also the area between Carnglaze and the sea. At a guess I think they must be smugglers or wreckers – that would explain the sound of the ponies. I have asked Professor Martineau to find out what he can. Even so, supposing another exorcism worked – which I doubt – what will come after that? There may be layers of hauntings going back for centuries.'

'You mean Carnglaze will never be an ordinary house?'

'The real problem for us at the moment is whether the voices will stay as just voices or whether there will be further manifestations designed to frighten us away.'

'So Mistress Annie feels we ought to leave?' Jael nodded.
Eliza relayed this conversation to Ewella who received it with scorn.

'A lot of nonsense! That Mistress Annie thinks she knows everything – just because she has some skills in herbal medicine. Some do call her a witch but I don't believe that!'

Then something happened which made up Eliza's mind. It was late. She went up to check that the children were safely tucked in but found Caroline wide eyed and far from sleep.

'Caroline?'

'At the door! Just standing there looking at me. Send him away, Mama!'

'There is no one there! The shadows cast by the flickering candles just make it seem so. Now you stop imagining things and get off to sleep.'

'Mama – I saw him! He was wearing big boots and a red scarf – and a strange hat. How would I know that if I had not seen him?' Eliza shuddered, pinned to the ground by the terrified eyes of her daughter.

'Caroline,' she said gently. 'You could write stories with the things you imagine. Now I shall stay here until you fall asleep. There is nothing to worry about.' What else could she say? Certainly there WAS something to worry about. She knew that lying to the children was wrong – but there was an outside chance that indeed the figure had been a picture from Caroline's fertile mind. She hoped it was but her innermost fears could not be so easily assuaged. Comforted by her mother, Caroline soon succumbed to sleep and Eliza could creep away.

Sleep did not come easily to Eliza that night. She was caught between warring factions. There was Ewella, scornful of the supernatural and disapproving of any move to the Manor. There was Seth who had both heard voices and seen the aftermath of the exorcism and yet refused to believe anything unusual was happening, his specious argument fuelled, no doubt, thought Eliza, by a determination to stop her accepting Austol's offer. On the other hand, Jael and her mother, Mistress Annie, were in no doubt and neither had Professor Martineau any difficulty in believing. Then Uncle Tobias, and Caroline and Richard in particular among the children, had experienced happenings, voices or visions, that were inexplicable in the cold light of day.

Despairing of sleep, Eliza stole downstairs, hoping to catch the last embers of warmth from the fire and make herself a hot drink. Her candle flickered but steadied into a bright flame. The shadows on the walls were still. Where was Seth? His desertion at such a time bespoke a lack of concern that was deeply hurtful. No doubt there was a good explanation but it would not be good enough for her. Ever since he had rescued her from Marah Cove, when she had sprained her ankle, she had felt a close connection with him and nurtured the entirely unwarranted assumption that she should always come first in his life. Never mind his marriage to Rose, nor her own to Barnabas, in times of need she expected him to be there for her. Childish in the extreme, she berated herself. A romantic and illogical desire. Did Seth think of her in the same way? Or feel any obligation towards her? Probably not. He had affection for her no doubt, but a pale shadow of what she wanted.

She rested her head upon the table, weary of her conflicting thoughts. A cold draught blew in from the door as if it had been left open. But she herself had bolted it fast. A pervading cold, chilling the air and nullifying the warmth from the fire, wrapped round her like a winding sheet. Suddenly and brutally awake she looked around with startled eyes. Her candle began to flicker wildly and then blew out. She was left with the shadows from the dying fire. This was too much. She needed to see Jael, however late it was and extract some comfort from another human being. She could not stay in the darkened room, so alone and uncertain and she knew that Ewella would merely heap more scorn upon her. Slowly she stood up. Nothing moved in the room. Only the bitter cold spoke of something unusual, something not of the earth waiting there. With relief she reached the door and unbolted it, the grating sound breaking the stillness. But nothing else happened and she found herself on the other side of the door and hurrying to Jael's barn.

Jael slept lightly and soon she had made Eliza a herbal drink, assuring her it would have a sedative effect.

'Now, wear this,' she said, proffering a rough cross made of twigs tied together with twine. 'Rowan twigs,' she said. 'Always a good protection. I'm afraid it will scratch under your dress but it may help. Now I shall walk with you back to the house and wait while you go in. You will sleep, now, I promise you.'

Shakily, Eliza nodded her head and the two stepped outside the barn into the faint light of a sickle moon. The rain clouds had rolled away at last. Gently Eliza pushed open the heavy wooden door and, as it swung to, the darkened room within was revealed.

'Like a mouth, waiting to swallow me.' The thought crept unbidden into her mind. She tried to tread softly over the threshold so as not to wake any of the sleepers and turned to wave her thanks to Jael. Then found she could not move. She wanted to climb the stairs up to her bedroom but could not. The dark room, supposedly empty, was still quiet but suddenly it came to her. She was not alone. Just ahead of her was a dark shape, darker than the rest of the room.

'Ewella?' she managed, in a quavering voice, though not with any real hope of the shape proving to be her sister-in-law. There was no answer. She still could not move, held still by unseen bonds. The shape moved imperceptibly closer. It was then anger took over.

'I don't know what you want – but we in this house have done you no wrong! Go away and leave us alone!' Her words flew like daggers, powered by rage. Silence followed. Perhaps it was only her imagination but the intense cold lessened slightly and this emboldened her. She fixed her eyes on the dark shape before her.

'There are no traitors here! No one has betrayed you. Leave us in peace!' She felt inside the neckline of her dress and dragged out the rowan cross. Then the strength left her legs and she stumbled to the table and collapsed into one of the wooden chairs.

'Leave! Just leave! This house is mine!' whispered a voice with startling clarity. So close was the voice that it seemed right next to her. It was more than she could bear and she shut her eyes tightly and put her head down on the table.

'Eliza, my dear. Why are you down here so soon?'
Slowly she raised her head and looked around. The grey light of early morning was struggling through the windows and Uncle Tobias, his white hair on end and his clothes all rumpled was gazing down at her.
'I-I couldn't sleep. I hope I did not wake you, Uncle.'
'No, no my dear. I am often awake at this time. Perhaps you would be kind enough to make me a hot drink. It is a long time to breakfast!' With a sweet smile, Uncle Tobias tottered back to his room. Eliza lit the oil lamp on the windowsill and a candle on the table, eager to dispel the last of the night. Then she attacked the fire, making it blaze up, and put the kettle on the range. The drink made her feel brighter as did Uncle Tobias, so cheerful in his cold room, so accepting of the discomforts the house provided. Gradually the aches in her limbs, caused by her uncomfortable sleep, dissipated. She peered through the window and saw that the coming day promised to be calm; the trees and thorn bushes were etched black against a pearly sky and nothing moved. She turned away, intending to make preparations for breakfast but was brought up short. In spite of the fire and the candles, the temperature was dropping. The cold was back. A renewed tension gripped her body, imprisoning her limbs so that again she could not move. There was another presence in the room. In the grey light of early day a shadow lurked by the door, insubstantial, evanescent, but still there, quietly menacing. It was the last straw.

All right!' exclaimed Eliza. 'You have won. We shall go! We shall leave this house and Carnglaze will be all yours!'

29

Eliza gazed out of the window at a very different view. No thorn trees, no tangled bushes, no derelict wall and courtyard, just green lawns, pine trees and glimpses of the sea. She heaved a sigh. She had failed. She had allowed the spirits to chase them all away from Carnglaze, fearing for her children and Uncle Tobias and, it had to be admitted, for herself. The ghosts had been getting closer and manifesting more frequently. No wonder the Lanivets had left. Ewella had not been afraid; she seemed immune from the psychic web that tangled Eliza.

'It would be a brave spirit who dared defy Ewella,' said Jael. She had refused to accompany Eliza, the children and Uncle Tobias for a 'little holiday' at the Manor, saying that she wanted to visit her mother in Liskeard. Eagerly, Ewella had declared that she would accompany her and visit some of her relations there. She did not approve of her sister-in-law's decision to take shelter at the Manor. So, for the first time, Eliza was left alone with her family. Austol offered them a warm welcome though he seemed surprised at Eliza's insistence that she would take up the role of housekeeper he had once offered as a way of repaying him.

'I am touched by your kindness,' she had said, missing the gleam in Austol's eyes at her words, 'But I should be happy to help until you find a permanent replacement.'

The staff at the Manor remembered Eliza from her previous visit though now she wore a dark blue twill dress with a capacious white apron and carried a chatelaine around her waist.

'She do mean business,' muttered one kitchen maid to another. And she did. In a matter of weeks she had the household running smoothly and established a reasonable relationship with the cook, who acceded to demands for a more varied menu.

'Another stargazy pie and I shall throw up!' whispered Joel. Fortunately only John heard him. Austol professed himself delighted with Eliza's management skills; she, however, found that she was actually missing Ewella. The time they had spent working together at Carnglaze had drawn them closer but she was unaware that Ewella still had her reservations. Seth for one. Another was her suspicion about Austol. Why was he being so good to both Eliza and Grace? No doubt he had felt lonely after the death of his wife, Eulalia, and then the departure of his son, Kenwyn, who had left the Manor while still suffering from his injuries. But to invite ALL the household, including Jael, to stay? He could have employed a housekeeper at a fraction of the cost. It was a situation that needed watching.

Austol stalked around his property, his cold eyes missing nothing. He noted the fires lit in the entrance hall, the main reception rooms and the studies, his and that of Uncle Tobias. He saw the furniture well-polished and the silver gleaming on the sideboard. Stains on the upholstery vanished as if by magic. Flowers from the conservatory appeared at regular intervals and were not allowed to droop and die as before. He discovered that his chief gardener was delighted by Eliza and her appreciation of his work.

'She is some interested in all the new plants and wants to learn about the unusual ones,' he announced to Austol, with pride. A pleasant surprise for the master of the house was to find, on one of his inspections, that the rooms belonging to his daughters were unusually tidy. No garments flung on the floor but put away in the vast commodes. Each girl had her own bed cover, spread over immaculate beds and the carpets, so expensive to buy, were cleaned as were the heavy velvet curtains. Regularly the windows were flung open and the fresh air from the sea fragranced the rooms, banishing the usual stifling atmospheres. The way Eliza worked was witnessed by Austol at first hand. The sound of someone in tears issued from the library. He looked through the open door and saw Eliza patting one of the maids on the shoulder. 'Don't cry, Susie. It is not your fault. That shelf is too high for you to reach. Now I shall help you put the books back and no harm is done.' He saw the two of them pick up the tomes scattered on the floor and feed them back on to the shelves and he heard Susie's stammered thanks to Eliza. 'Next time you dust them, use the steps,' smiled Eliza. However she scolded the boy who staggered in to the hall with a pile of logs for the fire. He was told in no uncertain terms that he should take off his boots and not scuff the shining wooden floor.

'Just a bit o' mud,' he muttered. But he obeyed her.
Later, Austol, reclining comfortably in his favourite armchair, smoking a cigar, reflected that rarely had he been so comfortable in his own

house. He enjoyed glimpses of Eliza, hurrying about her work, noting with approval her shapely figure, her trim waist, her neat gleaming hair so unfortunately covered with a starched white cap. She was a treasure indeed and he had to find ways of ensuring her continued presence at the Manor.

He cornered her upstairs in one of the children's bedrooms.

'Eliza, my dear. Have you heard from Barnabas yet?'

'No, I have not.'

'You know that I have instructed the mailman to redirect your letters here?'

'That is very kind of you, Austol,' replied Eliza, trying to keep the exchange as formal as possible. But Austol was having none of that.

'Surely you should have heard from him by now? How can he leave you and your family for so long without news?' He moved towards her and before she realised what was happening he had placed an arm round her shoulders. Ostensibly kind, it felt like an iron band.

'Be sure, Eliza, that you will always have shelter here at the Manor,' he said. His words were like ointment covering a wound. This was too much. Panic stricken, she looked up at him. Those stony eyes gleamed with something else, something proprietary, something possessive. He was close enough for her to smell the smoke of his cigar on his breath and the eau de cologne on his skin. He was too near her, too familiar.

'Austol, please!' She tried to move further away from him.

'My dear – we are family! Why else do you think I invited you all here! There is no need to treat me like your master. That would offend me!' Eliza ducked out from under his arm and stepped backwards, ready to flee. But Austol just laughed and turned to go. 'Time to return to your duties, Eliza.'

He left Eliza feeling awkward as if she had read more into his actions than had been intended.

'Mistress Eliza, at last I have tracked you down. I have been hoping to speak to you.' It was Edgar who had found her, exhausted and worried, sitting in the conservatory behind a large fronded plant. He parted the leaves and peeked through at her, making her laugh.

'Why so serious?' he asked, sitting down beside her in a cane chair. The temptation to confide in Edgar was overwhelming. He had not intruded on her since her arrival at the Manor and the only time she really saw him was at mealtimes, when Austol dominated any conversation. Not that there was much, as he was using the time to train his girls in the finer points of table etiquette, a process followed with interest by Nathaniel and Caroline but with boredom on the part of the others. Joel was exhibiting signs of outright rebellion and in this he was joined by Uncle Tobias who would have dearly liked to turn the conversation to mining.

'Well, yes.' It all tumbled out. 'He treats my children as if they are his. No doubt he feels justified since he has offered us a place to live but they resent it. And so do I. But that is not the real problem – ' she hesitated.

'I think I can guess,' said Edgar, soberly. 'I have seen the way he looks at you. I worry that he has further plans for you! And I do not want to alarm you but he usually gets what he wants!'

'What can I do?'

'You will have to decide that. I really cannot advise you.'

'I shall have to go back to Carnglaze!' said Eliza, in despair. 'I would rather be harassed by spirits than someone like Austol. I appreciate the kindness he has shown us but I cannot fill the role that he seems to have planned for me!'

'He believes that Barnabas is not coming back,' said Edgar, bluntly. 'And he plans for you to take the place of Eulalia.' There was no doubting the bitterness that had crept into his tone.

'Oh no! That will never happen. I have been carrying out duties as a housekeeper with great willingness and would help with the education of his younger daughters but that is all! I promise that I have never given him cause to think otherwise!'

'You will have to be careful how you break the news to him that you are leaving. He will not be pleased!'

'I shall suggest that perhaps some of the children are ready for school and I shall not be needed. Then he could employ a proper housekeeper now that I have the Manor running smoothly.'
Edgar held up his hands as if in defeat. The worried frown did not leave his face.

'I suppose you can try. But there are flaws in your reasoning. What about Tobias? And the children? They have their own rooms, a playroom and space! And they are safe. How will they react to returning to Carnglaze? And how will he treat Grace if her sister is not cooperative? Tell me that!'

Days passed and, to her relief, Austol left Eliza alone. She noted how her children and Uncle Tobias seemed so much happier and she began to feel that she was making a fuss about nothing. Then Grace came back. Accompanied by Nanny Hannah, Elestren toddling beside her, a pretty child with the same hair of spun gold as her mother, Grace swept into the hall. She looked superb. Her travelling costume was of a subtle pale green with fur trim and a matching hat swathed in veiling. Her sharp eyes missed nothing, not the flower filled hall, not the gleam of polish, not the sparkling mirrors. And who had wrought this change in the previously rather shabby appearance of the Manor? None other than her sister as she realised when Eliza appeared to show her into the reception room.

'Eliza! What on earth are you doing here? And dressed like that!'

'It is a long story,' sighed Eliza. 'But it is good to see you, Grace. You look wonderful and Aunt Gloria wrote to say how much better you were.'

'I should like to go up to our rooms and start unpacking. Please tell Austol we have arrived.' Grace marched off, trailed by Nanny Hannah and Elestren. Eliza went to find Edgar to pass on the news of Grace's arrival; this way she would avoid Austol. But she was not to escape so lightly. Edgar seemed to have vanished somewhere.

Later that evening Austol requested her presence in his study, a request she saw no way of refusing. She found him at ease in his favourite chair, brandy at his side on the table and a large cigar clamped firmly between his teeth.

'Please sit down, Eliza.'

She did as she was told and waited patiently for Austol to tell her what he wanted.

'I have heard,' he said, 'That you were thinking about returning to Carnglaze?' Eliza gasped. So someone had been tattling. Edgar perhaps? Austol observed the wave of colour that suffused her face and knew that he had his victim at a disadvantage.

'Austol, I feel that I have kept my side of the bargain, Eliza began, shakily. 'The Manor is running smoothly and you do not need me and all my brood here. You have been more than kind to put up with us for so long and we shall never forget it.' Austol appeared to consider, stroking his whiskers and puffing on his cigar. Then he came to a decision.

'I have to admit I am rather disappointed,' he said. 'However I do see that unwittingly I have put you into an awkward position. You are quite correct – the Manor is now well organised and I could hire a housekeeper to follow in your footsteps. But, dear Eliza, I worry about you and your children – and your Uncle Tobias. It may be seen as an act of defiance to return to Carnglaze and your 'spirits' may well take exception.'

'I did not think that you believed in our 'spirits' so wholeheartedly,' said Eliza, again taken by surprise. Sometimes it was difficult to fathom Austol.

'It would be foolish not to take account of such things here in Cornwall,' he smiled. 'Now, I do not wish to stand in your way. Of course you must return to Carnglaze if that is your wish. But please leave Uncle Tobias here. He is recovering so well from his time there that his cough is almost gone.'

'That is very thoughtful of you.'

'Perhaps some of the children would like to remain as they are happy here – and now Grace is back, young Richard will need some company. My girls are too old for him.'

Eliza was torn. What a relief it would be to know that her children were not in any danger and, furthermore, living in a comfortable house. But the thought of losing even one of them was bitter.

'I thank you, Austol, for your kindness. 'I need to think about this – and meanwhile I shall go and talk to Grace.' He watched her leave with an amiable smile, which vanished as soon as the door shut. He rubbed his hands together. He had no doubt that another frightening episode at Carnglaze would have Eliza scuttling back to the Manor.

Grace was unconcerned about Eliza's predicament. 'It is probably not a good idea for you, Eliza, to stay here,' she said. 'Morwenna tells me that there is gossip that you are setting your cap at Austol.' The blatant unfairness of this attack struck Eliza speechless. It also added to her determination to leave as soon as possible. Winter was nearly over and the spring would make time at Carnglaze easier. First of all she would have to visit Cubert Petherwin, the solicitor in Truro. If Barnabas did not return she needed to know her position. More urgently she needed to know if she could pay Austol for looking after her children now that she would no longer be employed by him.

'He won't let you pay,' said Edgar, when he heard her plan. 'He wants your gratitude. He wants you to be dependent on him.' Words which alarmed Eliza yet again. Then he added:

'I shall drive you back to Carnglaze and, if it is agreeable to you, I shall stay for a few days until we are sure that all is quiet.'
Eliza was about to protest but Edgar held up his hand.

'Don't worry, Eliza. Uncle Tobias will be coming back with us. He insisted that you were not to be left alone.'

30

Back at Carnglaze, Eliza had expected to feel unwelcome as she led the way through the door but the house seemed to be holding its breath, waiting for them, uncertain how to respond to this renewed invasion of unwelcome guests. She herself found it strange to be there without the usual bustle of children. She missed them already. Perhaps Ewella and Jael would soon return from Liskeard, and normal life could resume. What would they say, however, when they found that she and Edgar were there.....! Uncle Tobias was a comforting third of course but if Morwenna found out she would never let a little detail like that spoil a good story. Edgar broke into her thoughts by saying that he would light the kitchen range and put the kettle on. Perhaps she would like to light the fire in the other room and make Uncle Tobias comfortable? Hardly had they done so when there was a knock at the door. It was Mathey to Eliza's delight. He and Jed had been staying at Tull Farm and Mathey reported that Trembles was in good spirits and longing to be exercised. Edgar made a hot drink as they sat round the kitchen table and chatted, in a way that would have scandalised Ewella. The night was uneventful. No disturbances. Uncle Tobias was snug by the fire declaring bravely that he was more comfortable than at the Manor. Edgar seemed to be happier away from the Manor and his formidable brother-in-law and announced that he was determined to stay for several days until he was sure that Eliza was settled and unthreatened. A brief tour of the downstairs cupboards revealed them to be empty so he offered to go foraging for supplies.

In the morning, after Edgar had left, Eliza decided that hard work was the best way to prevent her thoughts from turning to the absence of her children - or the presence of ghosts. She tied her hair up, donned a calico apron and prepared to scrub the floor. On her knees, half way across the floor, there was a peremptory knock. Her caller did not wait for an answer but pushed open the door.

'S - Seth!' stuttered Eliza. Indeed it was Seth. There he stood, handsome, well dressed in a fine wool coat with a frill of lace on his shirt and, as usual, his black hair flopping over his forehead. Eliza was aware of his intense dark eyes but missed the fleeting touch of apprehension in his expression. She just had time to regret that he had caught her again in work attire, her hands red from scrubbing. But then hurt surfaced and her greeting was cold.

'We have not seen you for some time, Mr. Quinn,' she said.

'I came last week but the house was empty and I was told that you had moved to the Manor. And now you are back here. Perhaps common sense prevailed?'

Scowling, Eliza prepared tea for them both. How dare he criticise what she did! It did not concern him. She had not forgiven him for his hasty departure after their experiences on the path. She had felt so abandoned and she resented the sarcastic inflexion in his tone.

'There were reasons why we moved,' she said. 'Good reasons! And you? Have you been on some long holiday with Rose?'

'Yes.' The one word dropped like a stone into a pool. Eliza spun round from the range.

'And now you expect a welcome here? From me?'

'No. I know you too well, Eliza.' The pretence of formality was abandoned. 'But I do expect you to give me a chance to explain.'

It was an echo from her past. Barnabas, too, had asked for time to explain. And she had refused him. Now Seth. Another man who had cared for her and had never let her down before. She would not make the same mistake twice.

'Explain if you wish,' she said.

'Rose felt neglected that I spent so much time away from Penzance. Not just visiting you. I have been reconnoitring a number of mines in the area with a view to purchase. This has involved many visits to present and erstwhile mine owners and, I admit, has been time consuming. After my last visit to Carnglaze I returned to the Galleon to find her in a state of collapse. Nothing else would suffice but that I take her away at once to Scotland to visit a great Aunt, her last surviving relative - a disastrous idea as it happened because the old lady died two days after we arrived. And we had to attend the funeral.'

'Oh, poor Rose!' cried Eliza, jolted out of her accusatory mood. 'Seth, I feel I must see her. If she is well enough to travel to Scotland, surely you could bring her to Carnglaze to see me?'

At last Seth could relax. 'I'm sure she would be delighted!' They sat smiling at each other and the hastily erected barricades between them were swept aside. She allowed him to cover her hands with his. He stroked them and exclaimed over the redness and roughness and it did not seem to matter. They were in a bubble of sudden happiness, all the more welcome for previous misunderstandings. He leaned forward and loosened her hair then pulled her to her feet and untied the calico apron. She found she was standing close to him, so close she could feel the warmth emanating from his body and all thoughts, worries, and sadness were as nothing, engulfed by need, the need to be held by him. She allowed herself to nestle in to him, pliant and yielding; she heard his breathing quicken and felt his heart beat against her breast. Then he kissed her.

Hoof-beats outside and they drew apart, both flushed. It was Edgar bearing supplies of vegetables, eggs and a chicken from Farmer Tull. He was not pleased to find Seth being entertained by Eliza but his annoyance was superseded by Seth's poorly hidden rage.

'You are STAYING here?' he demanded.

'I am here until I know that Mistress Eliza is comfortable and settled,' said Edgar, an edge of defiance in his voice.

'Seth is here to arrange a visit with Rose,' said Eliza hastily. The tension was broken by Uncle Tobias hobbling in to find out who the visitors were.

'Seth, my boy!' he greeted him with pleasure. 'How good to see you. And how is Rose?' The conversation took on a lighter tone.

'There's someone else coming!' exclaimed Edgar. This time it was a surprise visit from Professor Martineau, who came in red faced with excitement and waving a sheaf of papers.

'My dear Mistress Eliza! I have struck gold at last!'

'Gold?' cried Edgar. 'Real gold? In a mine?'

'No, no, my dear sir. It is a metaphor! I have uncovered some interesting information in my researches!' Seth looked intrigued and abandoned his intention to leave.

'It seems that Carnglaze used to be the house of one Samuel Hooper, a famous smuggler,' the Professor began. 'In fact it was the centre of smuggling activity in this area for many years. Contraband was landed on the shore, loaded on ponies and transported up that path by the stream, to be hidden somewhere in this house or nearby.'

'How could they possibly do that?' interrupted Eliza. 'The path is so narrow!'

'It must have been wider then, I suppose, and has only more recently been overgrown with vegetation and blocked with rockfalls. It is a very well hidden path and only local people would have known about it. Also Carnglaze itself was reputed to be haunted even at that time so the locals also shunned the area.. Thus it was a safe route for the smugglers from the beach.' He beamed at Eliza, pleased with his findings. 'Well, to continue. Hooper was suspected by the Preventive Officers of being the ringleader but was never caught. Not, that is, until his wife betrayed him. A trap was set and several of his men were found with goods in their possession and imprisoned. But Hooper managed to give the Preventive Men the slip. He was only apprehended when he returned some weeks later, bold as brass, to collect kegs of brandy from Carnglaze. He might have escaped even then but he took time to strangle his wife – and the delay allowed the Preventive Men to catch up with him. He was duly hanged at Penzance Prison.'

Eliza shivered. 'A dreadful story. She must have hated her husband to betray him like that.'

'The story fits the haunting here!' exclaimed Seth. 'Samuel Hooper must be the one who says 'Mine' all the time. It was his house. And the men are angry because they, too, were betrayed.' Eliza hid her surprise. So Seth HAD heard the voices and his denials must have been to comfort her.

'They were left to languish in prison,' said the Professor. 'Their sentences were all the more severe because there had been instances of deliberate wrecking, which were never proved to have been instigated by Hooper's men but nevertheless they were suspect. Now Cornish men are not averse to collecting goods from the shore when ships are washed on to the beach or trapped on rocks by a storm, but deliberate wrecking died out many years before the time of Hooper and his smuggling friends and any suspicion that they had been involved would have antagonized the whole community.'

'Do you think they WERE involved in wrecking?' asked Eliza.

The Professor hesitated.

'I rather doubt it. There was no proof. In any case, those rocks out there, waiting like beasts with teeth, only need stormy weather to deliver their victims. No need for any lights or nonsense like that.'

'Do you know anything else about Samuel Hooper's wife? Why she betrayed him?'

'No. It could have been that they quarrelled. But I think it would take more than that for a wife to betray her husband – and cut off her source of income.'

'Perhaps she was bribed. Or fell in love with one of the Preventive Men,' suggested Eliza.

'We just do not know.'

It was late afternoon. Seth had taken himself off, citing a need to return to Rose and avoiding Eliza's gaze as he left. She was not angry. She now knew without doubt how he felt and hugged to herself the memory of those few moments they had had. Seth was an honourable man and would not leave Rose alone and she respected him for it. Her own part in this unfortunate relationship she did not care to scrutinise. Barnabas was not there and she had been a wife without a husband for a long time. A specious argument she well knew.

Uncle Tobias was back by his fire and Edgar was restless There was something about the atmosphere in the house that set his nerves on edge. Help came in the guise of Nathaniel and Caroline returning from the Manor with one of Austol's drivers.

'We missed you so much, Mama!' said Caroline.

Edgar took the chance to return to the Manor as Eliza was no longer alone. The twins were pleased to be back at Carnglaze. Nathaniel was scornful because none of Austol's girls could read as well as he could and provided no opposition when playing chess. Furthermore, they apparently showed little spirit and were appalled at some of Joel's antics which also earned rebukes from Edgar and Ewella, neither of whom were used to rebellious small boys.

'Caroline is more fun than the whole pack of them,' Nathaniel said. Caroline's face briefly registered some complacency at this.

'I do miss the others,' she said, rather wistfully.' 'I like having more space but I would rather they were here with us – even John!'

The next morning, Nathaniel came rushing in to report that Trembles did not seem well and was off his food. When Eliza went to see him, she found the little pony standing miserably in the corner of the barn, his head drooping.

'I don't know what can be the matter,' she said, blankly. 'Jael would minister to him if she were here. Perhaps we should wait until tomorrow and see how he is?'

'If anything happens to Trembles, Caroline will never forgive us,' stated Nathaniel. 'I'll fetch Mathey and see what he thinks. We may need the animal doctor.' Some hours later, Mathey put in an appearance. He looked grave as he examined Trembles.

'He dun't look good,' he admitted. 'He were all right yest'day, though.' It was clear he had no idea what was wrong and it seemed that they would have to resort to the animal doctor.

'I'll fetch him, Mama,' said Nathaniel eagerly. 'He lives on the other side of Rosmorren – '

'Out of the question!' said Eliza. 'It is too far for you to go. You would have to walk all the way and it is more than twenty miles. Besides it will be dark before you get there. No, we shall have to wait patiently until tomorrow and decide then.'

However, when it came to suppertime, Nathaniel did not appear. He had taken matters into his own hands.

Eliza, Uncle Tobias and Caroline shared a silent supper, all three now worried about Nathaniel as well as Trembles. Then Eliza crept out to the barn and was horrified to find Trembles sweating and restless. She did not know what to do for the best but resolved to spend the night in the barn with the little pony. She covered him with a blanket and spoke to him soothingly which seemed to help. Swathed in her warmest shawl in addition to another blanket, she settled down on some straw for her vigil. Her oil lamp burned strongly giving out a comforting light. But soon, against her will, her eyelids drooped and she fell into a heavy sleep. It was the cold creeping round her, deadening the feeling in her hands and feet, breathing ice on her face, which startled her into wakefulness. The oil lamp had gone out, taking with it the last vestiges of warmth and comfort. Surely this was no ordinary cold; it surrounded her with such menace that she felt rigid with terror, not daring to move. She had sensed such cold before – on the path to the sea, and in the house. The spirits were there, gathered round. She could not cry out. In any case, how could Uncle Tobias, a frail old man, help her? Then the whispering began. No loud individual voices but those undertones of anger which were just as frightening. Then, suddenly, a single voice, deep and filled with rage.

'You shall not escape me. Betrayer! This house is mine!'
Oh, where was Barnabas when she needed him? She could hear Trembles shifting restlessly and stamping his hooves on the straw. Perhaps he, too, could feel this dreadful cold? Hear the whispers? Hear that threatening voice? She would see that the poor creature was tended as soon as day came.

'Mama? Where are you?' Nathaniel's voice reached her at the same time as she became aware of encroaching daylight. It released her from her immobility and she scrambled to a sitting position, calling out for her son.

'Mama, I have Mr. Henry Pauncefoot with me! He brought me back on his horse! He says he knows you and has come to help!' Eliza could not stop smiling. Of course she knew Henry Pauncefoot. She would never forget him, the man who had helped her give birth to Joel and saved both their lives. And there he was, older and more grizzled, but still Henry with his big hands and his big smile.

'Seems Trembles d'ave the colic,' was Henry's conclusion after his examination of the little pony. He went on to dose Trembles with strong smelling liquid and recommend that he be taken on regular but gentle exercise. After he had joined them for breakfast and chatted to Uncle Tobias, he left again on his big horse, clopping down the track in leisurely fashion, but promising to call again if needed.

'Oh Nathaniel, you arrived in the nick of time!' cried Eliza. 'And Mr. Pauncefoot said how brave you were to walk all the way to Rosmorren.'

'It was easy. All I had to do when I reached the road was to follow it. But I was lucky to find him there,' said Nathaniel.

31

Jael returned from Liskeard, happy with her success at a local fair and happy to be back with Eliza and Uncle Tobias. She found Nathaniel feeding Trembles his medicine and had to listen to all that had happened since she had been away. Hearing their excited voices, Uncle Tobias emerged from his cubby hole like a tortoise from hibernation and joined Eliza and Jael at the kitchen table for tea and heavy cake.

'I never expected to say this,' he admitted. 'But I do miss the rest of the family. I should like them all back at Carnglaze – even that Ewella.' Eliza smiled at him. Trust Uncle Tobias to give voice to her own feelings. She would have to find a way of extracting her family from the Manor even if this move would be unpopular with several people – not least her own children. But there she miscalculated. On her next visit to the Manor, escorted by Edgar, she found that John, Nessa and Joel were actually anxious to come back to Carnglaze. Why, she could not ascertain. She tried to find out from Edgar but came up against a blank wall. The children were unusually reticent and Ewella, of course, had withdrawn from danger, like a hermit crab into its shell. She intended to go visiting to Liskeard, a fine escape from family problems. Only Austol was his usual self, complacent, and behaving as if Eliza was a close friend, with a bonhomie that grated. Most annoying of all, he had that look his eye when he spoke to her as if they shared some special bond. And he had a habit of placing a casual arm around her shoulders and looking surprised and hurt when she moved away.

'He has been very kind to my family,' she confided to Edgar, 'But he presumes a relationship with me that we do not have.'

'You need to be aware that Austol is a very determined man,' said Edgar, thoughtfully. 'In your place I should take my family home to Carnglaze. That is, supposing the - ah - spiritual activity in your house is quiet at the moment?'

'Yes it is,' lied Eliza. She suspected the spirits were always there, gathered round the house, but not always obtrusive.

Austol was displeased when he heard that Eliza wanted to take her children back to Carnglaze. But as he presided over the tea table, his profile stern and ever more hawk-like, Eliza felt that she had made a wise decision. This man had no softness, no real warmth in his nature. Good deeds and apparent kindnesses were ways of attaining what he wanted, though Eliza had no clear idea what that was. Her children in residence at the Manor ensured her frequent visits and her gratitude, but then she had helped him, had she not? He had no right to demand more of her and to make her feel under such obligation. Grace was another matter. Her decisions were hers alone and nothing to do with Eliza. She had made it clear on several occasions that she did not want to live at Carnglaze and was determined to remain in cushioned comfort at the Manor. Austol did not protest. Perhaps she was paying her way, Eliza thought with unusual cynicism. In any case, the Manor was large enough for contact to be a matter of choice.

Edgar drove them all home in the larger carriage which, of course, could not negotiate the track so the last part of the journey was on foot They set off, waving goodbye to Edgar, but found it an uncomfortable trek as rain began to fall, gently at first, then with increasing intensity. No one grumbled, however, and they raised a cheer when they reached the gate of Carnglaze.

'I did not think I would be glad to see this ruin again,' said John. 'But I prefer it to the Manor. All those girls! Ugh!'

'Mama, I am looking forward to seeing Caroline and Nathaniel,' piped up Nessa. 'And I do not ever want to live anywhere away from you.' Eliza smiled at her daughter. Wet through though she was, her ringlets like tangled string down her back, she could still find the positive in their mixed up back and forth lives.

'I shall see that the kettle is on and check the fire!' said Eliza but Jael had been busy and already the kitchen was warm, the kettle singing on the range. Uncle Tobias was sitting by the fire and showed his delight when they all struggled in from the rain.

'I can't believe that we are all here again,' said Eliza. 'It will be very crowded after all the space you had at the Manor.'

'We like it better here!' crowed Joel. 'No Austol to grumble at us and no silly girls.'

'Now then, young man,' reproved Eliza with insincere conviction. 'He has been good to you all, do not forget that.'

John had his nose pressed against the window. 'You can't see much because of the rain,' he reported. 'But those trees are not showing any new leaves. I thought it was spring.'

'There are primroses on the Morvah Road,' offered Nessa.

Nathaniel joined his brother at the window.

'Black trees with black thorns,' he said thoughtfully. 'Perhaps they are late because the sun does not reach this valley so easily.'

'Black is the right colour for this place.' Eliza thought.

As the day passed and the rain increased in intensity, battering at the windows, the happy atmosphere in the kitchen gradually leached away. Uncle Tobias was the first to retreat to his 'study', Caroline and Nathaniel splashed to the little barn to feed Trembles his second dose of medicine but agreed that any outdoor exercise for him was out of the question. The day grew darker, the temperature dropping, and Eliza began to grow uneasy. It was one thing to dismiss the spirits in the sunlight, quite another when the light was fast disappearing. It was then that Jael made a discovery.

'We are nearly out of oil for the oil lamps,' she announced. 'We had better not use them until we can get some more.' So supper was taken in the flickering light of candles, light which did not reach the corners of the kitchen where darkness lurked. Eliza noticed that Caroline was looking particularly nervous, looking over her shoulder towards the door. Jael had fallen silent and was deep in thought. The uneasy atmosphere was broken by a shout from John.

'Look! Under the door!' They all looked. Water was seeping in, gently but purposefully creeping across the kitchen floor, hesitating, then joining with a stronger surge from under the sitting room door. They all sat, paralysed by the sudden invasion.

'The stream has flooded! The stream has flooded!' shouted John and Eliza, riveted in her chair, saw the shadows cast by the candles were dancing in macabre glee.

The night hours passed in damp discomfort. The water was swishing through the ground floor but did not yet threaten to become dangerously deep. Eliza and Nathaniel took turns at keeping watch from the top of the stairs. Jael reported that the water was not flooding the courtyard to any depth and she and Trembles were safe in their respective barns.

'It's like there is a stream flowing through our house,' said John, puzzled.

'The main stream must have overflowed and we are in the path of a secondary tributary,' pronounced Nathaniel. 'When we picked herbs for Jael by the standing stone there was a sort of dent in the ground – like water used to flow there.'

'Like the dried bed of another stream,' concurred Caroline. 'Not very deep but that would explain the water running through our house when the main stream floods.'

Eliza had a flash of longing for Roscarne, high and dry on the cliff.

'That seems a very reasonable explanation,' she said. 'And maybe it will dry up soon when the rain stops.' She made a great effort to sound calm and encouraging but inside she was angry. The Lanivet brothers had not warned them that this could happen. Barnabas had consigned his family to a house that was not only haunted but prone to flooding. And what part did the spirits play in all this? Was this another frightening incident intended to oust them from Carnglaze? First poor Trembles and now an invading stream. What else could go wrong?

A gloomy dawn heralded another gloomy day. The atmosphere in the house was dank and the swirling water made the ground floor untenable. They all huddled upstairs without the warmth of a fire and no food for breakfast. Eliza made them all wrap themselves in their blankets and assured them with a confidence she did not feel that the water would go down soon and they would return to normal. But the hours passed and the water lapped at the lower stairs, showing no signs of retreating. It was Nathaniel who first lost patience and exhibited some of the fighting spirit that had been so evident in his father.

'I'm going to fetch help,' he announced. 'We can't go on like this.' He wrapped himself in his cape and splashed down into the flooded kitchen. Tea brown water swirled about his legs up to his knees, but he ignored it and struggled to the door. Through the upstairs window, the children watched him striding down the track, kicking the water aside with determination.

'He will never get through to the road. The bridge will be dangerous or it may be down already!' exclaimed Eliza. 'But I do see that my son is growing up!'

'Brave of him to try,' croaked Uncle Tobias. Nathaniel disappeared from sight as a new burst of rain curtained the window. Of

Jael there was no sign. Eliza persuaded the children to take to their beds to keep warm and wrapped up Uncle Tobias in her own blanket where he coughed piteously. There was nothing else they could do but wait. Gradually the day grew darker and still the rain fell. Poor Nathaniel would be soaked to the skin, Eliza thought but she was proud of his initiative and filed it away in her mind to tell Barnabas. When he came back.

It was still light enough to see that the water level was rising, stealthily and slowly. A gloomy Eliza sat on the top step, her chin on her hands, feeling the deep depression of failure. She had failed Barnabas when he needed her; she had failed Rose by allowing her feelings for Seth to take over; she had failed her children who were just then sleeping in a haunted, flooding house; she should have insisted that Uncle Tobias stay at the Manor as his cough had come back and he was looking increasingly frail. Then her son was making a heroic journey through beating rain to fetch help. And what was she herself doing? Nothing. Sitting and watching. She jumped up. She would forage for food in the kitchen. Surely there would be something left in the cupboards even though Jael had declared there was nothing. Paddling through the floodwater, ignoring the currents which shackled her legs in shocking cold, she splashed into the kitchen. But Jael was right. The cupboard was bare apart from two saffron buns, heavy with mould and inedible.

Then the whispering began. She could not believe it. Surely there was enough to contend with already.
'Go away!' she snapped. 'This house is unpleasant enough without you. We are doing you no harm!'
'Mine!' said a deep voice, so close she almost fainted with fear. 'This house is mine!'
'His house!' whispered the devilish chorus. 'Leave - leave - '
'Betrayer!' whispered another accusing voice.
'Danger - danger - danger……..' a tumult of threatening voices broke out, increasing in volume till Eliza felt she was being physically assaulted. This was too much. To be assailed by an intemperate, undisciplined stream, to suffer cold and hunger, and now to be threatened by a ghostly throng was beyond her capacity to bear. She wanted to scream, but was aware it would alarm the children so she huddled into her cape and put her head in her hands. Still the voices

scolded, deep and ugly…. Eliza put her fingers in her ears and tried to shut them out. In the gloom, the shadows no longer danced. They lurked in the corners, slow moving and menacing and beneath them, the water waited, spilled like ink across the flag-stoned floor of Carnglaze.

'Barnabas!' whispered Eliza. The answer, when it came, was unexpected.

'Mistress Trevannion! Mistress Trevannion!' A man's voice. Then Nathaniel.

'Mama! I have brought help. I have Farmer Tull with me – and Jed.'

32

Farmer Tull and Jed in boots and oilskins appeared out of the gloom. Eliza could have hugged them so great was her relief. With big smiles and jokes about the Cornish monsoon they shepherded the children out of Carnglaze with the intention of splashing their way along the track to the bridge and from there to pick up the farm cart on the road. It was clear that Uncle Tobias was going to have a problem with walking and kind Jed said he would carry him.

'Dun't think cart will 'ave room for everyone,' said Farmer Tull, dubiously. 'We s'all 'ave to make two journeys.'

'I'll stay behind,' offered Eliza. 'I want the children and Uncle Tobias to be warmed and fed, soon. We have had a long time marooned in the house.'

'And Trembles! What about Trembles?' shouted Caroline.

'Don't worry. He will be company for me! I shall bring him along, too.' Eliza watched the little party disappear along the track, then went to fetch Trembles from his barn. The poor little pony, weakened by his recent illness, was loth to leave his shelter but Eliza whispered to him and soothed him and eventually he followed her into the courtyard. Then a shocking thought assailed her. Where was Jael? She had not appeared out of her barn.

'Jael! Jael! Where are you?' called Eliza. Surely Jael would have heard all the commotion in the courtyard in spite of the noise of the drenching rain. She waded to Jael's barn and called again. Nothing. Carefully she felt her way inside and, as her eyes became accustomed to the dim interior she could see a figure lying on high piled straw. It was Jael. Her face was waxen and her eyes were shut. She did not stir when Eliza spoke to her.

'Oh Jael, please wake up!' begged Eliza. 'We can go to the farm to get dry and warm!' But Jael did not hear. Eliza was tempted to splash water into her face but felt perhaps there was already too much water about. Jael was breathing but not responsive. Now what was she to do? Had the spirits induced this strange sleep − another of their unkindnesses? But surely they would be glad that the family had been driven out of Carnglaze even if only temporarily. Then help came when she least expected it. A voice. Seth's voice. She must be hallucinating! He always seemed to materialise in times of trouble. He appeared out of the rain, wet but smiling.

'How – why? Why have you come here in this dreadful weather?' she stammered.

'I felt you needed me,' he said, simply. 'I wondered how you would manage cooped up in the house with all the children and the stream possibly flooding so you could not get out.'

'We would have managed! But the stream did flood AND poured through the ground floor of the house so we had no fire and no warm food. And now I can't wake Jael!' There was a note of hysteria in her voice and Seth put his arm round her and pulled her close. Wet through though they both were it was a comforting embrace, an embrace of warmth and kindness and not of passion.

'We shall get Jael to the farm and then try for the doctor,' suggested Seth. 'Whether any doctor will be able to get through before nightfall is doubtful but at least she will be warm.'

'The house will be pleased that we are leaving again,' said Eliza, not altogether lightly.

Farmer Tull and his wife were welcoming and kind to the bedraggled, hungry family from Carnglaze. As they felt the warmth from the blazing fire in the inglenook and recovered their spirits during the next two days, so the rain lessened and, at last, stopped. The clouds rolled away and sky of a washed blue appeared. Farmer Tull reported that the stream was back within its banks and the flood waters retreating and that soon they could return to Carnglaze. Only Jael was unhappy at the prospect. She had recovered consciousness, refused to consider calling a doctor but still was not her usual self.

'I feel we are threatened,' she whispered to Eliza. 'Not just the ghostly activity but something else.' Eliza had a healthy respect for Jael's powers of prediction and her words induced further anxiety. The children, however, were oblivious, delighted to be able to venture outside again, helping the farmer with his chickens and cows. Caroline fed the chickens and Joel, very proudly, herded the cows to be milked with just the aid of a stick. Nessa helped Mrs.Tull to do the baking and Nathaniel and John played war games in the muddy fields.

207

They returned to Carnglaze on a bright spring day and it was difficult to remember how it had been – so wet and gloomy and sullen in atmosphere. Eliza set to and worked with a will to eradicate the traces of the flood but she made Jael and Uncle Tobias sit quietly by the fire. Neither of them had recovered. Uncle Tobias was coughing continuously and Jael still seemed in another world, appearing white faced and fragile. It was not a surprise to Eliza when they had a visitor the very next day. It was Mistress Annie.

'My daughter needs me,' she said abruptly. 'And Mr. Trevannion – that's a nasty cough.'

'I am so pleased to see you,' said Eliza. 'I really don't know what to do for the best.' Mistress Annie looked at her with bright shrewd eyes.

'And you, Mistress Eliza, you are in need of care also. I shall do what I can.' She bustled into the kitchen, muttering that sage and honey would not be strong enough for Tobias and began chopping and grinding and mixing the herbs she had brought. Jael perked up at the appearance of her mother and Caroline followed her into the kitchen to watch what she was doing with great interest. Eventually she produced a blackberry coloured hot drink for Uncle Tobias and a thick white milky potion for Jael, who pulled a face as she drank it.

'Mistress Eliza, what you need I do not have,' Mistress Annie said. 'But I have a calming drink here for you. It is based on camomile. That will help.' Obediently Eliza drank it, wondering what it was that she needed. Barnabas perhaps? A return to Roscarne? Or Seth?

Mistress Annie left, refusing offers of food and shelter and the house returned to normal – as normal as was possible. Uncle Tobias coughed less but Jael still looked wan. Eliza was filled with foreboding. What would happen here in Carnglaze? How long were they doomed to stay, crowded and without comfort? And possibly running out of money! Eliza realised that a trip to see Cubert Petherwin, the solicitor in Truro, was long overdue. When Seth turned up the following week she begged a ride in his pony and trap to Truro.

'That will be fortuitous,' he said gravely. 'I have something to tell you and we shall not be interrupted on the journey.' He would say no more and Eliza was left wondering.

The pony negotiated the muddy track with dainty care and soon they were trotting more easily on the main road in the direction of Truro. It was chilly but fine and Eliza, huddled into her cape, wondered that Seth was so silent.

'It would be more fun if we were going to St. Michael's Mount,' she ventured. Seth nodded but his profile was still set and stern. What could be wrong? Eliza tried again.

'When are you going to bring Rose to see us? Carnglaze is all dried out now.'

'When we have spoken, perhaps you will not wish to see us,' was the response. Eliza was alarmed. It made her voice waspish when she spoke.

'For goodness sake, Seth, enough of this mystery! Pull up and talk straight to me!' He stopped the pony and trap beside a wooden gate and looked at her, despair in his face. Seth, usually so protective, so reliable, looked in need of comfort himself. He tried to speak but could not.

'Seth – tell me!' Now thoroughly alarmed, she put her hand on his shoulder. Without speaking, he covered her hand with his own.

'It's Rose......'

'Is she ill again?'

'Not ill – I thought she was because she was sick all the time. But she is not ill.'

Eliza could have shaken him. She jumped out of the trap and went to lean against the gate.

'Tell me, Seth,' she said quietly.

He joined her by the gate and surprised her by taking her in his arms. Pleased, she rested her head on his shoulder, feeling the warmth of his body, drawing comfort from his closeness. She could hear the beating of his heart but when she looked up, the distress on his face caused her to stand back.

'Eliza – Rose is carrying another child.'

Again Eliza's world collapsed. This could not happen, could not possibly happen again. The man she loved – and she had to admit to herself that she loved him – had betrayed her. Even though she knew her reaction was unreasonable she was stunned. Yes, he was married to Rose. Yes, she had lost her first child. But then they had come back from Arizona and Eliza had cherished the hope that somehow she and

Seth could be together. A childish hope as she now recognised. She loved Seth, but Rose was his wife and what could be more natural than that she would bear him another child?

'Eliza....?'

'I am pleased for you both,' she said tonelessly.

'Don't pretend! When there is real love'... his voice stumbled. 'Words are not necessary. You know how I feel and I know you feel the same way. But Rose has been distraught since she lost her first child and even though the doctor said she would not be able to conceive again she has never lost hope. And now she is sick – she has been so sick – but she is delighted all the same.'

'Rose is my very dear friend. I am glad for her,' said Eliza, managing to steady her voice. 'You must look after her. And I am glad that circumstances have prevented me from doing her harm. Please bring her over to see us very soon.'

The rest of the journey was completed in silence. Each of them had their own thoughts tumbling through their minds as they tried not to recognise the impasse they faced. Seth waited outside the solicitor, so morose of face that two girls, attracted by his dark good looks, decided not to stop and scurried by. When Eliza emerged from her meeting with Cubert Petherwin, Seth was encouraged to see that she looked more cheerful.

'I actually have some money left,' she said briefly. 'Mr. Petherwin thinks it will last about three months. What happens after that I do not know. Now – I need to patronise a dress shop. My best dress is in rags and that will not do.'

'Why...?'

'I may need to seek employment.'

Seth was reduced to astonished silence. She directed him to a shop with the name 'Miss Hetty' in ornamental writing over the door. There was one dress only in the window, elegant and very expensive. Unbelieving, Seth watched her enter the shop, her head held high. Half an hour later she emerged, carrying a white, gold ribboned box.

'Now I need sweetmeats for the children.'

The pony and trap rattled along the track and over the bridge. Carnglaze hove into view, dour and unwelcoming as usual.

'At least I know where I am with that house,' Eliza thought, with a wry grin. 'Not like the men in my life!' She had withdrawn from Seth and he might have been any driver, not one who meant so much to her. Seth himself was hunched over the reins and deep in thought. As they arrived, clattering over the cobbles, Eliza was startled to see a horse tethered at the front door. Edgar perhaps?

Seth scowled at the sight. He had no time for Edgar and his dislike was made worse because he realised that he had no right to resent Edgar's visits. He helped Eliza out of the trap but refused to stay for refreshment before his trip back to Penzance. In any case, the offer had been half hearted. There was no doubt that Eliza wanted no more of him.

'Please bring Rose to see us all as soon as possible,' said Eliza. Her voice sounded like ice clinking in a glass. Seth inclined his head. As he drove off, he was unaware that she gazed after him, all the hurt she had hidden from him in her eyes.

Wearily she pushed open the heavy door. Who was visiting? It was not Edgar. It was Ewella and a strange man.

'Ewella! I'm so glad to see you.' Impulsively she hugged her sister-in-law. Caught by surprise, Ewella could not hide a pleased smile.

'Eliza, may I introduce a cousin of mine?'

'Mistress Trevannion – I am Jasper Trevannion at your service.' He sketched a little bow. 'I am afraid I have had to beg your man – Mathey, I believe, to repair the wheel of the trap. We went over one pothole too many. When it is done I must take my leave. I do not like the idea of negotiating the track in the dark!'

'It was very kind of you to bring Ewella back to us,' said Eliza. 'We have missed her.'

33

It was **a** week later when Seth brought Rose for her visit to Carnglaze. His face was stern as he handed her down from the trap but Rose was all excited smiles. She threw herself into Eliza's arms and cried out with the pleasure of seeing them all.

'I am so happy for you, Rose,' said Eliza, warmly and sincerely. This was her good friend from Roscarne days and she was genuinely pleased that at last Rose was happy after all the tribulations she had endured. Her own disappointment she pushed to the back of her mind and set herself to making both Seth and Rose welcome. Uncle Tobias was delighted to meet Seth again, hoping to extract the latest news of the mining industry and Seth himself seemed relieved to chat on a subject dear to both of them. The children clustered round Rose asking her questions about her time in Arizona, while Ewella clattered pots and pans in the kitchen. Only Jael remained quiet, her face still and white, her eyes shadowed. She had watched in approval as Eliza put her own feelings to one side when greeting Rose but then relapsed into her own world again, a world that was providing her with worries and fears and strange premonitions. Outside the wind was rising and the trees were restless.

Ewella at last emerged from the kitchen with plates of ginger biscuits and saffron buns and bridled in pleasure as everyone exclaimed in delight. Eliza was able to scrutinise Rose at leisure as she talked to the children and what she saw did not please her. Rose's face was like parchment and her bones too prominent for a young woman. Her dress, though of a lustrous silken beauty, hung loosely on her and Eliza was frightened to see her hands were like claws. She drew Seth aside.

'Seth, I know Rose has been sick for weeks and that is why she is so thin. But she does not look at all well. Has she seen a doctor since you returned from Arizona?'

'No. She has refused. She says the last doctor told her that she should not have another child and she is frightened that a doctor here will say the same thing. But she is obsessed. Have another child she must and I fear for her mental stability if something happens to stop her.

It is already a miracle to her that she has conceived!' The worry on
Seth's face gave Eliza some inkling of what he had suffered himself.
There was probably guilt because he had not really wanted to marry
Rose; his marriage had been an escape from his unacceptable feelings
for Eliza. Then there was the sadness of loss and the efforts to assuage
their sorrow by returning to Cornwall. Then guilt again - a second child
on the way and yet the shocking revival of his love for Eliza, this
woman who was not his wife. However, Eliza knew that she wanted to
help both of them – to help Rose regain her strength, to erase the lines
of worry from Seth's brow and to minimise her own impact on their
lives. Seth would have to find a house for Rose and himself. Of course
it should be one near enough for her to visit – firmly she ignored the
protests of her uneasy conscience. Naturally she wanted to help her
friend, it was not just that she wanted to be nearer Seth.
Outside the wind began to moan and mutter round the house.

'Please tell me that Barnabas is to return soon,' said Rose
eagerly. 'Then you can all go back to Roscarne and it will be much
nearer for me to visit.'

'I wish I knew,' said Eliza. 'But we have not heard for a while.'
Her voice was bleak.

The window banged open suddenly and a cold draught swept through
the room. Eliza could see that the tops of the thorn trees were bending
and swaying in a weird witches' dance. Within the stone walls of
Carnglaze no one had been aware of the deteriorating weather.

'I think it would be prudent to leave quite soon or the drive will
be difficult,' said Seth. 'My new mare is easily spooked.' Nathaniel
opened the front door to look outside but it was snatched from his hand
and blown against the wall with a crash. Behind the noise of the wind
could be heard a strange roaring emanating from beyond the trees.

'The sea!' said Nathaniel. 'It must be the sea!'

'If we can hear it, the waves must be huge!' said John,
excitedly. 'Wish we were at Roscarne! There we could see them
crashing on the rocks and feel the spray in the air.'

Seth marched outside but came back hurriedly.

'Out of the question!' he said. 'We can't go back now.'

'The wind will probably die down as quickly as it began,' said
Rose, glad that there was a chance of staying longer with her friend.

'Shall I take your horse to one of the barns?' offered Caroline, ever protective of animals. 'I have to go out as I want to check that Trembles is not frightened.'

'I'll come too,' said Seth. 'And you can show me where to tether her.' Ewella decided to make hot drinks for everyone. She declared that the sound of the wind made her feel even colder.

The light faded slowly. The wind howled and screeched ever louder and became impossible to ignore even inside. The children looked nervously at each other. Eliza and Rose were chatting quietly and Uncle Tobias and Seth were playing chess. But Jael was unsettled and restless. She began muttering to no one in particular, wandering about the room, her face set and pale.

'Listen to the howl of witches riding on the wind,' she declaimed, after a particularly vicious gust. Eliza glanced at her in reproof. Jael looked back at her and her eyes were no longer grey but black as obsidian. 'Now hear the waves rise, they dance with the wind!' she went on, her voice rising in a wailing cadence. 'And hear the feet – hear the feet that tread heavy on the sand. See the broken come ashore.' A silence fell as everyone looked at her. She did not seem to notice. 'Death in the sea! Death on the land! Death waiting!' This was too much for Nessa who uttered a squeak of fright. That reached Jael. She looked round, bewildered, as if she did not know where she was.

'I'm sorry,' she said tonelessly. 'I shall go and lie down.' Before anyone could stop her she pulled the door open, braving the blast of the storm, and disappeared in the direction of her barn.

'Don't worry, Nessa. Jael is in one of her strange moods,' said Eliza, brightly, putting her arm around her daughter. She would not allow her own concern to show.

The door crashed open again and Seth and Caroline returned.

'What is the matter with Jael?' asked Caroline. 'She did not seem to see us when we passed her in the courtyard.' Seth nodded, frowning.

'The wind has sent her out of her mind,' said John, with a carelessness that made his mother cross. She sent the children to the schoolroom with Nathaniel in charge. No doubt he would enlighten Caroline as to what had happened.

The night closed in. Relentlessly the wind blew, battering the house, shrieking round corners and, in the background, the sea boomed, a sonorous bass in the mad orchestra of the storm. Eliza and Ewella decided to share beds with the children to allow Rose and Seth to use their room, tiny though it was. There was no chance of them driving back to Penzance that night. Eliza felt a sharp stab of envy that it was not she who could huddle in the warmth of Seth's embrace in that narrow bed. Sometimes the loneliness of being without her own man swept over her; however, she scolded herself, her main comfort was in having her children close to her. At the same time she realised that it was her duty to keep them safe, a loving duty but the constant worry was burdensome. Studiously she avoided catching Seth's eye as she and Ewella bustled round arranging linen and chasing the children to bed.

It was some time past midnight when Eliza woke. Something had disturbed her. She listened. Nessa was curled up next to her, thumb in mouth and breathing peacefully. Ewella, in with Caroline, was also unusually quiet. There was no sound from the room beyond. She crept out of bed and looked at the boys. Nathaniel lay like a soldier on guard duty, John was spread out starfish fashion and Joel in a tangle of bedclothes, looked as if he had been fighting sleep as usual. But now he was quiet. Then she heard it. There were noises outside. The creaking of carts, an occasional whinny, the jingle of a harness – what was going on? She realised that the wind had dropped and she could no longer hear the sea. But she could hear another sound, the sound of hooves on the stony track. Putting on her warm robe, she crept downstairs, without lighting a candle. The kitchen was bleak and cold, the fire dead in the range. She pressed her nose against the window and could just make out the courtyard and the track beyond – and a considerable number of ponies jostling restlessly at the entrance of the path leading down to the sea. They appeared and disappeared in wreathing mist but then she saw carts lined up behind them and a clutch of men, apparently talking earnestly and then dispersing one by one. She remained at the window, taking care not to be seen, until she began to shiver with cold. Nothing more seemed to be happening.

    'Open the door!' said a voice. It was Seth. He peered out of the window. 'Do it quietly and see what happens.'
    'But they might hear me!'

Unwillingly, Eliza did as she was told, but she could see nothing. The noises had stopped abruptly. No ponies, no creaky carts...just thick darkness.

'Where are they?' she whispered.

'I believe they are not there.'

'Of course they are there! I have just seen them!'

'They must be Free Traders,' said Seth.

'What do you mean - Free Traders?'

'You a Cornish girl and you don't know what a Free Trader is!' Seth mocked, gently. 'The other word is 'smuggler.' The difference is that smugglers bring boats in with goods to sell, so avoiding taxes, and do not rely on wrecks. But they all end up trading!'

'Oh!'

'Come inside and close the door. They have gone and we need to get warm.' He busied himself raking out the range and deftly relighting it. As the flames took hold, Eliza stopped shivering.

'What did you mean, Seth, when you said they were not there?' she whispered.

'I, too, have been doing some research, like the Professor,' he said in a low voice. 'I think a ship must have gone aground somewhere in the bay and the Free Traders are waiting to pick up their contraband.' His voice deepened. 'As they have done for years. These sounds are echoes from earlier times. The librarian at Helston tells me that a very rough sea seems to awaken them – the Free Traders I mean – and revive their activities. Other people have heard them – and accept them as part of the heritage of this coast.'

'You mean they are not real – they are phantoms?' Eliza whispered.

'Well, yes. Maybe they are just echoes of yesteryear. Not everyone sees them or hears them – only people who are sensitive. Apparently some locals say such stories have been circulated from time to time to frighten away the curious.'

'They are frightening me!' Eliza said, feelingly. 'But why?'

'You see there are still Free Traders living and active today,' said Seth. 'You need to realise that along this coast, and in most of Cornwall, many people live in dreadful poverty and the goods provided and extra luxuries are welcomed. The Free Traders, so called because they avoid the taxes, and sell their goods at lower prices, are accepted with enthusiasm in many quarters.'

'And of course,' he went on. 'The mine closures and the decline in tin mining have contributed to this poverty and so encouraged the activities of the Traders.'

'What happened in the past if the Free Traders were caught?'

'Prison. Some were hanged, depending on whether the seamen aboard the wrecked ship were left unharmed or murdered. At times, though, the Free Traders put their own lives at risk by saving men from drowning in the surf. They were not all bad.'

'I suppose some ships carry cargoes that are no use to the locals?' suggested Eliza. 'That must be disappointing.'

'Don't you believe it! It has been known for wrecks to be broken up for the timber!' Seth tried to lighten the atmosphere.' There have been times when the Preventive Men have arrived on a beach to find nothing but a few spars left.' An unwilling smile from Eliza encouraged him to draw closer and put his arms around her. She nestled against him, feeling grateful for his strong presence. Rose would not miss these few minutes when she had him to herself.

An apologetic new moon crept into view from behind the trees and the scene lightened imperceptibly. Then there was a flurry of movement and two ponies, heavily laden, appeared at the entrance to the path. The sound of their harnesses jingling took Seth and Eliza to the window again.

'They look so real!' shuddered Eliza.

'Sometimes they are – don't forget that. We still have Free Traders in action. They are not all ghosts! I shall go in to Penzance tomorrow and find out if anything has been happening. If there has been a real wreck they will know. It is amazing how quickly the news spreads! And half the town will be down on the shore if the wreck is here. They do not lose opportunities to salvage what they can. However, I think the bay just below here will be difficult to reach -there are no villages nearby.' Eliza felt bewildered. Real Free Traders as well as ghostly Free Traders!

She followed Seth up the stairs and was about to leave him for her own bed when he turned to her and pulled her close. Stroking her hair, he gently kissed her on her forehead.

'It is dangerous in this house,' he said. 'You must move somewhere else. You are mixed up in the troubles of a previous century and I do not want you to be at the mercy of vengeful spirits. Neither do I want you to fall foul of local Free Traders!'

His arms tightened protectively around her. She felt the heat from his body and instinctively leaned even closer, every nerve afire with need for him. But Seth, aware of the danger in such closeness, repeated, 'You must move elsewhere.'

'Why should she move elsewhere?' Rose appeared out of her room and Eliza grew rigid with shock. Had Rose seen the kiss? Had she seen how entwined they had been?

'Come to bed, Rose, and I shall explain,' said Seth. The door shut behind them.

34

Nathaniel was missing. Morning had brought in Professor Martineau for long delayed lessons but Nathaniel was nowhere to be found. The other children looked at each other in puzzlement but it seemed that no one had any idea where he had gone. Meanwhile Seth decided that he would take advantage of the break in the weather and take Rose back to Penzance – a Rose very disinclined to leave. His offer to help search for Nathaniel was met with a stony shake of the head and a reminder from Eliza that his priority should be his wife.

'We must come back soon,' Rose insisted. 'I feel so much better now that I have seen you all again. Eliza – beg Seth to come back soon!'

'She does not need to beg,' said Seth. 'I am delighted that you feel that way. I hope Eliza does not feel that we are taking advantage of her time and hospitality?'

'Of course not!' said Eliza, thankful that Rose could not have seen her with Seth. But it had been a close call. Why was it that the short moments she and Seth had shared with each other were always fraught with the fear of discovery? Rose had days with him but she, Eliza, had to be content with a few stolen minutes. Her appreciation of right and wrong was fading, the closer she was to Seth. The two of them were in another world where nothing mattered but the feelings they had for each other. She pasted a bright smile on her face and waved as they trotted out of the courtyard. There had been some consolation in the parting look Seth had given her, a look as longing as a kiss. It was unfortunate that Ewella intercepted that look.

Now – Nathaniel. Eliza had a shrewd idea where he had gone. Curiosity would take him down the path to the shore in the hope of seeing a wrecked ship and he knew that if he asked permission it would not be given. He had asked about the disturbance of the night before and Eliza had been surprised into telling him, something she now regretted. But she must find Nathaniel. She was wary of that path and its ghosts and did not like to think of him treading it alone. A bright early morning sun encouraged her to brave it herself and enabled her to negotiate the potholes, the boulders and the sudden slimy steps with more speed than usual. At last, the sea. Eagerly she scanned the sand below her for any sign of Nathaniel. Yes, there he was, a tiny figure, though not so tiny that he could not be recognised by his mother. The tide was low, the water an innocuous blue, with barely perceptible waves and Nathaniel was at the edge of the water, gazing eagerly at a wreck. It was a sad sight, a broken bird of the sea, stranded on sharp rocks, one of its three masts snapped and the remaining sails in ribbons, fluttering like washing on a line. There was no other sign of movement.

'Nathaniel!' Quite out of breath, after racing across the sand, she caught up with him. 'You should not be here on your own!' When he turned to look at her, she realised for the first time that he was a child no more. At nearly fourteen years old he was as tall as she was, his shoulders were broadening out his face was acquiring the leaner look of a man rather than boy. He regarded his mother with excitement in his eyes.

'Mama, I had to see the wreck! It is a barque from Boulogne! All the way from France! And I believe the goods it was carrying must have been looted - you can see the prints of hooves above the tideline!'

'Nathaniel, it is not safe to be here,' began Eliza, when there was a shout behind them.

'Hey, you! What are you doing!' A man in a navy uniform and big sea boots was chasing across the sand towards them, waving his arms. Not until he was closer did Nathaniel exclaim: 'Mama, I do believe it is Edgar!' Edgar it was. He halted suddenly, abashed to see them.

'Mistress Eliza! You should not be here! This place is not safe.'

'How can that be, Edgar? And how strange to find you here in the uniform of an official of some kind?'

'I am a Preventive Man!' admitted Edgar. Eliza looked round at the deserted beach, a vast stretch of sand at low tide, and then scanned the cliffs above.

'I do not see anyone at all in the vicinity,' she said, rather coldly. 'Perhaps you could explain further what is going on? I came down here to find Nathaniel, not to spy on Free Traders.'

Edgar sighed heavily. 'I am here to check that the 'thieves' – he laid emphasis on the word – 'have not returned to explore the wreck more thoroughly now it is low tide. You have no idea of the vultures that descend on a stricken ship like this! We hoped to apprehend them, catch them in the act – but I have to confess that I am the only one here.' He scuffed the sand with his heavy boot, looking disconsolate. 'There have been several wrecks during last night's storm and the Preventive boat is scouring the coastline and aiding the Revenue cutters where possible. Meanwhile I have been searching the caves behind us but there is no sign of anyone – or anything.'

'Maybe there is nothing to see?' she suggested. She was annoyed that Edgar had kept his occupation from her, part time though it was, and even more annoyed that he was presuming to warn her off the beach.

'Nathaniel and I will return to Carnglaze – Nathaniel? NATHANIEL!' Freed from the attention of both his mother and Edgar, Nathaniel had crept away and was now clambering over the rocks towards the wreck.

'Nathaniel – come back!' shouted Edgar. 'The little fool – he could injure himself! That boat is not stable – I can hear it grinding against granite with each slight movement of the water. The tide will be on the turn soon and it may well lift off and then sink!'

Eliza watched helplessly as her son climbed onto the listing deck and disappeared inside. She was not only worried that the barque would escape those dagger pointed rocks any time soon, even though it looked to be fairly well impaled, but Nathaniel could injure himself in other ways.

'I do not know what I should do,' said Edgar, sounding less sure of himself. 'The Preventive boat should be back soon to pick me up and it would not be a good idea for them to find you here.'

'Why ever not?'

'They may suspect that you know something of the Free Traders – or at least that you know where they are – and who they are – and the whereabouts of the ship's cargo!'

'That is ridiculous. We have just come from Carnglaze – '

'Exactly! Carnglaze has always been a centre of smuggling activity and a magnet for Free Traders – though of course the stories died down after the Lanivets took it over. It may be a case of give a dog a bad name – 'Eliza could not restrain a giggle at Edgar's inappropriate language. Edgar glared, feeling that his position as an important

Preventive Officer was being impugned. Eliza continued, innocent in tone.

'You do realise, Edgar, there may be no Free Traders, or smugglers here at all.'

Edgar did not pretend to misunderstand what she was saying.

'You have been listening to stories!' he growled. 'We have to make sure. Sometimes potential thieves take advantage of the ghost stories that haunt this place.'

'I want to find Nathaniel!' declared Eliza impatiently.

'We could wait a few minutes to see if Nathaniel appears,' he suggested. 'Otherwise I shall have to search the wreck.' He sounded anything but enthusiastic. However, Eliza was not impressed with this idea.

'I shall go myself,' she said firmly. 'I am lighter than you and less likely to disturb anything. Besides, Nathaniel will respond to my call rather than yours.'

'Out of the question!' exclaimed Edgar. 'It is not fitting for a lady to go scrambling over rocks!'

'This is not the first time I have climbed on rocks!' declared Eliza. 'And I do not intend to leave my son on that wreck at the mercy of the tide!' Before Edgar could protest further, she hitched up her skirt and hopped on to the first rock, then leapt from one to the other with agility until she could scramble on to a plateau like surface that stretched to where the stricken vessel was impaled.

'Nathaniel!' she called. There was no reply so she was forced to follow where she had seen him disappear. It was easy to clamber on to the listing deck. Ducking her head to enter the cabin she called again but Nathaniel was not there. The dank smell of soaking, rotting wood was overpowering and seaweed trailed on the floor. A broken oil lamp lay on its side, the oil long seeped away. She found it was slippery and difficult to retain her balance as of course the cabin was heavily canted to one side. 'Nathaniel!'

'Here, Mama! Come down the steps.'

With care clambered down the wooden steps, into the dim interior, fighting a claustrophobic feeling that she could be trapped.

There was Nathaniel crouched on the floor, a small chest opened in front of him. Piled around him were more chests, jumbled confusedly after the wrecking in a rough sea.

'Look what I've discovered!' He lifted out a swathe of lace to show his mother. 'There is more here – lots of beautiful materials. But I could not find any kegs of spirits. I thought there might be some left but I suppose they were moved last night.' She sat down next to him and searched through the open chest. There were bolts of shimmering silk, lace of different patterns, heavy taffetas and velvets – all goods which would fetch a high price in Truro or Penzance – and which would be fallen on in delight in her own household. Of course they were not as useful to the country folk as foodstuffs or the heavily taxed luxuries, brandy, rum and wine. No sign of any of those in the cabin. She wondered where all the kegs used to be stored in previous days while they waited for distribution; many could not be moved on the open road without attracting suspicion. And the crew? What had happened to the unfortunate seamen of this particular ship?

The barque shifted abruptly and the timbers shuddered. A wave smacked into its side.

'We must leave,' said Eliza. 'The tide is coming in. Close the chest, Nathaniel – we cannot take it.' Much as I would like to have some of those beautiful materials, she thought, wistfully.

'Mama, I just want to take a look in some of the other chests - you never know what we might find!'

'No, Nathaniel, we must go!' Nathaniel was not listening. He had opened yet another chest and was exclaiming over the contents.

'Look, Mama, wooden carvings!' He lifted out a beautifully crafted antelope from its nest of cotton. 'There are more here! This is made from ivory, I am sure!'

'Nathaniel! Come at once!' Eliza grabbed her son by the arm and tried to drag him away.

'I am just coming! Another few minutes won't hurt!'
Never had Nathaniel defied her before! In a temper, Eliza left him and began to climb up the steps to the upper cabin but as she did so, another abrupt movement of the barque made her lose her footing. With a scream, she crashed down the steps, hitting her head on the corner of one of the chests. She lay, unmoving. Aghast at what he had done, Nathaniel knelt down beside her.

'Mama! Wake up Mama! I'm so sorry. We should go at once!' But Eliza did not stir.

A frantic Nathaniel clambered up to the deck of the barque and screamed for help. There was no sign of Edgar, no sign of anyone on the sand or the cliffs. A wave broke over the listing deck and the spray bombarded him. He realised that the tide was indeed coming in - and fast. Water was already sneaking round the edges of the rocks and the waves were getting more imperious, one following the other as the tide gathered strength.

'Edgar! Edgar! Where are you?' Beside himself with fear, Nathaniel scrambled back on to the rocks, jumping from one to the other in his haste to get back to the sand. But his terror and hurried movements were his undoing. He slipped on a weed covered rock and one foot became trapped in a crevice. Frantically he tried to pull himself free but could not. The granite edges held him firmly. And still the tide advanced.

Wildly, he looked around him. Time passed. Gulls swooped and cried, the only signs of life in that panorama of sea, sand and sky. He pulled vainly, trying to free his foot and cried out with the pain. And his mother - how was she? He remembered her face, grey white and her eyes closed. It was all his fault! If only they were delivered from this he would vow total obedience in the future. His voice rasping, he screamed for help again. No one answered.

35

Slowly Eliza opened her eyes. She could see the wood ceiling of the cabin, in her nostrils the dank smell of water on the inside instead of water on the outside. She tried to move but a zig-zag of lightning pain made her cry out. The floor lurched beneath her as a wave broke over the stricken ship. Gradually the events leading up to her plight came back to her. She had fallen down the steps and must have hit her head. Cautiously she explored her scalp with her fingers. They came away bloody. The pain made her reluctant to feel further so she tried to sit up instead. Now her head was spinning and she closed her eyes again. Nathaniel! What had happened to Nathaniel? Her eyes snapped open. He would not have left her in such a predicament. Something must have happened to him!

'Nathaniel!' she croaked but there was no answer. Her son must be in danger and this prompted her to crawl on her hands and knees, ignoring the blackness that threatened to overwhelm her. She looked down the steps and could see the jumble of chests, including the one that spilled out the lovely materials, but Nathaniel was not down there. Next she crawled towards the half open door which turned out to be jammed so that she only had a limited view out. She could see a stretch of sand, part of the cliff in the distance, rocks – and water. No one was in sight. Not Nathaniel, not Edgar. A larger wave advanced over the sand. Another slapped the side of the ship, jolting it with mindless intent. Surely the tide must be further in than she thought and it meant that she had been unconscious for more than a few seconds. She pushed at the door but it would not budge. She could just thrust her head through the aperture and scream. Which she did, though the sound was quavery and shrill by turns.

'Mama – I can't move. I'm stuck!' Faintly, Nathaniel's voiced drifted in to her immense relief. He was out there and she had to get to him. Pulling herself up to her feet, where she swayed alarmingly, she picked her way down those steps again and found what she wanted - a loose plank of wood. Sweat beaded her brow as she climbed up again, slowly and carefully, then with all her strength, began striking the recalcitrant door, trying to make it open wider. So suddenly that it took her by surprise, the door shifted and she could wriggle out. She staggered to where the listing deck allowed her to step out on to the rocks, horrified to find that they were already awash with the first onslaughts of salt water. With nothing to hold on to and steady her progress she could only move slowly, pain still pulsing through her head. And there was her Nathaniel, up to his knees in water.

'Oh Nathaniel!'

'Mama, my foot! It's stuck!' her son wailed.

She splashed over to him and looked. There was nothing else for it, she had to act.

'You might be able to pull your foot out now, if I help you,' she said soothingly. 'The cold water will have reduced any swelling. Now, just pull when I say so.' Nathaniel waited while she felt around in the water for his ankle. She could see that it was trapped in the crevice at an awkward angle, making any movement more difficult.

'Now, Nathaniel, now!' She heaved on his leg, twisting it at the same time, making him shriek in pain but his foot was freed and he was able to hop clear of the importunate tide.

They sat, side by side, on the sand, breathing deeply.

'Nathaniel – where has Edgar gone? He was here was he not?'

'He was – you are not dreaming, Mama!' Nathaniel was rapidly regaining his spirits. 'I think he was picked up by the Preventive boat he was waiting for. He was anxious that they did not know we were here and he did not realise that we were in difficulties.' Eliza sighed heavily.

'That means we have to make our own way back along the path,' she said. 'Typical of Edgar! Always underfoot when he is not wanted and when he could be of real help he disappears!' This was unfair. Nathaniel glanced at his mother. It was not like her to talk in such a way in front of her children. But then she must be shaken up by her fall.

'Don't worry, Mama! I shall help you.'

'Yes, we need to get away from the tide. It is coming in fast.'

'Professor Martineau said it was time for the Spring tides and that they come in further and higher. Something to do with the moon,' said Nathaniel vaguely. Carefully he stood up and held out his hand to his mother. They shuffled over the sand towards the path that led up the cliff, at the best of times a scramble but now spitefully steep. Then they were on the final stretch of the path next to the stream. Idly, Eliza wondered what the spirits would make of their determination to return to Carnglaze. She was so tired, her head ached and black patches danced before her eyes – but her son was safe. She did not care about the spirits.

They had hardly reached the thorn trees when she stumbled.

'I must sit down for a few moments,' she muttered and leaned her head against a tree trunk. In the silence that followed Nathaniel heard other sounds, a crashing through the undergrowth and voices. But Eliza, her eyes closed, heard nothing.

'Eliza! Nathaniel! Thank goodness we have found you!' It was Jael – and behind her, Seth. Jael hugged Nathaniel and then fell to her knees beside Eliza.

'We must get her back to Carnglaze as soon as possible,' she said. 'Thank goodness you came back, Seth. I cannot manage her on my own.'

'I will carry her,' he declared. 'You two hurry back and get Mathey to go for Dr. Trevell. He will be needed! Nathaniel, don't worry about your mother, I shall take care of her.'

'She fell down the steps of the wrecked ship,' said Nathaniel, anxiously. Jael grabbed his hand and they set off towards Carnglaze. Meanwhile a concerned Seth hefted Eliza into his arms, and followed them at a much slower pace.

He knew the path was difficult at the best of times and he had to go slowly and carefully so that Eliza was not shaken up too much - or worse, that he should drop her. He stopped to rest briefly, a worried frown creasing his brow as she did not open her eyes. It was then that an uncomfortable sensation that he was not alone on the path crept over him. There must be someone ahead of him but unseen in the murky light. He continued at a steady pace but again he felt someone close to him, more than someone – several people. He could see nothing yet felt he was pushing through a crowd, a crowd that tried to bar his way.

'I'm taking her back to Carnglaze!' he snarled. 'Leave us be!' There was a brief respite in the pressure from the unseen and then a large branch, broken from a thorn tree, fell in front of him. He had to stop. His anger blazed, partly for Eliza, partly because of the antagonism he felt surrounding him.

'Leave us, I say!' he shouted. 'You are mistaken! She is no threat to you. And she will be departing from Carnglaze as soon as she is better! I guarantee that!' There was a flurry of whispering, a bluster of activity and the sudden cessation of pressure. The air around him lightened. Seth kicked the branch aside and continued his trek. Had he really been shouting at spirits, at phantoms? For the first time he appreciated how frightened Eliza must have been. And for the first time his wavering belief strengthened into acceptance.

At last he came to the end of the path and there was Carnglaze. His arms ached and delayed reaction to what had occurred was making him shake. Eliza and her family should not stay at Carnglaze, of that he was sure. He would see that she left if he had to carry her out himself. He glanced down at his burden and was surprised to see her eyes wide open, looking at him.

'Seth?' she said, uncertainly. 'How strange! I have been feeling so safe – and cared for. And here you are! Why are you carrying me?' He smiled encouragingly, pleased that she was conscious at last.

'Do you think you can stand?'

'I will try.' He supported her as she stood up and, step by slow step, they approached Carnglaze. He decided explanations could wait until Dr. Trevell had seen her. It seemed the doctor must have a new means of transport as a smart barouche waited outside the door. They made their slow way into the courtyard, the door was flung open and Jael, all smiles, came rushing out. Behind her was Ewella.

And then, another figure. A tall man with sleeked back red gold hair, a sharp planed face tanned to mahogany but eyes as blue as ever. A man of prosperous aspect, gold watch, gold cufflinks, fine leather boots. Not Dr. Trevell. It was Barnabas.

'Barnabas!' said Seth, tiredly. 'I hope this is the last time I have to return your damaged wife to you. It is becoming a habit!'

It was later. Seth had gone back to Penzance, to Rose. Jael had retired discreetly to her barn and Ewella was shepherding the excited children to their beds. Uncle Tobias, muttering about too much excitement for an old man, had tottered to his 'study' and his armchair.

Eliza and Barnabas sat at the kitchen table, Eliza with coffee and Barnabas with brandy. She had taken care to keep the kitchen table between them. There were things she needed to know. Why had he been away for so long? Why had communication from him lapsed? Why had he not let them know of his return? Until she knew and understood she could not run to him with delight and throw herself into his arms. He seemed a stranger, an affluent stranger. Confidence exuded from him. Even the way he sat betokened someone at ease with himself, in charge of the situation. Not the way he had been when he left Cornwall.

'I am pleased to see you back, Barnabas,' she said formally. 'You must tell me everything that happened in Australia.'

'Later. That would take too long, just now, my dear,' he smiled. 'I, too, am anxious to know what has taken place here since I have been away. The children do seem healthy and in good spirits. So it has not been as bad here as you imagined?' This was nearer a statement than a question. Eliza glared at him.

'It has been worse than I ever imagined!' she hissed. 'But I shall acquaint you with everything soon enough. First I need to know why you were away so long!'

'Part of the reason is because I languished in prison for nearly a year!' was the bald answer. Eliza could only gasp. She had imagined illness, money difficulties, but not this.

'What for?' she whispered eventually.

'Murder!' said her husband, laconically. 'It was an accident. New evidence was found and, they let me go. As you can understand, I am sure, I felt it was better to tell you face to face than write to you. Also I had several problems to sort out before I returned.'

'Did it not occur to you that we might be worried about you? At one time I thought you might be dead!'

'I am sorry — please believe me. I shall tell you all that happened in due course but it is a long story. I was buoyed by the thought that you were taking care of the children and I knew that you had great common sense. And Ewella to help you,' he added.
Eliza gazed at him. He had no idea, no idea at all of the life she had led without him. He rose to his feet.

'I shall return to my hotel in Penzance,' he said. 'I see you have no room for me here. I shall be back tomorrow and we can enlarge on our discussion.' And this stranger, who was her husband, kissed her on the cheek and left her.

36

The following day, Eliza took great care with her appearance. She extracted her new dress from Miss Hetty's out of its vast packaging of tissue paper and then peered anxiously into the one cracked mirror they possessed (in the room once occupied by Grace) to see if the deep lilac colour really did make her eyes look violet. Jael came in just in time to help pile up her hair. She was rewarded by admiring cries from her children and an appreciative nod from Uncle Tobias; only Ewella, angry with her brother for his long silence, raked her with contemptuous eyes, declaring 'He does not deserve it!'

After breakfast, Professor Martineau arrived. He sent the children to the schoolroom and indicated that he wanted to speak to Eliza privately. 'The wrecked ship in the bay,' he began. 'Smugglers! Bringing goods from France. The crew of five are in custody. Apparently Edgar Tallack was instrumental in tracking them down.' He regarded Eliza gravely. 'I only tell you this because it may be that our - your spirits in this house will be angry. Whether they will manifest their displeasure I don't know. However I advise you to send your children to the Manor or on some other visit for a short time – just in case.'

Eliza was appalled. Was there to be no end to this? The solemnity of Professor Martineau's words galvanised her into activity. 'I have to wait here for Barnabas,' she said. 'But perhaps Mathey could take them to the Galleon Hotel in Penzance for a visit to Rose and Seth Quinn? I do not feel that we should trespass on Austol's time anymore.' The Professor heaved a sigh of relief.

'I shall go with him and help with transporting the children. He will be unable to take all five in the cart!'

The silence, after they had left, was unnerving. Begging a lift from Mathey, Ewella had flounced off to shop in Penzance and Jael had left on an errand of her own before the Professor's arrival. Only Uncle Tobias remained, huddled in bed, still suffering from his heavy chest cold. After a few desultory tasks Eliza built up the fire in the range and sat at the kitchen table with a pile of mending. Waiting. The day passed slowly. She made soup for Uncle Tobias at lunch time but was unable to touch a drop herself. Barnabas was certainly taking his time. By late afternoon, a cold anger was building inside her. Away for nearly three years and now keeping her waiting all day! The thoughtlessness – no, the unkindness, was too much. She marched upstairs, took off her dress and repacked it. She tore the hairpins out of her hair and let it tumble untidily about her shoulders. Her blue twill working dress would do. Why should she make an effort? Barnabas was not coming, it seemed, and she had wasted a whole day in anticipation.

As dusk fell, she heard the sound of Mathey's cart. He came in, looking around him with some trepidation. 'Mistress Eliza the children are staying with the Quinns for two days and then Mr. Seth will bring them back. Professor Martineau has returned home but asked me to check that you were all safe. Safe? A strange word to use.' The old man looked worried.

'We are all safe,' said Eliza, soothingly. 'Jael and Ewella are not yet returned but I expect them soon. Thank you, Mathey for all your help today.'

After Mathey's departure, the silence rolled back in. Doggedly she sewed and darned and the pile of clothes needing mending reduced until there was nothing left. Uncle Tobias of course had his supper, but Eliza was unable to manage a mouthful. She lit the oil lamp in the window and also several candles to cheer the room, but then was sorry as they created shadows which cavorted over the walls in unseen draughts. Still no Ewella and no Jael. Outside was silence and blackness, a thick black as if the trees had been overdrawn with black crayon.

Then, much later, came the sound of wheels in the courtyard. The banging on the door was certainly not Ewella. Eliza peeped cautiously round the door. A tall shape loomed up.

Barnabas!' she exclaimed. 'What are you doing here, so late?'
Her husband came in and slumped down at the table.

'A long story,' he said. 'Have you any brandy?'

'No. We have no money for such luxuries.' Then honesty compelled her to add that perhaps Uncle Tobias had some but he was asleep.

'I see you really prepared for my arrival,' said her husband, with a fleeting grin. He had looked her up and down, taking in her working dress and untidy hair. Tired though he appeared to be, he was still surrounded with that aura of superiority and Eliza was grimly pleased that she had not remained in her new dress.

'Where are the children? In bed I suppose?'

'No.' She was about to say more but a familiar sound could be heard outside. The stamping of hooves, the jingle of harnesses, the creaking of carts. There were shouts and exhortations and it seemed a large body of men and ponies were gathering on the track. Eliza stiffened in alarm.

'What on earth is going on out there!' demanded Barnabas. He strode to the window just as the candles blew out, but could see nothing. Seeing him peering out with such puzzlement, the familiar horror gripped her.

'The – the Free Traders,' she whispered. At the end of such a day it was too much for her. The long wait, no food and the Professor's warning – and now the return of her 'spirits'! With a little sigh she slid off her chair on to the floor in a dead faint.

She came to and found that Barnabas was trying to pour water down her throat. In the light of the oil lamp she could see that he looked distraught.

'What happened, Eliza? Are you ill?'

'No.' She scrambled to her feet. 'Have you looked outside?'

'Of course not. I have been trying to revive you!'

'Please look. And tell me what you see.' He looked disbelieving that she should issue orders in such a way and raised his eyebrows. Eliza wanted to shake him.

'Just do as I ask! Tell me what is there!'

He opened the door and peered out.

'Nothing there,' he reported. 'Now Eliza, what is all this about? Free Traders?'

'Are you not surprised that after all the noises we could hear, now there is nothing and no one there? I tell you – they ARE there! They go too far, they encroach on my life – they HAUNT me!'

'Come here, my dear.' His tone was softer and before she knew what was happening he had pulled her on to his lap and was stroking her hair.

'Start at the beginning and tell me. I can see that something has seriously disturbed you and I need to know what is going on.'

Briefly, stumbling over her words, Eliza explained. Doubtful at first but increasingly angry as the story unfolded, Barnabas set her down on her feet, again strode to the door and opened it. This time a waterfall of noises poured into the room, louder than ever. An agitation of movement of carts and animals, the striking of hooves on stone, the whinnying of ponies and the muffled shouts of men.

'And they are not really there!' said Eliza. He looked. They were not.

He crept out into the courtyard to see if he could make out what was happening – if anything. He peered into the darkness but could make out nothing.

'There is no noise out there now!' he reported back to Eliza. 'But the darkness makes it impossible to see. Perhaps they, whoever 'they' are, have just gone by…?.'

'No!' said Eliza. 'They are still there!'

Hardly had she spoken when there was a loud crash and the door swung open again, so violently it rebounded off the wall. A rush of wind blew into the kitchen and swirled into the corners, making the range flare up and the oil lamp flicker wildly. Eliza screamed and buried her head against Barnabas' chest. Even so, she sensed the growing pressure of others close by, milling about the room; whispers grew louder and she could hear the words 'traitor' 'betrayer.' Unkind hands pulled at her so she felt she was being bruised and scratched and her dress likely to be torn from her body. Then, suddenly, another voice – deeper, louder and clearer.

'Leave, lads! 'Tis me she betrayed and I will revenge us all. She shall answer to ME!' The voice rose to a shout, a shout of rage that reverberated around the walls and the whisperers groaned, leaden with malice 'Punish her, punish her….!'

Eliza and Barnabas stood in the middle of the kitchen, arms tight around each other, unable to move in a room surging with anger made palpable by unquiet spirits still seeking retribution for wrongs perpetrated so long ago.

Then another voice spoke, a quavery old voice. It was Uncle Tobias. 'Shown yourselves at last, then,' he said. 'You are wasting your time here – she who betrayed you is long gone. These two are innocent' – his voice grew stronger – 'and they will go from this house! I promise you

233

that. It will stay empty for those who will not leave though they have perished from this earth.' The frenetic activity in the room lessened as if the spirits were listening. 'But SHE is still here. Samuel Hooper, find her, atone for what you have done, and then you will have peace.' Like the tide ebbing, the darkness in the room became thinner and seemed to flow out of the door, taking with it the heaviness of other presences. The oil lamp revived and glowed steadily, revealing Uncle Tobias in his robe, hair awry and looking bewildered.

'What is going on here?' he demanded. 'Such a noise, such shouting and I am supposed to sleep! Where is everybody?'

'You saved us!' breathed Eliza. 'What inspired you to say all that?'

'I said nothing! The noise was all in here!' He sounded irritable.

'Uncle Tobias. Perhaps you should go back to bed.' It was Barnabas intervening. 'I am so sorry we disturbed you.'

'Time you were back to take up your responsibilities, young man!' the old man threw over his shoulder as he hobbled back to his cubby hole.

Before either Barnabas or Eliza could utter another word, there was another knock at the door.

'Now what!' Barnabas flung it open. 'Jael!'

'And this is my mother, Mistress Annie.' Jael smiled sweetly at him and ushered in her mother. Mistress Annie went straight to Eliza and patted her shoulder.

'I am sorry you are having such a difficult time with these unruly spirits! I feel sure the worst is over now. Jael will fetch you both a calming draught of camomile and we shall talk tomorrow. I intend to stay with Jael in her barn and then we shall see.'
Still shocked, Barnabas and Eliza sat at the table until Jael brought them both her 'calming draughts' Then she and Mistress Annie took their leave. Barnabas shook his head after their departure.

'I seem to have returned to another world from the one I left,' he said ruefully. 'Where can I sleep, Eliza? The floor if necessary. I am well used to that.'

'Perhaps it would be better if you slept in my bed?' said Eliza, uncertainty in her voice.

'Well, we ARE married!' Barnabas smiled at her.

In spite of the heavy body next to her, appropriating most of the space, Eliza slept deeply and woke to sunshine struggling through the window. Barnabas did not stir. She realised his presence alone had enabled her to dismiss her fears and survive the night without dreams or sudden wakefulness. Whatever had happened between them before, she was grateful for that. Anger was a wasting disease she decided, a feeling that did not improve sentiments between people or bring about change and she was just overwhelmingly thankful that he had returned safely. No doubt he would explain the paucity of news and the reasons for his time in prison when they had more time. She looked down at him, tracing the new lines in his face, observing the threads of grey in his hair and whiskers and knew that his time away had not been easy. And Grace? She seemed too faint and far away to be a threat, just another ghost in their lives

Mistress Annie and Jael sat with Eliza close to the pleasant warmth from the range. Barnabas and Tobias slumbered on.

'Wherever you are intending to go, it should be soon,' said Mistress Annie. Jael nodded her head but Eliza was not convinced. Her gratitude for her husband's return had made her extra sympathetic to the turmoil of others – living or dead. A wave of sympathy flooded her senses for the unhappiness around her.

'So much unrest, so much bitterness - we cannot just ignore it and leave,' she protested. 'Do you remember what Uncle Tobias said? 'SHE is still here. Find her, atone for what you have done and you will have peace.' I am not sure what that means, exactly but I know there are at least two tortured souls here who need our help.' Mistress Annie nodded.

'Your concern does you credit my dear, but achieving anything helpful could be beyond us. After all, strange happenings have been going on for so long – for centuries and more! It is not for nothing that Carnglaze has the reputation for being haunted!'

'The Reverend Sithney and Professor Martineau managed to exorcise the spirit of the girl looking for her baby!' put in Jael eagerly.

'I know that was a more recent haunting and what is happening now has its origins further back in time – but surely, mother, we could try to do something about it?' Mistress Annie smiled at her daughter, then rose.

'I should like to walk round the house and land of Carnglaze again. Come, Jael.'

Barnabas came thundering down the stairs two at a time, his forceful personality displacing the air ahead of him in the way Eliza remembered so well.

'Eliza! You should have woken me. I have much to do!' He planted a kiss on his wife's cheek and smiled down at her, an open pleased to see you smile that jolted her memory back to early days.

'Perhaps Mathey could bring my horse from around the back? And is there anything to eat?' This was the old Barnabas, the man she had married, and a disarmed Eliza hurried to please him.

'Start packing up this house,' he instructed before he left.

'No,' thought Eliza. 'There is something still to be done here.' But she was happy to let him go, letting all the old resentments trail away. She would assert herself with tact when he came back as a return to their former combative relationship was unthinkable. Barnabas might not have changed but she had. Now, time to prepare breakfast for Uncle Tobias.

'Barnabas is back so everything will return to normal,' declared the old man hopefully.

'The standing stone is the key,' said Mistress Annie, when she and Jael returned. 'I feel it. But what it signifies I am not sure. I should like to meet with Reverend Sithney and Professor Martineau and we could share our knowledge perhaps?' Jael nodded eagerly.

'I'm sure that can be arranged,' said Eliza. 'I shall send Mathey with a message for the Professor. Meanwhile I have decided to pack up the house while the children are away - instructions from Barnabas,' she added with laugh, at the same time wondering that she could be so accepting of her husband after he was responsible for her weary sojourn in the bleak house that was Carnglaze.

'Ewella will help me – Ewella? Where is she?'

'I believe Ewella has gone to help Rose with the children. She said she would call in at the Galleon after her shopping.'

'She said nothing to me!'

236

'She said that perhaps you had forgotten that Rose is not well just now.'

'But Seth will be there!' snapped a now thoroughly irritated Eliza. 'She knows that! I would not leave Rose to manage on her own!' Always Ewella – when there was trouble Ewella managed to be involved, she fumed to herself. Of course she had remembered that Rose was poorly – but Seth, surely, would not think that she, Eliza, had been thoughtless?

It was late afternoon. Of Barnabas there was no sign. Ewella had not returned either and it had been left to Eliza to pack up what she could. Jael and Mistress Annie were back in the barn busy with chopping and grinding for a new potion, refusing to divulge what it was, as Eliza found when she paid them a quick visit. Uncle Tobias had taken advantage of the early sunshine and had hobbled out briskly for a walk. As a result he was sleeping again. Not until the sun descended behind the trees did Mathey return and with him, Professor Martineau and the Reverend Sithney. They, too, disappeared into Jael's barn. A long wait ensued. Eliza occupied herself by making a rabbit stew in the largest saucepan she possessed, feeling that she could at least feed whoever turned up. But rabbit stew was far from the minds of those in the barn. Only Uncle Tobias joined Eliza at the kitchen table for his supper. Still no sign of Barnabas.

Dusk fell, bringing with it a mist which gave the trees a wraith like quality and rendered surreal the world outside. Mistress Annie came bustling in. She looked purposeful and seemed to have decided on a course of action.

'Eliza, I think you should not be here.'

'I have nowhere to go. But in any case I should like to know what you are going to do.' Eliza was obstinate and Mistress Annie decided not to waste time trying to change her mind.

'Perhaps you could wait upstairs?'

With bad grace, Eliza did as was suggested but she took care to sit on the stairs where she could see the kitchen below, though out of view herself. Jael came in and lit the oil lamp. It smoked and guttered and finally went out. Jael clicked her tongue with exasperation and lit several candles instead. She and her mother whispered to each other and all Eliza could hear was Jael saying: 'Success is not certain!' A pause.

Then 'You need my help and there's an end to it.' She was unable to hear what was said next until the words, hissed by Mistress Annie. 'I KNOW! I can sense it. It's the standing stone - and she ....' The words were lost as they turned towards the door. Both of them then went out into the courtyard and Eliza realised they were taking the path which led behind the house – to the standing stone again? She shivered with the premonition that something dreadful was about to happen. Her hands and feet had become icy cold and she hugged herself, trying to keep warm. Next, in came the Professor and the Reverend Sithney, and both sat down at the table. 'We wait.' said the Professor gravely.

An hour passed. Two hours. Eliza stayed where she was, rigid with cold, as darkness advanced. Then, with a suddenness that made her jump, the door crashed open. Mist drifted in, veiling the walls, the table, and the two men so that she could hardly see. A pungent smell of ferns rose upwards with a distressing taint of earth and rotting vegetation behind it; the light from the candles dimmed and blurred, grotesque shadows creeping across the walls.

'She's coming!' It was the Reverend Sithney's voice, shaking with excitement. Drifts of mist were weaving shapes closer to the door and, within Eliza's horrified view, created the shape of a human form. Surely an aberration! But she could make out a dress and apron, a bonnet and possibly ribbons. The face she could not see. She wished she could tear the veiling mist apart like a ragged curtain and make out more detail but at the same time she knew in actuality she would be reluctant to do so. Slowly and impressively the Reverend Sithney stood and raised his arms. His black cloak made him look like a giant bat and Eliza wanted to dissolve into hysterical giggles. But then he spoke - and all desire to laugh vanished. His voice was deep and dark and seemed wrested from his innermost being while his eyes gleamed black as night.

'Where are you, Samuel Hooper?' he intoned. 'Samuel Hooper, come forth! It is time you showed yourself!' Eliza held her breath, wondering what would materialise next. Surely it was dangerous to call on denizens of the other world like this? She sensed the temperature in the room was dropping, dropping, and she shook, as much with fear as cold. Something else was about to happen and she was more than frightened – she was terror stricken. She wished she had done what

Mistress Annie had suggested and hidden in her bedroom, but it was too late.

This time the door groaned on its hinges and opened with agonizing slowness. Another spectre materialised, its outline muddied and opaque. It advanced into the room and, as the light from the oil lamp fell upon it, Eliza was horrified to see that it looked like Edgar. Not Samuel Hooper but Edgar, defiant in his uniform as a Preventive Man. Was he real or an hallucination? But what was Edgar, real or otherwise, doing at Carnglaze, a hotbed of phantom smugglers and Free Traders? And what was his connection to Samuel Hooper? Nearly fainting, Eliza watched the dimly lit scene below her, the interplay between the man and the misty figure of the woman. She seemed to be pushing him away, her hands defensively before her and he seemed to be pleading but she would have none of it. She drifted away across the room and he fell to his knees. She hesitated. Then she moved nearer to him, seeming to consider. Then she held out her arms. But there was space between them. And that space allowed other dimly seen shapes to interpose between the two, shapes crowding through the door, whispering, protesting, jostling. The whispering grew louder and louder, and the words 'Punish her!' rose above all.

Suddenly the door sprang open.
'Eliza, I'm sorry I am so late.' It was Barnabas, his appearance cutting through the melee of ghostly shapes which whirled and vanished, nebulous in the mist. But there was Edgar, real, solid Edgar, on his knees, dazed and disorientated. He could not speak. Surprised, Barnabas helped him into a chair and then demanded of Eliza who was slowly descending, as if in a dream:
'Who is this man? And what is he doing here?'
'It is Edgar. Austol's brother-in-law! I do not know why he is here. I need to tell you – ' Her voice cracked. But Barnabas was impatient. He had news of his own that he could not wait to share.
'First thing tomorrow we shall return to Roscarne!' he announced. The pride in his voice was unmistakeable. 'The house has been opened up and I have engaged servants to clean and make it ready!'
'Did I hear Roscarne mentioned?' Uncle Tobias demanded hopefully, having hobbled in.

'You did. Tomorrow morning early.' replied his nephew. 'You need to pack your things.'

'I possess very little,' was the reply. Obediently he returned to his cubby hole. Meanwhile the Reverend and the Professor remained silent, watching as Eliza tried to pour brandy down Edgar, worried about his strange appearance, his dazed condition and unseeing eyes. The momentous announcement made by her husband had not registered. With an effort, Edgar focused on Eliza and then clutched her arm.

'I was the cause of her death!' he cried, his voice despairing. 'They should punish ME – not her! I made her fall in love with me and then encouraged her to divulge the secrets of the smugglers! But Samuel Hooper took his revenge for her betrayal!' He looked around, fear in his eyes.

'They have gone,' she said soothingly. 'Edgar, you are here at Carnglaze. You are safe.' What else could she say? Barnabas looked at them, surprise and suspicion mingled in his eyes but Edgar subsided, muttering to himself: 'Why am I being used?'

The Professor and Reverend Sithney were whispering excitedly to each other and casting worried glances at Edgar. Then Jael and Mistress Annie came in and joined the two old men at the table where they talked long and earnestly. A puzzled Barnabas felt excluded. It seemed that Carnglaze was the focus of strange people and stranger shadows, a house full of strange happenings and he understood none of it. He was about to suggest that he would like to have some space to talk with his wife when the sudden silence was broken. The air crackled as in a thunderstorm. Slowly, menacingly, Edgar rose from his chair. Everyone looked at him. Eliza trembled when she saw that he seemed to have grown taller and his features were changing. His eyes were fixed and glaring. Surely his nose was more prominent than it had been? And the hair! It was white. Not Edgar's.

'Where is she?' demanded Edgar in a voice that was not his.

'Who is it you want?' Mistress Annie's voice was steady.

Eliza held her breath. The Professor and Reverend Sithney were still as stone, and only Barnabas moved restively. Mistress Annie moved to confront the figure that had been Edgar.

'Who is it you want?' she said again.

'My wife! The wife who betrayed me, who led me to the gallows!' the voice growled, dredged from the depths of time far away.

'The wife you murdered?' Mistress Annie's voice was still calm.

'She betrayed me with a Preventive Man!'

'But you took her life! You have both suffered. It is time to forgive!'

'Where IS she?'

'She is still here. She is buried here.' Mistress Annie's voice was soft. Uttering a cry of despair, the blurred, insubstantial, vaporous being that was Samuel Hooper left Edgar and swirled through the door which banged shut.

Edgar dropped back into his chair and put his head in his hands.

38

The next morning it was Ewella, carefully avoiding Eliza's glance, who served up breakfast to the dazed remnants of the household. Barnabas alone had left, promising to be back to help pack their belongings in the cart. Edgar was still there, communing deep within himself, and not answering even the simplest question.

'Do not worry,' whispered Mistress Annie to Eliza. 'The poor man has endured possession twice over – no wonder he is not himself. He will return to his normal self soon.'
Eliza, looking at him sitting there, spooning porridge like a child, his face white, his eyes blank, did not share Mistress Annie's optimism. How would Austol react to the return of such a severely shaken Edgar? Had he enough patience to allow Edgar to resume his normal life after what had happened?

'Mathey will take Mother and me to catch the Liskeard coach,' said Jael. 'Could he take Edgar back to the Manor as well?' Eliza nodded.
'The Professor has offered me a lift in his carriage,' put in Ewella. 'Perhaps then he will tell me what has been going on. You all seem to be in a trance!' She was resentful that she appeared to have missed something important and even more so that no one seemed inclined to tell her.
'Just tired, Mistress Ewella, that is all,' said the Reverend Sithney smoothly. 'Let me help you put your belongings in the carriage and then we can be off as soon as possible.'

Jed left later on in the morning escorting Uncle Tobias and a carriage full of household goods destined for Roscarne and promising to come back for Trembles waiting patiently in his barn. Finally Carnglaze was empty and Eliza alone in her lilac dress waiting for Barnabas. He turned up in a smart new trap with a beautiful chestnut pony which seemed to be high stepping with pride. He helped Eliza into the trap without answering the query in her eyes and soon they were trotting along the track, the stream grumbling along beside them until it turned after the bridge downhill to the sea. The dense woodland began to thin out and

Eliza smiled with delight as she saw the first primroses starring the verges. It dawned on her at last that she was escaping from Carnglaze! She looked back at the house, receding into the distance, a dark shape like a prehistoric beast crouching among the trees. She would never have to step inside that heavy door and face the gloom inside again. Never again would she feel imprisoned by those dismal stone walls, gazing enviously at the outside world and longing to be free of the house and its threatening darkness. The ghosts of Carnglaze could cavort and carouse in their new found emptiness and her family would no longer be there to be frightened.

As they trotted along the road to Rosmorren, the sea a dark blue edging to the fields on their left and the moorland crowned with granite tors to the right, all bathed in spring sunshine, Eliza felt the stirring of real happiness. There would be plenty to discuss about the last few years and probably many worries to face. But Carnglaze was left behind like a bad dream and she and her family were returning at last to a new life in Roscarne.

L - #0044 - 080319 - C0 - 210/148/13 - PB - DID2466021